WHAT COMES NEXT

JOHN KATZENBACH

A Mysterious Press Book
for Head of Zeus

First published in 2012 by Mysterious Press,
an imprint of Grove/Atlantic, New York.

First published in hardback in the UK in 2013 by Head of Zeus Ltd.
This paperback edition published in the UK in 2013 by Head of Zeus Ltd.

9 7 5 3 1 2 4 6 8

A CIP catalogue record for this book is available from the British Library.

Paperback ISBN: 9781781851425
eBook ISBN: 9781781853672

Printed and bound by CPI Group (UK) Ltd,
Croydon CR0 4YY.

Head of Zeus Ltd,
Clerkenwell House,
45-47 Clerkenwell Green,
London EC1R 0HT

www.headofzeus.com

WHAT COMES NEXT

For my old friend Bob

1

As soon as the door opened he knew he was dead.

He could see it in the quickly averted eyes, in the small slump of the shoulders, the nervous, hurried manner as the doctor moved rapidly across the room. The only questions that immediately leaped to his mind were: *How much time do I have? How bad will it be?*

He did not have to wait long for the answers.

Adrian Thomas watched as the neurologist shuffled his test results before squirreling down behind his large oaken desk. The physician leaned backward in his chair, then rocked forward before looking up and saying, "The test results rule out most routine diagnoses . . ."

Adrian had expected this. MRI. EKG. EEG. Blood. Urine. Ultrasound. Brain scan. A battery of cognitive function exams. It had been more than nine months since he'd first noticed he was forgetting things that were ordinarily easy to remember—a trip to the hardware store where he'd found himself standing in the lightbulb aisle with *no idea* what he had meant to purchase; a time outside on the main street in town when he'd run into a longtime colleague and had blanked on the name of a man who'd occupied the office next to his for over twenty years. Then, six days earlier, he had spent an entire evening hour pleasantly conversing with his long-deceased wife in the living room of the house they had shared since moving to western Massachusetts. She had even sat in her favorite paisley Queen Anne chair, near the fireplace. When the recognition of what he had done had become clear to him, he had also known that nothing would show up on any computer printout or color photograph of his brain structure. Nevertheless, he had dutifully made an emergency appointment with his internist, who had quickly shipped him over to the specialist. He had patiently answered every question and allowed himself to be poked, prodded, and x-rayed.

He had assumed, in those first minutes of shocked recognition after his dead wife had vanished from his sight, that he was simply going crazy—an unscientific and undisciplined way of defining psychosis or schizophrenia. But then, he had not *felt* crazy. He had felt quite good, really. It had been more benign, almost as if the hours spent in talk with someone who had died three years earlier was routine and pleasurable, a conversation not at all dissimilar to those they had frequently enjoyed in all the years of their marriage. They'd talked about his deepening loneliness and why he should take up some pro bono teaching at the university despite his retirement after her death. They'd discussed current movies and interesting books and what he should send his nieces in California for their birthdays. They had debated whether this year they should try to steal down to Cape Cod for a couple of weeks of rest in June, just after the bluefish and stripers started their annual run, before the suntan crowds showed up in coolers and umbrellas masses.

As he sat across from the neurologist he thought that he had made a terrible mistake in even considering for one second that the hallucination was part of an illness, and that he should never have allowed this alarm to frighten him enough to send him to the doctor's office. He should have thought of it as an advantage. He was completely alone now, and it would have been nice to repopulate his life with people he had once loved, regardless of whether they still existed or not, for however long he had left on this earth.

"Your symptoms suggest . . ."

He did not want to listen to the doctor, who had an uncomfortable, pained look on his face, and who was much younger than he was. It was unfair, he thought, that someone so young would get to tell him he was going to die. It *should* have been some gray-haired, God-like physician, with a sonorous voice weary with years of experience, not the high-pitched barely out of elementary school man rocking back and forth nervously in his chair.

He hated the sterile, brightly lit office, with its framed diplomas and wooden bookcases filled with medical texts that he was sure the doctor never opened. Adrian knew the doctor was the sort of man who preferred a couple of quick *clicks* on a computer keyboard or a BlackBerry to find information. He looked about and thought the office was oppressively clean and orderly, as if the natural messiness of a fatal illness wasn't allowed inside. He looked past the man's shoulder, out the window, and saw a crow alight on the leafy branches of a nearby willow tree. It was as if the doctor was droning away in some distant world that as of that moment he really wasn't much a part of any longer. Just a small part, perhaps. An inconsequential part. For an instant, he imagined that he should listen to the crow instead, and then he had a shock of confusion, where he thought that it *was the crow* that was speaking to him. That, he insisted inwardly, was unlikely, so he dropped his eyes and forced himself to pay attention to the physician.

"I am sorry, Professor Thomas," the neurologist said slowly. He was picking his words with caution. "But I believe you are experiencing the progressive stages of a relatively rare disease called Lewy body dementia. Do you know what this is?"

He did, vaguely. He had heard the term once or twice, although he could not immediately recall where. Perhaps one of the other members of the psychology department at the university had used it in a faculty meeting trying to justify some research or complaining about grant application procedures. Maybe he recalled it from his youth, when he performed clinical work in a VA hospital. He shook his head anyway. Better to hear it all unvarnished, from someone more expert than he, even if the doctor was far too young.

Words fell into the space between them, like debris from an explosion drifting down, littering the desktop. *Steady. Progressive. Rapid deterioration. Hallucinations. Loss of bodily functions. Loss of critical reasoning. Loss of short-term memory. Loss of long-term memory.*

And then finally the death sentence: "I'm sorry to have to tell you this, but typically we're talking five to seven years. Maybe. And I believe you have been suffering from the onset of this disease for some time, so that would be the maximum. And in most cases, things move much more quickly."

There was a momentary delay, followed by an obsequious, "If you want a second opinion . . ."

Why, he wondered, *would he want to hear bad news twice?*

And then an additional and somewhat expected blow: "There is no cure. There are some medications that can alleviate some of the symptoms— Alzheimer's drugs, atypical antipsychotics to treat the visions and delusions—but none of these are guarantees of anything and oftentimes they don't really help significantly. But they are worth trying to see if they will work to prolong functioning . . ."

Adrian waited for a small opening, before he said, "But I don't feel sick."

The neurologist nodded. "That too, unfortunately, is typical. For a man in his mid-sixties, you are in excellent physical shape. You have the heart of a much younger man."

"Lots of running and exercise."

"Well, that's good."

"So I'm healthy enough to watch myself fall apart? Like a ringside seat at my own decline?"

The neurologist did not immediately respond. "Yes . . ." he finally said. "But some studies have shown that the more mental exercises you do, coupled with continuing an active, exercise-filled day-to-day life, can delay some of the impact on the frontal lobes, which is where this disease is located."

Adrian nodded. He knew this. He also knew the frontal lobes controlled decision-making processes and the ability to comprehend the world around him. The frontal lobes were pretty much the part of his brain that had made him who he was and now were going to make him into someone much different and probably unrecognizable. He suddenly did not expect to be Adrian Thomas much longer.

That was the thought that filled him, and he ceased listening to the neurologist, until he heard, "Do you have anyone to help you? Wife? Children? Other relatives? There's not much time before you're going to need a dedicated support system. That will be followed by a round-the-clock care facility. I should really speak with these people very soon. Help them to understand what you will be going through."

The doctor said these words as he reached for a prescription pad and rapidly started to write down lists of medications.

Adrian smiled. "I have all the help I'm going to need right at home."

Mister Ruger 9mm semiautomatic, he thought. The weapon was located in the top drawer in the nightstand by his bed. The thirteen-shot clip was full, but he knew he would need to chamber only one bullet.

The doctor said some other things about home health care aides and insurance payments, power of attorney and living wills, long-term hospital stays and the importance of keeping all his future appointments, sticking to the medicines that he didn't think were going to slow the pace of the disease but which he should take anyway because they might work a little bit, but Adrian realized he no longer had any real need to pay more attention.

Nestled between several tracts of former farmland that had been developed into modern, upscale mansion-like homes on the outskirts of Adrian's small college town was a conservation area, where a wildlife sanctuary covered a modest hill that the locals called a mountain but in reality was a mere topographical bump. There was a walking path up Mount Pollux that snaked around through the woods before emerging at a spot that overlooked the valley. It had always bothered him that there was no Mount Castor next to Mount Pollux, and he wondered who had named the hill so pretentiously. Some academic sort, he suspected, from a faculty two hundred years earlier that sported black wool suits and starched white collars as they beat classical education into the students who matriculated at the college. Still, despite his questions about the name and the overall accuracy of the honorific *Mount* it was a place he'd enjoyed over the years. It was a quiet spot much beloved of town dogs, who could be let off their leashes, and where one could be alone with his thoughts. That was where he headed after leaving the doctor's office.

He parked his old Volvo in a pullout at the base of the path and started hiking up. Ordinarily, he would have worn boots against the early spring mud, and he thought he was likely to ruin his shoes before he'd gone too far.

He told himself that no longer made any difference.

The afternoon was fading around him and he could feel a caress of cold against his spine. He was not dressed for a walk, especially as the creeping New England shadows carried a breath of leftover winter. As with his rapidly soaking shoes, he ignored the chill.

There was no one else on the path. No bounding golden retrievers dashing into the underbrush in search of some scent or another. Just Adrian alone, walking steadily. He was glad for the solitude. He had the odd thought that if he'd met someone else, he would have been compelled to tell him: "*I've got a disease you've never heard of that's going to kill me, but first I'm going to be whittled down into nothingness.*"

At least with cancer, he thought, or heart disease, you got to stay who you were for as long as you could manage while it murdered you. He was angry, and he wanted to strike out, hit something, but instead he simply marched upward.

He listened to his breathing. It was steady. Normal. Not even labored in the slightest. He thought this unfair. He would have far preferred a tortured, sucking sound, something that told him he was terminal.

It took about thirty minutes for him to reach the summit, such as it was. The remaining sunlight filtered over the tops of some western hills, and he sat on a large ice age outcropping of shale rock, staring off into the valley. The first signs of the New England spring were well under way. He could see early flowers, mostly yellow and purple crocuses poking up through damp soil, and trees budding, which gave them a touch of green, and darkened their branches like a man's cheeks who has neglected to shave for a day or so. A flight of Canada geese stretched out in a V shape cruised the air above him, heading north. Their raucous braying echoed through the pale blue sky. It was all so distinctly normal that he felt a little foolish, because what was taking place within him seemed to be out of sync with the rest of the world.

In the distance he could make out the spires of the church in the center of the college campus. The baseball team would be outside, working in the batting cages because the diamond was still covered by a tarpaulin. His office had been close enough so that when he'd opened the window on spring afternoons he was able to hear the distant sounds of bat against ball. As much as any robin cruising the quadrangles in search of a worm, it had been a welcome sign after the long winter.

Adrian took a deep breath.

"Go home," he said out loud. "Shoot yourself now while all these things that gave you pleasure are still real. Because the disease is going to take them away."

He had always thought of himself as a decisive sort of person, and he welcomed the harsh insistence of suicide. He tried to come up with arguments for delay but none jumped to mind.

Maybe, he told himself, *just stay right here. It's a nice spot.* One of his favorites. A good enough place to die. He wondered whether the temperature would drop enough over the course of the night to freeze him to death. He doubted it. He imagined that he would just spend an unpleasant night shivering and coughing and live to see the sun come up, and that this would be embarrassing, even if he was the only person in the world who'd have seen sunrise as failure.

Adrian shook his head.

Look around, he told himself. *Remember what's worth remembering. Ignore the rest.*

7

He looked down at his shoes. They were caked with mud and soaked through, and he wondered why he couldn't feel the damp against his toes.

No more delays, he insisted. Adrian stood up, brushing some of the shale dust from his trousers. He could see shadows seeping through the brush and trees, the path down the mountain darkening with each passing second.

He looked back at the valley. *That was where I taught. Over there is where we lived.* He wished he could see all the way to the loft in New York City where he'd met his wife and fallen in love for the first time, but he could not. He wished he could see his childhood haunts and places he remembered from all sorts of moments growing up. He wished he could see the rue Madeleine in Paris and the corner bistro where he and his wife had taken their coffee every morning while on sabbaticals or the Hotel Savoy in Berlin, where they'd stayed in the Marlene Dietrich suite when he had been called upon to give a speech to the Institut fur Psychologie and conceived their only child. He strained, looking east toward the house on the Cape, where he'd spent summers since his youth, and the beaches where he'd learned to throw a fly to cruising striped bass or any of the local trout steams where he'd waded amid ancient boulders and water that had seemed to be alive with energy.

Lots to miss, he said to himself.

Can't be helped.

He turned away from what he could and what he couldn't see and started down the path. It was slow going.

He was only half a block from his house, cutting through the rows of modest middle-class, white clapboard homes that were filled with the eclectic selection of other college faculty and local insurance men, dentists, freelance business writers, yoga instructors, and life coaches that made up his neighborhood, when he spotted the girl walking down the side of the road.

Ordinarily, he would not have paid much attention, but there was something in the determined way the girl was pacing forward that struck him.

She seemed filled with purpose. She had dusty blond hair that was tucked up under a bright pink Boston Red Sox cap, and he saw that her dark parka was ripped in a couple of places, as were her jeans. What grabbed his attention was her backpack, which seemed stuffed nearly to overflowing with clothes. At first he thought she was just walking home after being dropped off by the late bus from the high school, the bus that distributed the kids who had been kept after school for disciplinary reasons. But he noticed fastened to her backpack a large stuffed teddy bear and he could not imagine why someone would take a childhood toy to high school. It would instantly have made her the object of ridicule.

He glanced at her face as he rolled past her.

She was young, barely more than a child, but beautiful in the way that all children on the verge of change are, or at least that was what Adrian thought, although it had been many years since he'd actually tried to get to know someone so young other than in a classroom setting.

She was staring ahead, fiercely.

He did not think she even noticed his car.

Adrian pulled into his driveway but did not get out from behind the wheel. He thought the girl—was she fifteen? sixteen?; he could no longer accurately judge the ages of children—seemed to wear a single-mindedness that spoke of something else. This look fascinated him, jolted his curiosity.

He watched her in his rearview mirror as she walked briskly to the corner.

Then he saw something else, which seemed just slightly out of place in his quiet, determinedly normal neighborhood.

A white panel van, like a small delivery truck but wearing no insignia on the outside advertising an electrician or a painting service, cruised slowly down his street. He glanced inside and saw that a woman was driving and a man was in the passenger seat. This surprised him. It should have been the other way around, he thought, but then he considered he was merely being sexist and clichéd. *Of course a woman can drive a truck,* he told himself. And even though it was getting late and the evening darkness was dropping rapidly through the trees, there was no reason to think that this truck was anything other than ordinary.

But as he watched he saw the van slow down and seem to shadow the marching girl. From his spot inside his car, he saw the van stop across from her. Suddenly, he could not see the girl—the van had blocked his view.

A moment passed, and then the van accelerated sharply around the corner and disappeared into the few twilight moments remaining before night.

He looked again. The girl was gone.

But left behind on the street was the pink baseball cap.

2

As soon as the door opened she knew she was dead. The only questions she had were: *How long do I have? How bad will it be?*

It would be some time before she got those answers. Instead, the first minutes were filled with a fierce terror and uncontrollable panic that obscured everything else.

Jennifer Riggins had not immediately turned as the panel truck crept up next to her. She was totally focused on quickly getting to the bus stop slightly more than a half mile away on the nearest main road. In the careful way she had designed the scheme of her escape, the local bus would carry her to the center of town, where she could connect with another bus that would take her to a larger terminal in Springfield, some twenty miles away. And, once there, she imagined she could go anywhere. In her jeans pocket she had more than $300 that she had stolen slowly but surely—five here, ten there—from her mother's purse or her mother's boyfriend's wallet. She had taken her time, collecting the money over the past month, hoarding it in a box inside a drawer beneath her underwear. She had never taken so much at one time that they would notice it, just small amounts that were immediately forgotten. When she'd hit her target number, she had known that it was enough to get to New York or Nashville or maybe even Miami or LA, and so, on her last theft early that morning, she had only taken a twenty-dollar bill and three ones, but she'd added to her stash her mother's Visa card. She wasn't sure yet where she was going. Someplace warm, she hoped. But anywhere far away and far different was going to be all right with her. That was what she had been thinking about when the truck pulled to a stop next to her. *I can go anywhere I want . . .*

The man in the passenger seat had said, "Hey, miss, could you help me out for a second with some directions?"

This question had made her pause. She had stopped walking and faced the man in the truck. Her first impressions were that he hadn't shaved in the morning and that his voice seemed oddly high and filled with more excitement than his ordinary question required. And she was a little annoyed, because she didn't want to be delayed; she wanted to get away from her home and from her smug neighborhood and from her small boring college town and from her mother and her mother's boyfriend and the way he looked at her and some of the things he'd done when they were alone and from her awful school and from all the kids she knew and hated and who taunted her every single day of the week. She wanted to get away before it got too dark, but it was still just dark enough so that no one would notice her leaving. She wanted to be on a bus heading *somewhere* that night because she knew that by nine or ten her mother would have finished calling all the numbers she could think of, and then she might actually call the police, because that was what she had done before. Jennifer knew that the police would be *all over* the bus terminal in Springfield, so she had to have made her move by the time all that was set in motion. All these jumbled thoughts flooded into her head as she considered the man's question.

"What are you looking for?" Jennifer responded.

She saw the man smile.

That's wrong, she thought. *He shouldn't be smiling.*

12

Her initial guess was the man was going to make some vaguely obscene, sexist remark, something insulting or belittling, a *Hi, good-lookin', you wanna have some fun* lip-smacking nastiness. She was ready for this and ready to tell him to go screw himself and turn her back and keep walking but she was a little confused, because she looked over the man's shoulder and saw a woman in the driver's seat. The woman had a knit watchman's cap pulled down over her hair, and even though she was young there was something harsh in her eyes, something very granite-hard that Jennifer had never seen before and which instantly scared her.

In the woman's hand was a small HD video camera. It was pointed in Jennifer's direction. This confused her.

Jennifer heard the man's answer to her question and it confused her further. She had expected he was asking for a neighborhood address or a direct way to Route 9, but that was not what came out.

"You," he said.

This made no sense. *Why were they looking for her? No one knew about her plan. It was still too early for her mother to have found the false note she'd left stuck with a magnet to the kitchen refrigerator . . .*

And so she'd hesitated at the very second in time when she should have run furiously hard or screamed loudly for help.

The truck door opened abruptly. The man vaulted out of the passenger seat. He was moving much faster than Jennifer had ever imagined someone *could* move.

"Hey!" Jennifer said. At least, later, she thought she had said *hey* but she was uncertain. Maybe she had just frozen. The only idea that went through her head was *This can't be happening* and that was followed by a dark, icy sense of dread because she *knew* in that second, as she saw something coming at her, what it truly meant.

The man had clubbed her across the face, staggering her. The blow had exploded in her eyes, sending a sheet of red hurt right through her core, and she had felt dizzy, almost as if the world around her had spun on its axis. She could feel herself losing consciousness, reeling back, and crumpling when he grabbed her around the shoulders, holding her from falling

13

to the ground. Her knees felt weak, her shoulders and back rubbery. If she'd had any strength anywhere it vanished instantly.

She was only vaguely aware of the panel truck door opening and of the man bodily rushing her into the back. She could hear the noise of the door slamming shut. The sensation of the truck accelerating around the corner drove her into the steel bed. She could feel the weight of the man crushing her, holding her down. She could barely breathe and her throat was nearly closed with terror. She did not know if she was struggling or fighting, she couldn't tell if she was screaming or crying, she was no longer alert enough to tell what she was doing. She gasped as a sudden great blackness came over her, and at first she thought she was already dead, then she thought she was unconscious before she realized that the man had pulled a black pillowcase over her head, shutting out the tiny world of the truck. She could taste blood on her lips, and her head was still spinning and whatever was happening to her she knew it was far worse than anything she had ever known before.

Odor penetrated the pillowcase: a thick oily smell from the floor of the truck; a sweaty, sweet smell from the man pinning her down.

Somewhere within her, she knew she was in great pain, but she could not tell precisely where.

She tried to move her arms and legs, pawing at nothingness like a dog dreaming of chasing rabbits, but she heard the man grunt, "No, I don't think so . . ."

And then there was another explosion on her head, behind her eyes. The last thing she was aware of was the woman's voice, saying, "Don't kill her, for Christ's sake."

With those words echoing within her, Jennifer slid out of control, tumbling swiftly into a deep, dark fake death of unconsciousness.

3

He held the pink hat gently, as if it were alive, turning it over carefully in his hands.

On the inner part of the brim he saw the name *Jennifer* scrawled in ink, followed by a funny drawing of a smiling ducklike cartoon bird and the words *is cool* as if they were the answer to a question. No last name, no phone number, no address.

Adrian sat on the edge of his bed. Resting starkly beside him on the hand-crafted, multihued coverlet his wife had purchased at a quilt fair shortly before her accident was his 9mm Ruger. He had gathered a large collection of photographs of his wife and family and spread them throughout the bedroom where he could look at them as he prepared himself. To make his intentions absolutely clear, Adrian had taken the time to go to his small home office, where once he had labored over lectures and lesson plans, click on his computer, and find a Wikipedia entry for *Lewy body dementia*. He had printed this out and then stapled it to a copy of the receipt for his bill from the neurologist's office.

All that remained, he told himself, was to write a proper suicide note, something heartfelt and poetic. He had always loved poetry and dabbled in writing his own verse. He had filled bookcase shelves with collections, from the modern to the ancient, from Paul Muldoon and James Tate, ranging back in time to Ovid and Catullus. A few years back, he had privately published a small volume of his own poems, *Love Songs and Madness*—not that he thought they were any good. But he loved writing, either free form or in rhyme, and he believed it might help him express the hopelessness he felt and the reluctance he had to try to face down his disease. *Poetry instead of bravery,* he thought. For a moment, he was distracted. He wondered where he'd placed a copy of his book. He thought it belonged on the bed, beside the pictures and the gun. Things would then be totally clear to whoever arrived at the scene of his self-murder.

He reminded himself that right before he pulled the trigger he should call 911 and report a shooting at his house. That would bring anxious policemen to the scene within minutes. He knew he should leave the front door invitingly wide open. These precautions would prevent weeks passing before someone found his body. No decomposition. No smell. Making it all as neat and tidy as possible. There was nothing, he thought, he could do about blood splatter. That couldn't be helped. But the police were professionals, and he figured they were used to that sort of thing. After all, he wouldn't be the first aging professor in the community to decide that a loss of the ability to think or reason or understand was a sufficient reason to end his life. He just couldn't offhand recall any other suicidal colleagues. This bothered him. He was sure there were some.

For a moment he wondered if he should write a poem about his planning: "Last Acts Before the Last Act."

That's a good title, he thought.

Adrian rocked back and forth, as if the motion could loosen thoughts stuck within him in blackened places he could no longer reach. There might be a few other small pre-suicidal tasks he needed to take care of—paying a few stray bills, shutting off the heating system or the hot water heater, locking up the garage, taking out the garbage. He found himself going over a minor checklist in his mind, a little like a typical suburbanite greeting Saturday morning chores. The odd notion occurred to him that he seemed to be afraid of making a mess of death and leaving it behind for others to clean up far more than he was scared of actually killing himself.

Cleaning up a mess of death. Memories tried to burst past the wall of his organization. More than once he had to do precisely that. He fought off images of sadness that echoed within him and focused hard on the task at hand.

Adrian looked over at the pictures surrounding him on the bed and perched on a nearby table. Parents, brother, wife, and son. *Be there soon,* he thought. Distant sister, nieces, friends, and colleagues. *Meet you later.* He seemed to speak directly to the people looking out at him. Lots of grins and smiles, he realized: happy moments at barbecues, weddings, and vacations—all fixed in film.

He looked around quickly. The other memories were about to disappear forever. The awful times that had come far too frequently over the years of his life. *Pull the trigger and all that disappears.* He dropped his eyes and saw that he was still tightly gripping the pink hat.

He started to put it aside and reach for the weapon, but he stopped. *It will confuse people,* he thought. *Some cop will wonder,* What the hell was he doing with a pink Red Sox cap? *It might send them on some inexplicable murder mystery tangent.* He wanted to avoid any suspicions.

He held the hat up in front of him again, directly in his view, like one would hold a jewel up to light to try and see the imperfections within.

The rough cotton beneath his fingers felt warm. He traced the distinctive *B.* The pink color had faded a little and the sweatband was frayed. That would happen only if the blond girl had worn it frequently, especially throughout the winter, preferring it to a warmer ski hat. This told him that the cap—for whatever hidden reason—was a favorite article of clothing.

Which meant to him that she wouldn't have abandoned it by the side of the road.

What had he seen?

Adrian took a deep breath and revisited each impression from earlier that evening, turning them over in his mind's eye in much the same way he was rubbing the baseball cap with his hands. *The girl with the determined look. The woman behind the wheel. The man at her side. The brief hesitation as they pulled next to the teenager. The rapid acceleration and disappearance. The hat left behind.*

What happened?

Flight? Escape? Maybe it was one of those cult or drug interventions, where the do-gooder types swept in and then harangued their target in a cheap rented motel room until the poor kid admitted to a change in attitude or belief or addiction.

He did not think that was what he saw.

He told himself: *Go over it again. Every detail, before they are all lost from your memory.*

That was what he was afraid of: that everything he remembered and everything he deduced would dissipate in the shortest of orders like a morning fog after the sunlight starts to eat away at it. He got up, walked to a bureau, and found a pen and small leather-bound notebook. Usually, he had used the thick, elegant white pages to keep notes for poems, writing down the odd thought or combination of words or rhymes that might lend themselves to development later. His wife had given him the notebook, and when he touched its smooth surface it reminded him of her.

So he played it all out again, this time jotting down a few details on a blank page.

The girl . . . She was looking straight ahead and he didn't think she had even seen him when he drove past her. She was in the midst of something. That he could tell, just from the direction of her eyes and the pace of her walk. She had *a plan*—and it was shutting out everything else.

The woman and the man . . . He had pulled into his driveway before the white van approached, he was sure of it. *Did they see him in his car?* No. Unlikely.

The brief hesitation . . . They had seemed to shadow the girl, even if just for a few feet. *It was as if they were sizing her up. What must have*

18

happened then? Did they talk? Was she *invited* into the van? Maybe they knew each other and this was just the friendly offer of a ride. Nothing more. Nothing less.

No. They departed far too rapidly.

What did he see as they went around the corner? *A Massachusetts license plate: QE2D . . .*

He tried to recall the other two digits but could not. He wrote down those he remembered. But what he really remembered was the sharp sound of the van accelerating.

And then the hat was left behind.

He had difficulty formulating the word *kidnap* in his imagination, and even when he did he told himself that this was a conclusion that simply *had* to be foolish. That sort of thing did not happen in the world he knew. He lived in a place devoted to reason, learning, and logic, with distinct sidelines of art and beauty. He was a member of a world of schools and knowledge. *Kidnap*—this ugly word belonged in some darker place unfamiliar in his neighborhood. He tried to remember *any* crimes that had taken place within the quiet rows of trim suburban homes that were spread out around him. Surely, he told himself, there had to be *some,* the hidden sorts of domestic abuses and disruptive teenage lives that were the stuff of television dramas. Sexual infidelities by adults and high school drug, booze, and sex parties had to have taken place in relative obscurity within blocks. Maybe folks cheated on their taxes or ran shady business practices—he could imagine those sorts of crimes taking place behind the veneer of middle-class life. But he could not ever recall hearing a gunshot or even seeing flashing police lights on any street nearby.

Those things happened elsewhere. They were confined to breathless evening news reports from nearby cities or to headlines in the morning paper.

Adrian looked down at the Ruger pistol. His brother's legacy. No one knew he owned it. He had never registered it, aware peripherally that his faculty friends at the college would find his possession of the weapon deeply shocking. It was a no-nonsense, ugly weapon that left little debate as to what its purpose was. He wasn't a hunter or an NRA type. He was contemptuous of the right-wing-get-a-gun-to-defend-yourself-from-terrorists mind-set. He was sure that over the years his wife had forgotten that it was in the house, if she had ever really known. He had never spoken of it with her, even after her accident when she had hung on but looked to him with longing for release.

If he'd been brave, he thought, he would have indulged her with the weapon's finality. Now, that same question and answer were left to him, and he knew he was a coward for using it in the same way it had been used once before. He wondered for a second if when he placed the barrel to his temple or into his mouth and pulled the trigger it would be only the second time the weapon had ever been fired.

It had a black, metallic skin that seemed heartless. When he hefted the weapon in his hand it felt heavy and ice cold.

Adrian pushed the weapon aside and turned back to the hat. It seemed to speak as loudly at that moment as the Ruger did. It was like being caught in the middle of an argument between two inanimate objects, as they debated back and forth over what he should do.

He paused, taking a deep breath. Things seemed to grow quiet in the room, as if there had been some noisy racket associated with self-murder that was abruptly silenced.

The least I can do, he thought, *is make a modest inquiry.* The hat seemed to be demanding that small amount from him.

He picked up his phone and dialed 911. He was aware there was a little irony in the idea that he was calling first about someone he didn't know, and that later he would make more or less the same call about himself.

"Police, Fire, and Rescue. What is your emergency?" The dispatcher's voice had a practiced calm to it.

"It's not really an emergency," Adrian said. He wanted to make sure that his voice didn't waver or sound hesitant, like the old man he thought he'd suddenly become in the hours after visiting the neurologist. He wanted to sound forceful and alert. "I am calling because I think I may have witnessed an *event* that might have some police interest."

"What sort of event?"

He tried to picture the person on the other end of the phone. The dispatcher had a way of clipping off each word sharply so that it was unmistakable in meaning. The tone of his voice had a toughened, no-nonsense timbre. It was as if the few words the dispatcher used were dressed in tight high-collared uniforms.

"I saw a white panel van . . . There was this teenage girl, Jennifer, it's written in her hat but I don't know her, although she must live in the neighborhood somewhere and one second she was there, then the next, she was gone."

Adrian wanted to slap himself. All his intentions of being reasonable and forceful had instantly evaporated in a sea of choppy, ill-conceived, and deeply rushed descriptions. He wondered, *Is that the disease punishing my language skills?*

"Yes, sir. And you believe you witnessed what exactly?"

The telephone line *beeped*. He was being recorded.

"Have you had any reports of missing children in the Hills section of town?" he asked.

"No current reports. No calls today," the dispatcher said.

"Nothing?"

"No, sir. Very quiet in town all afternoon. I will take your information and forward it to the detective bureau should there be a later report. They will follow up if necessary."

"I guess I was mistaken," Adrian said. He hung up before the dispatcher had time to ask for his name and address.

None of it made sense to him.

He knew what he'd seen and it was *wrong*.

Adrian looked up and out his window. Night had dropped and lights were clicking on up and down the block. Dinnertime, he thought. Families gathering. Talk about what happened that day, at work, at school. All very normal and expected. He suddenly burst out loud with a question that resonated in the small bedroom, as if it could echo in that small space like it would if he'd shouted above a canyon. "I don't know what I'm supposed to do now."

"But of course you do, dear," his wife insisted from the bed beside him.

4

The call came in shortly before 11 p.m. but by that time Detective Terri
Collins was already thinking hard about heading to bed. Her two children
were asleep in their bedroom, homework done, read to and tucked in.
She had just made that last maternal visit of the night—where she poked
her head in through the doorway, letting the wan light from the hallway
toss just enough illumination onto the faces of the two children so that
she could tell they slept soundly. No nightmares. Even breathing. Not
even a sniffle that might signal an oncoming cold. There were some single
parents she knew in the support group she occasionally frequented who
could hardly bear to tear themselves away from sleeping children. It was
as if during the night they were all vulnerable. All the evils that had created their circumstances seemed to have freer rein after sunset. A time that
should have been devoted to rest and renewal had devolved into one filled
with uncertainty, worry, and fears.

But all was right this night, she thought.

All was safe.

Everything was normal.

She left the door ajar just an inch or two and started to pad down to the bathroom when she heard the phone ring in the kitchen.

She glanced at a wall clock as she hurried to answer. *Too late to be anything but trouble,* she thought.

It was the night dispatcher at police headquarters.

"Detective, I have a distraught woman on the other line. I believe you've handled calls from her before. Apparently, we have another runaway."

Detective Terri Collins knew immediately who it was that the dispatcher had on hold. *Maybe this time Jennifer actually got away . . .* But this was unprofessional and getting *away* was only callous shorthand for trading a familiar set of terrors for a wholly different and potentially worse type.

"I'll be with you in a moment," Terri said. She slipped easily from mother mode into police detective. One of her strengths was her ability to separate the different dimensions of her life into neat, orderly groups. Too many years of too much upheaval had created in her a driving need for simplicity and organization.

She put the dispatcher on hold while she dialed a second number, one that she kept on a list by the kitchen phone. An advantage of having been through what she had experienced was the informal network of help available. Luckily, the woman she dialed was a dedicated night owl. "Hello, Laurie, it's Terri. I hate to bother you at this late hour, but . . ."

"You've been called in on a case and you need me to watch the kids?" Terri could actually hear enthusiasm in her friend's voice.

"Yes."

"Be right over. No problem. My pleasure. How late do you think you'll be?" Terri smiled. Her friend Laurie was an insomniac of the first order, and Terri knew that she secretly loved being called in the middle of the night, especially to watch over children, now that her own had grown up and moved away. It gave her something to do other than uselessly watching late-night cable or pacing anxiously about her darkened house talking to herself about everything that had gone wrong in her life. This was, Terri had learned, a lengthy conversation.

23

"Hard to say. At least a couple of hours. But probably late. Maybe even all night."

"I'll bring my toothbrush," Laurie replied.

She hit the HOLD button and reconnected with the police dispatcher.

"Tell Mrs. Riggins I'll be at her home within thirty minutes to talk to her and get an investigation started. Are uniformed officers there?"

"They have been dispatched."

"Let them know I'll be along shortly. They should take down any preliminary statements so we can put a time line together. They should also try to settle Mrs. Riggins down."

Terri doubted they would be successful at this.

"Ten-four," the dispatcher replied, disconnecting the line.

Laurie would be over within minutes. That was her neighbor's style. She hung up the phone. Laurie liked thinking she was an integral part of whatever investigation or crime scene that Terri was being called to, as important as a forensic technician or fingerprint expert. This was a harmless and useful conceit. Terri went back into the bathroom, dashed some water on her face, and ran a brush through her hair. Despite the late hour, she wanted to look fresh, presentable, and exceptionally capable in the face of frantic panic.

The street was dark and there were few lights on in any of the houses when Terri drove through the Rigginses' neighborhood. The only home with any outward activity was her destination, where the porch light shone brightly and Terri could see figures moving about in the living room. A single police cruiser was parked in the driveway, but the responding officers had left their flashing lights off, so it merely looked like another car waiting for the morning suburban exodus to work or school.

Terri pulled up in her battered six-year-old compact. She took a minute to breathe deeply before she gathered her things—a satchel with a mini–tape recorder and a bound notebook. She kept her badge attached to the strap of the satchel. Her weapon was holstered and on the seat next to her. She clamped it to the belt of her jeans, after double-checking to make certain the safety was on and no round was chambered. Another deep breath and she stepped out into the night and made her way across the lawn toward the house.

It was a trip she had made twice before in the past eighteen months. She could see her breath vaporizing in the air like smoke. The temperature had fallen, but not so far that any person in New England did anything other than wrap their coat a little more tightly around their chest and maybe turn up the collar. There was clarity to the cold, not the same as the frost of winter, but a sense that lines were still drawn in the air, even with spring fitfully making its start.

Terri wished she had stopped by her desk at the four-person detective bureau over at police headquarters and pulled her file on the Riggins family, although she doubted that there was any detail or note in those reports that she hadn't already committed to memory. What she hated was the sensation that she was walking into a scene that was something far different from what it purported to be. *An underage runaway* was how she would write it up for the department records and precisely how the detective bureau would handle the case. She knew exactly what steps she would take and what the departmental guidelines and procedures were for this sort of disappearance. She even had a reasonable guess about the likely outcome of the case. But that wasn't what was really happening, she told herself. There was some underlying reason for Jennifer's persistence and there was probably a far worse crime lurking within the teenager's single-minded dedication to getting away from her home. Terri just didn't think she would ever uncover it no matter how many statements she took from the mother and the boyfriend or how hard she worked the case.

She hated the notion that she was about to participate in a falsehood.

On the front stoop, she hesitated before knocking on the door. She pictured her own two children at home asleep, unaware that she was not right down the hallway in her little bedroom with her own door open and her sleep light, in case she heard any strange sound. They were still young.

Whatever heartache and worry they were going to produce—and there was surely to be some—was still to come.

Jennifer was considerably farther along that road.

Farther along a couple of roads, Terri thought. The double entendre made sense of the situation inside the house.

Terri took a final deep breath of the cold night air, like swallowing the last drop of water from a glass. She knocked once, then pushed the door open and stepped quickly into a small hallway. She knew there was a picture of a smiling Jennifer at age nine, pink bow in carefully combed hair, framed on the wall near the stairs to the upper bedrooms. There was an endearing gap between the girl's front teeth. It was the sort of picture beloved of parents and hated by teenagers because it reminded both of the same time, seen through different lenses and distorted by different memories.

To her left, in the living room, she saw Mary Riggins and Scott West—the boyfriend—perched on the edge of a sofa. Scott had his arm loosely draped around Mary's shoulders and gripped her hand. Cigarettes burned in an ashtray on a coffee table. Cans of soda and half-empty cups of coffee crowded the tabletop. Poised uncomfortably to the side were two uniformed officers. One was the late-night shift sergeant and the other was a twenty-two-year-old rookie who'd been on the force for only a month. Clearly the sergeant was still engaged in the breaking-in process for the younger man. She nodded in their direction, caught a slight roll of the eyes from the sergeant just as Mary Riggins burst out in a howl: "She's done it again, detective."

These words ended in a torrent of sobs.

She had been crying and her makeup was streaked, black lines scarring her cheeks, giving her a Halloween appearance. Crying had turned her eyes puffy, making her look far older than she was. Terri thought that tears were always difficult for middle-aged women—they instantly brought out all the years they tried so hard to hide.

Instead of launching into any further explanation, Mary Riggins buried her head into Scott the boyfriend's shoulder. He was a little older than she was, gray-haired, distinguished looking even in jeans and faded red-checked work shirt. He was a new age therapist who specialized in holistic treatments for any number of psychiatric illnesses and had a successful practice in the academic community, which was always receptive to different techniques in the same way that some people flit from diet to diet. He drove a bright red drop-top Mazda sports car and often cruised around the valley in the winter with the car open, bundled in a parka and lumberjack's floppy fur hat, which seemed more than merely eccentric and had a sense of defiance to it. The town police were very familiar with Scott West and his work; he and the Mazda collected speeding tickets with daunting frequency, and on more than one occasion the police had been forced to quietly clean up psychological messes created by his eccentric practice. Several suicides. A standoff with a knife-wielding paranoid schizophrenic he'd advised to stop taking Haldol and exchange it with Saint John's wort purchased from the local health food store.

The cigarettes and soda cans and coffee cups shouldn't be there, Terri thought. Scott came from the yoga-Pilates traditions that considered a Diet Coke or a Starbucks latte a sign of disconnect with the greater deep benign forces of nature. Terri thought his attitudes had more in common with astrology than psychology.

If she could have, she would have laughed at him and said something about the addictive powers of hypocrisy. But she had learned early in her police career that there was no end to the many contradictions people clutched in their lives, and pointing them out rarely did anyone any good. Terri liked to think of herself as a cold-eyed pragmatist, reasoned and ordered in her thinking, straightforward in her approach. If this style occasionally made her appear unfriendly, well, that was okay with her. She had already had her fill of passion and eccentricity and madness in her own life in years gone by, and order and process was what she preferred, because, she thought, it kept her safe.

Scott leaned forward. He spoke in a practiced, therapist's voice, deep, calm, and reasonable. It was a voice designed to make him seem like her ally in the situation, when Terri knew the opposite was much closer to the truth.

"Mary's very upset, detective. Despite *all* our efforts, on a nearly continual basis . . ." He stopped there, refusing to complete the sentence.

Terri nodded. She turned to the two uniformed officers. The sergeant handed her a piece of loose-leaf ruled notepaper, the sort that was in every high school student's three-ring binder. The handwriting was careful, a script formed by someone who wanted to make certain that each word was clear and legible. It was not something that had been rapidly scribbled by a teenager eager to head out the door and do what the note said she was going to do. It was a note that had been worked on. Perhaps it was even the third or fourth carefully constructed draft. Terri guessed if she searched hard she could find discarded alternatives in a wastebasket or in the trash containers out back. Before she responded Terri read through the note three times.

Mom,

I'm going to the movies with some friends I'm meeting at the mall. I'll get dinner there and maybe spend the night at either Sarah or Katie's house. I'll call you after the movie to let you know or else just come home then. I won't be too late. I've finished my homework and have nothing new due until next week.

Very reasonable. Very concise. A complete falsehood.

"Where was this left?"

"Stuck to the fridge with a magnet," the sergeant said. "Right where it couldn't be missed."

Terri read it through a couple more times. *You're learning, aren't you, Jennifer?* she thought. *You knew exactly what to write.*

Movies—that meant her mother would assume her cell phone was shut off, and it gave her at least a two-hour window when she couldn't reasonably be reached.

Some friends—not specified but seemingly benign. The two names she did provide, Sarah and Katie, were probably willing to cover for her, or were themselves unavailable.

I'll call you—so her mother and Scott would sit around waiting for the telephone to ring while valuable minutes were lost.

No homework—Jennifer removed from the equation the biggest external excuse for her mother to call her.

Terri thought it was clever the way Jennifer had bought a block of time, sent her mother in directions other than the right one, and hidden the real purpose of her plan. She looked up at Mary Riggins.

"You telephoned her friends?" she asked.

Scott answered. "Of course, detective. After the last showings at the theaters we called every Sarah and Katie we could think of. Neither of us could ever recall Jennifer talking about any friend with either of those names. Then we went through every other name we could remember ever hearing from her. None of them had been to the mall, and none had made plans to meet with Jennifer. Or had seen her since school ended in the afternoon."

Terri nodded. *Smart girl*.

"Jennifer doesn't seem to have that many friends," Mary said wistfully. "She's never been good at a lot of the social networking of junior high or high school."

This statement, Terri guessed, was a repetition of something Scott had said in many "family" discussions.

"But she could be with someone you don't know?"

Both mother and boyfriend shook their heads.

"You don't think she has some secret boyfriend that she's maybe hidden from you guys?"

"No," Scott said. "I would have picked up on those signs."

Sure, Terri thought. She didn't say this out loud but made a notation on her pad of paper.

Mary gathered herself together and tried to respond in some less tear-strewn manner. But her voice quavered, endowing each word with a shakiness that perfectly captured her fear. "When I finally thought to go to her room, you know, maybe there was some other note, or something, I saw that her bear was gone. A teddy bear she named *Mister Brown Fur*. She's slept with it every night . . . it's like a security blanket. Her father gave it to her not long before he died, and she would never ever go anywhere and leave it behind."

Too sentimental, Terri thought. *Jennifer, taking that teddy bear along with you was a mistake. Maybe the only one, but a mistake nevertheless. Otherwise you would have had twenty-four hours instead of the six you've successfully stolen.*

"Was there anything specific that happened in the past few days that would prompt Jennifer to try to run now?" she asked. "A big fight . . . maybe some event at school . . ."

Mary Riggins simply sobbed.

Scott West replied quickly, "No, detective. If you're looking for some outward, triggering action by Mary or me that might have prompted this behavior on Jennifer's part, I can assure you it doesn't exist. No fights. No demands. No teenage temper tantrums. She hasn't been grounded. She hasn't been punished. In fact, things have been blissfully quiet around here the last few weeks. I thought—as did her mother—that maybe we'd turned a corner and things were going to calm down."

That's because she was planning, Terri thought.

In the cascade of Scott's pretentious, self-justifying words, Terri believed there was at least one lie and maybe more. She would find it out, she knew, sooner or later. Whether learning the truth would help her find Jennifer was an entirely different matter.

"She's a very troubled teenager, detective. She's very sensitive and bright, but deeply disturbed and confused. I've urged her to get treatment, but so far . . . well, you know how stubborn teens can be."

Terri did. She just wasn't sure whether stubbornness was the issue.

"Do you think there is any specific place she might have gone? A relative? A friend who has moved to a different city? Did she ever talk about wanting to be a fashion model in Miami or becoming an actress in LA or working on a fishing boat in Louisiana? Anything, no matter how offhand or small, might provide a lead we can follow up on."

Terri knew the answer that would come. She had asked these questions the two prior times Jennifer had escaped. But neither of these two other times had Jennifer managed to create the lead time she had this night. She hadn't gotten far either of the other times: a couple of miles the first time; the next town over, the second. This occasion was different.

"No, no . . ." Mary Riggins said, wringing her hands and reaching for another cigarette. Terri saw Scott try to stop her by placing his hand on her forearm, but she shook him off and seized the package of Marlboros and defiantly lit up a new cigarette, even though a half-smoked one was smoldering in the ashtray.

"No, detective. Mary and I have tried to think of someone, or somewhere, but haven't come up with anything we think might help."

Terri nodded, thinking.

"I'm going to need the most recent photo you've got," she said.

"It's right here," Scott replied, handing over something he'd obviously already prepared. Terri took the picture and glanced at it. A smiling teenager. *What a lie,* she thought.

"I'm also going to want her computer," Terri said.

"Why would you want—?" Scott started but Mary Riggins interrupted him.

"It's on her desk. It's a laptop."

"There might be some privacy issues here," Scott said. "I mean, Mary, how will we explain to Jennifer that we just let the police take her private . . ."

He stopped. Terri thought, *At least he knows how dumb he sounds. Maybe, though, he's worried about something other than dumb.*

Then, abruptly, she asked a question she probably shouldn't have asked.

"Where is her father buried?"

There was a small silence. Even the near-constant sobbing coming from Mary ceased in that moment.

Terri saw Mary Riggins gather herself, lifting up as if what she wanted to say needed an injection of strength or pride between her shoulder blades, running down into her spine.

"Up on the North Shore, near Gloucester. But what relevance does that have?"

"None, probably," Terri said. But inwardly, she told herself, *That's where I would go if I was an angry, depressed teenager filled with an overwhelming need to get away from home. Wouldn't she want to make a last visit to say goodbye to the only person she believed had ever truly loved her before starting to run?*

She shook her head a little, a motion small enough that no one in the room would notice.

A graveyard, she thought, *or else New York City because that's a good place to start the process of getting lost.*

Actually, she wondered whether the two places were equally appropriate for a disappearing act.

5

In an office in Amsterdam . . .

In a bedroom in Bangkok . . .

In a study in Tokyo . . .

At an Internet bar in Santiago . . .

On a laptop in a library at a university in Nairobi . . .

. . . And fed into a flat-screen television mounted on a penthouse apartment wall in Moscow. The room where the television was located was filled with partiers drinking iced vodka from crystal glasses and eating fine caviar, as one might expect. They turned down the blasting techno music and instead focused their attention on the screen, which had been silently showing a replay of a soccer match between Dynamo Kiev and Lokomotiv Moscow. A man sporting a large Fu Manchu mustache held up his hand, signaling for the room to grow quiet. It was his party and his apartment overlooking Gorky Park. He wore an expensive black suit with a purple silk shirt left unbuttoned and gold jewelry with the requisite Rolex on his wrist. In the modern world where gangsters and businessmen often look fundamentally alike, he could have been either or maybe both. Beside him, a slender woman easily twenty years his junior,

with a fashion model's hair and legs, wearing a loose-fitting sequined evening dress that did little to conceal her boyish figure, said first in Russian and then in French and subsequently in German: "We have learned that there is to be an entirely new series on our favorite Web broadcast beginning this evening. It should be of considerable interest to many of you here." She stopped there, not offering any further explanation to any of the guests as to what they were going to see. The way the group crowded around the television, slipped into comfortable couches or perched on chairs, indicated that many were already familiar with the offering that came blinking to life in front of them. Indeed, the eagerness in their eyes perhaps suggested that the party was being thrown specifically in celebration of the images that were coming through the computer system into the penthouse.

A large PLAY arrow prompt appeared on the screen and the party host moved a cursor over the signature and clicked a mouse. Immediately, there was some music: Beethoven's "Ode to Joy." It was played on a synthesizer, followed by a large picture of the very young actor Malcolm McDowell, holding a knife as Alex in Stanley Kubrick's film A Clockwork Orange. The picture dominated the screen. He wore the white jumpsuit, eye makeup, hobnobbed boots, and black bowler hat that the collaboration between performer and director had made famous in the early 1970s.

This image prompted a smattering of applause from the older people at the party, who remembered the book, remembered the film, and remembered the performance.

The picture of young Alex disappeared, replaced by a black screen that seemed to pulsate with anticipation. Within seconds, vibrant red italicized writing appeared, slicing across the frame like a knife, carving the words: What Comes Next?

This faded into a second credit sequence: Series #4.

The image then shifted into an anonymous basement room. It had an oddly grainy, almost single-dimensional quality, despite a broadcast originating with a modern, expensive high-definition camera. The basement seemed a gray, destitute place. No windows. No indication where this scene was taking place. A place of total anonymity. Initially, all the viewers gathered in front of the television at the party could see was an old, metal frame bed. On the bed was a young woman, stripped to her underwear, a black hood pulled over her face. Her hands and legs were cuffed and attached to rings fixed dungeon-like to the walls. The young woman didn't move, other than to breathe in and out heavily, so the viewers at least at that moment could tell she was still alive. She might have been unconscious, drugged, or even asleep, but after perhaps thirty seconds she twitched, and one of the chains restraining her rattled.

One of the partygoers gasped. Someone said in French, "Est-ce-que c'est vrai?" But no one answered the question, except perhaps with silence and by the way they craned forward, trying to see more closely.

In English, another partier said, "It's a performance. She must be an actress hired specifically for the webcast."

The sequined woman looked over at the man and shook her head. Her reply was tinged with her Slavic accent, but delivered impeccably: "Many people thought that, at the start of the prior series. But eventually, as the days pass, one realizes that there are no actors willing to play these roles."

She looked back at the screen. The hooded figure seemed to shiver and then turned her head sharply, as if someone just out of camera sight had entered the room. The viewers could see her strain against the chains gripping her.

Then, almost as swiftly as it had arrived, this image froze on the screen, as if it had suddenly been caught like a picture of a bird in flight. It dissolved into black and once again there was a question in bloodred writing: Want to See More?

This inquiry was followed on the screen by a demand for credit card information and a subscription fee structure. One could purchase some minutes, up to an hour, or a multihour block. One could also buy a day, or more. There was a large fee cited for SERIES #4 FULL ACCESS WITH INTERACTIVE BOARD. At the bottom of the entries was a large electronic stopwatch, also in bright red. It was set to 00:00. This was followed by the words: Day One. All the party attendees saw as the clock suddenly clicked forward 1 second, then 2 . . . as it began to keep time. It was a little like the digital clock that marks the elapsed length of a tennis match at Wimbledon or the U.S. Open.

Just beyond that was a statement: Series #4 potential duration 1 week to 1 month.

At the party, someone shouted in Russian, "Come on, Dimitri! Buy the whole package . . . start to finish! You've got the money!" This was accompanied by nervous laughter and bursts of acclamation and agreement as the man with the mustache first turned to the gathering, arms spread wide, as if asking what he should do, before he grinned, made a small, theatrical bow, and punched in some credit card numbers. As soon as he did this the screen filled with a prompt for a password. The man nodded to the sequined lady and gestured toward his computer keyboard. She smiled and typed in some letters. One might have imagined that she wrote out her lover's in-the-bedroom nickname. The party host smiled and signaled a white-jacketed waiter at the rear of the penthouse to refill glasses as his well-heeled guests settled into a fascinated quiet waiting for a final electronic confirmation of the sale.

Others, around the world, were awaiting the same thing.

There was no typical user at Whatcomesnext.com although there were probably a much lower percentage of women than men and the public nature of the party in Moscow was an exception; most of the clients signed on to Whatcomesnext.com in private locations, where they could watch the drama unfold on *Series #4* in quiet solitude. The website had created a sign-on system filled with access identification through blind passwords, double- and triple-secured, followed by a dizzying sequence of high-speed transfers to various Web engines in eastern Europe and India. It was a system that had been set up by sophisticated electronic thinking and had survived more than one effort by police to penetrate it. But because it didn't seem to have a political view—that is, the site wasn't favored by terrorist organizations—and it didn't deal overtly in child pornography, it had survived these modest and only occasional intrusions. In truth, the infrequent efforts made by police gave the site a certain cachet, or what might have been considered an Internet street cred.

Whatcomesnext.com sought out a different sort of client. The client list was made up of people who would pay handsomely for a mixture of sexual suggestion and drama that was on an edge of criminality. It used electronic chat and Internet word of high-speed mouth to pass on invitations to subscribe to its service.

The designers of the site did not think of themselves as criminals, although they had committed many crimes. Nor did they identify themselves as killers, though they had murdered. They never would have considered what they did as *perversion* although many would argue that it was precisely that. They saw themselves as modern-day entrepreneurs, who provided a specialty service, very rare, very much in demand, and greatly of interest in darker places around the world and hidden inside men.

Michael and Linda had met five years earlier at an underground sex party in a suburban Chicago house. He was a slightly shy, soft-spoken graduate doctoral student in computer sciences; she was a junior executive at a high-powered advertising agency who occasionally moonlighted for an escort service to make ends meet. She had tastes that pushed boundaries; he had fascinations that he'd never allowed himself to pursue. She had an affinity for BMWs and stimulants such as Dexedrine and flirted with dependency; as a teenager, he was arrested for stealing a neighbor's small yapping dog. The animal had bit him on the ankle one morning as he passed by on the way to school. Police believed Michael sold the dog—a bichon frise—to a man in rural Illinois who provided bait to people who fought pit bulls. Twenty-five dollars in cash. The charges against Michael had been dropped when a confidential informant that had provided authorities with his name turned out to be involved in worse crimes than dognapping. More than one policeman had seen the teenage Michael exit the courthouse a free man, his juvenile record expunged, and thought it would not be his last time there. So far these policemen had been wrong.

They had each come from questionable backgrounds and troubled, violent pasts that the veneer of their achievements managed to hide. Straight-A student and class leader and up-and-coming businesswoman. Both were intellectually sophisticated and accomplished. Outwardly, they appeared to be the type of young people who had managed to rise above humble origins. But those were external perceptions, and each, independently, thought they were lies, because their true selves were concealed in places only they could access. But they discovered these things about themselves and each other much later. The night they met had been one devoted to a different sort of education.

The rules at the gathering were simple. You had to bring a partner of the opposite sex; you could use only first names; there was to be no exchange of phone numbers or e-mail addresses after the party; were you to accidentally encounter someone at a later point in a different context you had to promise to behave as if this person was not someone you'd engaged in rough, pornographic, and public sex with but was a total stranger.

Everyone agreed to the rules. Except for the first, no one truly paid them any attention. The first *had* to be honored, because otherwise you would be turned away at the door. It was a place for assignations, and an event that spoke of disloyalty and excess. No one walking into the trim, suburban split-level home was particularly interested in *rules*.

Contradictions abounded. Two children's bicycles were abandoned on the front lawn. A shelf was crammed with Dr. Seuss books. Boxes of Cheerios and Frosted Flakes were thrust into a corner of the kitchen—to make room for a mirror left flat on the counter with chopped-up lines of cocaine put out as party favors. A television set in the family room was playing triple-X-rated fare, although few of the thirty-odd guests were paying much attention to filmed versions of what they were actually doing. Clothing was shed rapidly. Liquor was abundant. Ecstasy tablets were offered like hors d'oevres. The oldest partiers were probably in their early fifties. Most were in their thirties or forties, and when Linda came through the door and began the process of dropping her clothing more than one man looked appreciatively in her direction and instantly made plans to approach her.

As required, both Michael and Linda had arrived at the party with someone else. But they left together. Michael's "date" for the evening had been another student, a sociology doctoral candidate ostensibly interested in real-life research, who had fled the party shortly after three naked and thoroughly aroused men had cornered her, completely uninterested in her schoolgirl questions about why they were there, unwilling to listen to her weak protests as they bent her over. There was an informal request at the party that no one be *forced* to do anything they did not want to do. This was a concept that lent itself to widely different interpretations.

Linda's "partner" for the evening had been a man who called her service, and then, after treating her to an expensive dinner, had told her where he wanted to spend the rest of the evening. He'd offered to pay her more than her regular $1,500 fee. She had agreed, as long as the money came in cash and in advance, without telling him that she probably would have accompanied him for free. Curiosity, she thought, was like foreplay. After they'd arrived at the party the "partner" had disappeared into a side room carrying a black leather paddle and wearing nothing more than a tight black silken facemask, leaving Linda alone but not lacking in attention.

Their meeting—like all the meetings that night—was chance. It was an across-the-room connection in their eyes, in the languid arc of their bodies, in the silken tones of their voices. A single word, a slight dip of the head, a shrug of the shoulders—some small act of emotional intensity in a darkened room devoted to excess and orgasm, filled with naked men and women coupling in all imaginable positions and styles—were what bought them together. Each was engaged with someone else when their eyes met. Neither was *enjoying* what they were doing at that very moment. In a room filled with what most people would have considered events that were wildly different, both were a little bored. But they saw each other and something deep and probably frightening sounded within them. In fact, they did not have sex with each other that night. They merely observed each other in the act, and saw some mysterious singleness of purpose amid the groaning and cries of pleasure. Surrounded by displays of lust, they made a connection that nearly exploded. They kept their eyes locked on each other, even as strangers probed their bodies. When Michael finally picked his way through sweaty figures to her side, he displayed an aggressiveness that surprised him. He usually hung back, stumbling over words and introductions, all the time letting his desires echo unchecked within him. Linda was being slobbered over by a man whose name she didn't know. She saw Michael approach out of the corner of her eye. That she knew instinctively he wasn't coming to her side to seek out some orifice spoke to her own sea-tossed feelings. She roughly disengaged from her partner, whose clumsy administrations had bored her anyway, leaving him surprised, uncompleted, and a little angry—shutting down his fervid complaints with a single fierce glance. Then, naked, she'd stood up and taken the naked Michael's hand as if he were someone she had known for years. Without much talk they'd left the party. Just for an instant as they went in search of their clothing, hand in hand, they looked like some Renaissance artist's rendition of Adam and Eve being driven from the Garden of Eden.

In the years they had been together since, they had not thought twice about how they met. It had not taken them long to discover in each other passions that went far beyond sex and that, if dark, were also electric.

The stench of gasoline filled his nostrils.

He nearly gagged, turning his head, trying to steal a breath of fresh air. The smell made him momentarily dizzy, and he coughed as he splashed more and more of the liquid about. When the corrugated floor glistened with the rainbow colors of the gas, he pushed himself out the door and frantically tore at the air beyond, drinking in darkness.

As his head cleared he returned to the task. He dripped more gas on the exterior, went around to the front of the van, made sure the front seats were soaked.

Finally satisfied, he tossed the red container into the passenger seat. He also threw a pair of surgical gloves inside. He had prepared a plastic gallon jug with detergent and soaked a cotton fuse, making a modest napalm-type bomb. He reached into his pocket for a lighter.

Michael looked around. He was deep in an abandoned place, behind an old, shuttered, and long-empty paper mill. Once it had provided a livelihood for many in the small streamside town. Now it sat sullen as a reminder of times and jobs long lost, its windows broken and shattered from years of passing kids tossing rocks. He had taken care to park the van well away from the building; he did not want to start a fire that would attract too much attention too rapidly. He merely wanted to destroy the stolen van utterly. He had developed some expertise in this. It was not all that difficult.

He made a final check, making sure he had left nothing behind. It took only a few seconds for him to unscrew the license plates. These he intended to toss in a nearby pond. Then he stripped off all his clothes. He bundled them up, made sure they, too, were soaked in flammable fuel, and tossed them into the panel van. He shivered as the cold crept over him. Then he lit his homemade bomb and tossed it into the open van door. He quickly turned away and started running, his feet crunching against the gravel and packed dirt, hoping that he wouldn't hit a piece of stray glass and slice up the sole of his foot. Behind him there was a *thump* as the makeshift bomb went off. He slowed, took a single glance over his shoulder to make sure that the stolen van was engulfed in flame. Yellow-red streaks of fire curled through the windows and the first billowing clouds of gray and black smoke streamed skyward. Satisfied, Michael hurried, picking up his pace. He wanted to laugh out loud—the sight of a naked man running through the darkness away from an exploding panel truck was something he would have liked hearing some shocked and tongue-tied passerby explain to a skeptical policeman.

He could still catch the scent of the fire with its intoxicating subtext of incendiary smells on the light night breeze. *Who was it in the movie?* he asked himself suddenly. *Colonel Kilgore: I love the smell of napalm in the morning.* Well, he thought, in the evening it was just as seductive and it meant the same thing: *victory.*

His clothes were waiting on the driver's seat of his old, beat-up pickup truck. The keys were underneath the seat, where he'd left them. A small package of disinfectant wipes—he favored the sort used by old people with hemorrhoids—were right on top. They had less of a perfumy smell than others, but they eradicated the leftover gasoline scent rapidly. He pulled open the door and within a few seconds had rubbed himself all over with the soaked tissues. It took only a minute to pull on jeans, sweatshirt, and baseball cap. He took a last look around. No one. This was as he expected. A hundred yards away, concealed behind the building, he could see a spiral of smoke like a lighter shade of night curling into the sky, a fire glow burning beneath. He shoved himself behind the wheel and started up the truck. He took a long sniff of the interior—as expected, the stench of gasoline was gone, killed by the sanitizing wipes. Still, he plucked an aerosol can of odor-removing stuff from the glove compartment and sprayed the entire interior. This, he thought, was probably a precaution he didn't need to take. But if he *were* to be stopped by a policeman for speeding or rolling through a stop sign or failing to yield the right of way or for any other simple reason, he didn't want to smell like an arsonist.

Thinking through matters, seeing all the angles in advance, imagining each possible variable in a sea of possibilities was what Michael enjoyed almost more than everything else. It made his heart beat faster.

He put the truck in gear, pulled the cap down close to his eyes, and fiddled with a set of earphones attached to an iPod. Linda liked to make him special mixes of tunes for when he went off to do some of the grunt work associated with their business. On the MENU screen he saw a play list: Gasoline Music. This made him laugh out loud. He leaned back as something by Chris Whitley that had a nasty bit of steel guitar in it powered through the speakers. He listened to the singer hit a few strings. ". . . like a walking translation on a street of lies . . ." *True enough*, he thought as he pulled out of the abandoned warehouse parking lot. Linda *always* knew what he liked to hear.

In a plastic bag on the seat next to him was the credit card belonging to some woman named Riggins that he'd taken from Number 4's wallet. One or two quick tasks on the road and in Boston and then he'd get back to Linda. The truck had warmed up and heat was pouring through the vents, wafting over him. It was still nasty cold and damp outside. He decided that their next Web broadcast should originate in Florida or Arizona. But that was getting ahead of the current series, which he knew was a mistake. Michael prided himself on a singularity of focus; once they were engaged, nothing got in the way, nothing was allowed to obstruct, derail, or distract from what they were doing. He believed any successful artist or business-man would say the same thing about his or her work projects. *Can't write a novel or compose a song, can't swing an acquisition or expand an offering without complete devotion to the task at hand,* he spoke inwardly to himself.

Linda knew the same.

It was why they loved each other so much.

He thought: *I am incredibly lucky.*

Michael settled in for the two-hour drive to the city. Back at the rental farmhouse she would have everything going. They were probably almost rich already, he thought. But it wasn't about the money for him or for her. The start of *Series #4* excited him and he could feel overwhelmingly pleasant warmth coursing through his core, warmth far different from the heat coming through the truck system. It beat time to the music that filled the truck compartment.

6

Inside the black hood that covered her head, Jennifer's entire world had narrowed to just what she could hear, what she could smell, and what she could taste and each of these senses was limited—by the pounding of her heart, the throbbing headache that lingered behind her temples, the claustrophobic darkness that enveloped her. She tried to calm herself but, beneath the silken black cloth, she sobbed uncontrollably, salty tears running down her cheeks, her throat dry and raw.

She wanted desperately to cry out for help although she knew none was close by. The word *Mom* slipped through her lips, but beyond the darkness she could see only her dead father standing just beyond her reach, as if he were outdoors and unable to hear her cries because they couldn't quite penetrate some glass wall. For an instant she felt dizzy, as if she were teetering on a cliff's edge, just able to keep her balance, with a strong gust of wind threatening her equilibrium.

She told herself, *Jennifer, you've got to keep control . . .*

She was unsure whether she spoke these words out loud or merely shouted them inwardly to all the warring confusions and hurts that were racing about within her. It was almost impossible for her to tell whether she was in pain or whether she was in doubt. Each seemed to hurt equally, but she knew she needed to make some sense of what was happening beyond the hood.

She told herself to take deep breaths. *Jennifer! Try!*

There was something oddly reassuring in speaking to herself in the third person. It reinforced her sense that she was alive, that she was who she was, that she still had a past, a present, and maybe a future.

Jennifer, stop crying!

She gulped at the stale, hot air inside the hood.

Okay. Okay.

It wasn't as easy as that. It took minutes for her to calm down, but the gasps and sobs of fear finally slowed and nearly stopped, although there was nothing she could do to halt the uncontrollable quivering that infected each muscle, especially in her legs. They were twitching fiercely, spasms that made her whole body feel Jell-O-like. It was as if there was something disconnected between what she could think, what she could perceive, and how her body was reacting. Nothing was synchronized. Nothing was coordinated. Everything was out of focus and out of control. She could not find any mental grip within her that she could seize so she might try to understand what had happened and what might still happen.

She shivered, although she wasn't cold; in fact, it was very hot in the room. For the first time she became aware that she was nearly naked. Once again, she shuddered through her entire body. She could not remember being undressed, nor could she remember being brought into the room. The only thing she recalled was the man's fist coming at her like a bullet, and the sensation of being thrown into the back of the truck. It all confused her; she was unsure whether it had really occurred. For a second, she imagined she was dreaming, and that all she had to do was stay calm, and then she would wake up in her bed at home and she could go down to the kitchen and fix herself some coffee and a Pop-Tart and remind herself of all her plans to run away.

Jennifer waited. Beneath the hood, she squeezed her eyes shut and told herself *Wake up! Wake up!* But she knew this was a hopeless wish. She wasn't nearly lucky enough to have it all dissolve into a dream.

All right, Jennifer, she told herself. *Concentrate on one thing. Just one thing. Make one thing real. Then go from there.*

She was suddenly terribly thirsty. She ran her tongue over her lips. They were dry, cracked, and she could taste more blood. She pushed against her teeth with her tongue. Nothing loose. She crinkled her nose. No pain. *All right, now you know something useful: no broken nose, no fractured teeth. That's good.*

Jennifer could feel something near her stomach that itched. There was also an odd sensation on her arm that she could not place. These confused her more.

She knew she had to take two different inventories: one of her self, one of where she was. She had to try to make some sort of sense out of the darkness and come up with some kind of clarity. Where was she? What was happening to her?

But these simple tasks eluded her. And the more she insisted on control, the more elusive it seemed. The blackness inside the hood seemed like it was taking over within her, as if the hood did more than merely prevent her from seeing out; it prevented her from seeing *in*. She had the sense that her entire world was descending into her stomach and painting over her mind; all she could imagine was a fierce terror of nothingness. And then, as this despair swept over her, she understood a truly awful idea: *Jennifer, you're still alive. Whatever it is that is happening to you, it's not going to be anything you've ever known before or ever even imagined taking place. It's not going to be quick. It's not going to be easy. This is just the beginning of something.*

She could feel herself spiraling down. A vortex. A whirlpool. A hole in the emptiness of the universe. Her legs shook and she was powerless to prevent the sobs from returning. She gave in to the fear, and her entire body was wracked with agonizing spasms right until the moment she heard the muffled sound of a door opening.

She bent to the sound. Someone was in the room with her.

She thought in that split second that being alone created the terror echoing within her. But in truth being alone was far better than knowing that she was not. Her back arced, her muscles tightened; if she could have seen herself, she would have imagined that her body reacted to the sound in the same way it would have to an electric current.

I have become an old man, Adrian told himself as he stared in the mirror above his wife's bureau. It was a small, wooden framed mirror and over the years she had used it to do little more than make a final check of her appearance before heading out on a Saturday evening. Women liked that last-second examination, making certain that things matched, blended, and complemented each other before they sallied forth. He was never that precise in how he'd appeared to the world. He affected a far more haphazard look—rumpled shirt, baggy pants, tie slightly askew—in keeping with his academic life. *I always looked like a caricature of a professor, because I was a professor. I was a man of science.* He reached up and touched the streaks of white-gray hair that fell from his scalp and rubbed his hand across the gray-flecked stubble on his chin. He ran a finger down a line creased in his flesh. Age had scarred him, he thought; age and all the experiences of life.

From behind he heard a familiar voice.

"You know what you saw."

He looked into the mirror.

"Hello, *Possum,*" Adrian said, smiling. "You said that already. A few minutes ago."

He stopped. Maybe it had been an hour. Two. How long had he been standing in the bedroom, surrounded by images and memories with a weapon in his hand?

He used his wife's nickname, one that had been shared only with the closest members of the family. She had acquired it as a nine-year-old, when a crew of the slightly more than rodents had moved into the attic of

47

the family's summer home. She had insisted to her brothers, sisters, and parents that *any* attempt to oust the unwanted invaders would be met with all the retaliatory resources that a dedicated child could muster, from tears to tantrums. So, for that one summer, at least, her family had put up with the nocturnal scratching sounds of clawed feet racing through the eaves, undefined threats of disease, and general distaste for the beasts, who had the unsettling habit of staring intently at the family members from the shadows. The possum family, for its part, had not taken long to discover the many wondrous attractions of the kitchen, especially since the creatures instinctively seemed to understand the unique status that their nine-year-old protector had bestowed upon them. *Cassandra was like that,* Adrian thought. *A fierce defender*.

"Adrian. *You know what you saw,*" she repeated herself, this time far more forcefully. Her voice had a familiar rhythmic insistence to it. When Cassie had wanted something done in all the years of their marriage, usually it had been expressed in tones more suited to a 1960s folk song.

He turned to the bed. Cassie was stretched out, languid, with a *come hither* look on her face. She was the most beautiful hallucination he could have imagined. She wore a loose-fitting cornflower blue shift with nothing underneath, and it seemed to him that a breeze pulled it invitingly tight to her body although there wasn't a window open, nor even a hint of wind within the bedroom. Adrian could feel his pulse accelerate. The Cassie looking at him from her perch on the bed couldn't have been more than twenty-eight, as she was at the beginning of their first year together. Her skin glowed with youth; each curve of her body—her slight breasts, narrow hips, and long legs—seemed like memories he could feel. She shook her dark mane of hair and frowned at him, her mouth turning down at the corners in a small way that he recognized; it meant that she was very serious, and that he needed to pay attention to each word. He had learned early in their life together the look that spoke to something more important.

"You look beautiful," he said. "Do you remember when we went to the Cape in August and went skinny-dipping in the ocean that one night, and then couldn't find our clothes in the dunes after the current knocked us down the beach?"

Cassandra shook her head. "Of course I remember. It was our first summer together. I remember everything. But that's not why I'm here. *You know what you saw.*"

Adrian wanted to run the tips of his fingers down her skin so that he could remind himself of every electric touch from their past. But he was afraid that if he reached out she would disappear. He did not fully understand his relationship with her hallucination, what the rules were. But he knew that he did not want her to leave.

"That's not altogether true," he replied slowly. "I'm not at all sure."

"I know it isn't exactly your field," Cassie said. "Not precisely. You were never one of the forensic boys—you know, the guys who liked to deconstruct serial killers and terrorists and then entertain their classes with gory stories. You liked all those rats in cages and mazes and figuring out what they were going to do with the right stimuli. But you absolutely know enough about abnormal psychology to assess the case at hand."

"It could have been anything. And when I called, the police told me—"

Cassie interrupted him. She pushed her head back, another familiar gesture where she looked for answers in the ceiling or the sky. This would happen when he was being obstinate. She had been an artist, and she had an artist's appreciation of events: *Draw a line, make a stroke of color on a canvas, and it will all become clear.* She always followed this *look to the heavens* gesture with something pointed and demanding. It was a habit that he'd loved because she had always been so absolutely certain.

"I *don't care* what they told you. She was there, on the side of the road, and then she was gone. It was a crime. It *had* to be. You witnessed it. By accident. Only you. So now you have a few stray pieces of a really difficult puzzle. It's up to you. Put them together."

Adrian hesitated.

"Will you help me? I'm sick. I mean, *Possum,* I'm really sick. I don't know how much longer anything is going to work for me. Things are

49

already sliding. Things are already coming unraveled. If I take this on—whatever *it* is—I don't know that I can survive it . . ."

"You were going to shoot yourself a few minutes ago," Cassie said briskly, as if that explained everything. She raised her hand and gestured broadly toward the Ruger 9.

"I wanted to be with you. And with Tommy. I didn't think it made any sense to wait any longer."

"Except you saw the girl on the street and she disappeared and this is important."

"I don't even know who she is."

"Whoever she is, she still deserves a chance to live. And you're the only one who can give it to her."

"I don't even know where to start."

"Pieces of a puzzle. Save her, Adrian."

"I'm not a police detective."

"But you can think like one, only better."

"I'm old and I'm sick and I can't think straight anymore."

"You can still think straight enough. Just this last time. Then it will all be over."

"I can't do it alone."

"You won't be alone."

"I could never save anyone. I couldn't save you or Tommy or my brother or any of the people I really loved. How can I save someone I don't even know?"

"Isn't that the answer we all try to find?"

Cassie was smiling now. He knew that *she knew* that she had won the argument. She always won, because Adrian had discovered within the first few minutes of their years together that it gave him far more pleasure to agree with her than to fight with her. Adrian said, "You were so beautiful when we were young. I never could understand how someone as beautiful as you wanted to be with me."

She laughed. "Women know," she said. "It seems a mystery to men, but it isn't to women. We *know*."

Adrian hesitated. He thought for a moment that tears were welling up in his eyes, but he didn't know what he had to cry about, other than everything.

"I'm so sorry, Cassie. I didn't mean to get old."

That sounded crazy. But it also made a curious sense to him.

She laughed. He closed his eyes for a moment to listen to the sound. It was like an orchestra reaching for symphonic perfection.

"I hate it that I'm all alone," he said. "I hate it that you're dead."

"This will bring us closer."

Adrian nodded. "Yes," he said. "I think you are right."

He looked over at the bureau. The prescription scripts from the neurologist were gathered in a pile. He had meant to throw them away. Instead, he picked them up.

"Maybe," he said slowly, "some of these will buy me a little extra . . ."

He turned, but Cassie had vanished from the bed. Adrian sighed. *Get started,* he told himself. *There is so little time left.*

7

She closed the door behind her and then stopped. She could feel a rush of excitement within her, and she wanted to savor it for a moment.

Linda generally arranged things in precise order, even her passions. For a woman with extravagant desires and exotic tastes, she was dedicated to routine and regimentation. She liked to plan her indulgences, so that every step of the way she knew exactly what to expect and how it would taste. Instead of dulling sensations, this quality heightened them. It was as if these two parts of her personality were in constant battle, tugging her in different directions. But she loved the tension that it created within her; it made her feel unique, and it made her into the truly extraordinary criminal she believed herself—and Michael—to be.

Linda imagined herself to be Faye Dunaway's *Bonnie* to Michael's Warren Beatty *Clyde*. She considered herself to be sensuous, poetic, and seductive. This wasn't arrogance on her part as much as it was an honest appreciation of the way she looked and the effect she had on men.

Of course, she didn't care for anyone who stared at her. She cared only for Michael.

She slowly let her eyes sweep over the basement room. Stark white walls. An old brown metal frame bed with a white sheet covering a dingy gray mattress. A portable camp toilet in the corner. Large overhead lights threw unrelenting brightness into every corner. The still, hot air smelled unpleasantly of disinfectant and fresh paint. Michael had done his usual good job at fixing everything up for the start of *Series #4*. She was always a little surprised by how handy he had become—his expertise was with the computers and Web operations that he had studied in college and graduate school. But he was also adept with an electric power drill and a hammer and nails. He was a regular jack-of-all-trades. Perhaps that was why she loved him as deeply as she did.

Linda believed the two of them were linked in a way that defined *special*.

She paused and took a detective's inventory. What could she see in the room that gave the basement any sort of recognizable identity? What might show up in the background of the webcast that indicated *anything* about where they were or who they might be?

She knew enough to realize that something as mundane as a pipe fitting or a water heater or a light fixture could lead an enterprising police officer in their direction—if one ever chose to look. The pipe fitting might be measurable in inches, not centimeters, which would tell this clever and deeply imagined detective—Linda liked to try to envision this person— that they were in the United States. The water heater could be manufactured for Sears and be a model that was distributed only in the eastern part of the United States. The light fixture might be identifiable from a lot shipped to the local Home Depot.

Having those details might just bring this fictional detective closer. He would be part Miss Marple, part Sherlock Holmes, with just a touch of gritty fake-slick television reality. He might affect a rumpled *Columbo* look, or maybe a high-tech, close-cropped *Jack Bauer* style.

Of course, she reminded herself, *he* wasn't really out there.

No one was, except for the clientele. And they were lining up, ready, waiting for their credit card charges to be approved and then eager to watch *What Comes Next*.

Linda shook her head and breathed in deeply. Seeing the world through the narrow lens of paranoia made her excited; the passion attached to *Series #4* was created in great part by the utter anonymity of the setting. It created the blankest of canvases on which they could draw their show. There was no way anyone watching could ever tell with any certitude what was about to happen, which was its great attraction. Linda knew most Internet pornography was about being totally explicit—images that left no doubt whatsoever about what was going on; theirs was the exact opposite. It was about suddenness. The unexpected. It was about creativity. It was about invention.

It could be about sex.

It could be about control.

It was about imprisonment.

It was violent.

It was definitely about life.

It might also be about death.

That was why they were so successful.

She closed the door behind her. She took a moment to adjust the mask over her face; for this first moment, she had chosen a simple black balaclava that concealed her shaggy blond hair and had only a slit for her eyes. It was the sort of headgear favored by antiterrorist SWAT teams, and she was likely to wear it frequently throughout the duration of *Series #4* even if it did feel tight and confining. Beneath that, she wore a white Hazmat suit constructed of processed paper that crinkled and made swishing noises as she took a step forward. The suit hid her shape; no one could tell if she was large or slight, young or old. Linda knew she had a considerable voluptuousness beneath the suit; wearing it was like teasing herself. The material pinched at her naked skin, like a lover interested in delivering small amounts of pain alongside larger amounts of pleasure.

She tugged on surgical gloves. Her feet were encased in the floppy blue sterile slippers that were de rigueur in an operating theater. Beneath her mask she smiled, thinking, *This is an operating theater.*

She took a few steps forward. *I am newly beautiful,* she thought.

She turned to the figure on the bed. *Jennifer,* she reminded herself. *No more. Now she is Number 4.* Age: sixteen. A suburban girl from a cloistered academic community, plucked almost by happenstance from a street. She knew Number 4's address, her home phone, her few friends, and much more already, all details she had gleaned from a careful examination of the contents of the girl's backpack, cell phone, and wallet.

Linda moved to the center of the room, still a dozen feet from the old iron bed. Michael had sunk rings into the wall behind the frame for the handcuffs. Like a television sitcom director, he had drawn a few faint chalk lines on the floor to indicate which camera would capture her image and placed X's in tape at key spots to stand. Profile. Full frontal. Overhead. They had learned in the past that it was important always to remember what camera shot was available, and what it would show. Viewers expected many angles and professional camera work.

As voyeurs, they expected the best, a constant intimacy.

There were five cameras in the room, although only one was clearly prominent and immediately visible, the main fixed Sony HD camera on a tripod aimed at the bed. The others were minicams concealed in the ceiling overhead and in two corners of the artificial walls. Only one would pick up the entrance, and that one was saved for dramatic purposes, moments when either Michael or Linda was entering the room. It would titillate the viewers because *something* was going to take place. Linda knew that at this moment it was shut down. This visit was preliminary, just the first move in the feeling-out process.

In her pocket was a small electronic remote control. She slipped her finger over a button that she knew would freeze the image being fed out electronically. She waited until the moment that the hooded girl nervously turned ever so slightly in Linda's direction. Then she hit the button.

They will know she heard something . . .

. . . But they won't know what.

She and Michael had long before learned the advantages of *the tease* in sales.

She walked slowly forward.

The girl was following her movements beneath the mask encasing her head. She had not said anything yet. Fear made some people rattle on aimlessly and helplessly, begging, pleading, reverting to infancy, while others managed a sullen, doomed silence. She did not know what Number 4 would be like. She was the youngest subject they'd ever employed, which made it an adventure for Michael and her as well.

Linda took up a position at the foot of the bed. She spoke in a flat monotone that concealed her own excitement. She did not raise her voice or emphasize any word. She remained utterly cold. She was practiced at the art of delivering threats, and equally practiced at carrying them out.

"Do not say anything. Do not move. Do not scream or struggle. Just pay attention to everything I tell you and you will not be hurt. If you expect to live through this, you will do exactly as you are told at all times, regardless of what it is you are asked to do and what you might feel about doing it."

The girl on the bed stiffened and quivered but did not speak.

"Those are the most important rules. There will be others later."

She paused. She half expected the girl to plead with her right at that moment. But Jennifer remained quiet.

"From now on, your name is Number Four."

Linda thought she heard a small moan, muffled by the black hood. That was acceptable, even expected.

"If you are asked a question, you must answer. Do you understand?"

Jennifer nodded.

"Answer!"

"Yes," she said rapidly, her voice gasping beneath the mask.

Linda hesitated. She tried to imagine the panic beneath the headgear. *Not like high school, little girl, is it?*

She did not say this out loud. Instead, she simply continued her monotone.

"Let me explain something, Number Four. Everything you knew about your life before has now ended. Who you were, what you wanted to be, your family, your friends—*everything that was once familiar*—no longer exists. There is only this room and what happens in here."

Again, Linda examined Jennifer's body language, as if looking for some clue that she understood.

"From this moment, you belong to us."

The girl seemed to stiffen and freeze. But she did not cry out. Others had. Number 3 in particular had battled them almost every step of the way—fighting, biting, screaming—which, of course, hadn't been an altogether bad thing once Michael and she had figured out what the rules had to be, because it created a different type of drama. That was part of the adventure and part of the attraction, Linda knew. Each subject demanded a different set of rules. Each was unique from the very beginning. She could sense excited warmth coursing through her own body but she controlled it. She looked over at the girl on the bed. *She is listening carefully,* Linda thought. *Smart girl.*

Not bad, Linda decided right then. *Not bad at all. She will be special.*

Jennifer screamed inwardly, as if suddenly she could let loose something within herself that reflected her terror and could travel beyond the mask, beyond the chains that confined her, past any walls and ceilings out somewhere where she might be heard. She thought that if she could just make some noise it would help her remember who she was and that she was still alive. But she did not. Outwardly, she choked back a sob and bit down hard on her lip. Everything was a question, nothing was an answer.

She could sense the voice was moving closer. A woman? *Yes.* The woman in the panel truck? *It had to be.*

Jennifer tried to remember what she had seen. It was nothing more than a glimpse of someone older than her but not old like her mother, wearing a black knit cap pulled down over her hair. *Blond hair.* She pictured a leather jacket but that was all. The blow that had crashed into her face and rocked her had obscured everything else.

"Here . . ." She heard the word, as if something was being offered to her, but she did not know what it was. She heard a metallic snipping sound, and she could not prevent herself from recoiling.

"No. Do not move."

Jennifer froze.

There was an instant—and then she could feel the loose folds of her mask being pulled forward. She was still unsure what was happening but she could hear the sound of scissors.

A piece of the mask fell away. It was over her mouth. A small opening.

"Water."

A plastic straw was thrust through the slit, bumping up against her lips. She was suddenly terribly thirsty, so parched that whatever was happening took a back seat to the desire to drink. She seized the straw with her tongue and lips and pulled hard. The water was brackish, with a taste she could not recognize.

"Better?"

She nodded.

"You will sleep now. Later you will learn precisely what is expected of you."

Jennifer felt a chalky taste on her tongue. Beneath the hood, she could sense her head spinning. Her eyes rolled back and, as once again she descended into an internal darkness, she wondered whether she had been poisoned, which didn't make any sense to her. Nothing made sense except the awful sensation that it did to the woman with the voice and the man who had punched her into unconsciousness. She wanted to shout out something, to protest, or just to hear the sound of her own voice. But before she could form some words and thrust them past her cracked dry lips, she felt as if she were teetering on a narrow ledge. Then, as the drugs clumsily concealed in the water took hold, she felt herself tumbling.

8

What she needed to do was to both hurry up and be patient.

Terri Collins knew that the best chances to find Jennifer were rapidly sliding past, so she had to move quickly in the few areas that *might* work. But she was filled with doubt, not only of the likelihood of a quick *Here she is* success but of the actual reasons behind Jennifer's third time running away from home. Too many questions, not enough answers.

By the time she got back to her office it was well past midnight, creeping into the early morning hours. Other than the phone dispatcher and a couple of overnight duty patrolmen, there was little activity in the building. The cops watching over the nearby colleges and suburban streets were all out on patrol or holed up at a Dunkin' Donuts fueling themselves with coffee and sweets.

She hustled to her desk. She immediately dialed numbers for the police substations at both the main bus terminal in Springfield and the downtown train station. She also contacted the Massachusetts State Police barracks along the turnpike and the Boston Transit Police. These conversations were brisk—a general description of Jennifer, a quick plea to keep an eye out for her, a promise to follow up with a faxed photo and MISSING PERSONS flyer. In official worlds, the police needed copies of the documents in order to act; in the unofficial world, getting some phone calls and some radio traffic out to the late-night shifts working the bus stations and the highways might be all that was necessary. If they were lucky, Terri hoped, a trooper cruising the Mass Pike would see Jennifer forlornly hitchhiking near an entry ramp or a cop taking a pass through North Station would spot her in line for a ticket and all would end up more or less resolved: a stern talking-to, a ride in the back of a squad car, a teary-eyed (that would be the mother) and sullen-faced (that would be Jennifer) reunion, and then everything that had been one way before would continue again—until the next time she decided to escape.

Terri worked quickly to create the circumstances that might lead to that rosy scenario. She tossed her bag, her badge, her gun, and her note-book on her desk in the small warren of offices that the college town police department called the detective bureau but which was sarcasti-cally referred to on the force as Gold Shield City. She dialed numbers rapidly, spoke directly to dispatchers and shift lieutenants using her best *try to move fast* voice.

Her next calls went to Verizon Wireless security. She explained to the person in a call center in Omaha who she was and the urgency of the situation. She wanted *any* usage of Jennifer's cell phone reported to her immediately along with the identification of the cell phone tower that processed the call. Jennifer might not know that her cell phone was like a beacon that could be traced back to her. *She's smart,* Terri thought, *but not that smart.*

Terri also alerted overnight security at Bank of America, who would report if Jennifer tried to use her ATM card. She did not have a credit card—Mary Riggins and Scott West had been adamant that this indul-gence was for affluent others and not Jennifer. Terri hadn't quite believed this.

She tried to think of anything else that might diminish Jennifer's invis-ibility. She had already gone past her department's formal guidelines because, technically, a Missing Persons report couldn't be filed for twenty-four hours and a runaway wasn't considered a crime. Not yet. Not until something actually happened. Terri was all too aware that the *something* that might happen was usually terrible. The informal idea was to find the child before it happened.

She did not believe for an instant they would be so lucky.

After she made the calls, Terri went to a large black steel case file container located in a corner of the office. The Riggins family file documented the two previous runaway efforts. After the previous attempt Terri had left the manila folder in the ACTIVE section, where it had remained for more than a year. It should have been sent to storage but Terri had known that this particular night was inevitable even if she didn't know exactly *why.*

She plucked the folder from the cabinet and returned to her desk. She had most of the relevant information stored in her memory—Jennifer wasn't the sort of teenager that one forgot easily—but she knew it was important to go over details, because perhaps a clue to where she was heading now had emerged in one of her prior attempts. Good police work is plodding and determined and relies to a great degree on looking at minutiae. Terri wanted to make certain that all her reports on this case that traveled up the bureaucratic chain of command displayed attention to every possibility for success.

She knew she wanted this, even if the chances of success were slight. She sighed deeply. Finding Jennifer was going to be hard. In truth, the best hope was that the teenager would run out of money before she'd been pimped into prostitution or addicted to drugs or raped and murdered and she would call home and that would be that, sort of. The problem, Terri realized, was that Jennifer had planned this escape. She was a determined teenager. Stubborn and intelligent. Terri did not think that giving up at the first sign of trouble was in Jennifer's DNA. The problem was, the *first* sign of trouble might also be the last.

Terri opened the case file and placed it on her desk, next to the laptop computer that she had removed from Jennifer's room. Jennifer had placed two bright red flower stickers on the outside and also a SAVE THE WHALES bumper sticker. Ordinarily, she would wait until morning and then contact the state attorney's office to have one of its forensic technicians examine the computer. Bureaucracy squared. But Terri had audited a graduate-level course at the local university on cyber crime and she already knew enough to get into the hard drive and make a ghost of what was contained there, and then to transfer all the data to a flash drive. She reached for the computer and opened it.

She took a single glance toward the window. She could see dawn light creeping through the branches of a stately brown oak tree on the perimeter of the department's parking lot. For a few moments she watched. The light seemed to seek out and penetrate the budding leaves and rough bark skin of the tree, pushing shadows aside briskly. She knew she should have been exhausted after the long all-nighter but her adrenaline gave her just enough energy to carry her forward a little farther. Coffee might help, she thought. She reminded herself to call her home soon, make sure that Laurie had awakened the kids and made their school lunches and hustled them out the door in time for the bus. She hated not being there when they awoke, although the kids would likely be pleased to see Laurie. They always thought it exciting when their mother was called away on some midnight police errand. For a second, Terri closed her eyes. She had a momentary shock of anxiety: *Would Laurie watch them get on the bus? She wouldn't leave them on the side of the street waiting . . .*

Terri shook her head. Her friend was more reliable than that.

Fear, she thought, is always something hidden just beneath the skin, waiting to burst forth.

She touched the computer's ON-OFF switch and the machine blinked to life. *Are you here, Jennifer? What are you going to tell me?*

She wondered whether every minute that passed was more valuable than the last. She knew she should have waited for the official go-ahead to probe the machine. But she did not.

Michael was inordinately pleased with himself.

After burning the stolen van he had stopped at a rest area on the turnpike, where he'd managed to leave a library card with the name *Jennifer Riggins* in the ladies' room. He had nursed a cup of black coffee in the food area, between a McDonald's and a shuttered frozen yogurt kiosk, eyeing travelers as they clattered through the area, waiting for the moment he could be certain that no one was in the bathroom. A quick check had ascertained that there were no security cameras in the vestibule leading to the doors marked MEN and WOMEN. Nevertheless, throughout his time, he'd kept a dark blue baseball cap scrunched down on his head, the visor cutting off any camera that might pick up his profile. He crunched up the coffee container, dropped it into a wastebasket, and made his way to the door marked MEN. But at the last second he'd swerved into the ladies' room. He was there only seconds—just long enough to drop the card faceup next to a toilet, where it was likely to be spotted by the next cleanup crew that entered to mop the floors.

He knew there was every chance that they would just toss the card in the trash. But it was also possible they might not, which would serve his purposes.

Back outside in his truck, Michael settled behind the driver's seat and pulled out a small laptop computer. He was pleased to see that the rest area was covered with a wireless Internet connection.

Like the van they'd used, the computer was stolen. He'd plucked it from a tabletop at a university dining hall three days earlier. This had been a remarkably easy theft. He scooped up the computer when a student had left it to get a cheeseburger. With fries, Michael guessed. The important thing had been *not* to grab it and run. That would have attracted attention. Instead, he'd slipped it into a black neoprene computer sleeve and walked to a table on the opposite side of the room, where he'd waited until the student returned, saw the loss, and started yelling. He'd put the stolen computer in a backpack so it was concealed, then walked over to the small group gathered around the irate student. "Dude, you gotta call campus security right away," he'd said, in his best graduate school, slightly older voice. "Don't wait, you gotta get on it." This sentiment had been met with many murmurs of agreement. And in the moments afterward, as cell phones popped out of pockets and confusion reigned, Michael had simply sidled away from the gathered undergraduates with the stolen laptop cavalierly hidden inside his backpack. He'd marched jauntily through the knots of students to a parking area outside where Linda was waiting.

Certain thefts, he thought, were incredibly easy.

Within a few seconds working the keyboard Michael had reached a reservation window for the Trailways bus lines in Boston. He continued clicking computer keys, feeding in the credit card number from the Visa card he'd taken from Jennifer's wallet. He presumed *Mary* was her mother.

He purchased a one-way ticket on a 2 a.m. bus to New York City. The idea was to create a modest trail for Jennifer—if anyone went looking for her. *A trail to nowhere,* he thought.

Then he had put the truck in gear and left the rest area. He knew of a Dumpster behind a large office building just outside Boston that had early morning pickups and he wanted to toss the computer there, beneath piles of trash. Anyone clever enough to trace the reservation back would find a most curious IP address.

The stop after that was the Boston bus station. It was a stolid square building with a haze of diesel engine smoke and a thick oily smell, illuminated by unforgiving neon lights. There was always an ebb and flow of passengers and buses, moving out onto the streets, passing through the city's attractions before heading out on Route 93 north or south or on 90 west. It reminded him of dropping a thermometer onto a hard floor and seeing little silver droplets of mercury spread out in all directions.

The bus station had electronic ticketing but he waited until several people crowded around the ATM-like dispenser. He joined them, swiped the stolen Visa card, and got the ticket. It had *Ms. M. Riggins* printed on it. He kept his head down. He knew there were security cameras covering much of the bus station, and he imagined that it might be possible for a cop to compare the time stamp on the ticket with video of the dispenser and see that no Jennifer was in sight. *Caution,* he told himself.

As soon as he obtained the ticket he headed for the men's room. Inside, he quickly checked to make sure he was alone and then locked himself into a stall. He opened his backpack and took out a different coat, a floppy bucket-style hat, and a fake beard and mustache. It took him only a few seconds to transform his appearance and head back outside and find a spot in a darkened corner to wait.

The station had a constant but bored police presence. Their main job was searching for homeless folks who were looking for a warm and safe place to spend the night but who disdained the many shelters available. The cops' other duty seemed to be preventing someone from being mugged, which might result in an unfortunate headline. The bus station was an edgy place; he could sense he was on the fringe between normalcy, respectability, and crime, one of those spots where different worlds rubbed uncomfortably up against each other.

Michael thought he looked like he belonged with the respectable folks, which was a nice type of camouflage against the truth.

Then he waited, seated in an uncomfortable molded red plastic chair, nervously tapping his toes, trying to remain unnoticed, until he saw what he needed: three college-age girls with one distracted-looking boyfriend accompanying them. They all carried backpacks and appeared unaffected by the lateness of the hour. But they also looked like the do-gooder types that would want to do the right thing when they found something that wasn't theirs. They would call someone. That was what he wanted. *Mystery layered upon mystery.*

He slowly pulled into line behind them, collar turned up, hat pulled down because he knew this time for certain there were security cameras taping everything. *The goddamn Patriot Act,* he joked to himself. Except it wasn't hard to find Internet postings that told him pretty much where those cameras were located and how they conducted surveillance. He waited until the crew of college-age kids crowded forward trying to get the harried late-night ticket man to handle their requests all at once. At that moment, he surreptitiously reached forward and slipped the Visa card into an open pouch on one of the backpacks.

Sleight of hand, he thought, *worthy of Houdini.*

This made him smile because, in their own way, what he and Linda had done was magic: *Jennifer had disappeared.*

In her place, handcuffed and hooded, a frozen image heading out into the cyber world, was Number 4.

9

Adrian stood across from the pharmacist and watched as she efficiently scooped various pills into containers. Occasionally she would look up at him standing at the drugstore counter and smile wanly. He could sense that she had a small comment on the tip of her lips, but she swallowed it each time it threatened to burst forth. It was a look that he was familiar with from the front of the classroom, when a student launched into some soliloquy that might be totally on point but also could be flying off on a disconnected tangent. For an instant he felt like a professor again. He wanted to lean across the counter and whisper something like *I know what all these pills mean, and I know you know it, too, but I'm not scared of dying. Not in the slightest. But what worries me is fading away and these are supposed to help slow that process down, although I know they won't.*

He wanted to say this but he did not.

Or perhaps he did, and she did not hear him. He was unsure.

The pharmacist approached him. "These are really expensive," she said, "even with comprehensive insurance from the college. I'm terribly sorry."

It was as if by apologizing for the outrageous cost of the medication she could actually tell him that she was sorry he was as sick as he was.

"It's all right," he said. He thought of adding something like *I won't need them for all that long* but, again, he did not.

He fumbled in his wallet and then handed over a credit card and watched several hundred dollars get charged to his account. He had a slightly humorous thought: *Don't pay it. Let's see the bloodsuckers try to get the money out of some old drooling fool who doesn't remember what day it is, much less even making the charges.*

Adrian carried a paper bag filled with medications outside the pharmacy into a bright morning. He ripped open the container and dropped an Exelon into his palm. This was joined by Prozac and Namenda, which were supposed to help with confusion, which he didn't think he needed yet, although he was willing to concede that this might be a sign of exactly what the pill was supposed to help. He only glanced at the long list of nasty side effects that accompanied each medication. Whatever they were, they could hardly be worse than what was awaiting him. There was also an antipsychotic in the bag, but he did not open this vial and was tempted to throw it away. He popped the selection of pills into his mouth and swallowed hard.

A start, Adrian told himself.

"Okay, now that you've taken care of that, let's get down to business," his brother said briskly. "Time to find out who *Jennifer* is."

Adrian turned slowly toward the sound of his brother's voice. "Hello, Brian," he said. He couldn't help but break into a smile. "I was hoping you would show up sooner or later."

Brian was perched on the hood of Adrian's old Volvo, knees drawn up, smoking a cigarette. Smoke curled up into the blue sky above the two of them. He was wearing filthy, tattered olive drab fatigues that were flecked with blood spatters. His flak jacket was ripped. His helmet was at his feet, sporting a peace symbol drawn in thick black ink and an American flag decal with the words *Death Dealer and Heart Stealer* scrawled beneath it. He had rested his M-16 between his legs, holding the stock in place with his jungle boots. Sweat streaked Brian's face, and he was pale and cadaverously thin and barely twenty-three years old. He was resting in a position similar to a photo that had been taken years earlier—a Larry Burrows picture, snapped on assignment for *Life* shortly before he was killed and that his brother had kept framed on his desk in his office as a reminder, as he had once told Adrian, although he wasn't specific as to what he was reminding himself of. The photo was now in a dusty box in Adrian's basement, along with many of his brother's other things, including the Silver Star he'd won and never told anyone about.

As Adrian watched, Brian stepped down from the hood with a slow, painful motion, as if he was exhausted, but which had a complacent laziness that Adrian recognized from their childhood. Brian was never hurried, even when things were exploding all around them. It was one of his best qualities—the ability to see clearly when others panicked—and Adrian had always loved his brother for the calmness he projected. Caught in a dangerous current, Brian could swim when others floundered and drowned. In all their years growing up, separated by just two years in age, whenever something—*anything*—had happened, Adrian had always looked first to his brother to gauge what his own reaction should be. Which had made his death all that much more incomprehensible to Adrian.

Brian shook himself like a dog unhappily rising from a deep sleep and pointed at his right arm, where the battle tunic sleeve was rolled up, leaving only a single patch visible—the solid bar and horse's head profile of the First Air Cavalry in yellow and black

Brian stretched his thin, muscled arms and slung his weapon over his shoulder. He looked up into the glare of the sun, shading his eyes momentarily.

"College town, oh brother of mine," he said. "Pretty tame. Not like Nam," he said with a half-joking snort.

Adrian shook his head. "And not like Harvard, or Columbia Law School. Or that big firm on Wall Street you worked for. And not much like the big Upper East Side apartment where you—"

He stopped. "Sorry," he quickly apologized.

Brian laughed. "Not like a lot of things. And don't worry about it. You want to talk about why I killed myself, well, there's still plenty of time for that. But right now, seems to me we've got work to do. The start of any investigation is where the heavy lifting happens. Got to make progress while things are still relatively fresh. Get going before the trail gets cold. I think you've already delayed too much. Didn't you listen to Cassie? She told you to get a move on. So let's get started. No more time for delays."

"I don't exactly know where to begin. It's still very . . ." He hesitated.

"Scary? Confusing?" His brother gave him a laugh. He often attached laughter to matters of deep concern, as if he could lessen the worries that went with them. "Well, the pills will help, I think. Just maybe hold things at bay a little bit, while we sort through what we know."

"But I don't really know anything."

Brian smiled again. "Sure you do. But it's a matter of pragmatics. Got to work steadily, see every question as a hole that needs to be filled in."

"You were always good at organizing things."

"The army trained me well. And law school trained me even better. That wasn't my problem."

"You'll help me?"

"That's why I'm here. Same as Cassandra."

Adrian paused. Dead wife. Dead brother. Each would see things a little differently. He didn't care *who* might spot him at that moment talking animatedly to no one. He knew with whom he was conversing.

Brian had removed the clip from the M-16 and was tapping it against the hood of the Volvo to make sure it was full. Adrian wanted to reach out and touch the worn clothing. He could smell dried sweat and jungle rot and a faint odor of cordite. It all seemed very real and, still, he knew it wasn't, but he didn't dislike that.

"I always thought I should have gone, too, just like you did."

Brian snorted. "To Vietnam? Wrong war at the wrong time. Don't be old and stupid. I went for all the wrong reasons. Romance and excitement and sense of duty—maybe that wasn't the wrong reason—but loyalty and honor and all those fine words that we assign to men going off to battle. And it cost me big time. You know that."

Adrian felt a little chastised. He had always gotten tongue-tied and stammered when he tried to speak with his older brother about emotional things. Everything about Brian had always seemed so perfect, so admirable. A warrior. A philanthropist. A man of laws and reason. Even when they were grown up and Adrian's education gave him a clinical understanding of PTSD and the dark depressions Brian continually suffered, translating the things he'd learned in a classroom into practical applications to someone he loved had been difficult. There were many things he wanted to say, but they always tripped on his lips and fell into the crevices of forgetfulness.

Brian slapped the tin pot helmet on his head, pushing it back a little, so that his blue eyes could sweep over the parking lot at the pharmacy.

"Good place for an ambush," he said, idly. "Ah well, can't be helped. First question: Who is Jennifer? Got to get an answer there. Then we can go about chasing down the *why*."

Adrian nodded. He glanced down toward the pink Red Sox hat on the seat of the car. Brian followed his eyes.

"That's right," the older brother said smoothly. "Someone will recognize that. You say the girl was on foot?"

"Yes. She was walking hard toward the bus stop."

"So she came from somewhere in your neighborhood?"

"That would make sense."

"Well," Brian said, "start there. Draw a mental perimeter. Pick a good six-block circle, a couple of klicks, and then be systematic. Keep notes as to where you go, what the address is, what the people say. Someone will see that hat, hear the name, and steer you right."

"But there has to be, I don't know, fifty, maybe seventy-five houses . . . That's a lot of doorbells."

"And you're going to ring every one."

Adrian nodded.

"Look, Audie," Brian said, using his childhood nickname. "Most police work is leg work. It's not Hollywood and it's not all that exciting. It's just hard work. Heavy lifting. Turning possibilities into details and facts and then piecing them together. Mystery writers and television producers like to imagine that they are like those big thousand-piece depictions of the *Mona Lisa* or a map of the world that has to be put together. But more often cases are like those wooden block puzzles they give preschoolers. Fit the picture of the cow or the duck into the cutout of the cow or the duck. Either way, when you're finished you can see something. That's what ultimately makes it so satisfying."

Brian hesitated. "Do you remember me telling you about the case I had over there? It was the summer after I came back and we were out on the Cape. We had a fire going on the beach and maybe a few beers too many and I told you about it . . . the one where I ended up interviewing every member of two different platoons at least four times before the story started to break."

Adrian did remember. Brian had rarely spoken about being in country and the combat he'd seen while pursuing military justice. This had been a rape case, in 1969. It had been filled with troubling ambiguities—the victim had been Viet Cong, Brian had been certain, as had the men accused of assaulting her. So she was the enemy—they were all sure of it—although there was no concrete proof. And so, whatever happened to her, well, she probably deserved it, or at least that was the justification for five men in a hooch, taking turns until she was nearly dead, which left them with only one remaining choice. It was one of those cases where there was simply no moral good side, where finding out the truth about what had happened in a small sideshow of the war had created no good. A rape took place. The commanding officer ordered Brian to investigate. People were guilty. But nothing happened. He filed his report. The war went on. People died.

Brian shouldered his rifle and pointed down the road.

"That direction," Brian said. "It might be tedious but it has to be done. Do you think you can keep remembering what you're supposed to ask? You don't want to forget . . ."

"You'll have to keep reminding me," Adrian said. "Things sort of slide out of my mind when I'm not paying enough attention."

"I'll be there when you need me," Brian said.

Adrian wanted to reply that he wished he'd been able to say the same. He hadn't been there when his brother needed him. Simple as that. It made him want to cry, and then he understood that desire signified he was having trouble controlling his swinging emotions. He knew he couldn't actually break into tears in the middle of a bright, clear, mild morning, standing in the parking lot of a pharmacy at the small, busy shopping center on the edge of his college town. It would draw unwanted attention. It wouldn't be appropriate.

Not for the detective he had to become.

Adrian slipped behind the wheel and started to drive home to his neighborhood, which suddenly seemed to him even in the bright spring sunshine to be far more dark and mysterious than he'd ever believed it could be.

Of the first score of doors he knocked on nearly half didn't respond, and the others weren't helpful. People were polite—they assumed he was selling something, or going door-to-door fund-raising for some cause, such as clean water or whale saving, and when he showed the hat and mentioned the name they were taken aback, but didn't know the girl.

He was alone with Brian marching just in front. His brother had slipped on aviator-style sunglasses against the morning glare and he had the energy of a young man, which usually put him a few strides ahead of Adrian.

Adrian felt very old as he walked along, although he wasn't tired and he was secretly pleased to feel his leg muscles taut and uncomplaining as he kept pace with his brother's ghost.

He stopped, letting the morning sun fill his face, staring up into shafts of light as they danced with shadows. It was always a contest between bringing light and finding darkness. This made him think of a poem; his favorite writers were always working on imagery that trod the line between good and evil.

"Yeats," he said out loud. "Brian, did you ever read 'Cuchulain's Fight with the Sea'?"

Brian unslung his rifle and paused a few feet ahead. He hunkered down, dropping to a single knee, staring ahead, as if it were a jungle trail he was

73

surveying, not a suburban neighborhood. "Yeah. Sure. Second-year seminar on poetic traditions in modern verse. I think you took the same class I did and got a better grade."

Adrian nodded. "What I liked was when the hero realized he'd killed his only son . . . the only recourse was madness. So he was enchanted and set to fighting with sword and shield against the ocean waves."

"*The invulnerable tide* . . ." Brian said, quoting the poet. He held up a fist, as if to slow a platoon of men in single file behind him instead of his only brother. Brian's eyes centered on a redbrick pathway. "Take the point, Audie," he whispered. "Try this house." These words were spoken softly, but Brian equipped them with the force of command.

Adrian looked up. Another trim, suburban clapboard home, like just about every other one. Like his own.

He sighed and went up to the door, leaving his brother behind on the sidewalk. He rang the doorbell twice, and just as he was about to turn and leave he heard hurried footsteps inside. The door cracked open and he came face to face with a middle-aged woman, a dish towel in her hands, red eyes and blond frazzled hair. She smelled of smoke and anxiety and looked as if she hadn't slept in a month.

"I'm sorry to bother you," Adrian started.

The woman stared out past him. Her voice quavered but she tried to be polite.

"Look, I'm just not interested in Jehovah's Witnesses or the Mormon Church or Scientology. Thank you, but no thanks."

As quickly as she had opened it the woman was shutting the door.

"No, no," Adrian said.

From behind him, he heard his brother's shouted command: "*Show her the hat!*"

He thrust the pink hat forward.

The woman stopped.

"I found this on the street. I'm looking for—"

"Jennifer," the woman said.

She immediately burst into tears.

10

By the time Terri Collins managed to get into the hard drive on Jennifer's computer and copy everything without simultaneously destroying it, it was midmorning and, even with a catnap on a couch outside of an interview room, she was still exhausted. The office around her had awakened. The other three detectives on the small force were at their desks, making calls, sorting through various open-case tasks. She had also received a summons from the chief's office, wanting a midday update, so Terri was scrambling to put together some sort of analysis of Jennifer's disappearance. In order to keep processing the case, she needed to create at least the impression that a crime was taking place because, otherwise, she knew the chief would tell her to do what she had already done—put out a picture and description and the appropriate statewide and national bulletins and then get back to work on cases that actually might result in arrests and convictions.

She looked guiltily at the stack of case folders cluttering a corner of her desk. There were three sexual assault cases, a simple assault—that was a Saturday night Yankees–Red Sox fistfight in a bar—an assault with a deadly weapon—what was that sophomore from the tony Boston suburb of Concord doing with a switchblade anyway?—and half a dozen drug cases ranging from a nickel bag of marijuana to a student over at the university arrested selling a kilo of cocaine to an undercover campus cop. Every file needed attention, especially the sexual assaults, because they were all more or less the same—girls taken advantage of after they'd had too much to drink at a frat house or a dorm party. Invariably, the victims wavered, imagining they were somehow to blame. Perhaps, Terri thought, they were. Inhibitions had been washed away in beery excess and provocative dancing, maybe they had heeded the catcalls of *show us your boobs!* that were commonplace at campus gatherings. Each case was awaiting toxicology results and she suspected they would all test positive for Ecstasy. These cases all started: "Hey, baby, let me get you a drink" in a crowded room, music pounding, bodies packed together, and the girl not noticing the slightly odd taste as she sipped at her plastic cup. One part vodka, two parts tonic, a dash of date-rape drug.

She hated seeing sexual predators skate away when the embarrassed and sobered-up girls and their equally embarrassed parents dropped all her carefully constructed criminal charges. She knew the boys involved would end up boasting of their conquests as they matriculated on to Wall Street or medical school or into some other high-powered profession. She thought it was her policewoman's duty to make sure that this ascension wasn't without some sweat and some scars.

Terri went and poured herself her fourth coffee of the long night becoming a long day.

She thought that every other case on her desk should take precedence.

Saving Jennifer Riggins from whatever emotional morass that had instilled in her the need to run was way beyond the detective's job description.

Yet she could not bring herself to just let her run. Terri knew the statistics far too well.

And, she reminded herself, she knew the necessity of running away with an intimacy that she would never forget.

You had to run once. Why do you suppose this is different?

She answered: *I wasn't sixteen. I was grown up and with two babies. Almost grown up.*

But you still had to run, didn't you?

The question reverberated within her and she plopped down and rocked in her seat at her desk, trying to imagine where Jennifer had gone. She leaned forward and took a long pull at the coffee cup. Hers had a large red heart and *World's Best Mom* written on the side and had been a predictable Mother's Day gift from her children. She doubted that this sentiment was true, but she was doing her damned best to try.

After a second she sighed, then took the flash drive copy of the hard drive on Jennifer's computer and plugged it into her own. She sat back and started to survey the sixteen-year-old's life, hoping that some road map would appear on the screen in front of her.

Jennifer's Facebook entry was surprising. She had friended a very small number of her classmates at the high school and several rock and pop stars, ranging from a surprising Lou Reed, who was older than her mother, to Feist and Shania Twain. Terri had expected the Jonas Brothers and Miley Cyrus, but Jennifer's tastes were very much outside the mainstream. Under the category Likes she had written *Freedom* and under Dislikes she had put *Phonies*. Terri guessed that word could be applied to any number of people in Jennifer's world.

In the Profile section, Jennifer had quoted someone named Hotchick99, who had written on her own Facebook entry: *"Everyone in our school hates this one girl."*

Jennifer had replied: *"This is kind of a badge of honor to be hated by people like her. I never want to be the kind of person she would like."*

Terri smiled. A rebel with any number of causes, she thought. It gave her a little non-cop respect for the missing girl, which only made her sadder when she considered what was likely to happen to Jennifer on the streets. Escape wasn't going to seem so great then. *Maybe she'll have the sense to call home, no matter how terrible that will seem.*

77

She kept looking through the hard drive. Jennifer had also tested a few computer games, made a number of Wikipedia inquiries and Google searches that seemed to correspond to courses she was taking in school. There was even a *Translate the page* inquiry, where she'd submitted something that Terri suspected was a Spanish assignment. Beyond the ordinary, Jennifer did not seem particularly computer-dependent. She had a Skype account but there were no names listed on it.

Terri raced through an American history paper on the Underground Railroad and an English paper on *Great Expectations* that she found under Word Documents. She half expected to find these were written by a term paper mill but was pleased when she did not. Her impression was that Jennifer actually did most of her own work at school, which made her the exception rather than the rule.

She also seemed to like doggerel. She had downloaded samples from Shel Silverstein and Ogden Nash, which were odd choices for a teenage girl in this day and age. She found a file called 6 Poems for Mister Brown Fur, which were rhymed couplets and haiku written for her teddy bear. Some—there were many more than six—were quite funny, which made Terri smile. *Smart girl,* she thought again.

She continued searching. There were frequent visits to vegan websites and new age entries, which, Terri guessed, were efforts to understand her mother and quasi-stepfather-slash-boyfriend.

Terri kept clicking through the computer's history. She hoped to find some heartfelt misguided teenage longings diary but could not. She wanted some document that outlined Jennifer's *plan,* such as it was. But this eluded her. She found stored pictures, but most were of Jennifer and a few friends laughing, hugging, cutting up at sleepovers or parties— although it always seemed as if Jennifer stood just at the perimeter. She kept searching the picture files and finally came across half a dozen nude shots that Jennifer had taken of herself. They couldn't have been more than a year old. Terri figured she had set up her point-and-shoot digital camera on a stack of books and then posed in front of it. They weren't particularly sexy, more like Jennifer had wanted to document the changes taking place in her body. She was slender, with breasts that barely curved away from her chest. Her legs were long, and she coyly crossed them, so that only the slightest shades of her pubic hair were visible—as if she had been embarrassed by what she was doing even though she was doing it alone in her room. Two of the shots seemed to have the teenage version of sexy *come hither* looks on her face, which only made her seem younger and more childlike.

Terri examined each one carefully. She kept opening them up on the screen in front of her, expecting to suddenly see a naked boy pop into the pictures. She wanted to believe that kids that age weren't sexually active. That was the mother part of her. The hard-edged detective part of her knew that they all had far more experience than any parent imagined. Oral sex. Anal sex. Group sex. Old-fashioned sex. The kids knew it all, and had experienced much of it. Terri was secretly happy that the only provocative photographs on Jennifer's computer were of herself alone.

She stopped and thought there was something sad about the pictures. Jennifer was fascinated by who she was becoming but, as naked as she was, she was still more naked in her solitude.

She had almost finished her search when a pair of Google requests caught her eye. One was for Nabokov's *Lolita,* which Terri knew wasn't on *any* high school reading list. The other was for *men who expose themselves.*

This inquiry had produced a wide range of responses. More than eight million entries. But Jennifer had opened only two: Yahoo Answers and a psychological forum website that was a link to an Emory University Medical School Psychiatry Department series of papers on the psychological ramifications of Peeping Toms and flashers. This second result contained medical jargon that was far too sophisticated for a sixteen-year-old, although that apparently hadn't stopped Jennifer.

Terri leaned back in her seat. She didn't need to know anything else, she thought. Right in front of her was a crime that couldn't be proved—it would be Jennifer's word against Scott's and even her mother was likely to err by believing *him*—but which made all the necessary pack your bag and run away sense.

Terri went back to the poems for Mister Brown Fur. There was one that began with the line: *You see what I see.*

Maybe he did, Terri thought, *but a teddy bear sure as hell can't testify about it in court.*

The phone on her desk rang. It was the chief demanding his update. She knew she had to be very careful with what she said. Scott was well known and had many powerful friends in the local community. He'd probably treated half the city council at some point or another, although *treat* was a word that Terri used cautiously. She said, "I'll be right up."

Terri gathered some notes and was halfway across the room when her phone rang again. With a muffled obscenity she hurried back and stabbed the receiver on the fifth ring, just before it went to voice mail.

"Detective Collins," she said.

"It's Mary Riggins," she heard. Sobs. Gasps. Barest controls over a voice that seemed wildly turbulent.

"Yes, Mrs. Riggins. I was just on my way to see the chief—"

"She's not a runaway. Jennifer's been kidnapped, detective," the mother on the other end half sobbed and half screamed.

Terri did not immediately ask for details on how or why Mary knew this. She listened to the sounds of maternal anguish leak over the phone line. She had a sensation that something akin to a nightmare was happening. She just didn't know precisely what.

11

Jennifer awakened to the sensation that something was different, but it took her a few moments to comprehend that her hands were free and her feet were no longer pinned to the bed. Coming out of the drug-induced fog, she felt like someone climbing a steep hill, scrambling to reach the top, clawing at loose dirt and stone, while gravity threatened to pull her down.

She lifted her hands to her face. The hood was still in place and she touched its silken exterior. She wanted to grab at it, rip it away, see where she was, but she had the sense to control her desire. She took a deep breath and felt something choking her. She slowly lowered her hands and touched a collar. It was cheap leather and studded with sharp points and was fastened tightly around her neck. She could feel the end of a stainless steel chain that leashed her to something but gave her a little leeway to move about. She reached down to her ankles and realized that those restraints had been removed.

She touched her skin, searching for injuries, but could find none, although this didn't reassure her that there weren't any. Her only clothing was her flimsy underwear. She leaned slowly back on the bed, staring inside the hood up to where she supposed there was a ceiling, then a roof, and beyond that, the sky.

She assessed her state. It was better than before—she was no longer spread eagled and her hands were free. But she was still restrained. She realized suddenly that she desperately had to go to the toilet, and that she was still parched with thirst. She knew she should be hungry, but fear filled her stomach. Where she had been hit felt bruised and ached. But she was alive. Sort of. She still did not know what was happening to her; she had only a vague memory of the brief conversation with the woman who had come into the room, but she knew it meant something. *Rules.* The woman had talked about rules. It seemed to Jennifer that the conversation had happened on some other day, some other year, maybe even in a dream. All sorts of possibilities flooded her imagination, but each was more frightening than the last, so she worked hard to blank her mind. She told herself that inside the hood everything would seem empty and impossible, but she was still breathing and that meant something. She cautiously ran her fingers down the length of the chain attached to the collar around her neck. Jennifer realized that she could move, but only the distance that the chain would allow. She did not yet try to take advantage of this new freedom.

She had an immense urge to tug on the chain, see if she could break it free from wherever it was fastened. But she fought this off. That, she knew, would be against the *rules.*

"She's awake!"

The man bending over his computer screen in London stiffened. He was alone in the small office near the back of his apartment, seated at a desk cluttered with proposals, figures, and schematic drawings. He was a draftsman, and nearby there was a tall table where he occasionally made illustrations in pen and ink, although most of his work was now done electronically with sophisticated computer imagery. He was a loner, a freelancer working out of his flat, in considerable demand, so there could have been a Jaguar in his car park, had he actually wanted one. He wished there were someone he could share his astonishment with, but that would defeat the purpose, he thought. Series #4 was to be enjoyed, considered, and digested in solitude and utter privacy.

He looked closely at the figure on the screen in front of him. Number 4 seemed to him to be deliciously young, barely more than a child. He had children from a failed marriage, but he rarely saw them, and at this moment they remained very far from his thoughts. He admired Number 4's slender figure, felt a rush of excitement pass through him. He imagined there was a pearly smoothness to her skin and his left hand twitched, trying to caress Number 4 right through the computer screen. As if someone were reading his mind, the camera switched to a closer view. Number 4 was reaching out, like a blind person seeking something tactile that she could read with her fingertips. Each touch of nothing—the air in front of her—or of something, such as the wall where she had been chained, sent a pleasurable shiver through the draftsman. "She's learning where she is," he said, again out loud to no one. "But she won't be able to tell."

Number 4 remained near the bed, playing a game of blind man's bluff. Each time she moved, even slightly, the man in London bent closer to the computer screen. In a way, he thought, he was as alone as she was, except he knew that many other people around the world were watching Number 4 with the same intensity.

She was a prisoner of all of their fantasies.

Jennifer instinctively understood that panic would serve her little, but it took a huge force of will to fight the waves threatening her. She was breathing hard and her pulse rate was climbing. She felt sweat and tears and everything associated with fear. She had to fight to keep her hands from shaking and her body was wracked with involuntary movements—spasms, twitches, shudders—all of which she could do little to control. She thought it was as if there were two Jennifers at that moment, the one who was fighting to make some sense out of what was happening and the other, who wanted to give in to black agony.

To stay alive, she knew the first had to prevail.

Context, she told herself. Fit yourself into something you can understand.

She had never seen Patrick McGoohan in *The Prisoner* on television. She had never gone into a library to read John Fowles's *The Collector.* She knew nothing of Barbara Jane Mackle and the news stories written about her, or the book or the subsequent television drama. She had not even seen the *Saw* movies that were popular with teenage boys who favored the combination of gore, torture, and naked breasts for entertainment, nor had she seen the more benign vision embodied in the film *The Truman Show.* Sir Alec Guinness sweltering in his corrugated steel box for refusing to order his officers to work beside enlisted men while building the bridge over the river Kwai didn't exist for her. She knew nothing of the art, literature, or criminality of confinement. She had not owned a pet growing up, not even a goldfish swimming in a bowl, constantly pressing up against the glass measuring the limits of its world.

That she was a little like all of these was beyond her.

Even so, Jennifer had some instincts that she was not able to articulate but which gave her some strengths. She told herself that three times she had the guts to run away. This would be another chance as long as she fought off the urge to descend into terror. She breathed in and out slowly, calming herself.

She lowered her hands and touched the sides of the bed: a metal frame and a mattress. There was a rough cotton sheet—she pictured a stark white—on the bed beneath her.

All right, she told herself. *Let's see what we can touch.*

Carefully, she slipped her feet over the edge of the bed and rubbed the floor with her toes. It was cement, cold to the soles.

That's what a basement floor feels like, she imagined. She half thought she was speaking out loud and wondered if her words tumbled through the small hole in the hood that had been cut for the drugged water. The lack of orientation made it hard for her to tell whether the thoughts that filled her head emerged through her lips. She *might* be talking out loud. She *might* not.

She moved her feet around to see if there were any obstacles. None.

Jennifer told herself to try to stand, and then repeated the command. She wanted to hear her own voice work. So she said softly: "*Stand up, girl. You can do it.*"

Hearing the difference between words spoken and words thought gave her a little confidence. She pushed herself up to her feet.

Dizziness almost instantly overcame her.

Her head spun inside the hood, as if the blackness in front of her eyes were abruptly liquid. She staggered slightly, almost tumbling back onto the bed or collapsing onto the cement floor. But she was able to steady herself, and slowly her head stopped spinning and she could feel some control in her weak muscles. She wished she were stronger, like some of the weight lifting–obsessed athletes at her school.

Still breathing hard, she took a tentative step forward. She was holding her hands out in front of her. She could feel nothing.

She swept them right and left and her hand bumped up against the wall. She half turned and, using the wall to guide her, began to move crab-like, feeling the flat plasterboard beneath her fingers. She could hear a rattling sound, which she understood was the chain around her neck playing out. She guessed it was striking against the bed stand.

Her knee bumped up against something and she stopped. Some of the thick smell of disinfectant penetrated the silken hood. Very carefully, she reached down and, like a blind person, ran her hands over the obstacle.

It was a camp toilet. It took her a few seconds to form a picture of what it was in her mind, but she could feel the seat and the supporting tripod. That she recognized it was only luck—her father had taken her camping when she was little, and she had made a particular whiny series of complaints about having to use something so primitive in the outdoors.

Now she was nearly overjoyed. Her bladder hurt and, with the recognition of what it was at her feet, it began to send sharp demanding pains through her stomach.

She stopped. She had no idea who was watching her. She could only guess that the rules allowed her to use the toilet. She did not know whether she had any privacy. She was almost overcome with a teenager's sense of violation. Propriety fought against embarrassment. She hated the idea that someone might *see* her.

Her groin screamed. She understood she had no choice.

She positioned herself above the seat and, with a single abrupt motion, pulled down her panties and sat down.

She hated every second of relief.

At the monitors in the room directly above where Jennifer was confined Michael and Linda watched every motion she made. The awkward, blind-folded, tentative actions were delicious in their pace. They could sense ripples of intrigue and waves of fascination out in the netherworld of their broadcast. Without sharing a word, both knew that, for hundreds of people, watching Jennifer was going to become a drug.

And, like any good pusher, they knew how to maintain just the right balance of supply to meet the demand.

12

Terri Collins looked over at the old man seated in the corner of the living room and thought, *He can't be the reason why I'm here.*

Adrian Thomas shifted uncomfortably under her gaze. The detective had an unrelenting stare, one that implied something beyond skepticism. He could feel thoughts tugging him in different directions and he hoped that he wouldn't get flustered, as he had when he'd called the police dispatcher. He replayed the few observations and modest details that he had in his head, like an actor preparing his lines. He tried to organize all these impressions into a coherent assessment of what he'd seen so that the detective wouldn't simply think he was a confused old man, even if that was precisely what he was. When she turned away to face Mary Riggins and Scott West, Adrian stole a quick glance around, hoping that Brian was concealed in a corner and might give him some advice about how to deal with the policewoman. He would know what to say, Adrian was sure. But at that moment Adrian was alone—or, at least, he was unaccompanied.

"Mrs. Riggins," Terri said slowly, "kidnappings are complicated crimes. Generally, they are either about ransom or else one estranged family member stealing a child from another."

Mary shook her head, although she hadn't been asked a question.

"Then there's the third type," Scott interjected with a nasty glare in her direction. "Sexual predation."

Terri nodded. "Yes. Rare. Not unlike being hit by lightning."

"I think that's what you should be focusing on," Scott said.

"Yes, but I'd like to rule out these others—"

"And waste time?" Scott interrupted.

She could tell that was the direction he wanted her to investigate. She just resented being forced into the position by someone she thought had been on the verge of sexual predation himself. She decided to turn the tables on him.

"Or maybe there's some element of this that you haven't been forthcoming about . . ."

Terri stopped, turning her stare over at Scott.

"Perhaps in your practice . . ." She started slowly but picked up a little momentum in her voice as the words tumbled out. "A patient maybe. Someone angry or disgruntled, maybe psychotic even . . . seeking to harm you and chose Jennifer as the means . . ."

Scott instantly held up his hand. "That is highly unlikely, detective. I am very much aware of *all* the issues my patients face and none of them are capable of that sort of thing."

"Well," Terri continued, "surely you have some . . . *cases* that have less than satisfactory outcomes?"

"Of course," Scott snorted. "Every therapist who has any self-knowledge understands that they cannot be ideal for every patient. There are inevitably failures."

"So it is not unreasonable to imagine that one of those less than successful cases might possibly hold some sort of grudge?"

She phrased the statement as a question, and then eyed Scott cautiously as he responded.

"It is unreasonable, detective." He sounded very formal. "To imagine that one of my patients would concoct an elaborate scheme of revenge . . . no. Impossible. I would be aware of that much resentment."

Sure, Terri thought. She had to remind herself not to let her own opinions about Scott color her judgment. Nor should she let what she had gleaned from Jennifer's computer influence the questioning. But inwardly she looked forward to asking those questions on some later day.

"Still, I might need a list of names from you at some point."

Scott made a small dismissive wave. He might have been agreeing or disagreeing. Either was possible. Or neither. Terri did not expect him to comply.

She turned back to Mary Riggins.

"Now, family . . . how about your late husband's relatives?"

Mary looked confused. "Well, my relationships with them haven't been great but . . ."

"Has Jennifer been a source of conflict with them?"

"Yes. Her grandparents complain that I don't bring her to see them nearly enough. They say she's the only part of their son left to them. And I've never gotten along with her two aunts. I don't know, but it seems like they have always blamed me for his death. But this hasn't escalated to the degree . . ."

Terri noted that Mary Riggins did not use her late husband's name. *David.* It was a small detail but one that struck her as odd. She took a deep breath and continued.

"I might want those names and some addresses as well."

Terri hesitated then. She was looking for the foundations of a felony, and so far she had heard a few things that made her think there might be something hidden in the family that might create a framework for Jennifer's disappearance—but not enough. She asked, "And ransom? I presume you've had no contact from anyone seeking money?"

Mary Riggins shook her head.

"We don't have much. I mean, those cases, those would be businessmen's sons or daughters. Or a politicians'. Or someone with access to real cash, right?"

"Maybe."

Terri could hear some exhaustion in her voice. She thought this was unprofessional.

"Sex offenders," Scott repeated, angrily. "How many live nearby?"

"Some. I will obtain a list. You know the chances that Jennifer was simply snatched from the side of the road by some unknown criminal—a serial killer or a rapist—are infinitesimally small? These random acts are really the stuff of movies and television . . ."

"But they do happen," Scott interjected.

"They do happen."

"Even around here," he continued.

"Yes. Even around here," Terri replied.

Scott had a smug look on his face. There was a lot, Terri thought, to dislike about him. She wondered how *anyone* could imagine he could *help* them.

"Students must go missing from the college and the university," he persisted.

"Yes. These are kids with drinking, drug, boyfriend, or emotional problems. Invariably—"

"What about that girl, the one from the next town . . . whose body was found in the woods six years after she disappeared."

"I'm familiar with that case. And the registered sex offender who was eventually arrested two states away and who confessed to her murder. I do not believe we've ever had a crime like that in our jurisdiction—"

"Not that you *know* of," Scott interrupted again.

"Yes. Not that we know of."

"But detective. Listen to what Professor Thomas says," Mary broke in.

Terri turned back to the old man. He was looking off into space, as if he were someplace else. It seemed to her that there was a gray fog behind his eyes, a smoky substance that she couldn't readily identify. It worried her.

"Tell me again what you saw," she said. "Don't leave anything out."

Adrian told her about the determined look on Jennifer's face. He told about the van that had appeared out of nowhere and slowed, shadowing her steps. He described as best he could the woman behind the wheel and the man who disappeared from view. He told about the brief pause, and then the tire-squealing departure. He mentioned the license plate letters he spotted. And finally he told about the pink cap left on the side of the street that had brought him to the street where Jennifer lived, to her house and finally to the living room. He tried fiercely to keep everything clipped and orderly, to make it sound straightforward and official. He did not utter any of the conclusions that the ghosts of either his wife or his brother had insisted he make; he left those to the detective.

The more he spoke, the more he saw the mother gaining in despair, the more he imagined the boyfriend was becoming enraged.

The policewoman, on the other hand, seemed to grow calmer with each added detail. Adrian imagined that she was like the professional poker players that he occasionally saw on television: whatever she was actually thinking was cleverly concealed.

When he paused, he saw her dip her head and review the notes she had taken. In that moment he heard a whispered voice.

"I don't think you convinced her," Brian said.

Adrian did not at first turn to the sound. He kept his eyes on the detective.

"She's thinking it over, that's good. But she just doesn't believe. Not yet," Brian continued. He sounded forceful and confident.

Adrian stole a quick glance to the side.

His brother was seated on the couch next to him. The young Vietnam grunt Brian had disappeared, replaced by the mature persona of the New York corporate lawyer that he'd become. His sandy hair had thinned a little, and there were streaks of gray—a distinguished color—touching the locks that flowed over his ears and shirt collar. Brian had always worn his hair long, not ponytail ex-hippie long but an antiestablishment unkempt. He wore an expensive blue pinstriped suit and a custom-tailored shirt, although his tie was loosened around his neck. Brian leaned back and crossed his legs.

"Nope. I've just seen that *lookaway* look too many times. Usually it's when your client wants to start lying to you but feels a little guilty about it first. What she's thinking right now is that what she thought all this was—you know, a teenage runaway—*might* be something bigger. But she's really not sure, not at all, and she wants to make sure that she does the right thing here, because a mistake could cost her that next pay bump."

Brian spoke in musical tones, almost as if his assessment of Detective Collins were one of the poems Adrian loved so much.

"You know, Audie," he continued, "this is going to be complicated."

"What should I do next?" Adrian whispered. He told himself not to turn his head, but he did, just slightly, because he wanted to see his brother's face.

"I'm sorry," Terri said, looking up and just catching the sideways glance at its very end.

"Nothing," Adrian replied. "Just thinking out loud."

The detective continued to eye him, to the point where he became uncomfortable. Neither the mother nor her therapist boyfriend had noticed the small exchange. They were too locked up in their own nightmare to engage in his.

"She's sharp," Brian said, a little admiration creeping into his voice. "I think she knows what she's doing, except she doesn't know what it is she's got to do. Not yet. You've got to explain it to her, Audie. The mother and the slimy boyfriend—they don't matter. Not a bit. But this detective, she does. Keep that in mind."

Adrian nodded, but he had no idea what to say, other than telling her exactly what he had seen and letting her reach her own conclusions.

"Now she's going to ask you a couple of detailed questions," Brian whispered in his ear. "She needs more information to take to her boss. And she's feeling you out. She wants to know just how damn credible a witness you are."

"Professor Thomas," Terri asked abruptly. "Or do you prefer *Doctor . . .*"

"Either is fine."

"You have a doctorate in psychology, right?"

"Yes, but I'm not a therapist like Doctor West. I was a *rats in mazes* type. A laboratory geek."

92

She smiled, as if the word defused some tension in the room, which it did not. "Of course. Now, I just want to get a couple of things clear. You never saw Jennifer actually getting forced against her will into the truck, did you?"

"No."

"You never saw anyone grab her or strike her or any other action that you thought was violent?"

"No. Just she was there. Then she was gone. From where I was seated, I could not see exactly what happened to her."

"Did you hear a scream? Or maybe hear sounds of a scuffle?"

"I'm sorry, but no."

"So if she got into that truck, it might have been of her own volition?"

"It didn't seem that way, detective."

"And you don't believe you could recognize the driver or the passenger again?"

"I don't know. I only saw them in profile. And even then it was just for a few seconds. It was gloomy. Nearly dark."

"No, Audie, that's not right. You saw enough. I think you'll be able to recognize them when you find them."

Adrian half turned to argue with his brother, but then he stopped, hoping the detective didn't notice the way he'd shifted about.

Terri Collins nodded. "Thank you," she said. "This has been really helpful. I will get back to you after I do a little more work."

"She's good," Brian said. He was leaning forward, almost touching Adrian's shoulder, and he sounded excited. "She's really good. But she is still blowing you off, Audie."

Before Adrian could say anything, Scott broke in. "What will be your next step, detective?"

He spoke with the sort of no-nonsense *we expect to see results* tone that Adrian imagined people usually paid money to hear from him.

"Let me see if I can find out anything about the suspect vehicle that Professor Thomas has described. That is something concrete I can work on. I will also check state and federal crime databases for similar types of abductions. In the meantime, please be alert to anyone contacting you."

"Don't you want to call in the FBI? Don't you want to set up a phone trap on our lines?"

"That's a little premature. But I will go back to headquarters and discuss precisely that with my chief."

"I think Mary and I should be there," Scott huffed.

"If you like."

"Have you ever worked on a kidnap case before, detective?"

Terri hesitated. She was not going to answer that question truthfully, which would have been, *No*. That would only make things worse, which in a cop's book of procedures was a large mistake.

"I think I should go with you, detective, and see how the chief reacts." He turned to Mary. "And you should stay here. Monitor the phones. Make sure you're alert for anything out of the ordinary."

Mary simply sobbed in response but it was a sound of agreement.

Adrian realized that in their minds—Scott's and the detective's—his own role had just ended. He heard Brian shifting position beside him.

"I told you so," he said quietly. "The asshole boyfriend thinks you're just an old fool who accidentally saw something important and the cop thinks now she's heard everything you have to tell her. Typical."

"What should I do?" Adrian asked. He was unsure, as before, whether this had been spoken out loud or he had merely thought it.

"Nothing. And everything," his dead brother said. "It's not like it's only up to you, Audie. But it sort of is. But don't worry. I have some ideas."

Adrian nodded in response. He looked around for his jacket. He was sure he'd left it on the couch, or maybe draped over the back of a chair, removing it when he'd entered the house. His head swiveled about and then he realized he was still wearing it. He smiled, but one other person in the room had noticed his awkward forgetfulness.

13

Adrian had spent much of his academic life studying fear. It was a far more complicated subject than he had expected when he first launched into his graduate work. He was drawn to the topic nearly fifty years earlier when he'd been on a very rough flight home from his first college semester. Instead of being frightened, he'd been fascinated watching the reactions of the other passengers as the airplane shook and careened about the black thunderstorm-laden sky, so fascinated that he'd forgotten his own anxiety. Prayers. Screams. White knuckles and sobbing. On one stomach-churning drop when the engine pitch had threatened to drown out all the cries, he had looked around and imagined himself to be the only observant rat caught in a terrifying maze.

As a professor he had run countless experiments in laboratory settings, trying to identify perceptivity factors that stimulated predictable brain responses. Visual tests. Auditory tests. Tactile tests. Some of his university funding had come from government grants—thinly concealed military financing, because the armed forces were *always* interested in finding ways to train fear out of soldiers. So Adrian had spent his teaching years bouncing between classrooms, lectures, and late nights in a laboratory surrounded by assistants as he prepared his clinical studies. It had all been rewarding, except that when he'd reached retirement he had understood that he knew both very much and very little about his subject. He understood how and why a snake, say, brought about rapid breathing, increased pulse, sweat, tunnel vision, and near panic in some subjects. He had run systematic desensitization studies introducing *National Geographic* pictures of snakes, furry toy snakes, and finally real snakes to subjects— invariably undergraduate psychology majors—measuring how familiarity diminished fear. He had also done what were called *flooding* studies, where subjects were abruptly confronted with large numbers of the feared object, sort of like when Indiana Jones found himself in the underground snake pit in the first of the series of Spielberg movies. Adrian had disliked these sorts of tests. Too much sweat and screaming. He preferred the slower pace of examination.

His brother had often playfully scoffed at Adrian's work. "What I learned in the war," Brian once told him, "is that fear is the very best thing we have going for us. It keeps us safe when we need it, gives us a way of seeing the world that even if skewed a little errs on the side of caution, which, as a general rule, brother, keeps your ass out of trouble and alive for another day."

Brian liked to swirl ice cubes with his finger in his whiskey glass, letting the clinking noise punctuate his words. "When you *think* you should be scared of something, well, you damn well should be, because it makes whatever you do *next* make sense."

Adrian remembered this as he walked across his old campus. He smiled, thinking how much he missed his brother's way of speaking. One minute Brian would sound like a tweedy philosopher from Oxford, the next a rough-edged, obscenity-driven street tough. The law had been a good profession for him. He could have been an actor, except that Brian had hated taking orders, and the first time some pretentious director tried to tell him what to do, he would have walked off the stage. But he was clever at adopting whatever role was necessary for the legal case he had taken on. His brother had split his time between high-paying corporate clients and pro bono work for the ACLU and the Southern Poverty Law Center. These had been death penalty cases in rural districts, where criminal defendants—more than a few of whom had been unjustly accused—had little chance of avoiding the electric chair until Brian had arrived.

Brian, he thought, had the ability to make anyone think that *he* was like *they* were.

Adrian shook his head. Maybe that chameleon quality wasn't so great, because one morning his brother, whom he had believed the strongest man alive, had placed the 9mm to his temple and pulled the trigger.

He didn't leave a note. That was wrong, Adrian thought. He should have explained himself.

Adrian understood, as a psychologist, that his life had been dedicated to unraveling mysteries. *Why are we afraid? Why do we behave like we do? What makes us feel what we feel? Where does fear come from?*

And yet, now, with his rational time dwindling, he thought he had no answers to all the big questions in his life and he had a disease that was making finding answers harder and harder.

Adrian continued along. There is a pace on the walkways of a university campus that he could always read like words in a book. There was the *I'm late for class* quickstep and the *I've handed in my assignments and finished up* slow march.

This day, he was moving slowly, deliberately. Age, in part, dictated his speed. But also he was sorting through memories as he tried to plan his next move.

"Brian?" he blurted out loud. "I think I need your help here."

A pair of undergraduate girls smiled in his direction before returning to their cell phones. They walked together, side by side, companions, but conversed with unseen friends.

He decided, *Not that different from me.* Except the person on the other end of his conversation was dead.

There was a story his brother occasionally told after a few drinks, when lights were low and there were only a few people listening, because it was a story he'd shared only with those who loved him, about being on patrol in the A Shau Valley.

"We were just two klicks away from the base. Last bit of marching at the end of a long, boring day. Hot, thirsty, goddamn tired."

Adrian looked around. He expected to see Brian beside him because the voice echoing in his ear, repeating a story told many times before, seemed to be booming from only inches away. But Brian was nowhere to be seen.

"In other words, Audie, it was the perfect time and the ideal situation to not pay adequate attention."

There were twenty men in the patrol and they'd come that same way three uneventful times before in the prior week. Brian had described the setting: a thick stand of dark jungle trees seventy-five yards away on the right side of a wide-open rice paddy, a few huts, and a pathway to the local village off to the left. A couple of farmers were working the fields in the late afternoon. It was a setting filled with familiar, benign images. There was absolutely nothing out of the ordinary.

When he told the story, Brian repeated this at least three times. *Ordinary. Ordinary. Ordinary.*

The word had seemed like a curse.

They were dog tired and they wanted to get back to the firebase, have a meal, rest, maybe get cleaned up at least a little. There was, he would tell his brother, no reason whatsoever to stop.

But this day—Brian always remembered it was a Tuesday—he did. The men he was leading slumped to the ground. Fifty-pound packs in hundred-and-ten-degree heat sapped the decision-making process, Brian liked to tell his brother. *Maybe you can study that,* he would say. There was some grumbling—it's often far more exhausting to stop than it is to keep going. The men sullenly sucked water from near-empty canteens and smoked cigarettes while Brian trained his binoculars onto the tree line. He had concentrated hard, slowly moving his vision over each shape and shadow. He'd seen nothing. Absolutely nothing. It only made him feel worse.

"Audie, you can tell, sometimes. When everything is right but it isn't really. And that is what overcame me that day. It was all too right. Too right by a half."

And so what Brian had done was chart out the entire tree line on his grid map, and then he'd called in the coordinates to the firebase after lying to the artillery officer telling him he'd spotted movement in the trees.

The first round had landed short and killed the two farmers and sent pieces of a water buffalo flying bloodily into the air. Brian had ignored these murders, calmly adjusted fire over his radio, and seconds later sent high explosives tearing into the jungle. The earth had shaken. The air had filled with the sucking noise of shells descending. The explosions ripped the tree line into shreds, sending deadly showers of wood and metal into the sky.

Within a few moments the barrage was ended.

The men in the platoon hadn't been eager to inspect the damage, but that was what he ordered them to do. They walked silently past the bodies of the farmers. Glistening viscera and body parts lay strewn throughout the green shoots of budding rice. Blood like oil seemed to ride the watery surface of the paddies. People were just emerging from the village and the first distant wails of despair rose into the afternoon heat. And then they'd arrived at something nightmarish.

There must have been more than a company of NVA waiting for them in the tree line precisely where Brian had directed the artillery barrage. Everywhere they looked there were bodies and parts of bodies. They were blown apart, tangled in tree stumps. Heads. Arms. Legs. Ripped torsos. The barely recognizable yet unmistakable results of direct hits by a 75mm howitzer shell. There were blood trails everywhere, shattered equipment, and a landscape soaked with gore. A few wounded men moaned. Others may have dragged themselves deeper into the jungle, whether to regroup or to die Brian had been unsure. He hadn't cared.

None of his men said anything. A few whistles and some rapid breathing as they stepped through pools of blood. They simply followed Brian's lead and systematically walked from each concealed emplacement shooting any of the wounded enemy. He said he couldn't remember giving that order, but he must have. Then he had counted the dead. More than seventy-eight were totaled up, a significant victory in something that hadn't even been a fight. It was a slaughter. Every man in the platoon had understood that if they'd done what they had done the other times they'd arrived at that particular rice field they all would have been killed in the ambush. No one ever questioned Brian's instincts after that. That was what he'd told his brother.

And command gave him a medal.

But, Adrian thought, he never said this with pride, only sadness.

His brother, he thought, was trapped by his own history.

He wondered if he could say the same about himself.

"*I think you can, Audie.*"

He turned around but he could only hear his brother, not see him.

Small groups of students were making their way between the classrooms, and a distant bell tower chimed 3 p.m. Adrian remembered that this was the same hour of the day his brother had called in the accidental barrage that had saved his life.

He hurried on. The university was a hodgepodge of architecture, the modern sidled up next to the antique. Buildings with sweeping curves and wide window expanses looked out over grassy lawns and old wooden framed houses that had been converted into dormitories.

He was pleased to see that nothing much had changed since he'd retired.

The psychology department was located in one of the mid-modern buildings. It was a brick-and-mortar square space, with wide doors and an undistinguished if ivy-covered exterior. Adrian had always liked the idea that it was such an unremarkable building. It lacked the insistence of design that the business school or the chemistry department had. He thought the advantage of such a nondescript place was that it gave freer rein to the ideas that were exercised within. It hid—instead of shouted—all their intelligence.

Adrian climbed the stairs to the third floor.

He reminded himself that he was heading to room 302, and his lips moved as he repeated the name of the man he intended to see. It was an old friend and colleague but he didn't want to display any of his disease inside the hallways of his department. *Keep it all straight,* he told himself. *Every detail.*

He knocked and then pushed open the door.

"Roger?" he said, stepping inside.

A trim, bald man with a basketball player's height and lanky build was crouched in front of a computer screen, an attractive young woman seated nearby, a nervous look on her face. The office itself was overflowing with books jammed onto black steel shelving. There was also a selection of WANTED posters issued by the FBI, making one wall seem like that of a post office. Across from that was a framed movie poster from *The Silence of the Lambs* signed in black ink by the director and the screenwriter.

"Adrian! The famous Professor Thomas! Come in, come in!" Professor Roger Parsons unfolded from his seat and clutched Adrian's hand in greeting.

"I don't mean to interrupt a student conference . . ."

"No, no, not at all. Miss Lewis and I were just going over her midterm paper, which was actually quite excellent . . ."

Adrian shook hands with the young woman.

"I was wondering, Roger, if I could call on your expertise a little."

"Of course! My goodness, it's been months since anyone has seen you around here . . . and now this unexpected pleasure. How have you been? And how can I help you?"

"Should I leave, professor?" the student interjected. Roger Parsons looked to Adrian for an answer. Adrian was glad because he wouldn't have to answer the first of his old friend's questions.

"Does young Miss Lewis know anything about unusual criminal patterns of behavior?"

"Indeed she does," boomed Roger.

"Then she should stay."

The young woman shifted about, a little nonplussed but clearly pleased to be asked to remain. Adrian wondered whether she knew who he was, but his younger former colleague filled her in instantly.

"This is the most distinguished professor, a mentor to us all, they are naming the faculty lounge after," he said. "And honored we are that he has dropped in, even with a question or two."

"I wish I knew more about abnormal psychology," Adrian said.

"Well, I think you underestimate yourself, professor. But what you don't know, I will be happy to fill you in on," Roger replied. "And what is your question?"

"Criminal couples," Adrian said softly. "Male and female partnerships."

Roger nodded. "Ah . . . fascinating. There are several different relevant profiles. What sort of crime are we talking about?"

"A random kidnapping. Snatching someone unknown from a neighborhood street."

Roger's eyebrows curved upward.

"Very unusual. Very rare."

"That's what I thought."

"And the purpose of this abduction?"

"Uncertain at this moment."

"Money? Sex? Or perversion?"

"I don't know. Not yet."

"Probably all three. And more," Parsons said, musing out loud. "Certainly nothing good, and probably much evil."

Adrian nodded, and his onetime colleague slid instantly into college-lecture drone.

"That makes it much harder. Most often, what we know about these sorts of criminals we glean *after* they've been uncovered. Sort of retroactively fitting the psychological parts of the puzzle together. It all makes perfect sense *afterward.*"

"Can't do that now. Have to move ahead on little bits of information."

Roger Parsons stretched out his long legs and thought hard. "Is this someone you know . . . This isn't just an academic inquiry, is it?"

"Not exactly. A young person I came in brief contact with. I'm trying to help out some neighbors."

Adrian hesitated, and then added, "Your discretion is important. And yours, too." He addressed this to the young woman, who seemed a little terrified at the direction the conversation was going. "It's a crime that seems"—Adrian hesitated—"to be unfolding. I can't tell you exactly how."

"The abducted . . . what do you know about her?"

"Young. Teenage. Very troubled. Very smart. Very attractive."

"And the police . . ."

"Trying to sort through. They are insistently concrete, which I don't know is going to be a help."

Roger nodded again. "Yes. You are right on that score. Facts might solve a crime when there's a body. But that isn't the case?"

"Not yet."

"Good. And you're absolutely sure it was an unknown man *and* a woman who stole her and not necessarily some people who knew her?"

"Yes. Certain. Or as certain as I can be."

The younger professor thought again.

"You want me to speculate? That's all it would be. Pure speculation."

Adrian didn't reply. He knew he wouldn't have to.

"Well, it's about sex, of course, in all probability. But it's also about control. The couple will likely get erotic pleasure out of enslavement. They will feed their own arousal on each other's enjoyment. So many possible factors. I would need much more information to give you an accurate profile."

"I don't have much more. Not yet."

Roger continued to think deeply. "Well, one thing, Adrian. And don't hold me to this if it ever comes up, but I think I would focus on *purpose* if I were you and trying to make sense of the situation you describe."

"Purpose? How so?"

"Well, how will the victim create grandiosity, importance, and a sense of power for the criminal couple? Beyond the sexual toying, what is it that they hope to gain . . . because there will be *something*. It might be hidden, it might not. Power. Control. Many psychological factors in this sort of crime. None of them, alas, very pretty."

"How would the police go about solving . . ."

Roger shook his head. "Unlikely. At least, not until a body was found. Or, like in the case of those Mormon cultists with multiple wives, the child managed to escape. Except usually they don't. Escape is very hard for these sorts of hostages. From the comfort of our own homes we like to think *Well, why didn't they just run away and call the cops* but that requires psychological leaps that are very difficult to make. No, not easy at all . . ."

"So the police . . ."

Parsons waved his arm in the air as if snatching a rebound off the glass. "When they actually have a body, either dead or alive, then they can back-track their way. Maybe. Probably not. In either situation, I would not allow myself to hope for a satisfactory outcome."

Adrian nodded. *There's something else.* He heard his brother's voice echoing in his ear.

"There's something else," Roger said quietly, as if the dead, too, had prompted him.

Adrian waited for an answer.

"There's a clock running on this sort of crime."

"A clock?"

"Yes. As long as the victim is providing excitement, titillation, passion, what have you, she is exceptionally valuable to the couple. But as soon as that stops or they tire of her or they exhaust the fund of arousal she brings then she is worthless. And she will be discarded."

"Released?"

"No. Not necessarily."

There was a momentary silence, as the two professors contemplated the circumstances before them. In that brief moment they both heard the young student sharply inhale, as if a cold breeze had entered the small office. They turned toward Miss Lewis.

She had her head down as if she was shy about what she was going to say, and her cheeks had reddened, flushed by the thought that had jumped into her mind. Her voice was soft and hesitant.

"Ian Brady and Myra Hindley," she said. "England, 1966. The Moors Murders."

Roger Parsons clapped his hands enthusiastically. "Yes," he said, his voice suddenly booming in the small office. "Absolutely, Miss Lewis. Bravo. A fine observation. Adrian, you might start there."

The student managed a smile, hearing her professor's praise in his tone of voice, although Adrian thought it must be hard, in a way, to know the names and depraved acts of notorious serial killers at such a young age.

14

Even in the darkness that encompassed her world, Jennifer was haphazardly building a picture of where she was. This was accompanied by just the first gleanings of understanding about what was happening to her. She knew she was in some sort of basement room and she knew that she was being kept alive for some reason. And she knew that nothing in her sixteen years had prepared her for what was taking place.

Then she hoped she was wrong, although she was unsure what she wanted to be wrong *about*.

She wrapped her fingers together, in her lap, like someone at prayer. Then, just as slowly, she undid her hands and clenched them into fists.

When she fastened on the real—the bed, the chain and collar around her neck, the camp toilet—she was capable of drawing a misshapen portrait of her surroundings in her head. But when she allowed her imagination to consider what was going to happen to her, fear overcame her. She was constantly on the verge of dissolving into tears, or even fainting with terror. She ricocheted between the rational and agony.

Inwardly, she repeated to herself, *I'm still alive. I'm still alive.*

When she had these moments of composure, she tried hard to sharpen her hearing and her sense of smell. Touch, she guessed, was limited but might eventually tell her something.

She was poised on the edge of the bed. Beneath her toes she could feel the cold cement of the floor. Her stomach growled with hunger, but she didn't know if she could actually eat. She was terribly thirsty again, but she was unsure if she would have the guts to take another taste of water—even if it was offered to her.

The room was quiet except for her breathing.

There were two rooms, really, she told herself. The black room inside the mask and the room she was being held in. She knew that she had to learn as much as she could about each. If she didn't—if she simply waited for things to happen to her—she knew there would be nothing left except despair.

And waiting for whatever *the end* would be.

Jennifer fought panic every waking second.

She told herself it did no good to revisit what had happened, other than to try to draw a mental picture of the two people who had stolen her from the street in her neighborhood. But when she pictured herself walking through the early spring gloom of dusk, on a sidewalk in a place that she had known since she was a baby, it plunged her into a darkness deeper than that created by her hood. She had been ripped from everything she knew, and even a brief recollection of where she came from nearly stopped her heart. She felt dizzy, but she insisted to herself that she needed to focus. It was what her teachers in the school she hated so much had always complained about: *Jennifer, you need to concentrate on the material. You'd be such a fine student if only you would . . .*

All right, she said as if answering their nitpicking. *Now I'll focus.*

So she sat still and tried. The man's eyes. The woman's hat pulled down. *How big were they? What did they wear?* She took a deep breath and it was as if she could still smell the man's scent and she was back pressed against the floor of the truck, unable to breathe, crushed by his strength. Suddenly, she was unable to prevent herself from slapping at her skin, trying to wipe away the sensation that he had somehow marked her. She itched and scratched at her arms, as if it were poison ivy covering her. But when she felt welts and sensed bleeding she made herself stop, which took more strength than she knew she had.

All right. The woman. Her flat voice had been terrifying. The woman had come into the basement room and been the one talking about rules but not saying how to obey them. Jennifer tried to recall every word the woman had said to her, but it was lost in the fog of the drug that had made her pass out.

She was sure that it had happened. She was certain that the woman had been hovering above her, given her the drink, told her to obey. All this *had* taken place. It was not a dream and not a nightmare. She was not going to abruptly wake up in her bed at home in the middle of the night and hear the sounds of her mother and Scott's furtive lovemaking through the thin walls. She remembered how much she hated this—and longed for it at the very same time. Jennifer felt as if she were caught in the midst of a half dream and she argued with herself, and for the first time she wondered whether she was dead already.

Jennifer rocked forward slightly. *I'm dead,* she told herself. *This is what it must be like. There's no heaven. There are no angels and trumpets and pearly gates rising above billowing clouds.*

There's just this.

She caught her breath sharply. *No. No.* She could feel pain from where she'd scratched herself. That meant she was alive. But *how much* seemed elusive and *for how long* was an impossible question.

She shifted her seat and tried to remember exactly what the woman had said, as if there might be a clue within the words that would tell her something important. But each phrase, each tone, each command—all seemed distant and faint and she found herself reaching out, as if she could grab a word from the air in front of her.

Obey, and stay alive.

That was what the woman had said. By going along with whatever was happening Jennifer could stay alive.

Obey what? Do what?

Her inability to remember what it was she was supposed to do made her catch her breath and a single sob burst through her lips, welling up suddenly within her and exploding past any control she might have had.

This thought terrified her and she shuddered deeply.

Jennifer warred within herself. Part of her wanted to descend into a mass of despair and simply give in to the awfulness of her situation—whatever it was—but she fought hard against this desire. She did not know what the point of battling was, but she told herself that fighting reminded her she was still alive and therefore was probably a good thing.

But what she was going to fight, and how, eluded her.

I'm Number 4. They've done this before.

She wished she knew more about prisons and how people existed inside them. She knew that some people had lived through kidnappings that had lasted months, even years, before they escaped. People were lost in jungles, abandoned on mountaintops, shipwrecked at sea. *People can survive,* she insisted. *I know it. It's true. It's possible.* This thought allowed her to calm the nearly overwhelming desire to curl up into a ball on the bed and wait for whatever terrible thing was going to happen next.

Then she told herself, *You were in a prison and that's why you were running away. You were able to pull that off. So you know more than you think you do.*

She shifted about on the edge of the bed.

The toilet. If they were just going to kill me right away, they wouldn't have provided the toilet.

Jennifer smiled. This was an observation that had value.

She told herself to constantly measure everything, to assign some quality of reality to anything that she could actually touch, hear, or smell. The toilet, that was real. It was six strides away from the bed. When she sat on it the chain around her neck tightened, so that was one limit. She had not yet searched the other direction but knew she would have to. She imagined that the bed was the center of the room. Like a draftsman's metal angle, she could travel a set distance in a semicircle.

She listened hard for any sound, lifting her head a little like an animal in a forest that happens upon a scent, or a noise signaling deep instincts to be alert. She held her breath so that *any* sound would be clear.

Nothing.

"Hello?" she said out loud. Her hood muffled the word but it still projected enough so that anyone in the room could hear it.

"Anyone there?"

Nothing.

She exhaled and rose to her feet.

As before, she held her hands out in front of her, only this time she was careful to count every step and to make certain that each movement was the same length as the one before. *Twelve inches,* she reminded herself, so she could begin to create real measurements.

Keeping her hands pressed against the wall, she moved toward the toilet. *One. Two. Three . . .* six steps before she felt the seat with her knee. She bent down and ran her fingers over the surface. As she had expected, she could feel the chain tightening when she leaned forward. *All right,* she thought. *Now move out slowly.*

Jennifer took a step and was abruptly scared. There was some safety in the sensation of the wall beneath her palms, as if it helped her maintain her balance. Stepping away put her into a void, blind, tethered only by the chain around her throat. She sucked in air and forced herself to move away from the solidity of the wall and the new familiarity of the toilet.

She did not try to assign a value to what she was doing. Jennifer knew only that it seemed important. It was what someone should do. And concentrating on distances gave her the sensation that she was trying to help herself. She guessed that she would have to do more later. At the very least, this was a start.

Michael and Linda lay naked on the upstairs bed, still sweaty from their coupling, glistening with excitement. There was a laptop on the coverlet in front of them and they watched attentively on the small screen.

Their room consisted of a single double bed with passion-twisted and stained sheets. A couple of sturdy suitcases and canvas duffel bags strewn on the floor contained clothing. A stark uncovered overhead bulb lit up the room. It had a monastic emptiness except for a single flat wooden table in the corner. On the tabletop were a variety of handguns—two .357 Magnum revolvers and a trio of 9mm semiautomatics. Next to those were a twelve-gauge shotgun and the familiar shape of an AK-47. Boxes of bullets and spare clips of ammunition were spread about. There was enough weaponry to equip half a dozen people.

The computer was a top-of-the-line Apple. It connected wirelessly to the main studio in an adjacent room.

"Give everyone a warning beep," Linda said.

She bent to the screen, studying the picture. She watched as Jennifer unsteadily stepped away from the wall next to the camp toilet.

"This is really cool," Linda added, admiringly.

Michael wasn't watching Jennifer. Instead he was concentrating on the curve of Linda's back. He ran his finger up her rear, all the way to the top of her spine, then circumscribed her shoulders, pushing her hair aside, and kissed the nape of her neck. Linda nearly purred as she said, "Don't forget the paying customers . . ."

"Maybe they can wait a few seconds," he said. Then he ran his tongue up toward her ear.

Linda giggled and shifted about, coming to a cross-legged position on the bed. She took the computer and theatrically placed it between her legs so that it hid her sex. Then she bent slightly over the top, dangling her naked breasts above the screen. "Here," she said with a grin. "Maybe if I do this . . . you'll pay more attention to our job."

Michael nodded and laughed. "No shit," he said.

He hit a series of keys, which sent out a small electronic noise to all the Whatcomesnext subscribers. The tone—there was a selection of downloadable songs, sounds, and alerts that subscribers could choose from—signaled that Number 4 was awake and doing something. Many people had taken advantage of an additional offering, where the signal was sent to a private cell phone number.

"There," he said with a grin. "Everyone knows. Now, do I get a reward?"

"Soon," Linda replied. "We need to see what she does now."

Michael made a fake face, as if he were going to start crying, and Linda laughed again. "It won't be long," she said.

Michael turned back to the screen and watched Jennifer for a moment or two.

"Do you think she will find it?" Michael asked.

He did not say what *it* was, only pointing to the computer screen.

"I put it where she can reach it, if she goes out the limit."

"Kind of depends on what sort of explorer she is," Michael said, and Linda nodded.

"I hate it when they just sit there," Linda said. "Number Three really pissed me off all the time."

Michael did not reply to this. He was well aware how angry Linda had been with some of Number 3's behaviors, which had resulted in surprising shifts in the show's process. "I should pan over, make sure that everyone can see it's there."

Linda nodded. "But slowly . . . because they won't get it at first. I put it so you can't really tell what it is unless you really look hard. But then, when they figure it out . . ."

She didn't need to finish her statement.

Michael stretched and sighed. "I should go to the other room. Play with the camera angles."

Linda put the laptop aside. It was her turn to reach out and run her fingernails across his chest. Then she leaned forward and kissed his thigh.

"Work first, play later," she said.

"You are insatiable," he replied. "Which I like."

Linda put her hands above her head, leaning back provocatively. He bent forward and kissed her. "Tempting," he said.

"But the job comes first," she replied, slowly closing her legs together. She laughed. The two of them dragged themselves from the bed and padded on bare feet down the stairs, like children on Christmas morning, to the living room, where Michael had set up the main studio. As in the other rooms in the rented farmhouse there was little furniture. What dominated the space was a long table with three large computer monitors. Wires went in various directions, snaking across the wooden floor and disappearing through drilled holes. There were speaker systems and several joysticks, along with keyboards and surge controls. An editing board and a sound board also filled the space. In short, Michael had assembled all the high-tech equipment necessary for broadcasting on the Web. Just outside the window there was a portable convex antenna. The room had the same quality as a military operation or a movie set: much expensive equipment, all with specialized capabilities, all operated from a pair of black Aeron desk chairs centered in front of the primary computer.

It was cool in the room, and Linda went to retrieve a pair of faux fur-trimmed L.L. Bean parkas from a hallway to cover their nakedness. She slipped into one and arranged the other across Michael's shoulders as he bent to the screen. She looked outside at the nighttime beyond the window. She could see nothing except black isolation, which was, at least in part, why they'd rented this particular farmhouse.

"Do you think Number Four even knows what time it is?" she asked.

"Nope." Michael thought, and then added, "Which means . . . make certain that we don't help her. You know, by giving her breakfast in the morning or something that is clearly dinner at night. Keep mixing up the meals. Feed her three straight bowls of cereal followed by some burgers. It will help keep her disorientated."

"I know that, silly," Linda said.

Michael smiled. He liked it at the moments the two of them discussed the ways that Number 4 could be manipulated. It was the part of the game he most enjoyed. It also energized Linda, which made their own sex more unbridled, more passionate. When it started to slow, that was when he knew to wrap things up.

He took a single joystick marked with a piece of white tape that said *camera 3* and moved it slightly. On one of the monitor screens, the angle shifted slightly, revealing an object placed to the side of the bed, opposite the toilet. He moved the joystick forward, giving a closer look.

Linda was at his side, working swiftly with a keyboard, typing rapidly, her fingernails clicking.

On the main monitor—the one that showed what was going out to subscribers—Linda's typing appeared in red script across the image of Jennifer moving cautiously about, hands outstretched.

There's something for Number 4 to find.

What is it?

Michael panned camera 3 briefly to a small, misshapen lump on the cement floor. It was at the periphery of the chain's allowance. Jennifer was still several feet away, and the only way she would discover it was if she continued searching at the limit of her travel. Linda continued at the keyboard.

Will Number 4 locate it?

Michael laughed. "Keep going," he whispered.

Will it help Number 4?

Linda was typing furiously.

Or will it hurt Number 4?

"Now ask them," Michael said.

A box appeared on the screen as Linda hit keys.

Find? was followed by a square where one could click a response.

No find? had the same box.

Then there were two more entries.

Help?

Hurt?

Linda turned to the side. An electronic counter was tallying numbers on a different screen.

"They seem to have confidence," she said, as numbers grew in various columns. "But they are split on whether it will help her or hurt her." Linda smiled again. "I knew this was a good idea," she said. "They're all logging in and they seem pretty damn fascinated."

Michael concentrated hard on the cameras.

On the main monitor they both watched as Jennifer moved slowly toward the camera. Her hands were out in front of her, her fingers stretched forward, touching nothing except air. Her picture grew increasingly large on the screen. Her hands seemed only inches away when she stopped. She had reached the limit of the chain, fingertips nearly touching the primary camera.

"They will love that," Linda whispered.

The camera seemed to explore Jennifer's body, lingering on her slender breasts and then panning down to her crotch. Her underwear seemed little more than a tease. Linda imagined that around the world viewers were reaching out toward Number 4 as if they could touch her through their computer screens. Michael instinctively knew that was what was happening, and he manipulated the cameras expertly, creating a dance with the images. It was stately, like a waltz.

Jennifer backed away and moved a little to her left.

"Ah, she's got a chance," Linda said.

She glanced over at the counters, which were rising rapidly.

"I think she'll get it."

Michael shook his head. "No way. It's on the floor. Unless her toe touches it. She's not thinking vertically enough. She needs to go up and down, to really explore the space."

"You're too much of a scientist," Linda said. "She'll get it."

"Want to bet?"

Linda laughed. "Stakes?" she asked.

Michael turned away from the monitor briefly. He grinned like any lover might. "Name 'em," he said.

"I'll think of something when I win," Linda replied. She touched the top of his hand on the joystick, letting her fingers stroke his. This was something of a promise and Michael shuddered with pleasure.

Then they turned back to see if Number 4 would succeed. Or not.

* * *

115

Jennifer counted each step silently to herself.

She moved cautiously. The bed was behind her but she wanted to reach the wall so that she at least understood the limits of her space. Each small step became a new number in her head.

She kept her hands out in front of her, moving them just slightly, but touching nothing except emptiness.

She maintained a constant tension around her throat, trying to imagine herself a little like a chained dog, but not wanting to throw herself to the limit, like the dog would.

Jennifer had reached *eighteen* in her count when her left toe brushed up against something on the floor.

It was sudden, unexpected, and she almost fell.

It seemed soft, furlike and alive, and she stumbled backward. Her mind filled with images. *Rat!*

She wanted to run but could not. She wanted to leap back on the bed, thinking that would keep her safe, and panic filled her. She swung out her arms, punching nothing, and she realized that she had screamed once, maybe twice, and now, inside the hood, her mouth was open wide.

The counting process had evaporated. Whatever numbers she had collected were gone. She took a step and tumbled into utter confusion. She no longer could determine where the wall was, or the bed. The darkness inside the hood seemed to be blacker, more confining, and she shouted, "*Get away!*" as loud as she could.

The sound of her voice seemed to echo in the room and was replaced by the adrenaline pumping in her ears like the roar of a swollen river. Her heart was pounding in her chest, and she could feel her entire body quiver. She touched the chain—thought that she should use it like she would a line tossed to a drowning person, go hand over hand back to the bed and get her feet off the floor, so whatever it was couldn't reach her.

She started to do this, then stopped. She listened.

There was no noise of tiny feet running away.

Jennifer took another deep breath. Once there had been a family of mice in the walls of their home, and her mother and Scott had dutifully placed traps and poisons around the house to get rid of them. But what Jennifer remembered in that moment was the unmistakable noise they would make late at night running through the empty spaces behind the wallboard.

There was no similar noise.

Her second thought was, *It's dead. Whatever it is, it's dead.*

She froze in position, sharpening her ears for any sound.

But she could hear only her own heavy breathing.

What was it?

She stopped thinking of a rat, even though it was a basement she was imprisoned in.

She replayed in her mind the instant sensation against her toe and what she might learn from that momentary impression. She tried hard to form a picture in her mind, but it was impossible.

Jennifer took another deep breath.

Retreat to the bed, she told herself, *and you will sit there terrified because you won't know.*

This seemed to her a terrible choice. Uncertainty versus going back and touching whatever it was to try and determine what the dead thing might be.

She twitched. Her hands shook. She could feel tremors up and down her spine and she was both hot and cold at the same instant, sweating yet chilled.

Go back. Find out.

Her lips and mouth were even drier, if that was possible. She knew her head was spinning with the choice presented to her.

I am not brave. I'm just a kid.

But she thought there was no more room left inside the hood for being a child.

"Come on, Jennifer," she whispered to herself. She knew everything was a nightmare. If she did not go back and find out what her toe had touched, the nightmare would just grow worse.

She took a step. Then a second. She did not know how far she had recoiled. But now, instead of measuring, she took her left leg and pointed it outward, moving it back and forth like a ballet dancer or like a swimmer unsure about the temperature of the water.

She was afraid of what she would find, afraid that it had disappeared. Something dead, something inanimate was far preferable to something alive.

She was unable to tell how long it took her to locate the object with her toe. It might have been seconds. It could have been an hour.

When her toe touched the object she fought off the urge to kick out.

Steeling herself, she forced herself to kneel down. The cement scratched against her knees.

She reached out toward the object with her hands.

It was fur. It was solid. It was lifeless.

She pulled her hands back. Whatever it was, it wasn't an immediate threat. She had the urge to simply leave whatever it was where it was. But then something different, something surprising spoke to her, and she reached out once again, and this time she let her fingers linger on the surface of the object.

Familiarity.

She wrapped her hands around the shape and pulled it closer. It shifted in her hands and, as if reading Braille, she ran her fingers over it. *A slight tear. A frayed edge.*

Recognition.

She immediately knew what it was.

She clutched the object tightly to her chest and moaned softly to herself, whispering: "Mister Brown Fur . . ."

It was her teddy bear.

Jennifer could not hold back. She sobbed uncontrollably and caressed the worn surface of the only item from her childhood that she had thought crucial to take with her on her escape from home.

15

Terri Collins told herself to remain professional. She reminded herself to stick to facts and not speculation. But she had nothing but doubts.

Back in her office, she started with the truck that Adrian described. It defied the small town police logic that she'd developed over years and had just seemed too convenient for Scott, who was the type who wanted to see huge governmental conspiracies or demonic plots in all sorts of mundane events. She was surprised by the electronic reply from the Massachusetts State Police that a set of license plates beginning with the letters *QE* had been stolen from a sedan parked in the long-term lot at Logan International Airport nearly three weeks earlier.

So when her computer screen beeped with the reply and she saw the single line of type, she scrunched forward, bending toward the information displayed in front of her, as if by moving closer she could determine its value.

There had been a delay in reporting the theft, because the thief had taken the time and risk to attach a different set of plates to the businessman's car. That second set had been stolen from a mall one hundred miles away in western Massachusetts a month earlier. The businessman probably would not have noticed that his plate was different—how often does a person look at his own license plate?—had he not been pulled over on a DUI. The duality of the paperwork—a theft reported in one part of the state, then found on a different vehicle being driven by an obnoxious, arrogant drunk who, in addition to a series of insults tossed at the trooper who pulled him over, hadn't had any intelligible explanation for where his assigned plates might be—created a DMV bureaucratic knot of red tape.

Two sets of stolen license plates were interesting. Someone was taking extra precautions.

"Well," she said, "that's something."

Professor Thomas, she thought, had managed to get the numeral and the third letter wrong. The *Quod Erat* was correct but the *Demonstrandum* was a mistake, although she thought it pretty typical of a college professor with an Ivy League doctorate and a pristine reputation like his to automatically expect a *D* after a *Q* and an *E*. It went with all that education.

Still, the similarity of two letters and the reported theft made her expand her computer inquiries. She went to databases for Massachusetts, New Hampshire, Rhode Island, and Vermont searching for a recent white panel van theft. If whoever was involved in this random kidnapping had gone to the trouble of stealing two different sets of plates, she doubted the person would use anything other than a stolen vehicle.

She found three: a brand-new van taken from a dealer's lot in Boston, a twelve-year-old clunker stolen from a trailer park in New Hampshire, and a three-year-old panel van that fit Adrian's description taken one week earlier from a rental lot in downtown Providence.

This truck was interesting. A large fleet—twenty, maybe thirty, all with the same basic look and configuration—would be parked in rows in the back of a lot in some blighted urban area. Unless the person who jacked the truck left obvious signs of entry—a chain-link fence ripped aside or a lock sliced by a high-pressure bolt cutter—it might take the rental company twenty-four hours to do an inventory and realize one truck was missing. And, Terri thought, if the guys working the lot were less than competent it might take longer.

None of the three missing vehicles had been recovered, which wasn't surprising. There were a number of crimes that required a single use of a stolen truck: a quick break-in at an electronics store, a single load of marijuana being hauled up to Boston. She also knew that each of them was probably discarded as soon as the job was completed.

She expanded her computer search.

One entry got her immediate attention. The fire department in Devens, Massachusetts, had reported being called to the scene of an auto fire, where a vehicle of the same make and model as the truck taken in Providence had been torched behind a deserted mill. A confirmation was pending—the suspect vehicle had been completely gutted by the fire. It was not the sort of case that any cop placed a high priority on, so it would take some time for an insurance investigator to get to the local auto wreck depository near Devens, crawl all over the filthy charred remains until he found one of the etched serial numbers that had survived the fire, and then compare that to the missing vehicle so that his bosses would eventually cut a check to the rental company.

All that would happen much faster, of course, if Terri contacted the state police and told them that the truck had been used in a felony kidnapping of a minor . . . if there was such a crime.

She was still not persuaded but she was much closer to imagining that something unusual was taking place.

Rising from her desk, she went over to a wall map. She traced her finger across distances. Providence, to the street where Jennifer disappeared, to an empty, forgotten part of Devens. A triangle encompassing many miles but many roads that carved through rural sections of the state. If someone had wanted to travel anonymously a more isolated route could hardly have been chosen.

She went back to her computer and punched a few keys. She wanted to check one other detail: the date of the fire department call.

121

She stared at her computer screen. She felt a hollow sensation inside her stomach, as if she hadn't eaten, hadn't slept, and had just run a great distance.

The fire department had responded to an anonymous 911 call shortly after midnight, making it the day after Jennifer disappeared. But when they arrived a vehicle was found that had already burned to a blackened hull. Whoever set the fire had done so much earlier.

She tried to do some calculations in her head. A phone call comes in to a central dispatcher. The dispatcher hits an alarm that sounds in the bedrooms of the volunteers in the fire crew. They drive to the station, change into their gear, and then drive to the scene of the fire. *How long did all that take?*

Terri internally posed rapid-fire questions. That was how she worked: she would try to see each bit of evidence from two perspectives—hers as a detective, and that of some anonymous criminal. She thought it important to be able to place herself into the bad guy's mind-set because, when she managed that, answers came to her. So she demanded: *Did someone know about that delay? Is that why they chose that particular spot to torch the truck? Maybe. If I wanted to get rid of a vehicle after a single use I wouldn't pick a place where firemen might arrive before the flames had done their job.*

Terri noted on the incident report that the fire lieutenant had drawn attention to *undetermined accelerants.*

No hair, fingerprint, fiber, DNA would be left in that truck, she thought.

Terri got up from the computer and walked across the cramped office to the battered, stained coffee machine that was a necessity in any police detective's office. She poured herself a cup of black coffee, then sipped at the bitter taste. Ordinarily she liked two sugars and more than a dollop of cream, but this day sweetness seemed the wrong taste to put in her mouth.

After a moment she returned to her desk. Her satchel was hung over the back of her chair. She reached inside and removed a small leather case and flipped this open. Inside, encased in plastic sleeves, were half a dozen pictures of her two children. She stared at each photo, taking the time to reconstruct the circumstances of each picture. *This one was a birthday party. This one was when we went to Acadia on a camping holiday. This one was the first snow two winters ago.*

Sometimes it helped when she reminded herself why she was a policewoman.

She picked up the picture on the police flyer she'd had made up for Jennifer. She knew it was a mistake to emotionally join things. One of the first lessons anyone learned as they worked up the police ranks was that home was home and work was work, and when the two collided nothing good happened, because decisions should be made coldly and calmly.

She looked at Jennifer's picture. She remembered talking with the teenager after the second runaway attempt. It had been fruitless because, as troubled as the young girl had been, she was clever and determined and most of all tough. Growing up in a town filled with the pretentious, the eccentric, and the precious, Jennifer had been hard-edged.

And not fake and laughable tough, with teenage posturing and *I want a tattoo and aren't I cool because I called my English teacher an obscene name to her face and I'm smoking cigarettes behind my parents' backs* tough. The detective had imagined that Jennifer was a lot like she was at the same age. And Jennifer had been responding to some of the same emotions that had saved Terri's life when she had run from an abusive man. It was as if she could see herself in the younger woman.

Terri sighed deeply. *You should walk away from this right now,* she told herself. *Give the case to another cop and get away, because you won't see things clearly.*

This was wrong and right at the same time. In some not fully formed way she had come to think that Jennifer was her responsibility.

Filled with warring notions of what she should do, she typed a quick e-mail memo to her boss, with a copy to her shift supervisor. *Some evidence being developed that this is not a routine runaway. Needs additional investigation. Possible abduction situation. Will update with details as I collect more information. Later assessment warranted.*

She signed her name to the e-mail and was about to send it, then thought better. She didn't want to alarm the chief, at least not yet. She was also concerned about any information leaking out to the local press, because the next thing she knew every television station, reporter, and crime blog fanatic would be parked outside the station, demanding interviews and updates and pretty much preventing them from accomplishing anything important, including recovering Jennifer.

If there was any chance.

This made her pause. She thought about all the milk cartons, websites for abducted and missing children, television reports, and newspaper headlines and believed that none of it does any good.

Terri took a deep breath. *Not usually. But sometimes . . .* She stopped herself. It did no good to fall into speculation one way or the other until she knew for certain what she was up against.

She removed the line *Possible abduction situation* from the e-mail.

She knew she had to find something concrete. She knew what the first question from her boss would be: *How can you be sure?*

There was a lot more to do at the computer. She needed to take the few details she had and run them against other crimes, looking for similarities. She had to do a thorough check of all known sex offenders within the triangle she had identified. She needed to see if there were any reports of unidentified sexual predators working in the area. Were there any false alarms? Had any parents called any of the local forces complaining about this man or that man cruising the neighborhood suspiciously? Terri knew she had lots of research that needed to be handled quickly and efficiently.

If Jennifer was kidnapped, the clock was running. If there even was a clock. Maybe it was just one prolonged rape and then murder. That was what usually happened. Gone, used up, and then dead.

She tried not to think about that.

Terri paused. *There had been two people in that truck. That's what the old man said he saw.* This simply made no sense to her. Predators worked alone, trying to create as much darkness and fog around their desires as they could.

She fidgeted slightly in her seat. Maybe in eastern Europe or Latin America there were kidnappings that were organized parts of the international sex trade, but not in the United States and certainly not in small New England college towns.

Where did that leave her? She did not know.

Terri considered Mary Riggins and Scott West and knew they wouldn't be any help. Scott was likely to complicate matters with opinions and demands, even more than he already had. Mary was likely to panic further as soon as she heard the word *predator*.

There was only one other direction she could go.

She did not know what was wrong with Adrian Thomas. He seemed a little like a flickering light. She pictured the way he had seemed distracted, curiously displaced, disconnected to the room he'd been in and the story he was telling her, as if he were somewhere else, in some parallel location. *Something was definitely not right,* she thought. *Maybe he's just old and that is what it will look like for all of us someday.*

This was a charitable thought that she didn't actually believe. At that moment, however, his was the only logical direction in which to turn.

16

He thought, *They were truly terrible*.

Of course, the word *terrible* hardly captured what they had actually done. The word was antiseptic.

Adrian stared at pictures of Myra Hindley and Ian Brady that adorned the jacket of *The Encyclopedia of Modern Murder* that his friend the ab psych professor had loaned him. He was both fascinated and frightened. The book contained so many horrific details that they became petty, almost routine, because they were bunched together in relentless volume. *This victim was killed with a hatchet. This victim's screams were tape-recorded. They took pornographic pictures. This child was abandoned in a shallow grave out on the Moors*. Reading the journalistic descriptions was like walking through a battlefield. If you see one dead body, it's awful and compelling and hard to tear one's eyes away. If you see a hundred they start to mean nothing.

Adrian let the pages rustle together like dry leaves tumbling in a fall breeze as he opened to the entry that described *The Moors Murders*.

Like any good scientist Adrian had immersed himself in his subject, trying to learn as much as he could in a short amount of time. There is a processing that teachers develop over the years, where controversial, even repellant, material leaps into their minds in a way that is accessible so that it can be re-formed and presented to students. He was pleased that his ability to absorb much in a short amount of time had not yet slunk away, as had so many of his other intellectual capabilities.

Adrian had entered into a realm where, after spending much of a night and the following morning surrounded by books and making computer inquiries, he knew he could speak intelligently about the curious connections between male-female criminal partnerships. *What will love make you do?* he asked himself. *Wonderful things? Or awful things?*

At the same time he hoped no one would come along and ask him to add six and nine together or question him about the day of the week, week of the month, or month of the year, or even what year it was, because he doubted he could answer correctly, even if he got an invisible and subtle assist from someone he once loved who was now dead. Ghosts, Adrian thought, were helpful—but only to a point. He was still unsure how practical the information they shared might be.

He was smart enough to know that every hallucination stemmed from memory about what Cassie or Brian might once have said, or what they might now say, were they alive to say it. He understood that all these things that seemed real were in fact a chemical imbalance in his frontal lobes, a short circuiting and fraying, but still it seemed to be helping somehow, which was all that he asked for.

A voice interrupted his reverie.

"What does it say?"

Adrian looked across his office and saw Cassie standing in the doorway. She looked pale, old, beaten. There was sadness behind her eyes, a look he remembered from the days before her accident, when she was distracted by grief. Gone was the sexy, slender, seductive Cassie from their first years together. This was the tired and sick woman who desperately needed death to come to her. Seeing her this way made Adrian catch his breath and reach out, wanting to find some way of comforting her, when he knew that not once in their final months together had he ever been able to do that.

He could feel his own tears, and so he ignored her question and tried to say something he thought he should have said before she died. Or maybe he had said it a hundred times but it had never resonated.

"Cassie," he said slowly, "I'm so sorry. There was nothing you or I, or anyone, could do. He was doing exactly what he wanted to do."

She dismissed this excuse with a single wave.

"I hate that," she said briskly. "The *there was nothing we could do* lie. There's always something someone could have said or done. And Tommy always listened to you."

Adrian closed his eyes. He knew if he opened them they would automatically shift to the corner of the desk where there was another photograph: his son, Tommy, in cap and gown on a sunlit graduation day, ivy walls in the background. Nothing but hope and promise.

He heard Cassie's voice slice through the start of painful memories. He slowly opened up toward her. She was insistent and forceful, the way she always was when she knew she was right. He had rarely resented this. He considered it her artist's prerogative. If you knew where to put the unequivocal first line of color on a blank white canvas you had the right to your opinions.

"All those books and computer inquiries, what do they say?" she demanded again.

Adrian adjusted the reading glasses perched on the end of his nose. This was an academic's notion of acting.

"It says they killed five people together."

He hesitated. "Five people that the police constabulary in rural England were able to identify. There might have been more. Eight was the number some criminologists believed more accurate. The papers over there called it the *end of innocence*."

"People?"

Adrian shook his head. "No, you're right. Need to be specific. *Children*. They ranged in age from twelve to sixteen or seventeen."

"That's just about Jennifer's age."

"Right. But it's a coincidence, I guess."

"I thought in your teaching you *hated* coincidences and didn't believe they ever happened. Psychologists like explanations, not accidents."

"Maybe the Freudians—"

"Adrian, you know."

"I'm sorry, Cassie. That was supposed to be a joke."

He smiled wanly at his dead wife. She had remained hanging in the doorway, the way she often would, when she didn't want to disturb him at his work but still had a question that needed an answer. She would hesitate in that transitional space, as if what she asked in that moment would disrupt him less, coming as it did from a slight distance.

"Aren't you going to come in?" he asked. He motioned toward a seat.

Cassie shook her head. "I have too much to do."

He must have looked a little dismayed because her tone softened. "Audie," she said slowly, "you know there's not much time. Either for you or for Jennifer."

"Yes," he agreed. "I know." He hesitated. "It's just . . ."

"Just what?"

"It's turning information into action. These two, the moors murderers—Brady and Hindley—they were tripped up when they tried to bring someone else into their perversion and the fellow they wanted to enlist called the police. As long as it was the two of them, feeding off each other, they were actually safe. It was only when they wanted to impress someone else, someone who turned out to be just slightly not as homicidally perverse as they, that they got caught."

"Keep going," Cassie said. Her face had caught a small smile, just the barest of upturns at the corners. She was pushing him forward. Adrian knew that was always the way they were in their relationship. The artist in her would pull his head out of the academic clouds, find a practical application for all his lab work. Adrian felt a rush of passion. *Why wouldn't he have loved the woman who made his imaginings relevant?* Emotions flooded him and, like so many dinner table, backyard, gathered around the winter fireplace conversations, he picked up his pace.

"The psychodynamics of murderous couples are elusive. There is clearly an overwhelming sexual component. But the linkage seems more profound. That's what I'm trying to understand. Relationships are like checks and balances—they mean something is processed outwardly, discussed, analyzed, what have you. At least, that's what they appear to do. But beyond that, Cassie, there is this enabling kind of action. It's as if the male wouldn't do what he does without the female there to give it some quality that is frightening. It's beyond authorization. It's about taking something to a really deep and dark place."

Cassie snorted but her grin remained. She stayed in the doorway as she gestured toward the books. "Don't intellectualize, Adrian," she said. Again, he was forced to smile. Her tone of voice echoed over all the years they'd spent together. "This isn't an academic situation. There's no paper to deliver or lecture to give at the end. There's just a little girl who will be alive or dead."

"But I have to understand . . ."

"Yes. But only so you can *act*," Cassie said.

He nodded, then gestured. "Come in," Adrian whispered. "Keep me company. This stuff"—he waved his hand over the encyclopedia—"it scares me."

"It should." Cassie remained in the doorway.

"This case, it happened back in the 1960s . . ."

"So? What has changed?"

He didn't reply. Instead he thought, *We are less naive than we were then.*

Cassie must have heard this, or sensed it, because she quickly interrupted, "No. People haven't changed. Only the means have."

Adrian felt exhausted, as if learning all about a series of murders was draining him slowly.

"How do I turn one kind of understanding—you know, the book stuff—into the kind of understanding that will find Jennifer?" he asked.

Cassie smiled. He could see her face soften.

"You know who it is you should ask," she said.

Adrian rocked a little in his seat and knew she meant Brian and wondered how exactly he could summon up one of these hallucinations on demand when he needed some prodding in the right direction.

He glanced at all the collected material about murder and suddenly shoved it aside, not far, just a few inches away on the desktop, as if he could avoid infection by not coming into contact with it. He turned to a bookcase and reached past texts and study guides to one of his shelves of poetry. In each of the many jam-packed bookcases in every room of the small house, there was at least one shelf devoted to volumes of verse, because he never knew when he was going to need an injection of eloquence.

Adrian's fingers played across the spines of books. He did not know what he was searching for but he felt a huge compulsion to find the right poem. *Something that fits my mood and my situation,* he thought.

His hand stopped over a collection of war poets. All the doomed young men from the First World War. He seized this and let the pages fall open. Wilfred Owen's "Dulce et Decorum Est" was the first he spotted. He read . . . *limped on, blood-shod.*

Yes, he thought, that was him.

He read the words of the poem three times, then shut his eyes and breathed in deeply.

It was the smell that came to him first.

Thick dark oil and a rusty metal taste on his tongue, smoky and unbelievably hot, as if everything in the world was on the burner of a stove turned high and nearing the boil. He coughed sharply. Behind his closed eyes he could smell something so thick and awful that its stench nearly made him gag. He told himself to wake up, as if he were asleep, and then he felt his entire body lurch forward, then slam back, and suddenly he heard a grinding noise, rising above the half drone, half roar of a laboring engine. He felt himself pitched wildly in his seat, as if being tossed in a raging sea, and he reached out into the air to try to steady himself when he heard a voice coming from beside him, right next to his ear, a tone so familiar it would have been musical if not for the terrible smell, the overwhelming noise, and the fierce shaking back and forth.

"Hang on, Dad, it's gonna get a lot worse."

Adrian's eyes shot open.

He was no longer seated at his desk, surrounded by books and papers, poetry and pictures, filled with memories.

He was lurching in the cramped back of a Humvee.

There was a banging sound and the engine accelerated. He turned to the person jammed into the seat next to him.

"Tommy," he said. He must have gasped, because his son laughed out loud, at the same time that he grabbed a hold rod in the ceiling with one hand and tried to steady his camera with the other. His black Kevlar helmet slid down, almost covering his eyes. His navy blue flak jacket was bunched up around his neck. He looked young, Adrian thought. He looked beautiful.

"Got to speak fast, Dad, we're coming up on the spot where I die."

From the front, the driver—a young marine in khaki camouflage fatigues and wearing dark wraparound sunglasses—tossed a few bitter words back over his shoulder. "*Fuckin' IED buried in the sand. No way to spot it. We were always gonna be fucked. Fallujah fucked.*"

This must have been a joke because there was some tense laughter.

Adrian looked around at the other marines jammed into the back of the vehicle. They were staring out the windows at a harsh, sand-colored countryside, weapons ready, but they nodded in agreement. "*Like this isn't the perfect goddamn place for an ambush,*" one said. Adrian could not see his face but his voice had both a harshness and a sense of doom to it, as if he knew there was nothing anyone could do about what was about to happen. The gunner manning the .50-caliber protruding through the roof bent down. He couldn't have been more than twenty-one years old and he was laughing behind sand-caked goggles and teeth stained with dirt and dust. "*We should never have gone out on this mission,*" he shouted above the roar of the engine and wind whipping through the open windows. *"You could tell it was trouble from the first mile."* From the shotgun seat in the front, a hard-eyed black lieutenant speaking on a radio-telephone put the receiver down and turned in his seat toward the squad crowded behind him. *"Stow it!"* he ordered sharply. *"Look, not everyone buys it. You Masters and you Mitchell, you walk out of this with a couple of scratches and a bloody nose. And you Simms, tough shit about your legs, but you live and get to fly the big bird home. And we waste a whole shitload of the ragheads when I call in the air strikes before I get lit up, so stop whining."*

Then the lieutenant suddenly lightened up, a grin creasing his face as he pointed at Tommy. *"And news boy there makes all your sorry asses famous, don't you, Tommy?"* Tommy grinned. "Sure do," he said.

One of the marines leaned over and slapped Tommy on the thigh and said, *"Made us into fuckin' Internet stars!"* He laughed as he sighted down his weapon.

Adrian slammed sideways in his seat as the vehicle accelerated and bounced over debris. He caught a glimpse of mud and brick buildings, walls black-scorched by fire, pockmarked from heavy weapons rounds. Shredded palm trees littered the roadside. Burned-out cars and a tank that was twisted into a nearly unrecognizable hulk, still smoking, halfway into a ditch. A charred body hung partway out of a hatch. He heard someone mutter, *"Never mess with the flyboys,"* as they roared past.

Tommy had bent forward, the big Sony video camera raised like a weapon, trying to get a shot over the driver's shoulder, as they rushed toward a measly collection of low-slung buildings. Dust and smoke seemed everywhere, and the smell persisted in Adrian's nostrils. Tommy was filming but he spoke to his father. "I know. It's pretty bad. But you get used to it. And anyway, that's just the cordite from the explosions and maybe some burning oil. Wait until you get a whiff of dead bodies left out in the heat for a couple of days."

He lowered the camera.

"I won an award, you know," he said. "I get the whole thing on film, right from the spot we get hit, right through the firefight. And even after I got shot I kept my finger on the trigger so the camera would keep filming. Before they put the footage on the Internet—did you know it got nearly three million hits?—then on *The Nightly News* the anchor called everyone together and made a nice speech. You know, where he talked about being a combat journalist and Robert Capa and Ernie Pyle and getting the real story. He talked about the guys in Vietnam—Uncle Brian probably knew some of them—who would go into fights with just their Nikons strapped around their necks or a notebook in their hands and not even wearing body armor. He spoke about tradition and dedication and even made getting the story sound like some higher calling, like the priesthood. But you and I, Dad, we know I was here because I loved taking pictures and I loved excitement, and nothing combines the two like following a squad of badass marines, even if it costs you your life."

"*That's right. Definitely badass!*" said the .50-caliber gunner, shouting above the wind noise.

"Tommy," Adrian choked.

"No, Dad, you've got to listen to me, because things are going to happen fast now. I'll try to come back to you later, when it's not so confusing. But I need to make a point."

"Tommy, please . . ."

"No, Dad, listen."

The Humvee accelerated. The marine behind the wheel gave a little *whoop!* and said, "*Shitstorm about to happen, boys. Hang onto your cocks, pull up your jocks, and get ready.*"

Adrian didn't understand how people who were dead could talk about their dying before it happened, although he knew it already *had* happened a half dozen years earlier. He gripped the side of the Humvee tightly as it swerved into a pile of sandy dust. Beside him, Tommy was talking steadily, calmly.

"Go back to what you already saw, reading the encyclopedia. Everything you need to know is right there. You just have to think in a more modern fashion."

"But Tommy," Adrian started, but his son pivoted toward him. There was anxiety in his face. "Dad! Think about why I came here."

"You were a documentary filmmaker. You got permission to embed with the Marines. I remember how excited you were."

"Don't make it sound like more than it was."

"Tommy, I miss you. And your mother, she was never the same after. It killed her."

"I know, Dad, I know. I know that losing a child changes everything. That's why Jennifer is so *goddamn* important."

"But I'm dying, Tommy. And . . ."

One of the marines, manning a machine gun, pointed out the Humvee window, turned, saying, *"Hey, old-timer! We're all dying from the day we're born. Suck it up! Listen to Tommy. He's being righteous."*

There was a general murmur of assent from the other men. They were all hunkered over the weapons.

"Jennifer, Dad. Keep focused on Jennifer. I'm gone. Mom's gone. Uncle Brian's gone. And there are others. Friends. Family. Dogs . . ." He laughed, though Adrian didn't know what was funny. "We're all gone. But Jennifer isn't. Not yet. You know it. You can feel it. It's something in all that education, all those lectures, something, isn't it, that tells you she's not gone. Not yet."

"Shit, here we go," the driver said abruptly.

Tommy grabbed his father's knee. Adrian could feel the pressure. He desperately wanted to throw his arms around his son, find a way of shielding him from what he knew was about to happen. He reached out but somehow, he couldn't understand why, his arms fell short, waving uselessly in the air.

"It's about the *seeing*, Dad. It's about being able to show what you're doing. That's where the excitement comes from. And, by putting it out

135

there, where anyone can see it, it gives you power, it gives you strength. It makes you *hard*. That's where the passion comes from. Don't you remember? When you were reading about that couple in England fifty years ago. *Pictures. Tapes.* Now, why would they do that? Come on, Dad, this is your territory. You should know."

"But Tommy . . ."

"No, Dad, there's so little time. It's about to happen. Don't you remember me once telling you why I wanted to film things? Because it's the purest truth. When I took my pictures no one could say it wasn't real or it wasn't true. That was why we all did it. It made us into something bigger than we really were. No lies behind a camera, Dad. Think about it. Jesus! This is it!"

Adrian wanted to respond but the explosion tore the air apart. The Humvee seemed to rise up, as if no longer connected to the earth or to the world. The inside of the truck immediately filled with smoke and flame and the force from the blast threw Adrian backward. He thought he lost consciousness because of the darkness that enveloped him. All the smells, all the tastes seemed to increase, and his ears rang with a high-pitched bell-like noise. He was dizzy. His body felt like it was mired in sand and dust. He tried to look around for Tommy, but at first all he could make out were odd forms and twisted shapes that a few seconds earlier had been marines but now were tangled bodies, shredded and mangled by the bomb hidden in the road.

And then, as if someone had miraculously advanced the track of a movie, he found himself outside. Pale blue sky above, unrelenting heat and noise and something he thought at first was a swarm of insects but then understood was small-arms fire. At his feet was a marine, missing one leg, screaming and pulling himself toward a small dirt wall. Adrian pivoted, still looking for his son, and he saw the marine lieutenant on the radio-telephone. The lieutenant was shouting loudly, but Adrian could not make out what he was saying. The noise seemed to increase, and there was a thundering sound of heavy-weapons fire as other Humvees in the column opened up. Adrian put his hands over his ears, trying to shut out the noise, and he called out, "Tommy! Tommy!"

When he turned he spotted his son. Tommy was bleeding profusely through the ears. Adrian could see where his leg was broken, and his son was dragging it uselessly along behind him. But he was filming, just as they said he did. He had the camera up on his shoulder, as if it were his only weapon, and he was taking pictures of the firefight. Adrian realized his mouth was opened and he was trying to scream his son's name, but no sound emerged. He saw Tommy swing the camera toward the marine lieutenant, who was lying in a dusty pool of blood. Adrian could hear the shrieks of approaching jet fighters, and he looked up and saw the unmistakable forms of two Warthogs coming in low, the sun behind them so that they appeared as black specks above the horizon. Adrian was standing in the midst of bullets and explosions, but everything suddenly seemed slowed down. He turned again to where he'd spotted Tommy and tried to yell at him, *Take cover!* But Tommy was exposed, in the open. Adrian wanted to rush toward him; he had some vague idea of throwing himself over his son, to shield him from what was taking place, but his legs would not move.

"Tommy," he whispered. He watched the small dust flowers race toward him. He knew they were machine-gun bullets, coming from a hut fifty yards away, directly in the path of the Warthogs. If only they were a little faster, Adrian thought. If only the pilots had opened up a second or two earlier. *If only* . . .

The line of bullets marched inexorably toward his son. Adrian watched as Tommy filmed his own death. It came just seconds before the hut vanished in a billowing explosion of fire.

Time, Adrian thought, *is too cruel.*

He put his hands up over his face, trying to prevent all the images that were coming at him from penetrating his eyesight and entering his imagination. And in that sudden darkness all the noise and terror dissipated, fading away like the end of a song on the radio, and when he pulled his hands away and opened his eyes he was alone, back in the quiet of his study, surrounded by books on murder and poetry.

Adrian felt as if he had died a little.

He wanted to say something to his son. He looked around for Cassie but she was not there. For a moment, he thought the force of the explosions had damaged his hearing; his ears filled with a ringing noise. It persisted, louder and louder, until he wanted to shout out, it was so painful, and then he suddenly realized that it was the sound of his front doorbell.

17

She had fallen asleep—she did not know for how long: minutes? hours? days?—but the sound of the baby crying awakened her.

She did not know what to do. It was a faint noise, very distant, and she was slow to recognize precisely what it was. She clutched Mister Brown Fur tightly to her chest. She craned her head first in one direction, then in another, trying to determine where the wails were coming from. They persisted for what seemed to her to be a long time—though it might have been only a second or two—before fading away. She wondered what this meant. Jennifer had little experience babysitting, and she was an only child, so her knowledge about infants was limited to those basic instincts that exist within everyone. *Pick the baby up. Rock the baby. Feed the baby. Smile at the baby. Put the baby back in its crib to sleep.*

Jennifer shifted about, afraid to make any commotion of her own that would obscure the noise. The sound of the child meant something, and she tried to sort through what it was, forcing herself to be analytical, organized, rational, and perceptive.

For a moment, she wondered whether the cries were part of a dream. It took her a few seconds to determine, *No. They are real.*

But something else was wrong. She shook her head, a feeling of apprehension creeping past leftover nightmares. *What is it? What is it?* she wanted to shout out loud.

Something had changed.

She could sense it. The hairs on her neck stood up. Her breathing grew raspy, panicky. She sucked in air sharply and suddenly, as if jolted by electricity. She screamed.

The sound of her voice echoed in the room. It terrified her even more.

She twitched. Her hands quivered. Her back stiffened. She bit down on her chapped and cracked lips.

The hood was gone.

Yet still she remained in darkness.

At first she thought she could see, that it was the room that was black. Then she realized that was wrong. Something still covered her eyes.

Confusion wrapped her up. She did not understand why it had taken her so much time to realize that the hood had been replaced. There had to be a reason behind the change, but she couldn't tell what it was. She knew the change meant something important but whatever this change signified eluded her.

Leaning back carefully she raised her hands to her face. She let her fingers play over her cheeks, then move to her eyes. A single silken mask tied around the back of her head had replaced the hood. She felt the knot. It was already tangled with strands of her hair. She touched the chain around her neck. That hadn't changed. She realized that she could remove the mask without too much trouble. It would cost her a chunk of hair maybe, as she ripped it free, but then she would be able to see where she was. Jennifer carefully placed Mister Brown Fur on the bed beside her, raised her hands, and began to work her fingers under the soft material. Then she stopped.

From somewhere far away the baby wailed again.

It made no sense. How could a baby be connected to what was happening to her?

She tried to arrange her thoughts. *A baby crying meant that she was someplace. An apartment? A house jammed close to another? Did the man and woman who had snatched her from the street have a baby?* A baby implied parenthood, responsibility, something normal—and nothing that was happening to her seemed normal in the slightest. A baby meant minivans and cribs and strollers and trips to the park but that seemed otherworldly now. *The hood is gone. Now I'm wearing a mask. I could take it off. Maybe that's what they want. Maybe not. I don't know. I want to do what I'm supposed to do, but I don't know what that is.*

Then she gasped deeply, as if she'd been struck hard in the stomach.

They were here. In the room. When I was asleep. They removed the hood and replaced it with this mask and they never woke me up.

For what seemed to her to be the hundredth time she was unable to hold back tears. Gasping. Sobbing. She could feel the tears dampening the fabric of her new mask. She reached out for Mister Brown Fur and whispered to him, *Thank God you're still with me, because you're the only thing that makes me think I'm not alone.*

Jennifer rocked back and forth in agony and solitude until she was able to regain control over her heaving chest. Her breathing slowed and the half gasps that had wracked her body subsided.

Just as her sobs ended the baby let out a long, heart-rending wail. It echoed. Distant. Elusive.

Once again, she tilted her head. It was as if for a single second or two the baby's cries had reminded her of the world that existed outside the darkness covering her eyes. Then, just as swiftly as they had penetrated her consciousness, they disappeared, leaving her in the same dark limbo of uncertainty.

Jennifer battled her emotions. *No more tears. No more crying. You're not a baby.*

She did not allow herself to think maybe she was.

For a terrifying instant she thought *she* was making the cries, that somehow the bleating and wailing was hers and that she was listening to herself as she retreated through years to infancy.

She breathed in hard. *No,* she told herself. *Not mine. I'm here. They are there.*

She admonished herself: *Take control.* Although she had told herself this before, and she didn't know yet what she could take control *of.*

She also was smart enough to recognize that every time she had insisted to herself to seize her emotions, something had happened that disrupted her efforts.

She thought, *They mean to do that.*

Again, she tried to sharpen her hearing. Jennifer was unsure whether to be encouraged or dismayed by the sounds the baby made. They clearly meant something important, and yet interpreting the noise was elusive. This frustrated her almost to the point of tears.

She leaned back on the bed. She was thirsty, hungry, scared, and in pain, although she could not say for sure that any part of her was injured. It was as if she had been cut in her heart. But even that sense was almost overcome by her parched throat—she hadn't had anything to drink since the spiked water. *When was that? A year ago?* Or anything to eat since midday on the day she had run away from home. Whenever that was.

She understood she was imprisoned, but the nature of her jail was something that existed outside of her sight. She thought that even the worst killers put in prison forever know why they're there. She had an image, stolen from some movie she'd seen that had no title or stars or plot, but what she remembered was a prisoner carefully scratching into the wall a mark for each day that passed. She couldn't even do that. Knowledge, she understood, was a luxury.

Any kind of comprehension eluded her.

The woman had said to *obey.* But no one had asked her to do anything yet.

The more she pondered all these things, the more she rubbed her fingers nervously into Mister Brown Fur's worn pelt. She was nearly naked, in a room she couldn't see. There was a door. She knew that. There was a toilet. She knew that. Somewhere, there was a baby. She knew that. The floor was cement. The bed creaked. The chain around her neck would tighten at six paces right or left. The air was hot.

She was alive and she had her bear.

Inside the darkness, Jennifer took a deep breath. *All right, Mister Brown Fur, that's where we will start. You and me. The way it's always been since Dad died and left us alone.*

She did not know how much longer she had to live.

She did not know what was in store for her.

She did not know what she was a part of.

Jennifer wondered then, for the first time, whether anyone was looking for her.

At the same time that this thought occurred to her, she heard another wail from the baby. A single high-pitched, desperate cry. Then, as before, it disappeared, leaving her and Mister Brown Fur alone. She did not fully realize it but the sound helped her, because it distracted her from the most despairing idea of all: *How would anyone know where to look for her?*

"Play it once more," Michael said. He was fiddling with the main camera and thinking he might have to do a little repair work on the electronic tracking system. "Don't want to overdo it. Just a little bit . . ."

Linda punched some keys on the computer board. The baby cried again.

"Are you sure she can hear it?"

"Yeah. Absolutely. Look at the way her head moves. She hears it all right."

Linda bent toward the primary feed camera. "You're right," she said. "You're sure the clients can hear it too?"

"Yes. But they will have to work as hard to figure it out."

This made Linda smile. "You don't like to make it easy for them, do you?"

"Not my style," Michael replied, laughing.

He put his hands behind his neck, linking the fingers together, and he stretched like any office drone working for a large company might after too many hours in front of a computer screen.

"You know, they're all going to love it when Number Four screams like that. It just makes it all the more *real* for them."

In a contradictory way, Michael felt both contempt and fascination with the many people who subscribed to Whatcomesnext. At one instant, he thought them weak because they could not control their impulses as they grew ever more fascinated with Number 4. But then he would stare at the screen as it filled with the fantasy narrative he created, and he would feel the stirrings of the same compulsions.

Linda tried not to imagine their clientele at all—or, at least, not in the way Michael did. They weren't people to her, with dark passions that drove them to the website; they were just so many accounts in so many countries. Many different fifteen-number credit card authorizations. She had a businesswoman's calculating sense—this many subscriptions meant this many dollars deposited in the blind, offshore accounts she had established for them. She rarely thought about who was out there, watching, except to crunch numbers and make sure that Michael was providing the right edginess to the program, so that *Series #4* would have a drama of its own.

Michael was in charge of the story of Number 4. She was in charge of the business. Both aspects were critical to their success. It was a relationship that she believed defined true love. In her spare time and in between the different series, she liked to read the fanzines and gossip magazines about movie stars and she paid special attention to who was with whom, and who was breaking up with a partner, week by week. She indulged in the fascination of trying to guess what Brad or Angelina or Jen or Paris was going to do next, and where they might be caught in some compromising situation. This was her greatest flaw, she thought, the notion that she took all these celebrity couplings and dismissals seriously. But she also considered this a benign flaw.

Many days, Linda longed for celebrity of her own. She imagined that if people could only appreciate the success of Whatcomesnext they would be writing about the two of them in *Us* or *People*.

She was dismayed that the criminal nature of the business prevented them from being famous. It seemed to her that what they did was so much more important than who they did it to, and that there ought to be some exemption. They were the salesmen of fantasy. *That,* she told herself, *ought to be worth something more than money.* They were stars, she believed, but the world didn't know it.

Michael knew Linda dreamed of prominence. The smart side of him preferred anonymity, although he also wanted to please her in any way he could.

"It's time to give her something to eat," he said.

"You or me?" Linda asked.

Michael reached across the bank of computers and shuffled through some loose-leaf papers. It contained a very flexible script. Michael was one for preparation; he had taken the time to write down many of the elements of *Series #4* long before they had started. There were checklists, *to do* details, and lengthy paragraphs on his sheets of paper that he called Impact Viewer/Impact #4. He liked to believe he was meticulous in his planning but that he had the mental agility to create. Once, when he was in college, he'd taken a film studies course and he'd written a paper about the moment in *On the Waterfront* when Eva Marie Saint dropped her white glove and Marlon Brando picked it up and the director, Elia Kazan, had the good sense to keep the cameras rolling through something unscripted, which became a classic moment in cinema. *I would have been the same,* Michael often told himself. He wasn't the type to yell *Cut!* and retreat into something predictable. He was fluid. And as he looked at the screen in front of him and saw Number 4 clutching her teddy bear and sobbing, he thought that all the great movie directors had nothing on him, because he was sculpting something unique and something real and something far more dramatic and unpredictable than they had ever imagined possible.

"I think you go," he said after a moment. "She still seems so scared. When I enter the room, we should play that for maximum shock."

"You're the boss," Linda said.

"The hell I am," Michael replied, laughing.

He pushed himself away from the computers and walked over to the table with weapons. He searched for a moment before picking up a Colt .357 Magnum. Linda took it from him as Michael turned back to his sheets of paper, flipping rapidly through them. "Here," he said. "Read this."

Linda ran her eyes over the page. "Okeydoke," she said, grinning. She looked over at a clock. It was shortly after midnight. "I think I'll make it breakfast," she said.

Linda opened the door slowly and stepped into the basement. She was dressed as before, in a crinkly white Hazmat suit and black balaclava that covered everything except her eyes. She carried a tray, the sort found in cafeterias everywhere. On the tray was a plastic water bottle with all brand and manufacturing labels removed. She had prepared a bowl of instant oatmeal, using an American recipe that was shipped all over the world. There was also an orange. There were no utensils.

She saw Number 4 pivot in her direction, stiffening at the sound of the door opening.

Linda moved onto one of the chalk X's that Michael had put on the floor. She heard a faint *whirring* as Michael adjusted electronically the direction of the camera.

"Sit still. Do not move," Linda said.

She then repeated this command in German, French, Russian, and Turkish.

Her command of languages was slight. She had memorized some phrases, some expletives, because they came in handy from time to time. Her accent, she knew, was poor, but she did not care about this. When she spoke in English, she occasionally used Britishisms, common substitutions, such as using *lift* instead of *elevator* or *bonnet* instead of *hood*. She did not believe that these small changes in language would ever fool a trained investigator with access to voice recognition systems. But Michael had assured her that the likelihood any police agency that sophisticated would pursue them was negligible. Michael—eternal student that he was—had carefully examined the jurisdictional dilemmas all their series of Internet dramas created. He was confident that no one agency had the patience to look into what they were doing.

They were, she thought, operating in the grayest of arenas.

"Face the front. Place your hands at your sides."

Again, she repeated the commands in a series of languages, mixing them up. She was sure that she got some of the words wrong. This made no difference.

"I will place a tray on your lap. When I give permission, you may eat."

She saw Number 4 nod.

Linda stepped to the side of the bed and lowered the tray. She stayed in position, waiting. She could see that Number 4 had started to shake and that her muscles were knotting in spasms. *That must be painful,* she thought. But Number 4 managed to remain tight-lipped and, other than the involuntary motions caused by fear, followed each command.

"All right," Linda said. "You may eat."

She made sure that she wasn't blocking any of the cameras. She knew that the clientele would be fascinated by the simple act of feeding Number 4. It was why their webcasts were so popular: they had taken the simplest, most routine parts of life and made them *special*. If every meal might be Number 4's last it took on a whole new meaning. The viewers understood this and it drew them inexorably closer. With so much uncertainty surrounding the fate of Number 4, the most ordinary things became compelling.

That, Linda knew, was the genius in what they had designed.

She watched as Number 4 lifted her hands to the tray and discovered the bowl, the orange, and the water bottle. She went first for the water and drank greedily, sucking down the liquid with abandon. *It will make her sick,* Linda thought. But she said nothing. She watched as Number 4 slowed, as if she realized that she might want to save a drink for the end of the meal. Number 4 then felt the bowl with the oatmeal. She hesitated and her fingers searched the tray top for a utensil. When Number 4 found none she opened her mouth, as if to ask a question, but stopped.

Learning, Linda instantly understood. *Not bad.*

Number 4 lifted the bowl to her mouth and started to shovel the oatmeal down. Her first bites were tentative, but after she got a sense of the taste she wolfed down the remainder, licking the bowl clean.

A nice touch, Linda realized. *Viewers will like that.*

She still hadn't moved from the bedside. But as Number 4 started to peel the orange skin away to get at the fruit inside, Linda slowly removed the .357 Magnum from inside the Hazmat suit. She tried to coordinate her movements with Number 4's so that the gun emerged at the same moment that Number 4 bit down into the orange.

She lifted the gun as the orange went into Number 4's mouth. She watched as some of the juice slid down from Number 4's mouth.

Linda thumbed back the hammer, cocking the pistol.

The noise made Number 4 stop in midbite.

She won't know exactly what it is, Linda thought, *but she will understand that it is deadly.*

Number 4 seemed frozen by the sound. The orange was just inches from her lips but not moving. Number 4's body shook.

Linda stepped forward, placing the barrel of the pistol millimeters away from the space between Number 4's eyes, almost resting against the blindfold. She waited for an instant before pressing the gun directly against Number 4's face.

The smell of gun oil, the pressure of the barrel, these things would be unmistakable to Number 4, Linda knew.

She held that position. She could hear a whimpering sound bubble up from Number 4's chest. But the teenager said nothing and didn't move, even though every muscle in her body seemed about to explode with tension.

"Bang!" Linda whispered. Loud enough for the audio pickup, but just barely.

Then she slowly dropped the hammer back into a resting position. She exaggerated her movements as she slowly pulled the gun back away from Number 4's face and replaced it inside her suit.

"Mealtime is finished," Linda said briskly.

She removed the remains of the orange from Number 4's hand and then lifted the tray from her lap. She saw Number 4's body convulse again, head to toe. She hoped the cameras had captured that. *Panic sells,* she thought.

Moving deliberately, her feet making only the smallest padded sounds against the hard cement, Linda exited the room, leaving Number 4 alone on the bed.

In the control room above, Michael was grinning. The interactive response board was lighting up. Lots of opinions, lots of responses. He knew he would have to go over them all later. He was always particularly careful to assess the chats that went on between clients on the board he'd created for *Series #4.*

Linda breathed in deeply, closed her eyes, and pulled off the balaclava. *I am an actress,* she thought.

Neither Linda, just outside the basement door, nor Michael upstairs at the monitors noticed what happened next. Some of their clients did, though, as they bent to their computers. Number 4 had leaned back after hearing the door close, leaving her once again alone in the room. She had picked up her teddy bear and clutched it to her chest, nestling the worn toy between her small breasts, rubbing its head as if it were a baby, all the time mouthing something silently to the inanimate object. No one watching was sure what it was she was saying, although some were able to make the lucky guess that she was repeating over and over again a single phrase. They were unable to tell that what she said was, *My name is Jennifer my name is Jennifer my name is Jennifer my name is Jennifer.*

18

Terri Collins walked back and forth in the driveway outside Adrian's house as he demonstrated where he was located when he spotted the van. She scuffed her feet and kicked at a stray stone as he slid behind the wheel of his car to show her where he had parked. She asked, "And that's exactly where you were positioned the evening Jennifer disappeared?"

Adrian nodded. He could see the detective measuring sight angles and distances, imagining the shadows that dropped on the street that night.

"She can't see it," Brian said.

He was seated on the passenger side. He, too, was looking at the spot on the street where the van had slowed, stopped, and then accelerated.

"What do you mean?" Adrian whispered.

"What I mean is this," Brian replied, with a forceful bluster. "She's not allowing herself to picture the crime. Not yet. She's staring right at the spot but she's still trying to see reasons *it didn't* happen, not reasons it did. This is where you come in, brother of mine. Persuade her. *Make* her take the next step. Gotta be logical. Gotta be forceful. C'mon, Audie."

"But . . ."

"Your job is to make her see what you saw that night. It's what any investigator does, although they might not want to admit it because it sounds crazy at worst and flaky at best. They envision everything that happened just as if *they were there* . . . and it tells them where to look next."

Brian was dressed in his faded fatigues again. He had propped ragged jungle boots up on the dash and leaned backward, smoking a cigarette. Young Brian. Older Brian. Dead Brian. Adrian realized that his brother was a chameleon of hallucinatory memory. From Vietnam to Wall Street. The same was true for Cassie, and for Tommy, and whoever else from his past chose to arrive in what little of his present he had left. Adrian inhaled and he could smell the pungent odor of smoke, mingling with a thick, damp, wet tropical sensation that covered him, as if Brian had brought the steaming jungle along with him. The crispness of New England's early spring was nowhere to be found. Or, Adrian thought, it was nowhere where *he* could find it.

"Why didn't anyone else see anything?" Terri Collins said. Adrian wasn't sure whether he was supposed to answer this question, because she said it in a quiet voice directed more to the falling streaks of daylight than to him.

"I don't know," Adrian said. "People go home. They want their dinner. They want to see their family. They shut the front door and close away the day. Who is looking out at the street at that time of day? Who is looking for something out of the ordinary? Not many, detective. People look for routine. They look for normalcy. That's what they expect. A unicorn could trot down the street and they probably wouldn't notice."

Adrian said this, and he closed his eyes for an instant, hoping his words wouldn't conjure up a white, horned mythical animal trotting down the street that only he could see.

"Someone had to have noticed something," Terri continued, as if she hadn't heard anything Adrian had said, which made him wonder whether he'd actually spoken it out loud or merely thought it.

"But they didn't. Just me," he said.

The detective turned to him. She did hear that, he realized.

151

"So what is there to go on?" she asked. She didn't really expect him to reply. She watched as Adrian shifted about in his seat before exiting the car. Once she had interviewed a schizophrenic in the midst of a psychotic episode who had constantly turned in one direction or another as he heard sounds that weren't there, but eventually, by being patient, she'd elicited a description of a robber that made sense. And there were many times that she'd probed the memories of college kids who were aware that something bad had happened—a rape, usually—but weren't exactly sure what they'd seen or heard or witnessed. Too many drugs. Too much booze. All sorts of things that cluttered the powers of observation. But her skin crawled slightly, a prickly sensation, when she confronted Adrian. Something was the same, something was different. He seemed slight, slender, as if something were eating away at him every second of the time she faced him. She had the odd feeling that he was fading a little, infinitesimally, with each passing second.

Adrian took a deep breath.

Brian whispered, "This is important. Don't lose her, Audie. Don't let her get away. You're going to need her to find Jennifer. You know it. Don't scare her off."

"I think, detective, that this is a helluva problem," Adrian said, as coolly and forcefully as he could. "If what I saw was indeed an abduction, as I believe it was, well, then it was a type that is pretty unfamiliar around these parts."

"Good," said Brian.

"Yes. I'm listening," Terri replied.

"Random. You know, that's a word psychologists hate. It acts as an excuse for failing to respond. You see, it was my job—and my profession was teaching—to show that there is *nothing* that is random. If you continue breaking all the elements down, eventually you arrive at a truth, which suggests the inevitability of an action. Ultimately, what happens all makes sense. A person schedules a plane trip. It becomes a hijacking that ends up in the South Tower. Perhaps there is some bad luck involved—picking out that flight on that day. But it makes sense. Someone *had* to be somewhere, at some time, and that flight was the logical choice. The odds that the person beside them in line was a nihilistic suicidal terrorist are infinitesimal—but measurable. The key factors, everything that created the terrorist and everything that created the victim, all coalesce in a psychologically defined way in a recognizable pattern. And there's the truth of it all."

Terri stepped back.

"You sound like you're preparing a lecture for a class," she said.

"Now!" Brian urged in a loud stage whisper. "Get her now!"

"Yes. A lecture. But if there is any hope for young Jennifer you will have to enter *my* territory."

"Good," Brian said. "A proposal that grabbed her interest."

Detective Collins appeared to be deep in thought. Brian's voice was energized. Adrian thought he sounded just like he must have in command of men at war, or when he came upon a courtroom moment in which he seized a truth from a reluctant witness. "Now," his brother urged Adrian, "think of what Tommy told you."

Adrian hesitated. He wanted to swing toward Brian and demand, *What? What did Tommy tell me before he was blown apart?* And then he remembered his son's hurried words: *It's about seeing.*

"Look, detective. If Jennifer was snatched from this street in this neighborhood just to entertain some perverse killer in some dark, hidden, remote location, well, then you might as well just go on home and wait until someone finds her body next week or next month or next year or next decade. And we already know she wasn't stolen for ransom, because no one has contacted her mother. And we know it wasn't anyone in her family because relationships weren't *that* strained. And you've already asked about the stepfather and his therapeutic practice—actually, I thought that was a clever series of questions—but still the purpose of that sort of abduction would already be clear. I mean if someone wanted to harass or punish Scott West, they wouldn't be doing it without letting him know they were doing it, because otherwise the message would be lost. Which leaves you and me with only one very modest remaining hope: she was taken for another reason. What that reason is, well, that's what we need to figure out, because that will be the only way to find her. Find her alive, that is."

Adrian seemed to be both determined and erratic.

"Jennifer, detective . . . *Someone needed her for something.* Any other explanation is useless because they all result in the same conclusion: *she's dead.* So it makes no logical sense to pursue those. The only course is to imagine that she's still alive and for a specific, well-defined reason. Otherwise, it's just a waste of your time and my time."

Brian snorted. "Damn straight!" he burst out. It was like a shout too close to his ear and Adrian twitched a little.

Terri thought this was all madness and that the old professor—whose eyes were blinking rapidly and appeared a little buglike and whose hands were quivering with some sort of electric force that she couldn't see—was out-of-his-mind crazy, even if she couldn't put a medical diagnosis to it. She looked around the neighborhood, as if hoping that maybe in that moment she'd be lucky and the white van would come squealing up to the nearby curb, slow down, and Jennifer would be tossed out of the door, a little bruised, maybe sexually assaulted, but in a condition where with some love and some therapy and some painkillers she would survive.

The night fell into darkness around her. The old professor seemed to be perched on the thin limb of an idea. She thought, *What options do I have?*

"All right," Terri said. "I'm going to listen."

There was a momentary pause while Adrian nodded. He was a little astonished that the detective was willing to hear him out, and a little hesitant, too, because he didn't know what he was going to say.

"Can you feel it," Brian hissed, but not unpleasantly. "That breeze. It's like Jennifer has a chance."

Adrian held the front door open for the detective, ushering her inside out of the falling night. He hesitated, as if waiting for Brian to slide past him as well, but his dead brother remained on the steps, a few feet away. "Can't go in there," he said briskly, as if this were obvious.

Adrian must have appeared surprised because Brian quickly added, "Even hallucinations have rules, Audie. They change around a bit, given

154

the circumstances, given the input, which is something you probably knew already. But, still, got to obey."

Adrian nodded. This made some sense to him, although he couldn't have said why.

"Look, you can handle this next bit. I know it. You know enough about behavior and you know enough about crime and your buddy over at the university pointed you in the only direction that has any likelihood of success, so that's what you've got to convince the detective of. You can do it."

"I don't know . . ."

He heard his wife's voice say something in his ear. *Yes you can, dear.* Cassie sounded totally confident, and when Adrian looked back at Brian he saw the ghost making a power fist of encouragement, because he too must have heard Cassie's voice.

"In here?" Terri Collins asked.

Adrian shook his memories away. "Yes. To the right. We should sit in the living room. Would you like coffee?"

He made the offer without thinking. He realized suddenly that he probably had no coffee in the kitchen, and he wasn't exactly sure how to make it, even if he had. And, for a second, he was unsteady, as if he didn't even know where the kitchen was. He took a deep breath, reminded himself that he had lived in this house for many years and the kitchen was just past the dining room, before the downstairs half bath. The stairs led up to his bedroom and his study and everything was where it was supposed to be.

The detective shook her head. "No. Let's get right to it."

She walked into the living room. It was cluttered with books, half-finished coffee cups filled with curdled milk and cereal, and leftover plates of food and stray silverware. Papers were stacked in various spots, a television played soundlessly—tuned to a sports channel—and a musty sense of enclosed space filled the still air. It was close to a mess, she thought. Not quite there yet. Nothing accumulated in such disarray that a single afternoon spent cleaning and organizing wouldn't solve. The room, and the house as a whole, she figured, displayed the same qualities shared by young children unaffected by stray toys and abandoned clothing and old people surrounded by heartfelt mementoes and bric-a-brac. Neither group cared all that much for organization.

"I live alone now," Adrian said. "I'm sorry for the disorder."

"I have young kids," the detective replied. "So I'm used to it."

She pushed some papers off a chair and sat down after noticing that on top of three-week-old copies of *The Boston Globe* were some forms from a doctor's office that had been only partially filled out. She tried to read what they were but was unable.

"Okay," she said. "Tell me what you think we can do."

Adrian too shifted books around and plopped into an armchair. He had a momentary surge of confusion, like tides changing within him, and he heard confidence slide from his voice. He had been pleased with his dynamic framing of the case, standing outside. He'd thought he sounded forceful. But now he could hear indecision creep into his words.

"You see, detective . . ." He hesitated. "I really want her to be alive. Jennifer, that is."

Detective Collins held up her hand, cutting him off.

"Wanting and being able to do something about it are far different things."

Adrian nodded in reply.

"It's important. It's important *to me*. I have to find her. I mean, it's nearly all over for me, but she's young. She has her whole life ahead of her. No matter how bad it's been for her, it doesn't mean it should end prematurely . . ."

"Yes," Terri replied. "Those are truisms. But they have little to do with police work."

Adrian felt uncomfortable. He had never dealt with the police before. When Brian had killed himself, the New York City homicide bureau had been quick, efficient, and unobtrusive because everything was so obvious. When Cassie had her accident, the local state trooper who'd called had been solicitous, direct, and to the point. But they weren't involved in the long weeks it took for her to finally die. And Tommy, well, that had been a perfunctory call from a military spokesman who had given him the details about the dying and a time and date to meet an overseas flight bearing his son's coffin. He closed his eyes tightly for an instant and, behind the darkness, he heard a cacophony of echoes, as if more than one person was trying to speak with him at the same moment, and he had trouble sorting through the jumble of words and tones and various urgencies.

"Are you okay, professor?"

He opened his eyes. "Yes, I'm sorry, detective."

"You seemed to fade out there."

"I did?"

"Yes."

Adrian looked quizzically at her. "How long was . . ."

"More than a minute. Maybe two."

Adrian thought that was impossible. He'd closed his eyes for only a second. No longer.

"Are you all right, professor?" Terri asked again. She tried to remove any harsh policewoman's tone from her voice and sound more like a mother leaning over a feverish child.

"Yes. I'll be fine."

"You don't seem fine. It's not my business but . . ."

"I've been prescribed some new medications. Still getting used to them."

He did not think Detective Collins would buy that explanation.

"Perhaps you should speak with your physician. If you were driving a car and—"

Adrian interrupted. "I'm sorry. Let me collect my thoughts. Where were we?"

Terri wanted to finish her statement about the dangers of getting behind the wheel in whatever condition Professor Thomas was in. But she bit off her words and returned to the more important matter.

"Jennifer . . . and why would—"

"Of course. Jennifer. Here's the thing, detective. Almost every scenario you or I would be familiar with ends in a simple quotient to a long equation. *Death*. So, from the scientist's point of view, it makes little logical sense to pursue any of those avenues, even if they have the greatest likelihood of success, because the answer is one that is too terrible to con-template. So turn it around. What equation is there that ends in *life*?"

"I'm still listening."

"Yes, of course. Here is what we know."

Adrian stopped, wondering what he *did* know. He looked across at Terri Collins and saw that she had pushed forward slightly in the chair. At the same moment, he felt something pressing him from his side, and he longed to look that way. Then he realized he didn't have to, because his wife had draped her arm around his shoulders, and Cassie fiercely whispered, "*It's not Jennifer. It's what she is, not who she is. Tell her.*"

So Adrian did. He said, "Look, detective, maybe this fits into the category of crime where it isn't about a specific person, it's about a *type* of person."

Terri slowly removed her notebook. She thought the old professor had moved in his seat uncomfortably and now he was hunched over as if out of balance, but what he was saying made sense.

"What do we know? A sixteen-year-old is snatched from a street. Every-thing that you know about Jennifer or her family isn't really relevant, is it? What we need to discover is why someone needed the type of person she is, and why they were cruising this neighborhood. And then we need to imagine why they wanted *her* when they spotted her. And we know that it was a male and a female. So we are talking about a very narrow range of crimes here, and predominantly the sort that end in murder."

Again, Adrian's voice had returned to the forceful, academic, assured style that he remembered from a hundred million hours in classrooms. It was as familiar to him as his favorite poems, Shakespeare's sonnets or Frost's verse. It made him feel much better to recognize the part of him that was disappearing making a return.

"But if it ends in murder . . ."

"I only said it ends that way."

"But . . ."

"We must interrupt it."

"But how . . ."

"There is only one way, detective. It is if Jennifer's abduction has a purpose other than murder. If her presence has meaning that is distinct from how it is that she will end up. And for us to have any hope of success it has to be a purpose that we can identify, and then track back to its source. Otherwise, we'd be better off waiting for a body to be uncovered."

He hesitated, then corrected himself. "Not *a* body. Jennifer's body."

"All right. What could that purpose be?"

Adrian felt his wife nudge him and then squeeze his shoulder. He looked off to the side and it was as if the copy of the *Encyclopedia of Murder* that his friend had loaned him suddenly floated up in the air before his eyes and the pages started to flutter, caught by a sudden turbulent breeze.

Macbeth, he thought. When Lady Macbeth hallucinated the murder weapon. *Is this a dagger I see before me?* Only here floating in front of him was an entry in a book documenting an endless series of episodes of murder and despair.

"I have one small idea," Adrian said. "Maybe the only idea."

19

By the time she got home that night Terri Collins was convinced that Adrian was completely crazy and that probably being crazy was the only realistic course to follow.

Her two children rocketed out from in front of the television when she pushed open the door. She was inundated by a sudden cascade of child needs and demands—most of which had to do with listening to tales about school and what happened on the playground or in reading class. It was a little like walking into a movie after it had already begun, where she would quietly try to collect enough observations and hear enough details to fill in the missing plot information. Laurie, her friend and babysitter, was in the kitchen hovering over a sink filled with dishes and called out a greeting that was partially a welcome home along with a question about hunger, which Terri had answered with a negative. Terri's oldest, eight years old and filled with little boy energy, asked, "Did you arrest any bad guys today?" His little sister, two years his junior and as quiet as he was loud, merely clung to her mother's leg with one hand while waving a colorful drawing in the air with the other.

"No, not today," Terri said. "But I think I will tomorrow, or maybe the next day."

"Real bad guys?"

"Always. Just the really bad ones."

"Good," said the eight-year-old. He peeled away from her side and went back to a seat by the television set. Terri watched him move across the room. She searched every gesture he made, every tone attached to any word he spoke, every look on his face for the telltale signs of his father. It was like living with a live hand grenade in the house. She did not know what part of her ex-husband had been passed on to her son, but it frightened her. Genetics, she thought, can be terrifying. She knew that the child already had his father's easygoing smile and loose seductiveness—he was extremely popular in school and in the neighborhood. She feared that it was all a lie, that like his father he would be charming and evil at once. Her ex was forever wearing a smile in public, telling a joke, making everyone feel good about themselves, till the moment they were alone and he'd suddenly turn dark and hidden and start to beat on her relentlessly. That was the concealed part that no one—except her—had ever seen. It was a mystery, and when she had fled she knew she was leaving behind many folks, family, friends, coworkers who were asking, *How can it be?* and saying *It makes no sense.*

The trouble was, it did. They just didn't know it.

She watched as her son plopped down in a chair, ignored the television, and picked up a picture book. She wondered, *Did I get away in time?* What kept her awake at night was the thought that somehow her ex-husband had left an infection within the child, and that it was biding its time, waiting for the right moment to burst forth violently. Every day she waited for the phone call from the school, the *We think there's a problem* call. And, every night, when it had not come, she felt relief and then renewed fear that the next day would be the day it arrived.

She had managed to flee, packing and running when she knew he was wrapped up for a few hours. She had been cautious, giving no signs of flight in the weeks leading up to her escape, performing every boring, routine chore she could, so that when she fled it would be unexpected. She left behind most everything except some pocket money and the children. He could have everything else. She didn't care.

She had a single mantra, which she had repeated endlessly to herself: *Start over. Start over.*

In the time that followed, she had obtained the restraining order keeping him away and the divorce settlement that limited his access to the children and had filed all the necessary papers with his commanding officer down in North Carolina at the base where the First Airborne was housed. She had endured more than one session with military counselors, who subtly and not so subtly tried to talk her into returning to her husband. She had refused, no matter how many times they called him "an American hero."

We have altogether too many heroes, she thought.

But there was never a full and complete escape, at least not one that didn't involve hiding, false identities, and moving from place to place, trying to be anonymous in a world that seems devoted to publicizing something about everybody. He would never be fully out of their lives. It was, in part, why she had gone back to school and worked so hard to become a policewoman. The semiautomatic in her satchel and the badge she wore carried an implicit message that she hoped served as a barrier between him and whatever poison he wanted to deliver.

She hugged both children and at the same time offered up a small prayer: another safe day. She wanted to light a candle in a church and ask for her ex to become an alcoholic, a drug addict, or to be redeployed into Iraq or Afghanistan, someplace where there were bullets and bombs and indiscriminate death.

This was cruel, heartless thinking, not in any way charitable. She didn't care.

Terri settled the kids into kid tasks—drawing, reading, watching the tube—and then walked into the kitchen. Laurie, who had been totally reliable since the first moment that Terri had received the call about the missing Jennifer, was putting together a plate of food.

"I figured you weren't exactly telling the truth," she said.

Terri looked down at the warmed-up meat loaf and cold salad. She took the plate, gathered a fork and knife, and still standing leaned back against the cabinets and started to eat.

"You should be the detective," she said between mouthfuls.

Laurie nodded. This was a significant compliment to anyone who spent as much time with Raymond Chandler, Sir Arthur Conan Doyle, and James Ellroy as she did.

In the other room, the two children occupied themselves quietly, which was something of a victory. Terri started to pour herself a glass of milk, then thought better and found a half-empty bottle of white wine. She took two glasses from a shelf. "Stay for a little bit?"

Laurie nodded. "Sure. White wine and putting kids to bed. I can't think of a better evening as long as I get back to the tube before *CSI* comes on."

"Those shows—you know they're not real."

"Yeah. But they're like little morality plays. In medieval times all the peasants gathered in front of the steps of whatever church and watched actors perform Bible stories in order to teach lessons like *Thou shalt not kill*. Today, we flick on the tube to watch Horatio What's His Name in Miami or Gus in Las Vegas inform us of more or less the same thing in a more modern fashion."

They both laughed. "Ten minutes!" Terri called out to the kids in the other room, an announcement met with predictable groans.

Terri knew that Laurie was eager to ask about the case but was too polite to broach the subject without an opening.

She took a bite of meat loaf. "A runaway," she said in answer to the question not spoken. "But we can't be sure. Maybe a kidnapping. Or maybe someone helped her run away. It's just not clear yet."

"What do you think?" Laurie asked.

Terri hesitated. "Most children that disappear are taken for a reason. And usually they show up again. At least that's what the stats tell us."

"But . . ."

Terri looked into the other room to make sure that her children remained out of earshot. "I'm not an optimist," she said quietly. She forked some of the salad and took a long swig of wine. "I'm a realist. Hope for the best. Expect the worst."

Laurie nodded. "Happy endings . . ."

"You want a happy ending, watch television," Terri said briskly. She sounded much harsher than she thought she should, but her conversation with the professor had left her seeing only gray and dark possibilities. "More likely to find one there."

It was, she thought, an unusual way of investigating crime.

It had turned late, Laurie had departed with her usual plea to call any time, day or night . . . the kids were asleep and Terri was on her third glass of white wine, surrounded by books and articles, a laptop computer near her elbow. She was in the strange realm between exhaustion and fascination.

"You see, detective, the crime that happened, right in front of me—it was only a beginning. Scene one. Act one. Enter the antagonists. And what little we know about it probably leads nowhere. Especially if the criminals are experienced in what they did."

She could hear the old professor's voice echoing in the sanctuary of her small, trim, toy-cluttered house. *Experienced.* She had not told him about the stolen truck and the torch job that in all likelihood eradicated any evidence inadvertently left behind. Someone who *knew* what he was doing would take those precautions.

"We have to consider the crime that is taking place, even as we talk."

The professor, she thought, was wild with suppositions, crazed with ideas. But lurking within were notions that made sense to her. She had listened to him carefully, trying to see a path through two mysteries. The first was the obvious one: *What was wrong with him?* The second was far more complicated: *How do you find a Jennifer that has been snatched out of the world?*

She had decided that she would simply bear with the professor. He was smart, perceptive, and extremely well educated. That he rapidly faded in and out of attention, seemed to drift into other lands, and responded to questions and statements that hadn't been voiced, well, as far as Terri was concerned this was all fairly benign. Somewhere in all his ramblings might be a path that she could follow.

On her lap, spread out, was the *Encyclopedia of Modern Murder.* She had read through the segment on the Moors Murders twice and then done a thorough Internet examination of the crime. It never ceased to amaze her what one could find lurking in odd corners of the cyber world. She came across autopsy photographs, crime scene maps, and original police documents, all posted on various websites devoted to serial killing and sexual depravity. She was tempted to order one of the several books about Myra Hindley and Ian Brady, but she didn't want this sort of material taking up bookshelf space next to *The Cat in the Hat* and *The Wind in the Willows* and *Winnie the Pooh.*

She was careful to clear her computer's memory of each of the murder-driven websites she examined. No sense in leaving behind something that her oldest just might know how to click on and open up. *Children are natural voyeurs,* she thought, *but all curiosity should have its limits.*

Even after she had moused and clicked everything away into computer purgatory, what she had read lingered within her.

The professor's point, she understood, was that what tripped up the homicidal couple was the need to share their excesses.

"*That's the key,*" Adrian had said. "*They needed to reach beyond the two of them. If they had simply shared their love of torture with each other, well, then they would have been able to go on more or less indefinitely.*"

Terri had written down a few notes as the professor had lectured her. *Short of making a mistake in planning, being spotted by some random person, they could have continued for years.*

She knew very little about this sort of crime, despite having spent some classroom time on celebrated murders and serial killings. A few years engaged in the routine of college town crime, with its very limited spectrum, had removed most of her recollections.

"*If I take two identical white rats and place them in the same psychological situation, it's possible to assess their different responses to identical stimuli. But there will still be a baseline of similarity that we can measure from.*"

He had been energized. She had imagined that, as he spoke, he could see himself surrounded by students, jammed into a darkened laboratory, watching the behavior of animals, carefully assessing behaviors.

"It is when the similar rats in the identical situation start to deviate from those norms that things become interesting."

But Jennifer's disappearance wasn't a lab experiment.

At least, she thought, leaning back in her chair, *I don't think it is.*

She was in a difficult position. She reminded herself to be cautious. She loved her job but she understood that each case was career defining. Screw up a campus rape and she'd be back driving a patrol car. Mess up a drug investigation or a burglary and in a small department such as hers the black mark on her record would be magnified. Instead of waving her gold shield at petty crooks and students who had drunk their way into a felony she'd be answering telephones.

A part of her burst into anger at Jennifer. *Goddammit! Why couldn't you just smoke pot and stay out late like every other disaffected teenager. Why not drink and have unprotected and far too early sex and get through your teenage years that way? Why did you have to run away?*

She was exhausted. She would already have dozed off if not for the combined images of two dead murderers from half a century earlier and Jennifer. She wanted to promise *I'll find you* but she knew that was still unlikely.

The chief of her department sat behind his desk. There was a picture on the wall behind him of the chief in a baseball uniform surrounded by children. A Little League championship season. Not far away were a cheap but glistening trophy and a framed plaque that declared him *The Best Coach Ever* that was signed by many barely formed signatures. The rest of the wall was devoted to diplomas from many training courses: an FBI professional development program, Fitchburg State College, and a graduate degree from John Jay College in New York—she knew this last was fairly prestigious. The chief liked to wear a uniform to work, but this day he was in a suit that seemed far too tight for his expansive stomach or for his weight lifter's arms. It gave her the impression that he was about to burst out in a number of directions, like a carton character filling up with balloon air.

He was nursing coffee and drumming a pencil against the modest report that she'd filed.

"Terri," he said slowly, "more questions here than answers."

"Yes sir."

"Are you suggesting we call in the state guys or the feds?"

Terri had anticipated this question. "I think we should inform them of the situation, as best as we can tell. But without any firm evidence they're just going to be as frustrated as I am."

He wore glasses. He had the habit of putting them on and then taking them off—removing them when he spoke, replacing them when he read—so that he was constantly in motion.

"So what you're saying . . ."

"A teenager with an established history of running away runs away for a third time. An unreliable witness says he saw her snatched from a street. Further investigation uncovers that a stolen vehicle similar to that he spotted may have been torched in the hours after the disappearance."

"Yes, and?"

"Yes, and that's it. No ransom request. No contact from the missing girl or anyone else. In other words, if there was a crime it stops right there."

"Jesus. What do you think?"

"I think . . ." Terri hesitated. She was prepared to rush into her answer when she abruptly realized that what she would say next was dangerous. She wanted to make certain that she protected her position cautiously.

"I think we should proceed carefully."

"How?"

"Well, the witness—Professor Thomas, he's emeritus from the U; I put his bona fides in the report—thinks we should examine possible abduction for sexual abuse cases. Go through all potential sex offenders. Try to find some avenue to pursue there. At the same time, we should increase the Missing Persons requests. If you want to inform your liaison with the Springfield FBI office, that might make sense. See if they want to get involved—"

"I doubt it," the chief said. "Not without something more concrete to go on."

Terri didn't continue. She knew the chief would.

"Okay, keep working the case. Keep it on the top of your platter. You know most of these runaways eventually show up. Let's hope that maybe the people the professor spotted were some friends that the mother doesn't know about. Let's just keep collecting information while we're waiting for an *I'm broke and I wanna come home* phone call."

Terri nodded. The chief saw the same problems she did. He wanted to make sure that he never had to get up in front of a bunch of cameras and reporters and say, "Well, we failed to take advantage of opportunities we had . . ." She had seen cops in other jurisdictions face up to the same music and watch their careers evaporate. She doubted that her chief—even with the solid support of the mayor and local government council—wanted to be the next one facing the steely eye of negative publicity.

It was easy for her to guess that he also didn't want to get up in front of the town council, even in private session, and say, "Well, maybe we have a serial rapist or killer in our nice, quiet little college town . . ." because that would be every bit as explosive.

So, as she suspected, what he was really saying to her was *Do your best. Cover every base. Follow every procedure. But don't take a chance. Don't go crazy. Just be steady and reliable . . . Because if anything goes wrong you will get the blame.*

She nodded. "I'll keep you posted if I develop anything relevant."

"Do that," he replied. He tugged at the tie around his neck. A speech, Terri guessed, maybe in front of the Masons or the local Lions Club. It would be the sort of place that wanted to hear about crime-statistic breakdowns and about how the department had handled every case with skill and professionalism. This was an impression the chief was adept at giving.

She decided she was going to do two things. Check cold cases. Maybe there was another Jennifer she didn't know about. And then she planned to identify every registered sex offender within her reach. A lot of visits.

She got up, crossed the chief's office, and left. She had not spoken a word about Professor Thomas's theories. Most crimes fit patterns, fit statistical norms, fit into frameworks that can be taught in classrooms and then applied to real-life situations. He wanted to step outside those parameters.

It didn't make sense to do it, she knew. But neither did it make sense *not* to.

20

Michael was pleased.

The inbox of responses for *Series #4* was crowded with ideas, suggestions, and demands. These ranged from the subtle *I need to see her eyes* to the considerably more predictable *fuckherfuckherfuckher* to the complex *Kill her. Kill her now!*

Michael knew that his replies were important, and he spent time crafting each. Like any good entrepreneur dealing with a multifaceted client base, he wanted to be certain that those merely making recommendations were given the same careful, teasing answers as he gave those who were more deeply enmeshed in *Series #4*.

Michael was always alert to the needs of subscribers entangled in the obsessive and compulsive demands created at Whatcomesnext. He liked to imagine himself as a writer for the new age, a poet of the future. He thought traditional authors who devoted months and years to building stories on a page were dinosaurs and clearly on their way to extinction. He proudly spoke a different language, one that wasn't limited to English or Russian or Japanese. He wasn't a painter confined to the barriers of a canvas; he constructed brush strokes that constantly shifted and changed. Unlike a film director working within a strict budget, he crafted images that were filled with uncertainty and surprise. He wasn't tied to any dialect or any medium. He was an artist for modern times, one that blended film and video with Internet and words and performance, a mixed media that spoke to the days that were coming, not the antique times that had passed. He thought of himself as part documentarian and part producer. His was a design of spontaneity.

It did not bother him in the slightest that his creation was built on a crime. All great advances in art took chances, he believed.

Linda was asleep, wrapped in tangled sheets on the bed, making small regular, peaceful breathing sounds. Her long legs were exposed and her skin glistened. She was halfway on her stomach, with a pillow pulled against her, and the curve of her breast was outlined beneath the sheet she'd tugged around her back and shoulders. He imagined her dreams were happy, filled with simple, magical sights.

Sometimes, when she slept, he found himself staring at her, and it was as if he could see her aging, her perfect skin fading and wrinkling, the tautness in her body loosening. He would imagine the two of them growing old together, and then he would think that was impossible; they would forever be young.

Occasionally he glanced toward the camera monitors to check on Number 4. At that moment she, too, seemed asleep—at least she had barely moved in the past hour. He suspected her dreams to be far less quiet. Number 1 and Number 2 had frequently screamed in their sleep. Number 3 had groaned, pulling on restraints, which had been a precursor to the way she had fought them when she was awake. It had cut *Series #3* shorter than he'd liked because Number 3 was just too hard and too demanding to handle. But he'd learned a great deal from Number 3 before the end of the show, and these were lessons he was employing with Number 4.

He punched a few computer keys and zoomed a camera into a close-up. Number 4's lips were slightly parted and her jaw seemed set in concrete. *She will scream soon,* he thought.

There are screams caused by what you dream. There are screams caused by what happens to you when you are awake. He was unsure which was worse. *Number 4 knows,* he thought.

He sighed, lifted his hands, and ran them through his long hair. He adjusted the glasses on the end of his nose. He wondered if he had time to grab a quick shower. As he watched, he saw Number 4 twitch and her hand involuntarily move toward the chain around her neck. *Dreams of drowning,* he guessed. *Maybe dreams of choking. Or nightmares of being trapped under the ground.*

He watched, thinking that Number 4 would probably wake up in the next few minutes. The dreams were so vivid, so frightening, that they often pitched subjects into wakefulness. At least that was what he believed.

One of the problems with guaranteeing her disorientation—which Michael knew was a key element of the entire show—was that she was likely to be awake at odd times, no longer roped to the rhythms of wake in the morning, stay up in the day, go to sleep at night. There was an advantage to this, Michael knew, because *Series #4* went to so many time zones in so many parts of the world that eventually every person was satisfied—because at some point or another, their time zone would contain something undeniably live and visually compelling. But this was a hassle for the two of them—often one of them had to do sentry duty while the other caught some sleep. Part of their own passion for the project came from sharing observations and their own arousal over what they were creating. But frequently these moments came when one was observing, which made for frustration.

In their first two efforts at Whatcomesnext.com this had proven to be an immense problem. They were constantly exhausted and, by the end, had barely the energy to complete the show.

After much discussion Michael and Linda had solved this electronically. They taped action, they taped moments of sleep, they created shows within the show so that the narrative thread of *Series #4* was constantly being renewed and rewound and replayed. He had become an expert at Final Cut and other editing programs and had learned how to paste together different sequences, so that when things felt like they were lagging he could send out something compelling.

Michael had come up with this idea when he studied modern pornographers and recognized that people would watch the same video of actors coupling over and over again, as if every moan and every stroke were happening for the first time.

But Michael had the sense to understand that no matter how explicit the pornography was eventually it turned stale. It was ultimately predictable. He got so that he could actually time the videos that streamed over the Internet—so many minutes for each element of each sex act, one after the other, all in military order until the eventual mouth open conclusion.

Michael had been determined to break those molds.

The beauty of *Series #4* lay in the art of unpredictability.

No one would ever know what might take place on camera. No one would ever be able to anticipate the next move. They could not measure the length of time it might last, or the actual theme.

A near-naked teenager chained to a wall in an anonymous room was a canvas that any possibility might be drawn upon.

He was immensely proud of this. And proud of Linda. It had been her insistence that they *find someone young and fresh* for *Series #4.* She had argued that the increased risk involved was dwarfed by the Internet word of mouth that would increase their paying customer base. She had been insistent and determined, using all her onetime business school and corporate knowledge to buttress her argument.

Michael admitted that in this—as in so many other things—Linda had been right.

Number 4 was going to be featured in the most interesting drama they'd ever created.

Behind him Linda stirred. In her sleep she was smiling. He smiled back and longed to stroke her leg, but as he reached out he stopped his hand. She needed her rest, and he shouldn't disturb her.

He turned back to the computer. There was an e-mail message from someone with the Web name Magicman88 asking: *Number 4 should exercise, so we can see her figure more excellently.*

Michael wrote back: *Yes. All in good time.*

He liked giving the subscribers the impression that they were helping to control the situation, and he made a note on his script to make Number 4 do some push-ups, sit-ups, maybe jog in place.

He sat back in his chair and asked himself, *If I make her exercise, what will that make her think?*

He wondered: *Does the lamb being fed extra food realize it's being fattened for slaughter?*

Michael whispered out loud, "No, she won't. She will believe it's all a part of something else. She won't be able to see the theater of it all."

Linda rolled over in the bed. He liked the idea that she was sensitive even to his whispers.

Back on the video monitor he saw Number 4 lift her hand to her face, her fingers touching the mask that hid her eyes. But her motions seemed involuntary and he understood she was still asleep.

He believed that this was part of his genius. Michael was able to imagine the psychological ramifications of every action that took place on the video screen. He considered not only how Number 4 was being affected but also how it would appear to those watching. He wanted them to both identify with Number 4 and, simultaneously, want to manipulate her.

Control was everything.

Again he glanced at the monitor and then let his eyes linger on Linda. When they had first devised the ideas that had led to *Series #1* he had immersed himself in the world of captivity. There wasn't a paper written about the Stockholm Syndrome that he hadn't read. He had devoured POW memoirs and obtained declassified U.S. military tracts assessing life in the Hanoi Hilton. He had even managed to obtain some of the CIA psychological operations unit's interrogation and risk assessment manuals for high-value targets. He'd read prison wardens' oral histories and biographies of the men they'd kept incarcerated. He knew the truth about

Birdman of Alcatraz and could have told any film history professor precisely how Burt Lancaster's famous performance had deviated from the reality.

He thought he knew as much about confinement as any expert. This self-assured knowledge always made him smile. The difference between him and some professional was that they were looking for information, or wanted to inflict pain, or merely needed to measure the passing of time.

Linda and he were creating art. They were unique.

She shifted again, and he quietly got up and made his way to the bathroom. A shower would refresh him, he told himself. He needed to be alert for the next dramatic moment with Number 4.

There was a small mirror above the sink and he took a second to stare at himself in it. He flexed his wiry muscles and thought he looked ascetically thin, monklike, or maybe configured like some possessed long-distance runner. He pushed his threads of hair away from his face and felt his scraggly beard. He had long fingers that once he'd thought would have been well suited to dancing across a piano keyboard. Now the music they made was playing with the keys of a computer. He splashed some water on his face. He thought he looked a bit pale. He and Linda needed to get out a little more, not be such recluses. Or maybe after *Series #4* was finished they should go south for some R and R. Maybe someplace hot, humid, and tropical, like Costa Rica, or perhaps exotic like Tahiti. They would have more than enough money for whatever first-class extravagance they wanted. *Series #4* was by far their most successful version yet. There were still subscribers logging in with new credit card numbers, forking over the funds electronically. He reminded himself that he needed to do an update, so that the newer viewers were as up to speed as those who'd been there from the start. Michael decided to shave, and he turned the hot water on full, almost instantly steaming up the mirror. He lathered his face with shaving cream, poised with a razor in his hand, and mimicked another famous movie: "It's show time!" he whispered confidently.

* * *

As before, Jennifer was unsure whether she was still dreaming or if she had awakened. Behind the curtain of black that covered her eyes, she could sense that things were starting to slide as if nothing in the world was attached solidly, gravity had lessened, and everything was loose and disconnected. She did not know whether it was night or day, morning or evening. She did not remember how many days she'd been held captive. Time, place, who she was—all was unraveling from minute to minute. Sleep did not mean rest. Food did not curb her hunger. Drink did not reduce her thirst. She remained buried behind the blindfold, chained in place.

Her fingers wrapped for the millionth time around Mister Brown Fur. It was the only thing left within her grasp that reminded her of anything that had been real in her life right up to the second that she had been swept away.

Her fingertips tickled at the worn synthetic bear. She wondered why they had let her have it. She recognized that it couldn't be to help her. It had to be helping *them* and for a second she wondered whether she should fling the familiar toy into the void where she could never find it. It would be defiance. It would be an act that would show the man and the woman that she wasn't going to just roll over and let them do whatever it was they intended to do.

She gripped her hand tightly around the stuffed animal's midsection and felt her muscles grow taut, like a pitcher readying to deliver a baseball to home plate.

She gasped.

Don't! she suddenly shouted to herself.

Or maybe it was out loud. She couldn't tell.

She listened for an echo but could hear none.

She pulled the bear to her chest and nuzzled him, running her fingers down the toy's backside. "I'm sorry," she whispered out loud. "I didn't mean it. I don't know why they let me find you, but they did, and so we're in this together. Just like always."

Jennifer craned her head to the side, as if expecting to hear the door, or the sound of the baby crying again, but there was nothing. All she could hear was her own heartbeat and she imagined that she was sharing that with the toy.

It made her feel a little better to hear her own voice even if it faded away quickly. It reminded her that she could still talk, which meant that she was still who she was, if only a little, but it was an important little.

She almost laughed. There were many evenings when she had lain in her bed at home, the lights out in her room so she was surrounded by night, curled up with Mister Brown Fur, pouring out all her hurts and tears onto the stuffed animal, as if he alone in the entire world understood what she was going through. Many conversations, over many years, about many troubles. He had been there for her throughout, from the first instant that she'd torn open the bright *Happy Birthday* wrapping that her father had placed somewhat incompetently around the toy. He'd been very sick then, and it had been the last thing he'd been able to give her before he'd gone off to the hospital. So there it was: he gave her a toy and then he died, and she hated her mother because she hadn't been able to do anything about the cancer that murdered him.

Jennifer breathed in and stroked the bear. *Maybe they're killers,* she thought harshly, as if she could pass the words in her head directly into the stuffed animal, *but they aren't cancer.*

She told herself that was the only thing in the world she really feared. *Cancer.*

Another deep sigh and she shifted on the bed.

"We need to be able to see," Jennifer whispered in the bear's ragged ear. "We need to be able to see where we are. If we can't see, we might as well be dead."

She hesitated. These words made her nervous probably because they were true.

"You look around carefully," she continued softly. "Memorize everything. And then you can tell me later."

She knew this was foolish, but she found herself pivoting the bear's head back and forth, so that the little glass beads that made up his eyes could survey wherever it was she was being held. Though she knew this was stupid and childish, it made her feel much better and a little stronger, so that when she heard the sound of the door opening she didn't stiffen quite as quickly, nor did her breathing get raspy. Instead, she turned toward the sound, hoping that it was something as routine as a meal or a drink, but nervous that it might be a signal of something new happening to her.

She knew right then that whatever was in store for her, it wasn't to be fast and sudden. This thought made her hand twitch with fear. But she was smart enough to know that every second that passed, and every new element that was introduced into the dark world she inhabited, might help her as much as hurt her.

21

Adrian lay curled on his bed, his head cradled in the lap of his naked, six-months-pregnant wife. He breathed in deeply, separating different scents, as if each said something unique about Cassie's personality. Cassie hummed some leftover sixties Joni Mitchell tune that seemed to come from a long-forgotten time. She slowly stroked his tangled gray hair in time to the music, pushing it back from his forehead, and then ran her fingers around his ears, gently massaging them. The sensation went way beyond seductive.

He remained motionless and thought that it reminded him of the long-ago moments after lovemaking. Exhaustion that soared.

Adrian wanted to close his eyes, tumble endlessly into the depths within him, and die, right at that moment. If there were a way to will one's heart to stop beating, he would have done it without hesitation.

Cassie bent her head toward his, whispering, "Do you remember how many hours you would spend lying like this, Audie, waiting to feel Tommy kick?"

He did. Not one wasted second. It was the happiest time of his life. Everything seemed filled with possibility. He had obtained his doctorate and his appointment to the university. Cassie had already had her first show, at a prestigious New York gallery, just off Fifth Avenue, and the reviews—*Art World* and the *New York Times*—had been respectful and almost glowing. His poetry habit—he had often thought of it in the terms one usually confined to an addict—was just taking root. Discovering Yeats and Longfellow, Martin Espada and Mary Jo Salter. Their son was about to be born. He had been filled with excitement every day, greeting the first shafts of morning sunshine with unbounded energy. He had taken up running just after the sun rose, pounding out six miles at a fast pace, just to keep all of his enthusiasm in check by expending effort. Even the college's cross-country team, which viewed running as the most positive obsession on earth, had thought the newly appointed psych prof who beat them out every morning was more than a little nuts.

"There was so much to love, then," Cassie said. Her voice had a lyrical tone.

"But it's all gone now."

He opened his eyes and realized that he was alone and that his head was scrunched up against a pillow and not his wife. He reached out, as if he could catch her and hold her the way she was in his memory.

He could feel her hand in his but he could not see her.

"You have work to do," she said briskly. Her voice seemed to come from behind him, above him, beneath him, inside him all at once.

Cassie was there. Cassie wasn't there.

Adrian sat up. "Jennifer," he said.

"That's right. Jennifer."

"I can hardly remember her name," he replied.

"No, Audie, you remember. You can see her in your mind. And you can see who she was. Remember her room? Her things? The pink hat? You remember all that. And I'm here to remind you. Find her."

This echoed, as if it were spoken at the edge of an immense canyon.

He looked outside and saw that night still gripped the world. *It will be cold,* he thought. *But not as relentless as the winter. If I walked outside, I could feel the spring. It would be hidden in the darkness, but it would still be there.*

He rose, intending to head out the front door, but he did not. He looked over at a mirror on Cassie's old bedroom bureau and thought that he looked thin, pounds melted away by disease. He tried to remind himself to eat properly. He wondered whether he'd been asleep for hours or only minutes. *Take some of the medication,* he told himself. *You've got to stop falling in and out of hallucination.* He understood that there was little chance of this happening, no matter how many pills he took. And he *liked* the visitations. They were a part of his life that he enjoyed a whole lot more than the dying part. He felt like a stubborn old man, which, he imagined, wasn't such a goddamn bad thing. But, even so, he went to his bureau, found some of the pills that were supposed to be helping him fight his dementia, ignored the notion that he couldn't remember when he last took any, and slugged a handful down. Then he marched out of the bedroom and over to his office and pushed aside papers and books and settled in front of his computer. The only thing he arranged beside him was a map of a six-state area. Massachusetts. Connecticut. Vermont. Rhode Island. New Hampshire. Maine. Then he turned to the computer and stared in on statewide Sex Offender Registry entries for each.

Adrian had little idea that Detective Collins had been busy doing more or less the same thing.

He punched a few computer keys and then clicked on a name.

A police mug shot came up on the screen in front of him. A man with beady eyes, thinning hair, and a sallow, furtive appearance. Exactly as Adrian would have expected. There was a listing of arrests, convictions, and court appearances. There was also an address and a simple narrative describing the man's predilections. There was a "dangerousness" scale and descriptions of his modus-operandi. It was all clipped and clear, written in police style, without flourishes and with little acknowledgment regarding the realities of what the man did. He exposed himself outside a mall—that was one arrest Adrian noted. Nothing that indicated what impact this had either on the offender or the people who'd been victimized.

Adrian sat back in his chair, sighing deeply. Perhaps the entries on the screen would mean something to a professional. But he had spent his life interpreting behavior. When he saw something—whether it was in a laboratory rat or a person—his job had been to extrapolate meaning from the actions. Anyone could identify an action; there was no art or understanding in recognition. His job had always been to find out what it meant, and what it said about others, and what it suggested for the future.

He clicked on another picture. Another man, this time thickset, bearded, with great sheets of curly hair and a body covered with tattoos. The entry had close-ups of many of these—fire-breathing dragons, sword-wielding Valkyrie maidens, and motorcycle insignia—before filling in the same crime information.

As he had the sallow-faced man before, Adrian stared at the picture and thought he could tell nothing from the flat vision of the criminal.

He thought there was no way that anything that popped up on a computer screen was going to tell him anything about the sort of people who had taken Jennifer.

"So if that's the case," Cassie said, as she leaned over his shoulder reading the information on the screen with him, "it seems there's only one thing to do." He could feel her hot breath against his cheek.

He nodded. "But . . ."

"Didn't you always say you had mixed feelings about reading the results of other people's experiments? You only really trusted the experiments that you ran yourself. When you were studying fear and its emotional impacts, didn't you always say you had to see it for yourself?"

Cassie was asking questions that she knew the answers to. Adrian was familiar with this approach. She'd used it successfully for years.

He hesitated. Gnawing questions seemed to chew at his imagination. Before he could stop himself, he asked something that had been reverberating inside him for years.

"It wasn't an accident, was it?" he asked back. "With the car, the month after Tommy died. It wasn't an accident at all, was it? You just wanted it to seem like it was. You lost control and hit that tree on a rainy night. Except you didn't really lose control, did you? It was supposed to be a suicide that no cop and no insurance agent could call a suicide. Except it didn't work, did it? You didn't expect to wake up crippled in the hospital, did you?"

Adrian held his breath. He had blurted out his questions like an overly enthused schoolboy, and now he was embarrassed, but he also wanted to hear Cassie's replies.

"Of course not," Cassie snorted her reply. "And when you have always known the truth, why is it so important to state it out loud?"

He didn't know what to say to this.

"We never talked about it," Adrian said. "I always wanted to, but I didn't know how to ask you when you were alive."

"Just barely alive."

"Yes. Crippled."

"Crippled more by Tommy's death than by any damn oak tree at sixty miles an hour. That's the way things shake out, Audie. You know that."

"You left me all alone."

"No. Never. I just died, that's all, because I had to. It was my time. I couldn't really handle Tommy's death. And you never expected me to be able to. But you're wrong."

"Wrong?"

"You've never been alone."

"I feel that way now that I'm dying too."

"Really?"

Cassie's hands rubbed his shoulders, kneading the flesh and muscles. She seemed older, frayed in the same way she was after they got the news about their only child. She had spent days staring at his picture, then other days obsessively searching the computer for news about other reporters, cameramen, and news people in Iraq. He thought then that she had wanted them all to die, so it would seem to her that her own child's death wasn't so unique and this would somehow make it less terrible. He thought he was acting the same way now, only he was trying to find something that would tell him where to look for Jennifer. He bent toward the computer and punched in a new entry.

"Well, look at that," he said softly, his voice filled with surprise. He had entered his own college town into the registry database and it had returned a list of seventeen convicted sex offenders living within a few miles of the college and all the elementary schools.

"When I put a rat in a maze, injected it . . ." he started. Cassie was close by, he could feel her and see her reflection in the computer screen, but he was scared to turn around, because he thought that would chase her ghost away and he liked having her close by. He paused, then laughed a little. A familiar statement: "I always wanted to ask the rat . . ."

What did you feel? What did you think? Why did you do what you did? Cassie finished his words for him with a slight lilting laugh that he recognized from better days.

She slapped his back resoundingly, as if signaling the end of the back rub. "So," he heard her say briskly, "go ask a rat."

22

Adrian had to wait only a half hour before the man he'd selected from the list of seventeen registered sex offenders appeared in his doorway and made his way quickly to his car. It was early in the day, and the man sported a cheap red tie and a blue cardigan sweater. He carried a worn black leather briefcase and didn't seem to Adrian much different from any other person heading off in the morning to a boring but regular job with a small but necessary paycheck attached to it.

There was nothing particularly unusual about the way the man looked, nor the street he lived on. He was a little shy of middle age, not very tall, slightly built, with sandy hair, and he wore black-rimmed glasses. He carried a simple gray jacket over one arm as if he didn't trust the day would ever truly warm up. He had a clerk's dowdy appearance.

Adrian watched from where he'd parked across the street as the man got into a small beige-colored Japanese car. The single-story ranch-style house where the man lived with his mother—according to the printout Adrian had with him—was kept meticulously trim, set back from the street and freshly painted. There were early season blue and yellow flowers in red-brick flowerpots placed in rows by the front door.

All in all, it gave the appearance of an undistinguished man living in a typical house in an unremarkable neighborhood. The surrounding area was closer to the rural world of farms and plowed fields being readied for corn planting than the more closely packed energy of the college town. This man lived just slightly removed from the mainstream, even if the mainstream that Adrian was familiar with—crowded coffee shops, standing-room-only pizza parlors, paperback bookstores, and handmade crafts outlets—was pretty tame. Not like New York or Boston or even Hartford. No daily rush hour, no frantic get-ahead dedication to jobs. The academic world that dominated Adrian's town was ambitious but defined ambition in a tenured professorship way.

The man Adrian watched did not seem to belong to any world Adrian knew. He seemed *separate*.

Adrian reminded himself: *Just because he seems humdrum and ordinary, that doesn't mean he is.* He hesitated, uncertain about what he was supposed to do next.

"No, go ahead, quick! Follow the son of a bitch," Brian urged. "You need to see where he goes to work. You need to get a handle on who he is!"

Adrian glanced in the rearview mirror and saw the reflection of his dead brother. It was the middle-aged-lawyer Brian, leaning forward, waving his hands as if to push Adrian into action, urging him to get moving. Brian's long hair seemed tousled, unkempt, as if he'd spent the night awake at his desk. His silk Brooks Brothers rep tie was loose around his neck, and his brother's voice was urgent and decidedly impatient.

Adrian immediately put the car in gear and pulled out behind the sex offender. He saw his brother slump back in the seat, exhausted and relieved.

"Good. Goddammit, Audie, you've got to stop being so . . . *hesitant*. Every time, from now on, when you want to look at someone or something or some bit of evidence or information with all the slow, steady, cautious style of a professor and an academic, well, tell yourself to get a damn move on."

Brian's voice seemed almost reedy, weakened, as if he was summoning up the strength to speak from deep within. At first Adrian wondered if his brother was sick and then he remembered that his brother was dead.

He steered the old Volvo out onto the roadway.

"I've never tailed someone before," Adrian said. The Volvo engine made a whining, reluctant sound as he punched the gas.

"Nothing to it," Brian replied with a sigh, relaxing, the mere act of moving forward lessening some tension within. "If we were really expecting to stay hidden—you know, do this like professionals—then we'd have three cars and we'd do an overlapping style . . . you know, trade him off, one car to the next. Same thing works when you're on foot on the street. But we're not going to be that fancy. Just follow him to wherever he's heading."

"And then what?"

"Then we see what we shall see."

"Suppose he guesses that I'm following him?"

"Then we see what we shall see. Makes no difference. By the end of the day we're going to talk to the guy."

Adrian saw that Brian was staring at the computer printout, reading everything listed there.

"I see why you chose this creep," Brian said. He laughed a little, although there was no joke that Adrian was aware of in any of the pages from the website registry.

"It's the age similarity," Adrian said out loud, as he steered around a corner and then accelerated to keep pace. "He's been convicted or pled guilty to three separate offenses, each time with young girls ranging in age from thirteen to fifteen."

Brian spoke with the certainty of a lawyer who has the facts and the evidence on his side. "A sweetheart, no doubt."

This last observation was spoken with ringing sarcasm. It was exactly what Adrian had told himself when he'd gone through the list of seventeen men. The trick was to look at the grouping scientifically and not get stymied by the details of what they'd done but to focus on the underlying disturbance. Most of them were convicted rapists. Some were involved in domestic issues. This man had been different. There had been an arrest for possession of child pornography. Charges had been dropped by an ex-wife, regarding a stepdaughter. Several busts for exposure.

All rats. But one different rat.

"He exposed himself to them."

"A weenie wagger. That's what the cops used to call 'em," Brian said, with a blustery tone. "At least, in the city, that was the phrase they used. I doubt it's any different up here in the sticks."

"That's right, probably not. But Brian, look at the last conviction and you'll see . . ."

Adrian stopped. He switched his eyes between the tan car ahead of him and Brian in the backseat, reading.

"Ah, he did jail time for . . . Well, Audie, I'm impressed. You seem to be getting the hang of this."

"False imprisonment."

"Yes," Brian said. "You understand, that's a lesser charge than kidnapping . . . but it's on the same page, isn't it?"

"I think so."

Brian snorted. "Young teenage girls. And he wanted to grab one, didn't he? I wonder what he wanted to do then? Well, says a great deal." He laughed again. "But one thing . . . "

"I know. No accomplice. That's what I need to understand."

"Don't lose him, Audie. He's heading to town."

Some of the traffic had picked up. Several sedans and a pickup truck blocked the man in the tan car. Behind Adrian a school bus had pulled close to his bumper. Adrian maneuvered the car, keeping pace with the man.

"I remember, Brian, when you had that fancy sports car."

"The Jaguar. Yeah. It was cool."

"It would be a lot easier to keep up if we were in that."

"I sold it."

"I remember. I never understood why. It seemed to make you happy."

"I drove too fast. Always too fast. Too reckless. I couldn't get behind the wheel without pushing it way past not just the speed limits, Audie, but the limits of sanity. It made me wild at a hundred, crazy at a hundred and twenty, and genuinely psychotic at a hundred and thirty. And I liked it, going that fast. It felt like freedom. But I was clearly going to kill myself. I almost lost control so many times. I knew I was risking something big; it was too dangerous, so I sold it. Biggest mistake I ever made. The car was beautiful, and would have been a better way to . . ."

Brian stopped. Adrian saw his brother cover his face with his hands.

"I'm sorry, Audie. I forgot. That's what Cassie did."

Brian's voice seemed distant, soft. "She and I, we weren't alike at all. I know you think we didn't get along, but it's not true. We did. It was just that we saw something in each other that frightened us. Who would have guessed that we'd both go south in similar ways?"

Adrian wanted to say something but was unable to form the words. There were tears welling up in his eyes. All he could hear was pain in his brother's voice, which matched the pain he remembered from his wife's.

"I should have known. I was the psychologist. I was like a shrink. I had the training . . ."

Brian laughed. "Didn't Cassie absolve you of that guilt? She should have. Hey, pay attention! The dude's turning in. Well, I'll be damned. Isn't this the sort of place you'd expect a freak like him to work?"

Adrian didn't reply. He saw the beige car rolling into a large home appliance and fixtures store that occupied nearly an entire block just on the outskirts of town. He watched as the man drove around the back, past a sign that said EMPLOYEES PARKING.

Adrian pulled into a space in front. He waited for fifteen minutes in silence. Brian seemed asleep in the back. At least the hallucination was quiet. Adrian tried to think of something he could purchase inside that would make his trip seem about something else. But he knew all he really wanted was to make sure that the man was at work.

"Let's go," he said to Brian. "Got to make sure that this is where he'll be today."

Adrian exited and walked across the giant lot, scuffling his feet against the macadam. There were pickup trucks and minivans moving in. He saw a cross section of contractors, plumbers, carpenters, and harried suburban-dad types heading inside. He followed the steady stream of people, not turning to see if Brian was following, although he felt alone, even in the midst of the crowds.

Inside the cavernous area he felt a momentary despair. The place was huge, divided into dozens of sections—for gardening, roofing, kitchen appliances, power tools—a huge list of devices and wares lined up in aisle after aisle. Men and women wearing red vests and name tags scurried about, directing customers and offering advice. Cash registers were already beeping and ringing up sales. Adrian started to wander up and down arrays of tile and wood paneling, stainless steel sinks and faucets, Spackle and hammers and power drills. He was about to give up when he spotted the man, working in the section devoted to home electronics. He watched for a moment as the man energetically spoke with a couple of do-it-yourself types, a man and a woman who looked to be in their early thirties. The man was shaking his head but the woman seemed animated, as if she'd been persuaded that the two of them, with the right tools and the right advice, could rewire their house. The man had the look that young husbands sometimes have, knowing that they are being saddled with more than they can handle, but he was helpless to prevent it. Adrian would have laughed at the picture—having been more than once in the same position with Cassie—except he knew that if the couple were aware of who it was they were speaking with they would have recoiled in horror.

He watched for a few more seconds and then, understanding that he could return in eight hours after the man's shift, he turned and left. He felt as if he'd achieved something, but he wasn't sure what. Perhaps it was just the sensation of being closer to someone who could tell him what he should be looking for.

But forcing it out of the man was going to be a challenge, and Adrian did not know how he was going to meet it.

* * *

He spent the rest of the day in anticipation, although unsure exactly why. More research led him deeper into what he considered perversion. But nothing told him where to find Jennifer. He did not have to hear Cassie or Brian insisting that he move faster, that time was wasting, that every second meant she was closer to dying—if she was still alive. All these admonitions were true. Or maybe not. There was no way for him to tell, and so he simply assumed that the opportunity to save her still existed.

He thought: *Save her. You never saved anyone except yourself.*

And he had a sudden fear that, were he to stop looking, Cassie and Brian and even Tommy would disappear and leave him alone with nothing except jumbled, disjointed memories and the disease that was twisting them around inside of him like a rubber band stretched to breaking.

So, alone now, wondering where Brian was, wondering why Cassie couldn't leave the house, and why Tommy had visited him only once and hoping that his son would come back again to his hallucinatory world, he found himself outside the home warehouse store once again. The day was fading around him and he feared he might have trouble seeing the man when he left work.

The beige car pulled out from the rear of the store just about the time that Adrian had estimated the eight-hour workday had ended. Adrian pulled in as close behind it as he could manage and kept an eye on the man through the windshield of the car ahead of him, although that was getting increasingly difficult as the daylight faded.

He expected a return to the trim house, maybe a stop at a grocery store, but that would be it for delays.

He was wrong.

The man turned off the main road and headed into town on a side street. This took Adrian by surprise and he pulled across traffic dangerously, causing someone to honk rudely at him.

The old Volvo labored to keep pace.

The beige car was about thirty yards ahead, on a street just behind the main thoroughfare. It was a place with some offices and apartment buildings and an artist's studio or two, just past a Congregational church and a computer repair store. Adrian saw the car turn in and scoot into a small parking lot, slipping between half a dozen cars into the only remaining slot.

"What's he doing?" Adrian asked out loud. He expected Brian to answer, but he did not appear. "Damn it, Brian!" Adrian shouted. "I need your help right now! What should I do?"

The backseat remained silent.

Cursing, Adrian accelerated down the street. It took Adrian several minutes to find a free parking place in a metered lot a block away. The college town had all sorts of parking restrictions designed to keep students from leaving cars jamming the sidewalk areas. In the summer it was empty. During the semesters it was overcrowded.

Adrian pushed himself out of the car and slammed the door behind him. He walked as quickly as he could back to where he'd last seen the man.

From the street he could see the beige car. But there was no sign of the sex offender. There was just a single, older building. It was a stately wooden-framed, white clapboard two-story house that had been cut up into offices. Adrian could see a main entranceway where once had been a front door and he walked over. He told himself to assume the man was inside somewhere, but where, he didn't know.

Adrian stepped inside. On the wall by the door was a single sign, delineating six different offices. It was all beneath the heading: VALLEY EMOTIONAL HEALTH SERVICES.

Three MDs and three PhDs.

It was quiet in the lobby. A single sound-deadening white noise machine hummed in a corner. A couch where people could sit was arranged across from a few chairs, making the whole vestibule into a waiting room. Adrian saw that three offices opened onto the ground floor. Three were up a single flight of stairs. There was no receptionist. This was typical of places for therapy. People knew when their appointments were, rarely arrived more than a few minutes early, and weren't made to wait long.

So, Adrian thought, *one of six.*

There was, he imagined, no way to determine which of the six offices the man had gone into. But Adrian still turned to the wall where the names of the therapists were located. It was a small town, and he suspected he would know most of them.

But there was one he'd met only once: that was Scott West.

"So," Brian said smugly, whispering into Adrian's ear, as if he'd known all along what Adrian was going to find inside the building, "Jennifer's mother's boyfriend is treating a known sex offender. That's a curious connection. I wonder if he bothered to mention that to Detective Collins when she questioned him the other day?"

Adrian didn't turn to his brother. He could feel him hovering right behind. Nor did he say, *Where were you when I called for you.* Instead he nodded, then replied hesitantly.

"He could be in one of the other offices."

"Sure," Brian said. "He *could* be. But I don't think so. And neither do you."

23

When Detective Collins looked up she was surprised to see Adrian Thomas standing in the doorway to the detective bureau. He was accompanied by a uniformed officer, who shrugged and gave her the *I didn't have a choice* look as he pointed the old man in her direction.

Terri had just gotten off the phone with Mary Riggins, who, in her constantly teary, distraught, hesitant way, had told her that she had just received a call from Visa security that her lost credit card had been returned to a bank in Maine. "And it had been used," Mary Riggins said bleakly, "to buy a bus ticket to New York City."

Terri had dutifully taken down the information and the contact number for the credit card security. She was unsure how the card had managed to travel in one direction when the ticket was headed in another. This was illogical. But it had given her the start of a new time line, and she was searching for the phone number for the Boston police bus station substation when she saw Adrian.

Her desktop was cluttered with documents and stray bits of information concerning Jennifer's case and she rapidly collected it all into a pile and turned it facedown. She guessed that the professor had seen her do this and would recognize it for what it was, and so she readied a response that would deflect any inquiry without being rude. She wasn't going to mention anything about the Visa card. But Adrian, without greeting, simply asked, "Have you obtained a current list of patients from Scott West? I remember you asked for that."

She was slightly taken aback. She hadn't thought he had been paying that much attention when she had met with Scott and Mary in their home.

Adrian filled the momentary pause with a second question: "He said he would give it to you, and he scoffed at the idea that anyone he'd ever treated would have any connection to Jennifer's disappearance, didn't he?"

She nodded. She waited for another question from the professor but he merely bent forward and fixed her with a look that she suspected had been reserved for wayward, ill-prepared students in decades past. It was the *try another answer* look.

She shrugged. She remained noncommittal.

"He is supposed to bring that list to me tomorrow. It will be confidential, professor, so I would not be free to share any information with you."

"What about a list of known sex offenders? I thought I made it clear that was the next step."

Adrian was being forceful in a way that Terri had not seen before. She was put off. She had thought that the professor wanted to work in the gray areas of speculation, theory, and supposition. She had expected a tweed jacket, leather arm patch, pipe-smoking sort of academic, happy to sit in an office surrounded by books and learned papers, occasionally chiming in with an observation or an opinion—just as he had when he'd lectured her about Myra Hindley and Ian Brady and the Moors Murders. She had not expected that he would ever arrive at her office. He seemed different, like a baggy shirt that had shrunk to tightness in the wash. The same but barely recognizable.

"I have been looking over those lists, professor. And I have read a great deal about the British case back in the sixties that you referenced. But concretely connecting these things to Jennifer's disappearance might seem obvious to a university professor, but to a police officer . . ."

This was spoken in the practiced tones of a cop who wants to reply without saying anything. He interrupted her swiftly.

"Does the name *Mark Wolfe* mean anything to you."

She hesitated. The name had a little electricity to it, like a minor charge of current. Something that buzzed in the back of her memory. But she did not immediately place it.

Adrian spoke without waiting.

"Convicted sex offender. A serial exhibitionist with a particular predilection for teenage girls. Lives not far outside of town. Does that help you?"

The buzzing increased. She knew that the name was on one of the sheets of paper she had concealed from Adrian's eyes on her desktop. She nodded, while inwardly she was trying to sketch a picture of the man. *Glasses.* Thick black-rimmed eyeglasses. She remembered those from a mug shot.

She rocked back in her chair and motioned Adrian toward a nearby seat. He remained standing. She thought he seemed rigid, and she wondered where the distracted, eyes-wandering, *I'm someplace else* look had vanished to.

"I saw him today."

"You saw him?"

"Yes. And—"

"How did you happen to know who he was?"

Adrian reached inside his coat pocket and removed a sheaf of crumpled-up papers. He handed these over and Terri saw that they were printouts of local sex offenders available to anyone who knew how to do a simple Web search.

"And Wolfe . . . why did you choose him?"

"He seemed the most logical. From a psychologist's perspective."

"And what exactly is that perspective, professor?"

"Exhibitionists live in a curious kind of fantasy world. Often they derive titillation and sexual gratification from exposing themselves and triggering the fantasy that the women—in this man's case the very *young*

196

women—who witness their exposure will be magically attracted to them as opposed to repulsed, which, of course, is the reality. The act of exposing themselves triggers their imaginations."

Terri could hear the measured tones of the classroom in every word.

"Yes. Fine and good, but what has he to do—"

Adrian interrupted her.

"I saw him going into Scott West's treatment office after he finished work this evening."

Terri did not instantly react. This was Cop 101. Maintain a poker face. Inwardly, she felt an eruption. There were several aspects of the statement that deserved her attention. *How did the professor know it was after work? Why was he following him?* She pursed her lips together and decided to play obtuse. She asked. "Yes, and?"

"This does not strike you as odd, detective? Perhaps relevant?"

"Yes. It does, professor."

This was a reluctant piece of honesty.

"I recall he was quite adamant that *none* of his current or former patients could have anything to do with—"

"Yes. I heard that as well, Professor Thomas. But you are making assumptions that I would not yet . . ."

She stopped. She did not want to sound like a fool.

Adrian seemed to narrow his glance, his focus directly on her.

"Do you not think it calls for some investigation?" He said this last word with emphasis.

"Yes. I do."

There was a momentary pause between the two of them.

"You know, detective, if you won't look for her, I will."

"I am looking, professor. It's not like I just turn over a rock, or open a drawer or look behind a door, and there she is. She's gone and there are conflicting elements . . ."

Again she cut off her own words.

She reached under the papers collected on her desktop and removed the flyer that she had prepared. It had Jennifer's picture at the top under the word *Missing* and it listed all her vital statistics and contact numbers. It was the sort of flyer that is seen every day in police stations and on the walls of government buildings. It was only slightly more comprehensive than handmade missing dog or missing cat flyers that people tack to tree trunks and telephone poles in suburban neighborhoods.

"I am looking," she repeated. "That has gone out to departments and state police barracks throughout New England."

"How hard will those people look?"

"You don't expect me to answer that question, do you?"

"You know, detective, there's a difference between looking for someone and waiting around for someone to say *I just spotted someone.*"

Terri's eyes narrowed. She did not enjoy being lectured to by a professor about her job.

"That is a distinction I'm familiar with, professor," she replied coldly.

Adrian stared at the flyer. He looked down at the picture of Jennifer. She was smiling, as if she hadn't a care in the world.

Both of them knew this image was a lie.

Adrian hesitated. He saw his hand tighten and start to crumple the paper flyer, as if he needed to grip it tightly, otherwise it would slip free.

He took a step back. He could hear odd noises echoing in his head— not the voices he was familiar with but sounds like paper ripping or metal twisting. He felt empty inside, a sort of gnawing hunger, although he could not think of the food he wanted to eat. Muscles tensed in his arms and he could feel his back tighten, as if he'd been bent over in the same position for too long. He felt a runner's stiffness, a hot day's overexertion, and he battled against the desire to rest, arguing within himself that he could not stop, he could not pause, he could not shut his eyes for an instant, because that would be the moment when Jennifer would be lost to him forever.

Jennifer, he thought, was just like all the hallucinations in his life. She existed once, and now he had to fight hard to keep her from fading away. She was still real, but only barely, and anything he could identify that gave her substance was a step toward finding her.

The pink baseball cap. He wished that he hadn't returned it to Jennifer's mother. It would be something real, something he could touch. He wondered if he could act like a bloodhound, pick up her scent from the hat and track her.

He was breathing rapidly.

A known sex offender connected to Jennifer's family.

Adrian believed it had to mean something. He did not know what.

"Professor?"

He would go by himself.

"Professor?"

He would confront the man. Force him to tell him something that would help lead to Jennifer.

"Professor!"

He looked down and saw that he had gripped the side of Detective Collins's desk, and that his knuckles had turned white.

"Yes?"

"Are you okay?"

Terri watched Adrian's red face slowly return to a more normal color.

He took a deep breath. "I'm sorry? Is something . . ."

"It seemed like you were someplace else. And then you were like trying to pick up my desk or something. Are you okay?" she repeated the question.

"Yes," he said. "I'm sorry. It's just old age. And that new medication I mentioned the other day. I get distracted."

She looked at him and thought two things: *He isn't that old* and *This is a lie.*

Adrian slowly exhaled.

"I apologize, detective. I have become quite engaged with this case of the missing girl. Jennifer. It, ah, fascinates me. I cannot shake the idea that my expertise and background in psychology is useful. I understand that you have procedures, and that you need to follow protocols. These things were once very important in my line of work. Knowledge without established procedures is often useless, no matter how seemingly valuable."

This sounded once again like something of a lecture to Terri, but this time she didn't resent it. The old man meant well. Even if he did seem to fade in and out every time they spoke together. And she was certain that it wasn't simply medication. She stared at Adrian as if by a singleness of gaze she could diagnose what made him so erratic. He seemed to take her stare indifferently, shrugging his shoulders.

"If you like, I will simply pursue matters on my own . . ."

This she did not want.

"You should leave police cases to the police."

Adrian smiled.

"Of course. But from my perspective this is not the sort of situation that wholly lends itself to a policeman's approach."

"I beg your pardon?"

"Detective," Adrian said, "you're still trying to figure out what crime took place so you can categorize it and follow some established process. I have no such restrictions. I *know* what I saw. I also know human behavior and have spent my life studying identifiable responses in both animals and humans. So *your* behavior in this situation doesn't actually surprise me all that much."

Terri was momentarily speechless.

"I suppose it was naive of me to assume the police would do anything," Adrian continued. Terri looked at him closely as he spoke. She could not understand how one second the old professor would seem completely centered, decisive, and clear and then the next as if he'd been blown into some other place by a wind she could not see or feel or hear.

"I think I will go."

"Wait," she said. "Go where?"

"Well, I have not often spoken with sex offenders—at least not that I was aware of, because you never really know everything about the people you come into contact with on a day-to-day basis—but I think this fellow is a good place for me to begin."

"No," Terri said. "You will be obstructing my investigation."

Adrian shook his head and grinned wryly. "Really? I don't think so. But you don't seem to want my assistance, detective, so I should just make my own path, so to speak."

Terri shot out her hand and seized Adrian's forearm. This wasn't done in the tough-cop strong-arm fashion as much as it was just to stop him from leaving.

"Wait," she said. "I think we need to understand each other better. You know I have a job and—"

"I have an interest. I am involved in all this, regardless of what you might say. I'm not at all sure that your job trumps my involvement."

Terri sighed. There is a perception a good policeman gets about people that tells them just exactly how much of a problem or a help someone will be. Adrian, she thought, gave every indication of being some of both.

This was typical. Her fault for living and working in an academic community where everyone seemed to think they knew each other's business better than anyone else.

"Professor, let's try to do this right," she said. She understood that she was cracking open a door that perhaps she shouldn't, and one that was better left slammed shut, but at the moment she didn't see an alternative. She did not want this half-crazed ex–college professor trampling on her case—if there was a case—willy-nilly. She thought, *Better to indulge him with a dose of reality and be done with it.*

In her experience, thanks to popular culture, people unfortunately romanticized police work. When they got a taste of what it actually entailed—all the boring paperwork and sturdy, steady assessments of details and facts—it generally scared them off and they eagerly went back to whatever it was they were doing beforehand.

For a moment, she glanced at the collection of documents on her desk. What she wanted to do was to call the Boston bus station police and obtain the security tapes for the night Jennifer disappeared. She sighed inwardly. That would have to wait a couple of hours.

"All right, professor," she said. "I will go ask some questions, and you can come with me. But after that, I want you to restrict yourself to maybe calling me on the phone with ideas before you come stomping in here. And no more of this investigating on your own. I don't want you following people. I don't want you questioning people. I don't want you pursuing this at all. You have to promise me that."

Adrian smiled. He wished that Cassie or Brian were there to hear the detective make this modest concession. They were not. But he realized maybe they didn't need to hear things to understand them.

"I think," he said calmly, "that would make some sense."

It wasn't really a promise he was making but it seemed to satisfy the detective. He also liked using the word *sense*. He did not believe he would be able to make sense of things for too much longer, but while he still could, even if only a little, he was determined to do so.

"Look," Terri said. "Keep your mouth shut, unless I ask you something directly. You're just here to observe. I'll do all the talking."

She glanced over at the old man in the seat beside her. He was nodding in agreement but she did not expect that he would follow her rules. She eyed the house with the small beige car parked outside. The evening dark made each shadow wider. The few inside lights fought against the falling night. There was a metallic gray television glow coming from one room, and she could see a form moving behind a thin curtain that blocked off the living room window.

"All right, professor," she said crisply. "This is detective work at its simplest. No good-looking actor with psychic abilities in charge of the case. I ask questions. He answers. He probably tells me some truths and tells me some lies. Enough of each to keep himself out of trouble. Pay attention."

"We're just going to knock on the door?" Adrian asked.

"Yes."

"We can do that?"

"Yes. Convicted offender. His probation officer has already cleared us inside. There's nothing Wolfe can do about this without getting himself into trouble. And trust me, professor, what he doesn't want is the sort of trouble I can make for him."

Adrian nodded. He looked around, expecting Brian to be close. Usually whenever there was something even modestly legal, Brian showed up, or his voice echoed in Adrian's ear with lawyerly advice. He wondered whether Brian would have been on the side of the detective or whether his civil libertarian views would have sided with the sex offender.

"Let's go," Terri said. "Element of surprise and all that. Stay right behind me."

She pushed open her car door and quickly walked through the darkness. She was aware that Adrian was struggling to stay on her heels. She stopped at the front door and pounded with a closed fist.

"Police! Open up!"

Adrian could hear shuffling sounds coming from behind the door. In a few seconds it swung open and a woman perhaps a dozen years older than he peered through the darkness at the detective and her companion. She was overweight, with uncombed gray hair that seemed wiry and explosive in spots and thin in others. She wore a pair of thick eyeglasses, just as her son did.

"What is it?" the woman asked, and then, without waiting for an answer, said, "I want to watch my shows. Why can't you leave us alone?"

Terri pushed directly past her into the small mudroom entranceway. "Where's Mark?" she demanded.

"He's inside."

"I need to talk with him."

Terri gestured for Adrian to accompany her as she stepped forcefully into the small living room.

There was a slight musty smell, as if windows were rarely opened, but the room itself was neat and tidy. Hand-crocheted throws adorned each piece of worn and threadbare furniture. In contrast, there was a large-screen high definition television standing on a Swedish-design stand dominating one half of the room, with two yard-sale reclining chairs situated directly in front. The sound was low but she was watching a rerun of *Seinfeld*. Adrian spotted a large soft bag stuffed with yarn and knitting needles by one of the chairs. There were some framed pictures on one wall; Adrian could make out a steady progression of life—a couple with a single child, going through the years from childhood to the present. Mother-father-child, mother-father-child, mother-father-child until around age nine, when the father disappeared from the pictures. Adrian wondered whether this was death or divorce. Regardless, it all seemed completely normal and routine, unremarkable in every way except one. For some reason, completely concealed in the ordinariness of the house, the only child had become a sex offender.

He thought there was far more mystery in the room than there were answers. He wondered whether Detective Collins saw the same. She seemed forceful, demanding, and her stiff-backed requests were designed to make an impression, he decided, rather than acquire one.

Behind them, the old woman lurched off in pursuit of her son. On the screen, Kramer and Elaine were enthusiastically trying to persuade Jerry to do something he was reluctant to do. Knitting needles were on the recliner, where the woman had put them down. He could smell something cooking but Adrian was unsure what it was.

"Keep alert," Terri whispered.

She turned and saw Mark Wolfe standing in the passageway that led back to a small dining area and kitchen.

"I haven't done anything wrong," was the first thing he said.

The second thing he said was, "Who's that?" as he pointed at Adrian.

24

They had made her exercise before eating a meal. The woman had entered the room and gruffly ordered her off the bed and onto the floor. She was told to perform a series of jumping jacks followed by sit-ups and stomach crunches and ending by running in place—all a little like gym class from elementary school, except there was no counting out loud.

She could feel sweat dripping off her forehead and she was breathing hard at the end, not understanding why they had ordered the workout but realizing that it probably did her some good. Jennifer could not imagine why they wanted to do *anything* that might improve her condition, but she was willing to take whatever good came with the bad. In fact, after the woman said, "That's enough for now," in a moment of defiance Jennifer had reached down and touched her toes five times in quick succession, hoping that the stretching would help her. The woman had spoken sharply, "I said, *that's enough!*" Jennifer had wordlessly climbed back onto the bed, neck chain rattling slightly, and been rewarded with dinner.

Jennifer was finishing her meal—a cold bowl of processed spaghetti with greasy meatballs delivered from a can—and gulping down her bottle of water, all the time aware that the woman was in the room watching her silently and waiting. There had been no further conversation as she ate—no threats, no demands—and nothing had changed in her situation, as best as Jennifer could tell. She remained clothed only in her skimpy underwear and blindfolded, restricted by the dog collar and chain around her neck. She had grown accustomed to moving a few feet from the bed to the camp toilet, which someone must have emptied while she slept. She was grateful. A powerful stench of disinfectant overcame any odor that the food might have carried.

Under most circumstances, she would have turned up her nose and complained and thrust aside the disgusting food offering. But the Jennifer who would have done that belonged to some prior life that no longer seemed to exist. It was a fantasy Jennifer, a remembered Jennifer, who'd had a cancer-dead father and a whiny mother and a perverted soon-to-be stepfather, a dull suburban house, and a small room where she hid out alone with her books and computer and stuffed animals and dreamed of a different, more exciting life. That Jennifer went to a boring school where she didn't have any friends. That Jennifer hated just about everything in her daily existence. But that Jennifer had disappeared. Maybe that Jennifer had once lived, but no more. The new Jennifer, the imprisoned Jennifer, recognized she needed to cling to life—if *they* told her to exercise, she was going to exercise. Whatever food was offered, she was going to eat no matter what it tasted like.

She licked her bowl clean, trying to steal every bit of nourishment and protein, anything that might give her strength.

She stopped when she heard the door open.

There was a slight rustling sound as the woman reached down and took away the food tray and moved toward the door. Jennifer's head swiveled in the direction of the noise and she waited for some exchange of words.

She heard whispers. She could not make out what was said.

She heard a *sloshing* noise. She tried to picture in her head what it could be. It was like a wave approaching.

She could sense someone crossing the room. Jennifer did not move, but she felt the closeness of another's presence, and she sniffed the air and picked up the scent of soap.

"All right, Number Four, you need to clean yourself."

Jennifer gasped.

It was the man's voice, not the woman's.

He gave orders in a cold, flat monotone.

"Two feet from the edge of the bed is a bucket of water. Here is a towel and a washcloth. Here is a bar of soap. Stand next to the bucket. Give yourself a bath. Do not attempt to remove your blindfold. I will be close by."

Jennifer nodded. Had she been older—a Peace Corps type, or someone with military training, even an ex–Girl Scout or an Outward Bound or NOLS graduate—she would have known exactly how to give herself a thorough cleaning with only a bar of soap and a small amount of water. But the few camping trips she'd taken with her father before he died had featured locations with baths and showers or a river or pond to dive into. This was something different. She recognized that it was about precision.

She carefully swung her feet over the bed. She reached out with her toe and located the bucket. She bent down and felt the water. Lukewarm. She shivered.

"Remove your clothes."

Jennifer froze.

She felt a rush of heat pass through her. It wasn't embarrassment precisely. It was more humiliation.

"No, I—" she started.

"I did not give you permission to speak, Number Four," the man said.

She could feel him come closer. She imagined he had cocked his fist and that she was inches away from being beaten. Or worse.

Electric confusion riveted her. Inhibitions that she should no longer have had, desires to maintain some sense of herself, doubts about where she was and what was expected of her, and the constant question *How do I stay alive?* flooded through her.

"The water is getting cold," the man said.

She had never showed herself to a boy or a man.

She could feel her face flush, her skin redden with embarrassment.

She did not want to be naked—even if she had already been close to it, and knew she probably had been watched as she used the toilet. But there was something about taking off the two flimsy items of clothing remaining to her that frightened her beyond embarrassment. She worried that once she removed them she wouldn't be able to find them or the man would take them away, leaving her totally exposed.

Like a baby, she thought.

Then, in the same instant, she realized that she had no choice. The man had been specific.

He underscored this by growling, "We're all waiting, Number Four."

She slowly unlatched her bra and placed it on the edge of the bed. Then she stepped out of her panties. This was almost painful. One hand instantly descended past her waist, trying to cover her pubic region. The other she clasped across her small breasts. Behind her blindfold she could feel the man's eyes burning her, scouring her body, inspecting her like a piece of meat.

"Get busy," the man demanded.

She bent down as coyly as she could and dipped the washcloth into the water and then rubbed the soap against it. Then she stood and slowly, systematically, began to clean herself. Feet. Legs. Stomach. Chest. Underarms. Neck. Face—being careful not to dislodge the blindfold, trying to be as modest as she could.

To her surprise, the feel of the soapsuds against her skin was nearly erotic. Within seconds she realized that she had never once felt anything quite as wonderful as the sensation of cleaning herself. The room, the chain around her neck, the bed—all disappeared. It was like washing away fear and her inhibitions abruptly dropped aside. She ran the washcloth over her breasts and then over her crotch and thighs. It felt like she was being caressed. She thought maybe once, skinny-dipping and diving into early summer salty surf on the Cape, or playing in the cool fast water of a river on a hot August afternoon—those were feelings that came close to what she was experiencing. But now, she scrubbed her skin hard, wanting to peel off a layer like a snake shedding an old skin, so that she would glisten. She was aware that the man was watching, but every moment that some self-consciousness about her body tried to creep past the delight of washing she simply repeated to herself *fuck you fuck you fuck you, you bastard* like some Eastern mantra. It made her feel even better.

She reached for her upper arm and suddenly she heard: "No. Not there." She stopped.

The man's voice continued, softly but insistently.

"On the lower part of your abdomen, adjacent to your hip and near your crotch, you will feel a slightly raised Band-Aid-like thing. Leave that alone."

Jennifer touched the area and felt what the voice described. She nodded.

"My hair," she said. She desperately wanted to wash her hair.

"Some other time," the man said.

Jennifer continued, alternating dipping the washcloth in the bucket and using the soap. She redid her face. She took an edge of the cloth and, even though it tasted terrible, she rubbed it against her teeth and gums. She reached for every part of her body that she could, once, then twice.

"You're finished," the man said. "Place the washcloth in the bucket. Use the towel to dry yourself. Replace your underwear. Return to the bed."

Jennifer did precisely as she was told. She rubbed the rough cotton towel over herself. Then, like a sightless person, she groped around the bed until she found the two items of clothing and she struggled back into them, slightly covering her nakedness.

She heard the sound of the bucket being picked up, and then muffled footsteps crossing the room toward the door.

She did not know what came over her right at that second. Perhaps it was the energy that exercising had given her heart and muscles, or the sense of strength the meal had given her, or the feeling of renewal that bathing provided, but she leaned her head back and reached her hand up to her face and impulsively lifted the edge of the blindfold, just for an instant.

* * *

By the time Michael had put the water bucket away, removed his tight, black long underwear and the balaclava that concealed his face from the cameras, slid into a pair of worn jeans, and got up to the bank of computers in the control room, Linda was already typing away furiously. She was still dressed in her crinkly Hazmat suit. Without lifting her head, still concentrating on her keyboard, she said, "Look at this! The board has lit up!"

The interactive message screen that accompanied Whatcomesnext.com was filling with instant messages from around the world. Passion, excitement, fascination redoubled. The viewers had loved Number 4's nakedness, they had loved her exercise, they had loved her animal-like devouring of the food. Testimonials of love.

More than a few wanted to know much more about Number 4. They demanded a chance to experience a greater depth of understanding. *Who is she? Where does she come from?*

Both Michael and Linda saw these requests and were troubled. They knew there was a fine line between anonymity and exposure. They knew they needed to be cautious about demands that came from hidden places.

"I feel as if she is *my possession*," a man wrote from France. Linda had punched the message into a Google translation service before reading the words. "Like my car, or my house or my job. I need to be even more intimate with Number Four. She belongs to me."

Another viewer from Sri Lanka wrote, "More close-ups. Extreme close-ups. We need to be even closer to her all the time."

This, Michael understood, was a technical request that could easily be managed with any of the cameras inside the room. But he was also smart enough to understand that *close-up* meant something different than merely a camera angle.

He turned to Linda.

"I think we need to speak about the direction all this might go in," he said. "And I damn well think I might need to make some adjustments in the scripts."

Michael stared down at more responses flowing into their computers.

"It's important," he said, "that we *always* keep control. Stick to the scripts. Stick to the plan. It's got to *seem* spontaneous out there . . ."

He gestured at the screen.

". . . But we always need to know where we're going."

Linda was both uncertain and excited. Her voice picked up momentum as she spoke. "I think Number Four just might be the most popular subject we've ever had," she said. "That's going to make us money. A lot of money."

Michael nodded. He touched the back of her hand. He grinned, although there wasn't a joke being told.

"Who would have guessed that snatching a teenager would make people so . . ." He hesitated. "I don't know. *Fascinated?* Is that the right word? Is the whole world made up of people who want to seduce sixteen-year-olds?"

This comment made Linda laugh out loud. "You might be right," she said. "Except *seduce* is the wrong word." She looked over at Michael, who was smiling. There was something in the skewed way he twisted his upper lip when he considered something to be amusing that she found utterly endearing. She thought that the two of them were the only pure items left in the world. Everyone else was twisted and perverse. They had each other. Her shoulders twitched, and a shiver went up her back. She believed that every minute *Series #4* was being broadcast brought her and Michael closer. It was as if the two of them were on a completely different plane of existence. It was all erotic. All fantasy. The danger aroused her.

Linda turned back to the screen and finished typing a reply, which was limited to *Number 4 lives today—but what will happen tomorrow?*

She hit the SEND button and the reply soared through the Internet to thousands of subscribers.

She got up from the computer bank, taking one last look at Number 4. The girl was back on the bed and clutching her stuffed bear. Linda could see that Number 4's lips were moving, as if talking to the toy animal. She turned up the volume on the in-room microphones but there was no sound. Number 4, Linda realized, wasn't actually speaking out loud. She pointed at the computer screen with the live feed.

"See that?" she said to Michael.

He nodded in reply. "She's really a whole helluva lot different from the others," he said.

"Yeah," Linda said. "She's not crying and whining and screaming and . . ." She stopped, looked back at the image of Number 4. "Or at least she's not *anymore*."

Michael seemed to be thinking hard. "We've got to create more for her, because she's so much . . ." They were both aware that Number 4 was much more *something* but they were unsure *what*.

Linda turned and suddenly began pacing back and forth across the room. "We've got to be careful," she said, making a fist. "We've got to give them *more* to appreciate. But we can't give too much, because then, when we reach the end, it will be too hard . . ."

She didn't need to finish. Michael was acutely aware of the dilemma she was describing. *You can't make people fall in love with something that they're going to watch die,* he thought.

"It's because she's young," he said. "It's because she's so . . . *fresh*."

Linda knew exactly what he was saying. The first three had been different sorts of prisoners. Number 4 was compelling to all the viewers for reasons she was only beginning to understand. She had demanded someone with no hard edges. Acquisition had been more dangerous, but more rewarding. She took a step forward and wrapped her arms around her lover. She could feel a quickening in her pulse. It was not like the sensation she felt when Michael slipped between the sheets of their bed late at night and, even if they were both exhausted, she could feel his insistence; nor was it like the sensation of achievement she got when she totaled up their earnings. This was something unusual. She had expected Number 4 to be—within reason—like the others, and now, for the first time, she thought Number 4 was far better, far more advanced, and far more compelling. It was a contradiction, she thought. Number 4 was much younger than Numbers 1 through 3. Number 4 had been seized under different circumstances, with a different intention in their minds.

She thought they were on the verge of something special with Number 4, something that she had not imagined and not anticipated.

Linda shook with excitement.

Risk, she told herself, was like love.

Michael seemed to be feeling the same thing. He suddenly bent down and ran his lips over hers, gently, suggesting. She immediately tugged him toward their bed. Both of them were like teenagers, laughing, almost giggling with excitement, nearly overcome with the sense that they were artists creating something that went far beyond truth.

Their own passion immediately eclipsed their attention, because had they been alert they would have seen an instant message that came from Sweden. A client with the screen name Blond9Inch wrote a single line in his own language, which neither of them understood. *She lifted her blindfold. I think she peeked.*

This was followed by dozens of other, far more predictable messages, in many different languages, all commenting on various aspects of Number 4's body and filled with suggestions as to what Linda or Michael should do to it in the near future, and thus Blond9Inch's clever observation was obscured.

25

That Mark Wolfe, three-time convicted sex offender and serial exhibitionist, sounded so normal surprised Adrian but not the detective beside him.

"I haven't done anything," Wolfe repeated. "And who is that?"

He continued to gesture toward Adrian while directing his questions at Terri Collins. From the other side of the room Wolfe's mother chimed in, "What's this about? It's time for our show. Marky, tell these people to leave. Is it dinner yet?"

Mark Wolfe turned impatiently to his mother. He picked up a remote control from a table and clicked off the television. Jerry, Elaine, and Kramer and whatever they were bent out of shape about disappeared. "We've had dinner," he said. "The show will be on shortly. They'll be leaving in a minute or two."

He glared at Detective Collins. "Well, what is it?"

"I think I should be knitting," his mother said. She took a step toward the recliner adorned with needles.

"No," Mark Wolfe said abruptly. "Not right now."

Adrian glanced over at the mother. She had a skewed half grin on her face. Her voice had sounded concerned, even upset, but she was smiling. *Early-onset Alzheimer's,* he thought abruptly. The rapid-fire diagnosis was unsettling to him; Alzheimer's affected the same part of the brain and destroyed many of the thought processes that his own disease did. It was simply more insidious, more patient, and therefore much harder to handle. His was relentless and fast, but the woman he saw unsure as to whether to laugh or start crying was gripped by something as determined as the morning tides steadily creeping up a sandy beach. Staring at the mother was a little like staring into a distorted mirror. He could see himself, but not clearly. It threatened to terrify him, and he could hardly tear his eyes off the wild-haired woman, until he heard Detective Collins say, "This is Professor Thomas. He's assisting me in an ongoing investigation. We have some questions for you."

Again, Mark Wolfe's broken-record reply: "I haven't done anything . . ." But this time he added, ". . . wrong."

The detective's firm voice seemed to drag Adrian back from some edge, and he focused on the sex offender. He found himself wrestling with his own memory, insisting that he had spent hours watching the behavior of laboratory animals, and then run countless experiments on student volunteers, assessing different types and degrees of fear and interpreting a wide range of behaviors. This moment, he insisted, was the same. He eyed the sex offender, looking for telltale signs of inner panic, searching for signs of deception, listening for signs of dishonesty. A twitch of the eye. A turn of the head. A change in his tone of voice. A quiver in his hand. Sweat on his brow.

"The conditions of your parole require you to maintain employment—"

"I've got a job. You know that. I sell electronics and major appliances."

"And you are not allowed in playgrounds or near schools . . ."

"You seen me break any of the rules?" Wolfe asked.

Adrian noted that he hadn't answered: *No, I haven't been in any playground or near any school.* He hoped Terri Collins had noticed the same thing.

"And you are required to check in with your parole officer on a monthly basis."

"I do that."

Of course you do. Adrian understood. *Making that call keeps you free.*

"And you are required to undergo therapy."

"Yeah. Big deal."

Terri hesitated. "How's that going?"

"That isn't your business," Wolfe blurted out.

Adrian thought the detective would reply with a demanding anger of her own but he was impressed when Terri Collins maintained a flat calm bureaucratic voice.

"You are required to answer my questions—whether you like them or not—otherwise you are in violation of the terms of your release. I'm more than willing to call your parole officer right now and get his assessment of your refusal. I happen to have his number in my notebook." Adrian guessed this was a bluff, but he heard an uncompromising tone that indicated the detective didn't really need to resort to anything other than a threat of a phone call and that she and the sex offender both knew this.

Wolfe hesitated. "The doc says that my therapy is supposed to be private. You know, between him and me."

"In most cases that is true. Not yours."

Wolfe hesitated. He glanced over at his mother, who had settled into a chair in front of the big-screen television as if Adrian and Detective Collins and her son weren't in the room at all. She was reaching for the remote control. "Mother!" he said suddenly. "Not now. Go to the kitchen."

"But it's time," she said, complaining.

"Soon. Not yet."

The woman reluctantly stood up and left the room. Adrian could hear her shuffling in the kitchen. This was followed by the sound of a glass shattering in the sink and a howl of frustration cut off by a torrent of obscenities. The son looked that way, a scowl crossing his face, but as if anticipating his response the mother called out, "It was just an accident. I'll clean it up."

"Goddammit," Wolfe said. "That's *all* we have. Accidents." He turned and glared at Terri Collins. "You see how hard this is, she's sick and I got to . . ."

He stopped. He understood that Terri didn't care in the slightest about the difficulties of living with someone in the tendrils of that disease.

"Your therapy," she said sharply.

"I go every week," Mark Wolfe answered glumly. "I'm making progress. That's what the doc tells me."

"Tell me what you mean by that," Terri asked.

Wolfe looked a little hesitant. "Progress is just progress," he said.

"You're going to have to be more precise, Mark," Terri said. Adrian noticed that she used the man's first name. *Disarming,* he thought.

"Well," Wolfe said, "I'm not sure what . . ."

Terri stared hard at him. An unmistakable detective's *you have to do better* look. Adrian thought this wasn't all that different from a silent stare he'd used on promising students who had fallen short of his expectations.

"He's helping me curb my wishes," Wolfe said.

Wishes, Adrian believed, was a poor substitute for *desires.*

"How?"

"We talk."

"What did you say your doctor's name was?"

"I didn't."

"Why not?"

Wolfe shrugged. "I see Doctor West in town. You want his number and address?"

"No," Terri replied. "I already have those."

Adrian was listening carefully. Cognitive behavior therapy. Aversion therapy. Reality therapy. Acceptance-based therapy. Twelve-step programs. He was familiar with the wealth of treatment programs and the small likelihood of success for a paraphilia such as exhibitionism. What he wanted to hear was how a new age therapist like Scott West treated someone suffering from a prehistoric condition.

"Where do you meet Doctor West?"

"At his office."

"Ever meet anywhere else?"

The sex offender made the mistake of hesitating briefly.

"No."

Terri paused. Harsh glance.

"I'll try again. Ever meet—"

"He took me in his car once."

"Where?"

"He said it was part of the therapy. He said it was really important for me to show myself I had control over—"

"Where did he take you?"

The sex offender looked away. "He drove me past a couple of schools."

"Which schools?"

"The high school. An elementary school two blocks away. I forget the name."

"You forget?"

Again the sex offender hesitated. "Kennedy Elementary," he said.

"Not Wildwood School or Fort River Elementary?"

"No," Wolfe blurted out. "We didn't go past those."

Terri Collins paused again. "But you know the names, and I bet you know the addresses as well."

Wolfe turned his head but he didn't try to move. He didn't answer the question because it was clear he knew. Adrian figured that the sex offender could also tell them the daily schedule, when the students arrived, when they left, when they filled the playground for recess. The detective slowly wrote down a couple of notes before continuing.

"So you drove past the schools. Did you stop?"

"No."

Adrian knew this was a lie.

"You were convicted of false imprisonment—" Terri started, but the sex offender interrupted her.

"Look, I gave that girl a ride. That's all. I never touched her."

"A ride with your pants unzipped."

Wolfe scowled and didn't reply.

"Ever go to your doctor's house?"

This took the questioning in a direction that must have surprised the sex offender. He blurted out his response.

"No."

"You know where he lives?"

"No."

"Ever meet his family?"

"No. That's not a part of the therapy."

"Tell me what you talk about."

"He asks me about what I'm thinking and feeling when I see . . ." He stopped at that word, breathing in deeply. "He wants me to talk about everything that goes through my head. I tell him the truth. It's hard, but I'm learning to control myself. I don't need to . . ." Again he stopped.

Adrian was nearly mesmerized by the way Terri probed the sex offender without indicating what it was she was searching for. But when he heard Wolfe's last comment, something stirred in the back of his own imagination. He wasn't certain what it was, but he thought he'd heard something critical. He tried to remember his own studies, clinical moments in laboratories. *Stimulus,* he thought. A subject would have a normal series of responses to a situation, until an extra stimulus was bought into the equation. Then the ability to control emotions was changed and sometimes abandoned. In a movie theater, when the knife-wielding bad guy jumps out from the darkness, we scream. When a car skids out of control on a wet pavement, heart rate, glandular activity, brain waves all increase as we fight panic. *Out of control.* He wondered whether his wife had been frightened when she steered her car into the oak tree. *No,* he thought, *she was relieved because she was doing what she thought she wanted.* Adrian cocked his head, trying to listen for his wife's voice, but it wasn't there. Something was. He had the sensation that there was a hand on his shoulder, trying to get him to turn and see something. The feeling tightened, as if he were being gripped urgently. But instead he stared over at the exhibitionist. Place the ordinary reality of schoolchildren in front of him and it triggers fantasy. Other people see

219

children at play. Mark Wolfe saw objects of desire. Adrian suddenly wanted to hate instead of understand. Hate is much easier.

"Look, detective, I'm a lot better. Doctor West has really helped me. You maybe don't believe it but it's true. You can ask him."

Terri nodded. "I will. You understand that even driving by those schools with your therapist was a violation?"

"He said it wouldn't be. He said my parole officer approved it. And we didn't stop."

Terri nodded again. *She doesn't believe this,* Adrian realized. *And she's right not to.*

"All right, I'll check. We're finished here."

She closed her notebook, gestured to Adrian, but then stopped and abruptly demanded, "Who is Jennifer Riggins?"

Mark Wolfe looked confused.

"Who?"

"Jennifer Riggins. Where is she?"

"I don't know any—"

"If you lie to me, you will be going back to prison."

"I don't know that name. Never heard it."

Terri took out her notebook once again and wrote something down. "You know that it is a felony to lie to a police officer?"

"I'm telling you the truth. I don't know who you're talking about."

Adrian saw many things in the sex offender's face. *Remarkable,* he thought, *how he mixes truth and lies.*

"I think I will be back to speak with you again," Terri said. "You don't have any plans to leave, do you?"

This wasn't really a question. It was an order.

She turned to Adrian. "Okay, professor, we're finished here for tonight."

Adrian thought he'd had a hundred questions but he could not immediately think of any. He took a step forward and felt as if someone beside him were whispering in his ear. *Brian. It had to be.* He thought for a moment. *No. Maybe it was Tommy.*

"Do you have a computer?" he blurted out.

Terri stopped at the door. This was a good question, she thought. "Tell him, Mark. You have a computer?"

The sex offender nodded.

"What do you use a computer for?"

"Nothing. Like e-mails and getting sports scores."

"Who e-mails you?"

"I know some people. I've got some friends."

"Sure you do," Terri said. "I'll take it."

"You need a warrant."

"Do I?"

Wolfe hesitated.

"I'll get it. It's in my room."

"We'll go with you."

They followed Wolfe through the kitchen. He glared at his mother when the old woman asked, "Can I knit now? Who are your friends?"

He opened the door to his bedroom. Adrian saw some work clothes strewn about. A few tattered sex magazines, a couple of books, and a small desk with a laptop computer. Wolfe walked over and unplugged the machine. He handed it to Terri.

"When do I—"

"A day or two. What's your password?"

Wolfe hesitated.

"What's your password?" she asked again.

"*Candyman,*" he replied.

Terri took the machine. "Yeah," she said. "Making progress."

As she tucked the computer under her arm, Adrian thought, *He gave that up much too easily.*

It didn't make sense to him. Still, he rapidly turned and tried to take in as much as he could about what the room said of the man who occupied it. He wished he could read the titles of the books. He suspected there might be a drawer filled with DVDs as well. But the room had a stark, empty quality. A single bed, a chest of drawers, the desk, and a stiff wooden chair. Not much that said much.

Except, he guessed, maybe it did.

As he turned to leave, right behind the detective and the exhibitionist, he heard a whisper. *Substitute.*

The thought came so quickly that it almost slid through his mind like sand through his fingers.

He turned around but no one was there. He didn't understand the word, but it troubled him as he trailed the detective out the front door.

The old professor and the detective drove in silence.

She had placed the computer on the backseat, knowing it wasn't evidence and would probably be just wasted time when she searched through its files. The relationship between the offender and Scott West troubled her but she couldn't see past the strong possibility that it was mere coincidence. She knew there were lies in what Mark Wolfe had said to her, but her antennae hadn't picked up the sort of falsehood that might steer her in one direction or another. She drummed her fingers against the steering wheel as she drove through the darkness toward the old man's house.

He was singularly quiet.

"What's bothering you?" she asked abruptly.

He seemed to reel in whatever memories or thoughts he was processing before replying.

"Jennifer," he said softly. "What are the chances that we'll find her, detective?"

"Not good," she replied. "It's not as hard to disappear in our society as people think. Or make someone disappear."

Adrian seemed to think deeply. "Do you imagine there's something on that computer—" She cut him off.

"No."

He half turned in his seat, as if the answer needed expansion. She obliged.

"It will have some troubling things. Maybe some run-of-the-mill pornography. I wouldn't be surprised if there was some kiddie porn hidden in some file. Maybe something else that indicates that the good Doctor West isn't doing quite as good a job at therapy as he probably imagines he's doing. But something about Jennifer? What would the connection be? No. I don't think so. I'll look. But I'm not optimistic."

Adrian nodded slowly.

"I found the entire meeting to be provocative," he said. His voice was only barely above a whisper. "I've never spoken with a man like that before. It was enlightening."

"Did you hear anything that might help?" Terri asked this question more to be polite than because she thought he actually might have noticed something important.

"Is that what detectives do?" Adrian replied. "Do they process information so quickly?"

"Not like the classroom, professor. Sometimes there's not much time and one has to see answers pretty damn fast. In homicides they like to talk about the first forty-eight hours. In fact there's a damn television show called that. The window is smaller for some crimes, a little larger for others. But you need to see, if not answers, at least *where* you will find answers pretty damn fast."

Terri sighed. "We've already gone way past Jennifer's window."

Adrian seemed to consider this. "Jennifer needs more time," he said. "I hope she has it."

Terri realized that she didn't dislike the old man. She understood he was sincere in his efforts to help. Usually civilians managed only to clumsily get in the way of law enforcement. Too many folks had seen too much television and thought they actually knew something. *Obstacles, not help,* she thought. This was a part of her training and her experience. But then the old man seated beside her, who seemed to drift from acute observation to demanding insistence to a different planet, wasn't like most of the busybodies and do-gooders she was accustomed to.

She steered the car to a stop in front of his house.

"Door-to-door service," she said.

"Thank you," Adrian said as he exited. "Perhaps you will call me with any information you might acquire . . ."

"Professor, leave the police work to me. If there is something I think you can help with, I'll be in touch."

She thought the old man looked crestfallen.

Jennifer is gone, she thought, *and he blames himself.*

There is a distinction between the police—who find the deepest tragedies to be a part of their daily routine—and the people who feel they have been made special by the sudden engagement with a crime. It is so beyond their ordinary existence that it not only fascinates but can be obsessive. But to a cop like Terri it was nothing more than normal. Tragic, but normal.

Adrian stepped away from the car and watched as it disappeared down the road.

"She's a good cop," Brian said. "But she's limited. The super-clever, innately intuitive, quasi-intellectual detective is a trick of mystery writers. Cops are really straightforward problem solvers. Tic-tac-toe, not 'The Lady or the Tiger.'"

Adrian trudged toward the front door. "Was that you in the house?" he asked.

"Of course," Brian admitted. He sounded coy, as if inviting another question. Adrian turned to his dead brother. It was lawyer Brian, fiddling with his silk tie, working the tight crease in his two-thousand-dollar suit. Brian looked up. "You learned something."

"But the detective said—"

"Come on, Audie, from square one this hasn't been about finding someone culpable. At least, not yet. It's about finding where to look for Jennifer. The only way to do that is to imagine who took her. And why."

Adrian nodded. "Yes."

"And that sure as hell isn't the way a nice little college town detective thinks, even if she seems pretty competent."

This seemed true to Adrian. It was chilly. He wondered where the warmth of spring was hiding. The air seemed deceptive, as if it might promise one thing and deliver something different. Untrustworthy time of year, he thought.

"Audie!"

He turned back to Brian. "It's getting harder," he said. "It's like every hour, every day, a little more of me slips away."

"That's why we're here."

"I think I'm too sick."

"Hell, Audie," Brian laughed. "I'm *dead* and that's not slowing me down."

Adrian smiled.

"What did you see in the creep's house?"

"An old woman who suffers . . ." What did he *see*?

"I saw a man who acted compliant, as if he had nothing to hide, who probably wants to hide everything."

Brian grinned and clapped his brother on the back.

"What does that mean?"

"It means I missed something."

Brian put his hand to his forehead, right to the spot where he must have placed the barrel of the gun that Adrian now had inside on his bureau top. He made a shooting motion but didn't seem to think this was ironic.

"I think we both know what to do," Brian said.

Adrian scrunched down in his car seat, hoping that his prior visit hadn't made Mark Wolfe more alert to the idea that someone might be watching him. There were morning shadows carving out spots of shade where the rising sun was blocked by trees just starting to fill out with leaves. The world outside his window seemed to Adrian to be not quite naked, but not clothed either. Sometimes he thought the change in seasons had moments where some natural force was awaiting permission, a go-ahead, to gather momentum and turn the day from winter to spring.

He did not know how many changes he had left. Nor did he know how much longer he would be able to perceive them.

He shifted in his seat, to ask Brian, but his brother was no longer with him. He wondered why he couldn't conjure up his hallucinations when he needed them. It would be reassuring to have someone to speak with and he wished his brother's confident tones would help his own resolve.

He thought what he intended to do was borderline illegal. If it wasn't against the law, it ought to be. Immoral, as well, which his brother the big-time lawyer would be particularly helpful with. Lawyers were always more comfortable with moral shades of gray.

"Brian?"

Silence. He expected this.

He peered up over the lip of the doorsill. Mark Wolfe should be coming out soon, he told himself, as he shivered.

He thought about his brother. When they were little it had always surprised him that Brian was so fearless. If Adrian and his friends were doing anything—swimming, playing ball, making trouble—Brian was always tagging along, and first to volunteer for whatever mischief was in store. Adrian remembered a moment where they had been called on the carpet by their parents. After being admonished, Brian had been sent off to his room. He had been called out further. *You're supposed to watch out for your little brother* and *Adrian, how could you let him* . . . He had been unable to explain that even with their difference in age it was Brian who seemed to be the leader. *Backwards,* he thought. *Our growing up was backwards.* But then, he said out loud, "But that still doesn't tell me why you shot yourself."

Adrian thought that everything in his life was a mystery except his work. Why did Cassie love him? Why did Tommy die? What was wrong with Brian that he hadn't been able to see what he was going to do?

He thought his disease had one thing going for it. All these questions and all the sadness that had stalked him were going to disappear in a fog of loss. He breathed out. *I'm dead already,* he thought.

He heard a car door shut.

A quick glance and he saw Mark Wolfe pulling out of his driveway, just as he had the day before. The sex offender drove off.

Adrian looked down at his watch. It had been a gift from his wife on their twenty-fifth anniversary. Waterproof—although he rarely went into the water. Shockproof—although he never dropped it. A lifetime battery—*Well,* he said to himself, *pretty good chance it will still keep time after I'm gone.*

Adrian planned to wait fifteen minutes. The second hand was almost hypnotic as it swept relentlessly around the clock face.

When he was certain that Mark Wolfe had headed off to his job at the home store, Adrian exited his car and walked quickly up to the trim house.

He knocked on the door loudly, then pushed a doorbell buzzer.

When the door cracked open and the slightly vacant eyes of the mother peered around the edge, Adrian stepped up.

"Mark's not here," she said immediately.

"That's okay," Adrian replied. He pushed against the door insistently. "He told me to come and spend some time with you."

"He did?" Confusion. Adrian took advantage. He thought he knew the woman's disease better than he knew his own.

"Of course. We're old friends. You remember now, don't you?"

He didn't wait for an answer. He just pushed his way into the house and immediately went to the living room, standing almost in the same spot as he had the night before.

"I don't remember you," she said. "And Mark doesn't have many friends."

"We spoke before."

"When?"

"Yesterday. You remember."

"I don't . . ."

"And you said to come back because there was so much to talk about."

"I said to . . ."

"We were talking about so many things. Like your knitting. You wanted to show me your knitting."

"I like to knit things. I like to make mittens. I give them to the neighborhood children."

"I bet Mark takes them around for you."

"Yes. He does. He's a good boy."

"Of course he is. He's the best boy there could possibly be. He likes to make the kids happy."

"With mittens in the winter. But now . . ."

"It's spring. No more mittens. Not until next fall."

"I forget, how are you friends with Mark?"

"I wish you would make me mittens."

"Yes. I make mittens for the children."

"And Mark takes them around. What a good boy."

"Yes. He's a good boy. I forget your name."

"And he watches television with you."

"We have our shows. Mark likes special shows. We watch together all the funny shows, early, and we laugh, because they get into such trouble on all those shows. And then he makes me go to bed because he says his shows come on later."

"So he watches your shows with you, and then he watches his shows on the nice big television."

"He got that for us. It's like having real people here visiting. Not many friends come over."

"But I'm your friend and I came."

"Yes. You look old like me."

"I am. But we're friends now, aren't we?"

"Yes. I suppose."

"What are his shows like?"

"He won't let me watch."

"But sometimes you can't sleep, isn't that right. And you come down here."

She smiled. "His shows are . . ." She laughed out loud. "I shouldn't say the words."

She had a coy, childish look on her face. Adrian watched her bounce between old and sick and childlike. He knew he had learned something, and he was struggling inwardly to sort it out himself. He could feel his wife, his son, his brother, all surrounding him, there but not there, trying to tell him what it was, tugging at his ability to perceive. He looked over at the woman. *Two crazed people,* he thought. *I can understand her but she can't understand me.*

Adrian thought it was all a foreign language and this made him think of Tommy, who died in a place that was so distant he could barely think of it in anything other than images coming across a screen. And this made him turn toward the big-screen television set and recall something that the woman had said and something that he remembered his son had told him, except it wasn't really his son but his son's ghost.

Knitting, he thought. *She knits.*

"Where is *your* computer?" he asked. "Do you keep it with the knitting?"

The woman smiled. "Of course." She went over and grabbed the bag with yarns and swatches of material that was next to the recliner, just where Adrian had seen it the night before. She brought it over to him. Beneath a skein of pink and red yarn was a small Apple laptop. There were computer wires attached.

He looked over at the television. *He runs the computer through that big television screen after his mother has been sent to bed.*

"I'm going to take this to Mark," he said. "He needs it at work."

"He leaves it here," she said. "He always leaves it here."

"Yes, but the policewoman who came will want it, so he should take it to her from his work. That's what he wanted."

Adrian knew all his lies would work, even if the old woman seemed reluctant. It was perverse. The childhood phrase *taking candy from a baby* leaped into his mind.

He took the computer and started toward the door.

It will be protected.

Password? Mark Wolfe hadn't struck Adrian as stupid. And he remembered the contemptuous look that Detective Collins had on her face when she'd taken the computer that the sex offender had offered up so easily. *Candyman.* How obvious, he thought. A password so pregnant with associations that anyone examining the machine would have to believe it would lead to incriminating evidence, when all it traveled was some innocent dark and dead end.

The computer in his hands—the mother's computer—that was the one. He looked over at the gray-haired, wild-eyed woman.

"Did Mark ever have a pet, growing up . . ."

"We had a dog named Butchie."

Adrian smiled. *Butchie. That was one possibility.*

"Mark had to put him down. Butchie liked to hunt things and he bit people."

So does your son.

The old woman suddenly looked as if she was going to cry. Adrian thought for a moment, and then he carefully asked another question. "And what was the name of the neighbor's daughter, you remember, the one that lived next door, or was it just down the street when Mark was a teenager?"

The old woman's face changed in an instant. She scowled. "This is like a memory game, isn't it? I can't remember very many things anymore and I forget stuff . . ."

"But that girl, you remember her, don't you?"

"I didn't like her."

"Her name was . . ."

"Sandy."

"She was the one that got Mark into trouble for the first time, right?"

The woman nodded.

Sandy.

Adrian started toward the door once more, the computer under his arm, but he paused as he reached for the handle and asked, "What's your name?"

She smiled. "I'm Rose."

"Like the beautiful flower?"

"I used to have the reddest cheeks when I was young and married to . . ."

She stopped. She put her hand to her mouth.

"Where did he go?"

"He left us. I don't remember. It was bad. We were alone and it was hard. But now Mark takes care of me. He's a good boy."

"Yes. He is. Who left you?"

"Ralph," she said. "Ralph left us. I was always Ralph's Rose and he said I would be in bloom forever, but he left and I don't bloom no more."

Ralphsrose, Adrian thought. *Maybe.*

"This has been so much fun, Rose. I'll come back and we can talk about knitting again. Maybe you will knit me those mittens."

"That would be nice," she said.

26

Jennifer was singing softly to Mister Brown Fur when the door opened. It was not a specific song as much as she was blending together every lullaby and children's ditty she could remember, so that "Row, Row, Row Your Boat" and "Itsy Bitsy Spider" joined with "The Bear Went Over the Mountain" and "I'm a Little Teapot." She mixed in the occasional Christmas carol, as well. Any lyric, any verse, any thread of music she could recall was hummed and sung quietly. She stayed away from rap and rock and roll because she couldn't imagine how they would comfort her. She caught her breath when the sound of the door interrupted her, but just as swiftly she kept going, raising her voice, increasing volume. "God rest ye merry gentlemen, let nothing you dismay, remember Christ our Savior was born on Christmas day . . ."

"Number Four, please pay attention."

"Oh, the bear went over the mountain, the bear went over the mountain, the bear went over—"

"Number Four, stop singing now, or I will hurt you."

It was the woman speaking in a monotone. Jennifer had no doubt that the threat was sincere.

She ceased.

"Good," the woman said.

Jennifer wanted to smile. *Small rebellions,* she told herself. *Do what they want but.*

"Pay attention," the woman said.

I know where you are, Jennifer thought. She didn't know why this was important to her, but she knew it was.

The few seconds that she had peeked beneath her blindfold had done much for her sense of strength. It had orientated her in the room. She knew about the video camera pointed in her direction. She had taken in the stark white walls, the gray color of the floor. She had quickly measured the size of her space and, most critically, she had seen her clothes stacked near the doorway. They were all folded neatly, placed next to her back-pack, as if they had been laundered and were waiting for her. It was not the same as actually being dressed, but the mere possibility of climbing back into her jeans and a sweatshirt had given her a sense of hope.

The camera had given her plenty to think about.

She could sense its unerring eye, watching her.

Jennifer understood it meant there was no privacy.

At first, it had reddened her face, and she felt a wave of violation com-ing over her. But, nearly as swiftly, she had understood that whoever was watching wasn't really watching *her* as much as they were watching *a pris-oner.* She was still anonymous. She was still hidden. Maybe her body had been exposed but not Jennifer. It was as if there was a distinction between who she was and what she did. The two were separate. Actions were being carried out by some Jennifer look-alike called Number 4, while the *real* Jennifer clutched her bear and sang songs and tried to figure out what she was trapped inside. She knew she had to work hard to protect *Real Jennifer* while making *Fake Jennifer* seem real to the man and the woman. Her jailers.

And there was one other thing she managed to understand about the camera. It meant that she was needed. Whatever drama was being played out she was the main actor.

She did not know how long this necessity would keep her alive. But it meant she had some time and she was determined to use it.

"Number Four, I am going to place a chair at the end of the bed. You are to make your way to it and sit down."

Jennifer swung her feet over the bed. She stood. Then she stretched, lifting one leg up, then the other, flexing her muscles. She rose up on her tiptoes and lowered herself several times in quick succession. Then she twisted one arm behind her back, stretching her torso. She repeated this movement with the other arm. She could feel her muscles contracting, then releasing, and stiffness exiting from her bones.

"It is not exercise time, Number Four. Please do as I say without delay."

Jennifer rolled her head, loosening her neck, then carefully walked to the foot of the bed, keeping a hand against the frame to steady herself. She reached out and felt the wooden back of a chair and maneuvered into it. She sat primly, hands folded on her lap, her knees pressed together, a little like a mischievous schoolgirl in a catechism class, afraid of the teacher nun.

She could sense the woman moving closer to her. She half turned in her direction, awaiting further orders.

The blow was unexpected and savage.

An open hand, delivered across her cheek, nearly knocking her to the floor. The shock was as painful as the blow. Behind her blindfold she could see stars and her face screamed out in pain, as if nerve ends all over her body had been subjected to an electric current. Dizziness mixed with pain in a concoction that made her head spin. She gasped for air. She knew she made some animal-like whimper noise of hurt, but she couldn't tell whether it had echoed in the room or only inside of her head. She gripped the chair seat, trying to steady herself, knowing, although not knowing *why,* that if she fell she would be kicked and hurt even more.

She wanted to say something but no words made it past her lips, only choking sobs.

"Are we a little clearer about things now, Number Four?" the woman asked.

Jennifer nodded.

"When I give you an order, you are to comply. I believe we had made this clear to you before."

"Yes. I was trying . . . I didn't realize . . ."

"Stop whining."

She stopped.

"Good. I have some questions for you. You will answer them carefully. Do not volunteer more information than is asked for. I want you to keep your head steady and looking straight forward."

Jennifer nodded. She sensed the woman leaning forward, closer to her, and she heard a whisper that echoed a hiss. "The answer to the first question is *eighteen*," she said.

Behind the mask, Jennifer blinked, as if surprised. She understood *that was for me only.*

She could hear the crinkling sound of the woman's outfit as she moved backward, maneuvering a small distance away. There was a pause, and Jennifer fixed herself, robot-like, back into the schoolgirl's position and stared straight ahead, even if she was looking into the blackness of the blindfold.

"Good. Number Four, tell us how old you are."

Jennifer hesitated then blurted out: "I'm eighteen."

A lie, she thought, that saved her from some pain. The woman continued.

"Do you know where you are?"

"No."

"Do you know why you're here?"

"No."

"Do you know what will happen to you?"

"No."

"Do you know what day it is? Or perhaps, the date, the time, or even if it is day or night?"

She shook her head, and then stopped herself. "No," she said. This time her voice cracked slightly as if the word *no* was expensive porcelain and would shatter at the smallest slip.

"How long have you been here, Number Four?"

"I don't know."

"Are you frightened, Number Four?"

"Yes."

"Are you afraid of dying, Number Four?"

"Yes."

"You want to live?"

"Yes."

"What will you do in order to survive?"

Jennifer hesitated. There was only one answer available.

"Anything."

"Good."

The woman's voice was coming from a few feet away. Jennifer suspected that she had moved behind the camera, so that her answers went directly into the lens. She felt a small surge in confidence. *I'm being filmed.* The ability to comprehend, even if only slightly, what was happening to her helped. She felt her muscles tense. *They don't know how strong I can be,* she told herself. Then doubt crept into her imagination. *I don't know how strong I can be.* She wanted to cry, give in to sobs and despair. Or else fight back, but she did not know how. She was trapped between two poles, as the woman's questions followed relentlessly.

"Stand up, Number Four."

She did as she was told.

"Pull down your underwear."

She could not help herself; hesitation crept into her hands. But Jennifer sensed the woman's fist curling, getting ready to smash her again. She did as she was told. She told herself it was like going to the doctor's office, or being in a locker room after a sweaty workout. There was no shame in her nakedness. But behind her blindfold even she knew this was a lie. She could feel the camera probing her and she was humiliated. Tears were close when the woman said, "You may return to your seat." She grabbed at her flimsy panties and tugged them into place and sat down. It was as if something had been cut away from her. It was worse than when the man had forced her to bathe naked. This had been an inspection. A meat inspection.

"Before you came to this room, what was your greatest fear?"

She needed to think. Her mind was crowded with embarrassment.

"Greatest fear, Number Four?" The woman's voice was insistent.

Jennifer struggled to come up with a reply.

"Spiders. I hate spiders. When I was little a spider bit me and my face swelled up and ever since then—"

"That is some *thing* you fear, Number Four. But what is your greatest fear?"

Jennifer hesitated.

"Sometimes I would get scared that I would be trapped in a room filled with spiders."

"I can make that happen, Number Four"

Jennifer shivered involuntarily. She knew the woman could. She imagined that she had only scratched the possibilities of the woman's cruelties. And she expected the man's to be worse.

"But what is your greatest fear, Number Four?"

The same question hammered her. She wondered, *What was wrong with my answer?*

A word or two caught in her throat and she coughed. She had another idea.

"That I would never get out of the little town I lived in and that I would be stuck there forever."

The woman paused. Jennifer thought that maybe she'd taken the woman by surprise with her answer.

"So, Number Four, you hated your home?"

Jennifer's head bobbed up and down as she replied.

"Yes."

"What did you hate?"

"Everything."

Again the woman spoke carefully. Her voice hammered at Jennifer. The steady beat of the questions felt like blows raining down on her heart.

"And so you wanted to escape, correct?"

"Yes."

"Do you still want to escape, Number Four?"

Jennifer felt sobs crushing her chest. She wasn't sure whether the woman meant escape from her home or escape from her cell. This indecision hurt.

"I just want to live," she said. Her voice quavered.

The woman paused before continuing. The questions were relentless.

"What have you loved in your life, Number Four?"

She was flooded with childhood memories. She could see her dead father standing in the midst of her blindfold darkness, except now he was alive and wearing a familiar grin that lit up his face and beckoned for her to come to him. She could remember parties and playgrounds. She could recall moments that were ordinary, picnics and a family trip to Fenway Park for a summer afternoon's ball game and hot dogs. Once during a school excursion to a nearby farm she had crawled into an enclosure where newborn puppies were being nursed by their mother, and she had marveled at the tiny energy and softness of life. She could see a picture of herself and her mother, whom she truly believed she no longer had a reason to love, swimming in a river in a state park, where a little waterfall cascaded cold water over their heads and the two of them had battled the goose bumps because it felt so wonderful. All these images accelerated around her, like being caught in a fast action movie inside the darkness. She breathed in sharply. All these thoughts belonged to her and she knew she had to protect them.

"Nothing," she said.

The woman laughed.

"Everyone loves something, Number Four. I repeat. What have you loved?"

Jennifer felt ideas rushing toward her. All sorts of images jumbling together. A torrent of memories. She had to fight them off, keep them hidden. She hesitated before speaking briskly.

"I had a cat . . . actually, I found a stray kitten. It was wet and scrawny and lost. I was allowed to keep it. I named it Socks because it had white paws. I fed it milk and it would sleep on my bed every night. For years she was my best friend."

"What happened to Socks, Number Four?"

"When she was seven she got sick. The vet couldn't save her. She died and I helped bury her. We dug a hole in a garden and put her into it. I cried for days afterward, and my parents offered to get me a new kitten but I didn't want something new, I wanted the one I'd had who died." She hesitated then briskly added, "There. That's something I loved."

"Touching, Number Four."

Jennifer was about to say *you asked* but she didn't want to be hit again. She steeled herself to hide a derisive grin but indulged in an inner sarcastic glee. The story of Socks was a complete and total lie.

No cat, you bitch. No dead cat at all. Fuck you.

"One last question, Number Four."

Jennifer did not move. She waited.

"Are you a virgin, Number Four?"

She could feel thickness in her tongue, a sour taste on her lips. They were dry and she licked them several times. She did not know what the right answer was. The truth was *Yes* but was that a good or bad reply? She could feel fear creeping into her. The vague implication about sex was stifling. *They want to rape me,* she thought.

"Are you a virgin, Number Four?"

If she replied *No* was that some sort of invitation? If she indicated she had had sex before, was that like giving them permission? Was her naivete a good thing or a bad thing?

She hated making a decision. She didn't know what was right.

"Yes," she said. Her voice cracked slightly.

The woman laughed.

"You may return to the bed," she said. Her voice was tinged with mockery.

27

At more or less the same time in different locations, Adrian and Terri were both staring at computers that belonged to the same person, but they had reached opposite conclusions.

One saw dead ends.

The other saw infinite possibilities.

What Terri discovered on the machine centered on her office desk was very much what she had expected. Some low-rent pornography—nothing that surprised her with exceptional exoticism or dark edginess—and a selection of mostly boring excursions to sports websites, medical chat rooms discussing Alzheimer's, an offshore betting site, and a predictable number of online video games such as Full Tilt Poker and World of War. There was, in her estimation, nothing on the computer that even suggested that Mark Wolfe was reengaging in the sort of activities that had gotten him arrested. Nor was there anything that overtly indicated he might be moving up the sexual predator food chain. The computer seemed to her to contain nothing relevant to the missing Jennifer. And even if she cringed a little at the pornography she found, she guessed that it wasn't anything different from what she would find on the home computers of half the policemen in her department.

She was ready to file Mark Wolfe and his connection to the soon to be stepfather of a missing girl under the category of wasted time. Indeed, the entire electronic search for Jennifer was pretty much stalled, in her mind, despite the eagerness of the old man. She knew she had to follow up on the credit card that had been returned in Maine, which might lead her somewhere, but she had her doubts.

Terri closed up the computer and breathed out slowly. The pain of it was she would have to return the damn thing to Wolfe. She reached for her telephone and called the home store where he worked.

"Mark Wolfe, please," she told the receptionist who answered. "This is Detective Collins calling about an ongoing sex abuse case."

Making Mark Wolfe squirm was one of her priorities. She doubted that anyone where he worked knew his background and she wondered how long it would take for the receptionist to mention at some coffee break that a police detective had called for one of the salesmen. This would lead to speculation. And speculation would lead to some nasty details being circulated around the workplace. The trouble she was making for him didn't bother her in the slightest. She understood that this wasn't a very enlightened or forgiving attitude but she didn't care.

When Wolfe came on the line she was blunt.

"You can come around to my office and pick up your computer," she said. "I'll be here until six p.m."

He merely grunted in reply.

She had some time before he would show so she shoved the computer aside roughly and picked up the credit card report. She dialed the number for the bank in Waterville, Maine.

A computer, Adrian thought, is like a funhouse mirror. It reflects much about who someone really is, when one sees past the contortions and blurred shapes.

The puzzle lay in finding the keys to open it up.

Wolfe's mother had given him some of the right words to open up encrypted files when Adrian had played around with combinations. *Roses-knitting* had opened one door that contained a portfolio of photographs of young women—all in various states of undress—posed provocatively. The first notion that leaped to his head was *kiddie porn*—but he recognized that wasn't quite accurate. The pictures were provocative and filled with the enticements of fantasy. They made Adrian uncomfortable, until he forced himself to inspect them closely, and he realized they were only *suggestions* of slightly older than children. The models in picture after picture were shaved and coy, selected for their immature bodies and childlike faces. But they only *looked* young. In Adrian's mind, they were probably all within days, or weeks, of the eighteen years they needed to avoid being classified as illegal child pornography. As he flipped through them, the pictures increased in intensity. There were shots of teenage boys coupling with the models, joined by pictures of significantly older men, middle-aged and beyond, doing the same. Lechery trumped, he thought.

The *Rosesknitting* files were unsettling but, he knew, not the sort of download that would be flagged on some Interpol computer, or even draw the attention of the local police. He found a link to sites called Barely 18 and Just Old Enough. He didn't bother to examine these.

There were other files, which he had trouble opening, that made him wish he had a younger person's expertise with the machine. He tried a series of variations with the word *Sandy*. He guessed that the only reason that name had penetrated the fog of the mother's disease was because it had been in use in the house. He knew some concoction with that word would open up something in the computer. But every combination he tried was rejected.

Past becomes present, influences the future, Adrian knew. This was something of a mantra for psychologists. Things, events, people, experiences scored into memory affect steps taken in the present and dreams about the days ahead. Mark Wolfe, sex offender, was no different from anyone, except that his damage was more virulent and had created someone with potential. Where it had come from was a mystery. Where it currently resided was clear from the computer screen. Where it would take him was uncertain.

He typed in the password *KillSandy* and images immediately leaped onto the screen.

He stared at a picture of a young girl bending to accept an old man's erection with her lips. The images made him feel as if he needed to wash his hands and get himself a glass of ice water.

Adrian started to push away from the seat at his desk. He thought he should find a book of poetry, read some subtle, rhymed verse, something that had a pristine and honorable quality to it. Perhaps some Shakespearean sonnets, he suggested inwardly, or Byron. Lines that spoke of love in a silken, pure fashion, images that created passion—not pictures of hairy men forcing their engorged energies on women that were closer to girls.

He shifted about in his seat but stopped when he heard his son whisper into his ear, "But Dad, you haven't looked hard enough. Not yet."

Adrian turned around quickly, his arms spread, as if he could embrace his son's ghost and press him to his chest, but he was alone in the room. Tommy's voice, however, seemed to be right at his side.

"What is it you are seeing?" his son asked him. Tommy had a musical tone in his words. It was like listening to a nine-year-old Tommy, not the adult Tommy. Adrian remembered when his son was young there was nothing he liked more than hearing him call out. It was like an invitation for the father to share something with the son, and it had a precious, jewel-like quality.

"Tommy, where are you?"

"I'm right here. I'm right beside you."

It was like hearing a voice penetrate thick fog. Adrian desperately wanted to be able to reach through the clouds and touch his son. *Just one more time,* he thought. *That's all. Just once. A single hug.*

"Dad! Pay attention! What is it you are seeing?"

"It's just some disgusting pornography," Adrian replied. He felt a little embarrassed that his son was looking at the same things he was.

243

"No, it's more than that. Much more."

Adrian must have looked confused, because he could hear his son sighing. It was like a breath of wind blowing through the stillness of the house.

"Come on, Dad, connect who you are with what you are seeing."

This made no sense to Adrian. He was a scientist. He was a student of experience. That was what he had taught for so many decades. On the screen in front of him were contorted bodies. Nakedness. Explicitness. All the mystery removed from love, acts boiled down into hard-core, no doubts reality.

"Tommy, I'm sorry, I don't understand. It's so much harder now. Things don't match up the way they should."

"Fight it, Dad. Make yourself stronger. Take more of those pills. Maybe they'll help. Force your mind to remember things."

Tommy's voice seemed to change, back and forth. Child Tommy. Adult Tommy. Adrian felt buffeted between the two.

"I'm trying."

There was a momentary hesitation, as if Tommy was thinking about something. Adrian wanted to be able to see him, and his eyes began to cloud up with tears. *It isn't fair,* he thought. *I can see the others, but now it's Tommy and he won't show himself.* It was a little like the great conundrum all parents know, that one day they look at the child they raised and he or she has grown up and entered into a world of their own that seems alien and incomprehensible. *The people we love the most become strangers to us,* he thought.

"Dad, when you read a poem . . ."

Adrian spun about in his seat, as if he could catch a glimpse of his child by darting his eyes about the room.

"What is it you are trying to see in the words?"

He sighed. Tommy's voice was faded and distant and it hurt to listen to it. He could feel pinpricks on his skin.

"I wanted to be there for you. I can't stand it that you died somewhere on the other side of the world and I wasn't there for you. I can't stand it that I couldn't do anything about it. I can't stand it that I couldn't save you."

"The poetry, Dad. Think of the poems."

He sighed again. He looked over at a picture of Tommy that he kept above his desk. High school graduation. A snapshot stolen when his son hadn't been watching. He was grinning, filled with everything that was possible about the world and none of the heartache or trouble that was an inevitable part of it. Adrian almost thought as if the picture were speaking to him, except that Tommy's voice was insistent and coming from behind his head.

"What do you see in the poems?"

"Words. Rhymes. Imagery. Metaphor. Art that evokes ideas. Seduction. I don't know, Tommy, what is it . . ."

"Think, Dad. How can a poem help you find Jennifer?"

"I don't know. Can it?"

"Why not?"

Adrian thought everything was reversed. Tommy had been their only child, and it had been Adrian who protected him and encouraged him and steered him along, and now it was like he was the child and Tommy knew things that he didn't. Except, he understood, it was he himself that knew things, but they were hard to reach, so Tommy was there to guide him even though his son was dead.

He wondered for a moment, *Are the dead always there to help us?*

"What do you see?"

He turned back to the computer.

"Just pictures."

"No, Dad. It's not really about the image. Just like in a poem, it's about how the image is perceived."

Adrian breathed in sharply. He remembered this phrase. For years he had taught a popular course at the university, Fear and its Uses in Modern Society, that not only examined the nature of fright physiologically but also then branched into horror films and scary novels and the way fear was a part of popular culture. It was a spring semester senior- and graduate-level course, very popular with students who had spent too many evenings hunched over white mice in laboratories and who were overjoyed to be

245

seated listening to Adrian opine about *Jaws* and *Friday the 13th* and Peter Straub's *Ghost Story*. This was the phrase that he concluded his final lecture with.

"Yes, Tommy, I know, but—"

"Jennifer, Dad."

"Yes. Jennifer. But how does this—"

"Dad, think hard. Focus."

Adrian grabbed a yellow legal pad from a corner of his desk. He seized a pen and wrote:

Jennifer runs away from home.
Jennifer is snatched from the street by strangers.
Jennifer disappears.
Jennifer is not ransomed.
Jennifer is lost.

It was like a poem on a page. "The Missing Jennifer."

Adrian looked at the naked figures on the screen. The models weren't coupling because they loved each other or because they desired each other or even because they wanted pleasure.

Money. Or exhibitionism. Or both.

"But they didn't ask for ransom, Dad, did they?"

Tommy's voice had dropped to a whisper. It seemed to be echoing somewhere inside his head.

"But how can someone make money off of . . ." Adrian stopped. The entire world made money off of sex.

"Connect, Dad. *Connect.*" Tommy was pleading with him.

He felt stupid. He felt uneducated and caught in some sort of brain mire.

"How do I . . ." He stared, then he hesitated as Tommy interrupted him.

"You know who can tell you," Tommy said. "But he won't tell you what you need to know easily. Take help. Take persuasion."

Adrian nodded. He closed up the computer and placed it in a satchel. He found his coat and tugged it on. He looked down at his wristwatch and checked the time. It read 6:30. He did not know whether this was morning or evening. He did not know how he knew this, but he was certain that Tommy would not accompany him. *Maybe Brian,* he thought. He looked around for Cassie, because he could use a word of support and encouragement. *They were both braver than I ever was,* he thought. *My wife. My son.* But Tommy's voice seemed to have faded away and she was absent, although in the next instant he could feel her, as if Cassie were right in front, pulling him along. "I'm coming, I'm coming," he said, as if she were impatient. He remembered that when they were young, sometimes he would be working, engrossed in some psychological study, or a piece of scientific writing, or trying to construct one of his poems, and she would come into the room where he was and wordlessly take him by the hand and, with a small nod and a laugh, lead him to the bed to make really abandoned love. But this time there was some other, far more pressing need waiting in the upstairs bedroom for him and he could feel her dragging him insistently in that direction.

It was dark and he could hear the voices raised in anger right through the door. The shouting seemed to come mostly from Mark Wolfe, with his mother wailing pathetically in response. He listened intently for a few minutes, standing outside, letting the night chill creep inside his skin. The door muffled just enough of the rage so that he could recognize only the intensity of the argument, not the subject, although he guessed it had something to do with the computer in his satchel.

Adrian wondered if he should wait for a lull, and then he simply knocked on the door.

Immediately the shouts stopped.

He knocked again and took a single step back. He expected the anger to buffet him like a wave against the beach when the door opened. He heard a lock being unfastened and light poured over him as the door swung wide.

There was a moment's silence.

"Son of a bitch," Mark Wolfe said.

Adrian nodded. "I have something of yours," he said.

"No shit. Give it here."

Mark Wolfe reached for him, as if by seizing Adrian's coat he could repossess the computer.

He did not know who was shouting instructions in his ear—*Brian? Tommy?*—but he lurched back, avoiding the sex offender's reach, and suddenly he realized he had his brother's 9mm automatic in his hand, and it was pointing directly at Wolfe.

"I have questions," Adrian said.

Wolfe recoiled. He eyed the weapon. The presence of the 9mm seemed to throw a blanket of calm over his rage.

"I bet you don't even know how to use that," he choked out.

"It would be unwise for you to test that theory," Adrian replied pedantically. He was shocked at the ice that each word contained. He thought he should be scared, nervous, maybe crippled by his condition, but he seemed oddly focused. It wasn't an altogether unpleasant sensation.

The gun had Wolfe's full attention. He seemed to be caught between diving back out of the line of fire and leaping forward and trying to wrestle it away. He was frozen like a freeze-frame picture.

Adrian lifted the weapon slightly, pointing it at Wolfe's face.

"You're not a cop. You're a professor, for Christ's sake. You can't threaten me."

Adrian nodded. He felt wondrously cool.

"If I shot you, do you think *anyone* would care?" he asked. "I'm old. Maybe a little crazy. Whatever happens to me would be irrelevant. But your mother . . . well, *she* needs you, doesn't she? And you, Mister Wolfe, you are still young. Do you think this particular moment is one worth dying over? You don't even know what it is I want."

Wolfe hesitated. Adrian wondered whether the sex offender had ever actually stared at a weapon before. He thought he had entered into a strange, parallel world, one that seemed alien to the rarefied air of the academic world he knew. This was something far more real. The sensation should have been offensive and terrifying but it wasn't. He thought he could feel his brother close by.

"You came here and stole my mother's computer."

Adrian didn't say anything.

"What sort of freak are you? She's sick. You can tell. She's not in control of her . . ."

He stopped. He snarled like an injured dog.

"I want it back. You have no right to take my mother's computer."

"Whose computer?"

Adrian used the barrel of the gun to point down at the satchel. "Maybe I should take it to Detective Collins. I can do that. I know she has more expertise in these things than I do. I'm damn certain that she will find out what you've been using it for. She'll be real interested in the *Rosesknitting* and the *KillSandy* files, won't she? So, really, it's your choice. What should I do?"

Wolfe stood in the doorway, teetering with the urge to attack. Adrian could see his face contort. He thought that men who lived secret lives hidden from everyday run-of-the-mill, routine existence hated to open any window that might expose who they really were and what they really wanted. All those perverse thoughts cascading around inside, concealed from the authorities, from friends, from family. He sensed that Mark Wolfe was on that edge of anger. Adrian saw him swallow, his face still locked in fury, but his voice now under control.

"All right. It's mine. It's private."

Wolfe spat out each word.

"You can have it," Adrian said. "But first I want something from you."

"What's that?" the sex offender grunted reluctantly.

"An education," Adrian replied.

28

The baby started crying again. Piteously. Much louder than before.

Jennifer was pulled from a half sleep by the sound penetrating the walls. She did not know how long she had drowsed off—it might have been twelve minutes, it might have been twelve hours. The constant darkness defined by the blindfold had ruined her sense of time. She was constantly disoriented. It was like the waking moments when some particularly vivid and troubling dream clings to consciousness. She twitched, alert to the sound.

Then she did something she had not done before. She clutched Mister Brown Fur tightly and swung her feet from the bed, like anyone would upon waking up in the morning. Still linked by chain to wall, she began to move about, as if by taking a step in one direction or the other she could narrow the range of distance and gauge where the baby's cries were coming from.

She thought she must appear on the camera to be animal-like, trying to form a mental picture of threat just by sniffing the air. She was acutely aware that she had only a few of her senses available, and she told herself to use what she had as best she could.

The cries increased in volume. And then, just as quickly, they ended, as if whatever sadness had prompted them was eradicated. She hovered, still chained to the wall, but in the empty space between the toilet and the void, her head still cocked to where she *thought* the cries had come from, she was suddenly aware of a new sound, something very different.

It was *laughter*.

More than that, it was children laughing.

She stopped, trying to hold her breath. The sounds of play seemed to fade in and fade out, as if they took steps closer to her and then ran away. She recalled times when she was detained in an elementary school classroom for some transgression, punished while the remainder of the class had been shuffled off to the playground, and their play sounds trickled through an open window, too high for her to see out of but loud enough so that she could picture the other children at play. Kickball. Freeze tag. Jump rope. Hanging from the bars of the jungle gym. All the rapid-fire games that filled recess.

Jennifer was enveloped by confusion; she *knew* she was in the anonymous basement but suddenly it seemed as if she were also trapped in a school that existed only in her past.

She told herself, *It can't be real.* But as she listened the sounds seemed so accurate that she was unsure.

The playground noises were so close she thought she could touch them. The sounds of play beckoned to her, inviting her to join in.

She tentatively reached out her free hand.

She told herself that if she could seize a sound from the air, then she could put it in the palm of her hand, stroke it, manipulate it, and somehow come to be a part of it.

It was wrong to imagine that sound could transport her away. But it was tempting and possible. She stretched her hand forward, fingers extended in hope.

She knew she was reaching into nothingness, just the stale air of the basement, but she could not help herself. The sound was so *close*.

Where she had expected nothing—sensation.

Beneath her fingertips, a smooth, papery feel.

Jennifer gasped, pulled her hand back. It was like touching a live wire. *Someone's here!* raced through her consciousness.

She heard a low, harsh whisper. It came from the darkness like heat lightning bolting across a hot summer sky.

"You are never alone."

Then there was an explosion in the black of her vision, red pain and sudden shock, as the woman punched her hard in the jaw. Jennifer staggered back, tumbling onto the bed. She almost dropped Mister Brown Fur as her head spun dizzily. The blow stunned her; it seemed so sudden, it was worse than the moment when the man had smashed her face as he seized her from her street, because this had a completely different type of unexpectedness. It was filled with contempt. It stung.

Jennifer curled into a fetal position on the bed. She could taste the salt of tears and a little blood dripped from her lip.

The room had turned electric hot.

"That is the second time you have forced me to hit you, Number Four. Do not force me again. I can do far worse."

The woman's voice continued in the droning monotone that Jennifer had come to expect. She didn't understand this. If the woman was angry her voice would have been high-pitched. If she was frustrated it would have reflected that in tone. Jennifer could not understand how she could sound so calm in a situation that seemed to defy normalcy.

Jennifer gasped. *It's what a killer sounds like.*

She waited, half expecting another blow, but it did not come. Instead she heard the door close with a thud.

She stayed in position, listening, trying to separate sounds, although her racing heart and buzzing head nearly obscured everything. Her whimpering sobs cluttered her hearing. It took an immense force of strength— she could feel the muscles in her stomach and in her legs tighten—to stop the demands of despair. The woman, she thought, either closed the door on her way out or maybe just closed it and was still standing right by the bed, hand drawn back, readying another strike.

Jennifer choked in the stale air.

She could sense different parts of her screaming for attention. The hurt part. The scared part. The despairing part. And, finally, the *fight it* part. This last managed to quiet the others, and Jennifer felt her pulse slow down. Her chin still seemed blistered but the pain faded.

The clothing she wears crinkles when she moves, Jennifer reminded herself. *Her feet make scuffling noises on the cement floor. She always takes a deep breath before she speaks, especially when she whispers.*

Jennifer slowly, surely, eliminated all of her sounds and listened only for the woman's.

Silence overwhelmed her. She was alone despite what the woman said. Despite the camera she knew was watching her.

The happy playground laughter in the background disappeared. There was a momentary quiet and she heard the baby in the distance cry once more, then abruptly stop.

The Tokyo businessman drank warm and weak scotch that had been watered down long before the ice cubes in the glass melted. The bottle it had been poured from was expensive, but he doubted the liquor was anything but a replacement, a cheap local brand, and he curled his lip in disgust. He had an iPhone in one hand and the drink in the other and he sat on an outdoor veranda in a wicker chair that dug into his naked skin. The Thai sex worker was poised diligently between his legs, administering to him with overly faked enthusiasm, as if nothing on earth could possibly be more erotic than satisfying him. He hated every false groan and moan she made. He hated the sweat that glistened on his chest. He did not know the girl's name, nor did he care to know. He would have been bored by her touch, had it not been for the images that he watched on the telephone screen.

The businessman was middle-aged, and he had a daughter back home with his dowdy wife. His daughter was about the same age as both the Thai girl plying him with her tongue and Number 4, but he did not think of his own child other than to continually remind himself to bring her back a present from his trip. Something colorful and silk, he told himself. He cleared his mind and stared at the small iPhone screen. Instead of the Thai sex worker, he allowed the eroticism of Series #4 to stimulate him. The sudden punch to Number 4's face had titillated him. It had been unexpected and dramatic and taken him by surprise. He shifted about in his seat and looked over the screen down at the raven-colored hair of the Thai girl. He joined the two in his mind—the sex worker and Number 4. He could feel his own hand clench tightly into a fist, as he contemplated striking the girl just to see what it felt like. Notions of pain and pleasure jumbled together in his head, and he reached out and wrapped his fingers through her hair. He wanted to twist it so she would cry out. But he stopped himself. Number 4, he realized, had barely made a noise when she was hit. Other moments that he had seen, Number 4 had cried and sometimes shouted and even once had screamed, but this time, when she was struck, she had fallen backward but maintained a stoic silence.

Her discipline was something to deeply admire.

He leaned back in the seat and closed his eyes. For a moment he tried to imagine that the Thai girl had vanished and that it was Number 4 busy between his legs.

He breathed out. He felt stirring throughout his body and he gave in to the conjoined fantasies with a newfound enthusiasm.

Linda was put out. Her hand hurt and Michael wasn't as instantly sympathetic as she expected him to be.

"Number Four has a prizefighter's jaw," she said. "Damn." When she had struck Jennifer, her little finger had been cut against the teenager's teeth. There was blood pulsing from a slice near the nail and she sucked on it as she complained.

Michael was amused, which she didn't appreciate. He was hunting through the medicine cabinet of the farmhouse, searching for some antiseptic and a Band-Aid. "If you close your fist and punch her," he said, "it might be better if you wore protective gloves. There are some on the table by the main computer."

He found what he was looking for. "This might sting," he said, as he dripped some sodium peroxide on the cut. "Did you know that the human mouth is one of the most dangerous, most bacteria-filled spots on the body?"

"You've been spending too much time at the Discovery Channel," Linda responded.

"And that the Komodo dragon on that island in the Pacific can kill you with a bite not because its teeth are sharp but because the infection it dispenses isn't treatable by modern antibiotics."

"Animal Planet?" Linda asked. She grimaced at the disinfectant dripping on the cut. "So, maybe for *Series Five* we will steal a dragon?"

"Sorry," Michael said. He looked down at the cleaned cut. "It's pretty deep. Do you think you want to go to the emergency room and get a stitch or two? The nearest hospital is probably forty-five minutes away, but you might actually need them."

Linda shook her head, but said, "What do you think?"

"I think we could do either. If I apply some pressure, it will heal up, but it might be sore for a day or so."

Linda held a small washcloth over the wound and walked across their bedroom to a window.

"Is there anything we need out there?" she asked, gesturing with her wounded hand.

Michael took a quick glance around as he did an inventory in his head. "Nothing immediate. We have plenty of food, even if it isn't what I'd call gourmet. We have weapons. We have all the electronics we need. I think we're okay for the next few days."

"Then no trips," Linda said decisively. "Not unless we actually need something. It makes no sense to let anyone see us."

She lingered for a moment, staring out of the farmhouse window. It was late in the afternoon and a slight breeze was pulling at the leaves that had started blooming on a line of trees marking the gravel drive that led out to the roadway, which would take them toward town had they any pressing need to go. There was a weather-beaten red barn to her right, where they had stored their Mercedes and covered it with a tarpaulin. Michael's dented truck was poised outside. It was a typical vehicle for where they were. Beaten enough by hard winters, used on enough back roads to show every bit of wear and tear. She thought the truck made them seem ordinary and local, like a pair of cheap jeans and a sweatshirt, when, in truth, they were silk and high couture. She loved the world of illusion that they'd created for *Series #4*. They were the nice young couple who had rented an isolated farmhouse in a forgotten and ignored part of New England. They had told the realtor who had found it for them that Michael was finishing his dissertation and she was working on sculptures and this blending of academic and exotic had ended any questions about the need for solitude that had been their primary desire. False names. False backgrounds. Virtually the entire transaction was done over the Internet. The only physical contact had taken place when Linda had dropped into the realtor's office and paid cash for a six-month lease. Someone with a suspicious mind might have questioned the stack of hundred-dollar bills she had produced, but in an economy buffeted by so many high-profile headline-grabbing flaws the sight of actual money stopped almost every inquiry.

No one had been able to see them unload their expensive audiovisual equipment. No one had been close enough to hear the sounds of construction as Michael had prepared the studio where Number 4 was being filmed.

Linda did not know it consciously but, in a way, they were as isolated as Number 4. For Linda, the sense of owning and controlling a world of their own became a part of her pleasure. It was all taking place in an old farmhouse miles from any urban center. No neighbors poking around nosily, bringing over a *let's be friends* casserole. They had no connection to where they were. No friends. No acquaintances. They did not participate in any world other than *Series #4*. Nor did she suffer any part of the outside world to intrude on theirs.

She held her finger up to the light coming through the window. She hoped she would not develop a scar. A rush of deep-red anger overcame her, a rage at the idea that Number 4 had inadvertently left a mark on her skin. Any flaw on her body frightened her. She expected always to be perfect.

"I'm okay," she said. She wasn't sure she believed this. She wanted, in that moment, to *hurt* Number 4 in some unforgettable way.

"Let me bandage it," Michael said.

She held out her hand and he took it like a bridegroom standing at the altar. Tender. He had changed his approach. No more laughter. He turned it to the light and dried it by dabbing it with cotton. Then he lifted her hand, like a medieval courtier, and kissed it.

"I think," she said slowly, finally breaking into a smile, "that it's time for Number Four to learn something new."

Michael nodded.

"A new threat?" he asked.

Linda smiled. "An old threat, reinvented."

29

Adrian used the gun to gesture toward the inside of the house, pointing it in the direction for the sex offender to move. The weight of the weapon seemed to fluctuate—light, almost airy one second, iron, anvil-like the next. He tried to force himself through a checklist: *Full clip in the handle?* Check. *Round chambered?* Check. *Safety off?* Check. *Finger on the trigger?* Check.

Willingness to shoot?

He doubted he could do this, even with his threats to the contrary and even taking into consideration the amount of evil that Mark Wolfe was clearly willing to deliver to innocent children. He heard Brian's voice whispering in his ear: *If you shoot him, you will be arrested and there will be no one left to search for Jennifer and she will be gone forever.*

The practical lawyer argument was his brother's. The matter-of-fact tone was his brother's. But he knew Brian wasn't with him, not at that moment. *I'm on my own,* he thought. Then he contradicted himself. *No I'm not.* He fought his own confusion.

Adrian looked at the shifty-eyed way the sex offender seemed to slink back into his living room. It nearly overwhelmed him to be in the presence of a man who cared so little about the impact of his desires. Ordinary folks consider consequences. The Mark Wolfes of the world do not.

The 9mm seemed suddenly cold to his touch, and then, in the next second, almost red hot, as if it had just been pulled from a refiner's fire. He tightened his grip. *But maybe I am the same.*

The man wore a grin that Adrian believed was indicative of a sickness he could only imagine. At least his own illness had a name and a diagnosis and a recognizable pattern of madness and disintegration. But Mark Wolfe's compulsion seemed to enter into a different realm, one where medicine lost its grip and was replaced by something far darker.

"Okay, old man," Wolfe said with a mocking familiarity. "Stop waving the cannon around and tell me what you need to know."

He stepped into the living room. There was little in his voice that suggested he felt terribly threatened by Adrian, despite the gun wavering in the air between them.

"But first I want that computer."

Adrian hesitated.

"It's important, is it?"

Wolfe smiled.

"You wouldn't be here, if you didn't know the answer to that question already."

From behind him, Rose entered the living room. She had a dishtowel in her hand and she smiled when she saw Adrian.

"Oh, Marky, your friend is back," she said enthusiastically.

Wolfe kept his eyes on Adrian. "That's right, Mom," he said slowly. "My good friend the professor has come to visit again. He brought your computer with him."

Rose had not seen the automatic in Adrian's hand, or else she didn't understand why he held it, or maybe even what it was, because she did not mention it. "Are we all going to watch our shows?" she asked.

"Yes, Mom. I think that's why the professor is here. He wants to join us watching television. You can start knitting now."

Rose smiled and moved over to her chair. Within seconds she had plopped herself down and the subtle *click clack* of needles and yarn dropped into the background.

"I don't show her my personal stuff," Wolfe said. "Even if she can't really wrap her head around it. I still make her go to bed before I hook it up."

Touching, Adrian thought. *He hides his sick pornography from his mother. What a good son.*

"So . . ." Adrian started. He stopped just as quickly.

"You will have to wait," Wolfe said. "This is my house, and my schedule."

Adrian nodded. He moved to a seat on a threadbare couch. "We'll wait together," he said. The weapon remained in his hand, trained on Wolfe's chest.

"You know," Wolfe said slowly, "people like me, we're not really dangerous. We're just . . . curious. Didn't Doctor West tell you that?"

Not dangerous. What a lie, Adrian shouted inwardly. But outwardly he maintained what he hoped was a clinician's poker face.

"I haven't spoken to Doctor West about you," Adrian replied. A small look of surprise flitted into Wolfe's eyes.

"That's interesting," the sex offender said. He sat down heavily across from Adrian and picked up a television remote control. He pointed it at the cable box beneath the flat-screen television and, as the device came to life, he muttered, "Because the good doctor seems to me to be pretty much the same as you."

"What do you mean?" Adrian asked as a channel guide came up on the screen.

"He wants to learn," Wolfe said. A quick burst of laughter jumped through his lips. "Except he doesn't need to point a gun at my chest to find out what he wants."

Adrian felt dizzy. He wanted help. He needed help. But all his dead visitors were quiet.

"What do you think, professor," Wolfe asked abruptly. "A rerun of *M*A*S*H* or maybe the old *Mary Tyler Moore Show*? My mother doesn't get the humor in *The Simpsons*."

He didn't wait for an answer. He punched a button and the screen filled with olive-drab army helicopters circling over a Southern California hillside pretending to be 1950s-era Korea. Familiar music poured out of the speakers. "Oh, good," Rose said brightly. "It's Hawkeye and Major Burns." The knitting needles *clicked* energetically as she bent forward toward the television.

"She can remember them," Wolfe said. "Radar. Hot Lips. Trapper John and Klinger. But not her sister's name. Or any of my cousins. They're all strangers now. Of course, they don't show up as regularly as Alan Alda and Mike Farrell. No one does. It's just the two of us. All alone. Except for the people on the screen. They're her only friends."

The sex offender turned slightly in his seat to follow the action in the show, ignoring Adrian almost to the point of behaving as if he and the weapon were no longer in the room, except Adrian saw Wolfe stiffen when he moved the satchel with Rose's computer to a spot on the floor between his feet. He did not know how long he could hold the weapon in his hand steady, and he wondered if it was like a diver's weight that would pull him into an abyss.

They sat through an evening of old sitcoms. The 4077th Mobile Army Surgical Hospital characters changed into Archie and Meathead. They were followed by Diane and Sam. For two hours antics filled the screen. Rose laughed frequently, occasionally when there was an actual joke, but that didn't necessarily seem a crucial part of her enjoyment. Mark Wolfe lounged in his seat, oblivious to the weapon pointed in his direction. Adrian shifted about in the couch, half paying attention to the comedies but also eyeing Wolfe. He had never held someone at gunpoint before. It didn't seem to him that he was doing a good job, but he wasn't sure that was entirely relevant.

He felt as if he were on some avant-garde stage but there was no prompter to feed him his lines.

The end theme from *Cheers* filled the room and Mark Wolfe took the remote control and shut off the television.

"That's enough for tonight, Mom," he said. "The professor and I need to finish our business. Time for you to go to bed."

Rose looked sad. "It's all over for tonight?" she asked.

"Yes."

The woman sighed and put her knitting back into the basket. She looked up. "Hello?" she said to Adrian. "Are you one of Mark's friends?"

Adrian didn't answer.

"Bed, Mother," he said. "You're tired now. You need to take your pills and go to sleep."

"It's bedtime?"

"Yes."

"Isn't it dinner?"

"No. You ate earlier."

"Then we should watch our shows now."

"No, Mother. Finished for tonight."

Mark Wolfe stood up. He went over and half lifted his mother from her chair. Then he turned back to Adrian, who still held the weapon in front of him, but to what point seemed to have dissipated in the rush of sitcom canned laughs and Rose's fading in and out memory.

"You going to keep an eye on me?" Wolfe said. "Or are you willing to wait until I come back?"

Adrian stood up. He knew that letting Wolfe out of his sight would be wrong, although precisely why in the midst of the theater of the absurd was elusive. He smiled at Rose.

"Let's go, then," Wolfe said, taking his mother by the hand.

Adrian thought he was being invited in on some sort of hidden ritual, like an anthropologist that finally wins the trust of a deep Amazon Indian tribe. He watched from a few feet away as the son monitored his mother preparing for bed. He helped her out of her clothes right to the edge of propriety; he put the toothpaste on the brush for her. He arranged a series of pills on a bureau top for her and handed her a glass of water. He made sure that she used the toilet, patiently waiting outside the bathroom door and calling out questions such as "Did you use the toilet paper?" and "Did you remember to flush?" Then he tucked her in to bed—all with Adrian, weapon still in hand, standing a few feet away. It was like he was invisible.

Few things he had ever seen in his life frightened him as much as watching the ritual of Rose getting ready for bed. It was not that she was child-like, though she was. It was that the ordinary routines of life had lost their connection to her thinking. In every action, every small moment that reflected her loss of grip on the world, Rose displayed what Adrian feared was barreling toward him. *It will be the same, but worse, for me.*

He hung back. Embarrassed. He was tumbling headlong into something so intimate that he could not put a word to it.

Mark Wolfe, the sex offender, kissed his mother's forehead tenderly. As he clicked off the bedroom light he turned to Adrian. "See?" he asked, but it was a question that didn't require an answer because Adrian clearly could see. "That's what it's like. Every night."

Wolfe pushed past him. He was heading back toward the living room. "Close that," he muttered, waving to the bedroom door. Adrian turned and stole a final glimpse of the woman lying like a lump in the shadowy darkness.

"Maybe she'll die in her sleep tonight," Wolfe said. "But probably she won't."

Adrian shut Rose away and followed.

"That cop," Wolfe said, "the one you came with before. She's like all the other cops I've ever run into. They like to harass me. Take my computer. See what magazines I've got. Check on my therapy. Hassle me at my job. Make sure I'm not doing anything they don't like, like visiting a school or a playground. They want to try to take the me out of me." He laughed. "Fat chance."

Wolfe looked over at Adrian. "So you want a little tour of my life, huh?"

The sex offender didn't wait for an answer. He merely moved back into the living room. He went to the window and lowered the blinds.

"You know that every day I get up and go to my job, just like a nice little parolee?"

Adrian nodded his head. He kept the gun pointed to the front.

"And now you've seen me and my mom. Ancient sitcoms and changing adult diapers. Real nice, huh?"

Adrian guessed that the weapon wavered in his grip. He tried to steady his hand.

"You're not going to shoot me," Wolfe said. "In fact, you're going to agree to what I want, because otherwise I won't help you. And you do need help, don't you, professor?"

He said this in a mocking, aggressive tone.

Adrian kept quiet. He wanted to push the weapon forward. He didn't understand why when he held a gun it didn't scare Wolfe. He tried to sort through this equation in his head. The gun was appropriate stimulus. *Violent painful death.* The reaction should have been readily clear and instantly identifiable. *Cowering unbridled fear.* That it was not confused him.

"So time for a little bargain, professor."

"I don't make bargains with people like you," Adrian weakly replied. This was woefully inadequate, he thought.

"Sure you do. As soon as you knocked on my door there, you were selling something. Or maybe you wanted to buy something. We just have to get the terms of the sale right before we get to continue on to the good part."

Wolfe seemed relaxed for a man facing a gun barrel.

"I want my mother's computer back. For obvious reasons. The hard drive is mine and mine alone. Personal stuff. Now, tell me what you want and we can arrange a price."

"I need to find someone."

"Okay. Hire a private cop."

"I am the private cop," Adrian replied.

Wolfe burst out with a short, harsh laugh.

"You don't look much like one, except for that heavy-duty artillery piece you keep waving about. You know, for starters, professor, you should keep two hands on the weapon. That will steady it, allow you to sight down the barrel more accurately."

Wolfe smiled. "There. A little bit of education, and I won't even charge you for it."

Adrian balanced conflicting notions in his head. He could lower the weapon, put it away, start negotiating. Or he could try to threaten Wolfe the way he imagined Terri Collins might, but he doubted he had the cop gravitas to make that believable. He was trapped, trying to consider his options, when he heard Brian whisper, "*Use who you were, and who you are, and who you will be . . . That might work.*"

He nodded and felt his brother helping to steady his grip. He raised the gun and pointed it directly at Wolfe. He sighted down the barrel and slowly tightened his finger against the trigger. He installed a little quaver in his voice.

"I'm sick," Adrian said quietly. "I'm very sick. I'm going to die soon."

Wolfe looked at him quizzically.

"Your mother, how much do you trust her? Do you think she knows what she's doing? If it was *her* waving this gun around, how certain would you be she wouldn't inadvertently pull the trigger and blow a nice huge damn hole in your face and *not have a clue why she did it or how.* And even if she only put a round in your stomach, and you had maybe just a little chance to live through it, do you think she would know enough to call 911? Or do you think maybe she'd start knitting and watching television?"

Wolfe's eyes narrowed and his face lost its mocking grin.

"Well," Adrian said slowly. "What I've got is something like what your mother has. Only it's worse. It makes me do all sorts of things that are erratic as hell and I don't understand at all why I do them. So there's a real good chance that any second now I'm going to forget why I'm here and maybe this cannon, as you so eloquently put it, Mister Wolfe, will go off, because I won't remember what I need from you and only that you're a major league sex offender and an all-round piece of excrement that deserves to go directly to hell. I'm just like that. Unsteady. Like standing on a slippery deck, waves rocking the boat. And I don't have much time to barter."

Wolfe seemed to recoil slightly. Adrian had spoken quickly, his voice rising and falling like the waves he'd used to give the whole speech a poetic ring.

"*That should make him think and really fuck him up,*" Brian snorted gleefully. "*Good job, Audie. You've got him off balance now. Nail him.*"

"Okay, professor." Wolfe was calculating just as rapidly as Adrian was. "Tell me what you need."

"I want a guided tour of your world. The midnight world."

Wolfe nodded.

"It's a big place. A big fucking place, professor. I need to know why."

"A pink hat," Adrian answered. Nonsensical. But it would keep Wolfe unsettled. He took a step forward, keeping the gun at eye height, using both hands. "Is this what you meant?" he asked. "Yes. I see. This seems like a much better way to hold the gun."

Wolfe recoiled. Adrian saw a flicker of fear in his face.

"You won't kill me."

"Probably not. But it seems like a foolish gamble on your part."

There was a momentary silence in the room. Adrian knew what the sex offender would say next. There was only one logical way out.

"Okay, professor. Let's do it your way."

A concession. Probably a lie, but Adrian thought he had managed to balance the authority in the room. It was Wolfe's home and they would be entering his territory. But Adrian's mystery—just how erratic was he?—trumped the sex offender's cold, rational self. Adrian had never thought he'd been particularly clever, but this made him smile. His dying madness was just slightly more compelling than Wolfe's psychopathic desires. Adrian thought that now he just had to bring these two elements together.

Adrian nudged the satchel with the computer toward the sex offender. "Show me," he said.

"Show you what?"

"Everything."

Wolfe shrugged, a motion contradicted by the eagerness with which he reached for the computer.

Time dissolved into a cascade of images. They were all different yet all the same. Races, ages, positions, perversions flooded the television screen after Wolfe hooked up some wires to Rose's laptop. Like a maestro directing an orchestra, Wolfe displayed to Adrian what was out there in the Internet netherworld. It was a dizzying, never-ending ocean of mind-numbing sex. Passion faked, it had everything to do with being explicit, nothing to do with real connection.

Wolfe was an expert guide. A Virgil to all of Adrian's inquiries.

He did not know how long they had been at it. He felt adrift. And the discomfort at the explicit intimacy that rolled up in front of him dissipated rapidly. He felt chilled by the constancy of it all.

Wolfe clicked on a couple of keys and the images on the screen changed. A woman encased in skin-tight black leather bondage stared out at them, inviting them into a room for discipline. Membership was a single, one-time fee of $39.99.

"Watch carefully, professor," Wolfe said.

He typed in a new set of instructions and leather-clad Woman #2 replaced leather-clad Woman #1. She was offering the same disciplinary system, only her price was euro 60 and she was speaking in French. Another rapid-fire series of clicks and leather-clad Woman #3 appeared in front of them. Her price was in Japanese yen and she spoke in that language.

The lesson was not lost on Adrian.

"So, professor, you need to tell me what you're looking for. Specifically."

The sex offender grinned. He was clearly enjoying himself.

Wolfe clicked on site after site. Children. Old people. Fat people. Torture. "What intrigues you, professor? What fascinates you? What rings your bell? Maybe gets a little blood pumping? Because whatever it is, it's out there somewhere."

Adrian nodded, but the acknowledgment rapidly turned into a head-shaking denial.

"Show me what *you* are interested in, Mister Wolfe."

Wolfe shifted about. "I don't think we share the same desires, professor. And I don't think you want to go along with me all that much."

Adrian hesitated. He had used the gun to get that far. But as he stared at Wolfe's eyes, he did not think that the sex offender would let him into his own private world. There had to be another route, though.

He could feel his brother behind him, as if Brian were pacing rapidly in the small space, back and forth, tossing over the dilemma in his mind. He could hear the *clip-clop* of his brother's footsteps, resounding against a hard-wood floor, even though there was carpet everywhere in the sex offender's home. Adrian sensed Brian stopping, leaning forward, whispering in his ear, like an adviser to the crown. "*Entice him, Audie. Seduce him.*"

Easier said than done. "But how?"

He must have said this out loud because he saw Wolfe stiffen in surprise. "*Who do you both know?*"

Adrian nodded. "That makes sense," he said. "He doesn't really know why I'm here."

"Who are you talking to?" Wolfe asked nervously.

Adrian didn't answer him.

"I need to find Jennifer. Jennifer is young. Sixteen. She's beautiful."

"I don't get it," Wolfe said. "Now you talking to me?"

"Jennifer is gone," Adrian continued. "But she is somewhere. I need to find her."

"This Jennifer, she your granddaughter or something?"

"I need to find her. I'm responsible. I could have stopped them from taking her, but I wasn't fast enough."

"Someone stole this Jennifer girl?"

"Yes."

"From around here?"

"Yes. From in front of my house."

"And you say I know her? That doesn't make sense. They don't let me anywhere near kids that age."

"You don't know how you know her but you do. You are connected."

"You're not making sense, professor."

"I am. You just don't see how. Not yet."

Wolfe nodded. Somehow this seemed reasonable.

"And the cops . . ."

"They're looking. But they don't know where."

Wolfe looked frustrated and a bit unsettled. "And you think she's in here somewhere?"

He pointed at the computer.

Adrian nodded. "It's the only place to look that holds out the least possibility of hope. If someone stole Jennifer to use her and then kill her, there's no chance. But if someone stole her to make something . . . money, maybe . . . before discarding her, well then . . ."

"Professor, if this girl is acting in porn movies or posing for sex tapes or engaged in this industry, hell, there's *no* way we can sit here and find her. Needle in a haystack. There are millions of sites, with millions of girls, eagerly specializing in everything that anyone might possibly think of. Volunteering to do *anything*. Everything under the sun is in here, somewhere. I mean, there is no way."

"She won't be a volunteer, Mister Wolfe. She won't be willing."

Wolfe hesitated, mouth slightly agape. Then he nodded.

"That narrows the search down," he acknowledged.

Adrian looked around the small living room, as if searching for one of the voices to direct him, but he was trying to determine what to say without saying too much. When he did speak, it was in a low, fierce voice.

"I get it."

He narrowed his gaze, fixing it on the sex offender with intensity. He could hear Brian urging him on in the background.

"So you have to look at pictures. It's the only thing available to you, isn't it, Mister Wolfe? Pictures aren't quite the same as the real thing, but for the time being they're an acceptable substitute, right? And then you allow your imagination to take over. That helps you to control things, doesn't it, Mister Wolfe? Because you need to buy time. You can't go to prison again, not now, because your mother needs you. But it's still there, isn't it, the big desire? Can't hide that. So you have to compensate because those wants, they just don't go away, do they? And that is what the computer gives you. A chance to fantasize and speculate and just balance things out, until something in your life changes and you can go back to doing what you want to do. And you're feeling not so bad about this, because you go to your job, and you see your therapist, and you think you've got him snowed completely, don't you? Because you've figured out that he's pretty curious about all this dark sex and you can tease him into anything. It's about control, isn't it, Mister Wolfe? Right now, you've got all these things in your life under control and you're waiting for the right moment when you can get back to doing what it is you want to do more than anything else."

Adrian paused. "*Make him show you!*" Brian was ferocious, right beside him.

"Open up one of those personal files," Adrian said.

The gun came up again. But this time it seemed to have a glow in his hand and he was determined that if he had to he would use it. Wolfe must have sensed the same thing.

He snarled, but it was the weakest look he'd managed since he'd opened the door to Adrian.

Wolfe glanced over at the computer and then to the television screen. He punched a few keys. A picture of a very young girl—maybe eleven—flashed up. She was naked, staring coyly out as if inviting with a knowing look, a glance that would have been professional on the face of some woman twice her age.

Wolfe breathed out hard. "You think you know me, don't you, professor?"

"I know enough. And you know that."

He paused. "There are places," he said slowly, "that cater to *unusual* interests. Very deep places. You don't want to enter those zones."

"But I do," Adrian said. "That will be where Jennifer is."

Wolfe shrugged. "You're crazy," he said.

"I am, indeed," Adrian replied. "Maybe that's a good thing."

"If this girl got kidnapped, professor, and even if she's somewhere in here"—he gestured toward the computer—"you'd be better off just figuring she's dead. Because that's what she'll be sooner or later."

"We all will, sooner or later," Adrian responded. "You. Me. Your mother. Everyone has a time to die. It's just not Jennifer's. Not yet."

He said this with conviction backed up by nothing.

Wolfe seemed to be both intrigued and put off, two conflicting sensations battling within him.

"What do you think I can do for you?" he asked, though the question had been reverberating in the room throughout the evening.

Adrian could feel his brother's hands on his shoulders, gripping him tightly, pushing him slightly forward.

"Here is what I want, Mister Wolfe. I want you to use your imagination. The same way you do when you walk past a school yard at recess . . ."

Wolfe appeared to stiffen.

"I want you to put yourself in some shoes. I want you to consider what you would be if you had Jennifer. I want you to tell me what you would do with her, and how, and where, and why. And I want you to imagine that at your side is a woman. A young woman, who loves you, and who wants to help you."

Wolfe was listening hard.

"And I want you to imagine how you would make money off of Jennifer, Mister Wolfe."

"You want me to . . ."

"I want you to be who you are, Mister Wolfe. Only more so."

"And if I do this what do I get?"

Adrian paused, thinking. "*Give him what he wants,*" Brian said.

"But what is that?" Adrian said. Wolfe eyed him again.

"*There's only one thing. It's what everyone like him wants.*" Brian spoke with certainty.

Privacy, Adrian thought.

"What I *won't do* is tell the detective what you're doing. And I won't tell her about your mother's computer. I won't tell anyone about it. And, after you find Jennifer for me, you can go back to being who you really are and waiting for the day when you've got everybody fooled and no one is paying attention to you."

Wolfe smiled, not unpleasantly. "I think, professor, that finally we've arrived at a sales price."

30

Terri Collins spent the morning caught between looking at grainy black-and-white images on a bus station security videotape and listening to confused lies from a pair of college sophomores who were unsuccessfully trying to give a benign explanation for the dozen computers, television sets, and PlayStations that had been discovered in the back of their car by an alert patrolman. He had pulled them over for speeding. *What sort of idiot crooks speed recklessly away from burglaries?* she wondered. It had simply been a matter of splitting up the two young men, repeatedly questioning them, waiting for their stories to diverge, which was inevitable. Terri had taken the time to contact the university security head as well, and she informed the operators who took the local 911 calls to be on the lookout for irate fellow students who had returned to school to find their off-campus apartments ransacked.

Every year she handled several of these types of cases, and the inherent stupidity of these break-ins bored her. She wondered how new students had imagined they must be the first criminal masterminds to think up the unique advantages of ripping off their classmates. She knew that sooner or later one of the two would give up the other and describe the entire foolish scheme. She had already typed up the felony arrest forms for the pair, but she doubted much would happen. They would spend a night or two in jail and then the legal system would find some way to plead them out. They were going to have to do some explaining to family and future employers. This, she thought, went directly into the *tough luck dumb fuck* category.

She hurried through her paperwork. It took time away from the images on the video that fascinated her and troubled her, because of both what it showed and what it didn't show.

Primarily: no Jennifer.

It had taken her a series of calls to track down the person who had returned Jennifer's mother's credit card to a bank in Lewiston, Maine. This, too, was a college student, who told a story that made little sense but which was undoubtedly true. The student had been in Boston with two roommates and a boyfriend, visiting old high school buddies. They had caught a late bus back to their own school. This was the sort of thing that took place hourly in a city dominated by colleges and universities. Where the tale had departed from the rational was when the student described emptying out her travel backpack and coming across the strange credit card. It was issued by a bank where she did not have an account. It was under a name she did not recognize and how it had gotten into the outside pocket of her pack was a mystery to her.

Under most circumstances, she simply would have tossed it out, but by happenstance she had to visit her own bank that day, so she had turned it in to a teller there, who had diligently called the issuing bank's security department, who had, in turn, called Mary Riggins.

It was a slow, winding trail.

The bus ticket the card had purchased was for New York. The East Coast runaway's mecca.

It made no sense to the detective. Why not simply toss the card away?

A mistake? Then she thought, *No.*

This was about misdirection.

She asked the college student three times whether she or any of her friends recalled seeing a teenager that fit Jennifer's description in the bus station. Each time the response was no.

Did she see anyone else? Anyone stand out? Suspicious?

No and no and no.

Terri's imagination churned and she felt a rush of anxiety that hid behind her detective's cold resolve. In her imagination there was an odd conflation. She had spent time that day speaking with the dumbest of criminals. And she wondered whether she was on the edge of something from the smartest of criminals. It was like being caught between two poles, nightmare and boring routine. Somewhere between all this Jennifer fit.

The security tape lacked clarity. The overhead placement angle didn't lend itself to precision.

What she could see was a man using the self-serve kiosk at the time the ticket transaction was time-stamped. He was not recognizable from the images captured by the camera, although she knew that more sophisticated police agencies would have photo enhancement equipment that might give her a much clearer look.

She saw the same man seated apart, waiting for the bus, in a later image. Hunched over. Hat pulled down, obscuring his face.

In short, she recognized a man who knew he was being photographed and was taking steps to avoid being caught on film, at the same time behaving in a manner that wouldn't stand out.

She saw the trio of students getting in line in front of a ticket counter. She saw a different man—she could make out a beard where none had existed before—sliding in behind them. She advanced the video long enough to see that this man did not actually make it to the ticket counter. He peeled off—not to visit a window with less traffic or to use a self-serve machine. As best she could tell he left the station through the front entranceway, not through the back loading area.

She looked again.

The man had no bags other than a small shoulder pack.

She played this over and over, trying to memorize every sight of Man #1 and then Bearded Man #2. She measured their physique, the way they walked, the manner in which they slumped their shoulders and kept themselves hidden beneath hats.

She tried to picture the man that Adrian had described for her. There was not enough to persuade her that the man in the grainy security video and the man glimpsed on the street were the same.

But, she insisted to herself, any other conclusion was nonsensical.

Terri pushed aside the burglary report and gathered all the information she had about the missing Jennifer. It was a jumble of pieces, less a jigsaw puzzle than the detritus of a plane crash, where investigators fit together what hasn't been destroyed, what is twisted and burn-scarred, and what is recognizable in a way that is designed to tell them something concrete about what happened.

A rebellious runaway teen.

An old man.

A burned panel truck.

No ransom requests.

No cell phone usage.

A bus ticket to nowhere.

A man disguising himself where there should have been Jennifer.

Terri reeled in her seat. She could feel her detective's skepticism falling away from her. There is a particular sense of despair that infects police detectives when they realize that they are up against the worst possible sort of crime, one that engages anonymity and evil. Crimes are solved because of connections—someone sees something, someone knows something, someone says something, someone leaves something at a crime scene— and eventually a clear-cut picture emerges. There is always some elemental connection that defines the detective's course.

Jennifer's disappearance defied that.

If there was anything clear-cut in what she knew, it was that she didn't know what to do.

But it was equally apparent to her that she had to do something that went beyond what she had been doing. She looked around her desk, as if this *what to do* should be obvious. Then she lifted her head and stared at the cubicle around her, decorated with pictures of her family, some colorful child-art watercolors and crayon drawings, juxtaposed against cold gray police reports and FBI alerts.

She had—she believed—done everything appropriately. She had done everything required by department standards. She had done everything that any official would do.

None of it had brought her any closer to the missing Jennifer.

Terri rocked forward, as if she had a cramp in her stomach.

Jennifer was gone. Terri pictured the teenager, seated across from her on one of the prior escape efforts, sullen, noncommunicative, waiting angrily for mother and boyfriend to arrive and return her to the place she was so eager to flee from while Terri lectured her about the mistake she'd made. Terri realized that the time to save Jennifer had been then. All she had to do was lean across the desk and say, *Talk to me, Jennifer* and open up some sort of line of communication. Now what was she doing? Filing papers and reports, taking useless statements from a deranged retired professor, interviewing a sex offender who didn't seem to have any link to the runaway, sending out needle-in-a-haystack, shot-in-the-dark inquiries to other police agencies. But, Terri understood, she was mostly just waiting for the day in the future when a hunter scouring dark woods for deer found Jennifer's skeletal remains, or her decomposing body was hooked by a fisherman probing a lake for smallmouth bass.

If the detective was that lucky.

Terri punched some computer keys and the image of the man in the bus station came up on the screen in front of her. She blew it up, clicking computer keys until the picture filled her entire screen.

All right, she said to herself, *I think I will find out who you are.*

This was easier imagined than done. But she reached for the phone to call the state police lab, which could run some image recognition software on the tape. Maybe she would get lucky, but she doubted it. She was also aware that this was a step that might not be approved by her superiors.

Mark Wolfe walked swiftly across the expanse of black parking lot mac-adam to where Adrian was waiting next to his car. Adrian could feel Brian's presence beside him, almost hear his brother's rapid breath, wondering for an instant why he would be nervous. Brian, Adrian understood, was always in control and never hurried, never anxious. And then he realized it was his own labored sounds he was hearing.

As he approached Adrian, the sex offender looked warily about. Adrian had the odd thought that Mark Wolfe was supremely confident inside his own home, but like a prairie animal out in the open he needed to lift his head and check for predators every few seconds. This was backward, Adrian imagined. Wolfe was the predator.

Wolfe wore a skewed grin.

"I'm not supposed to take a long break," he said. "Wouldn't want to miss a major appliance sale. Hey, professor, you need a big-screen TV and surround sound system? They're on special and I can get you a great deal."

This wasn't said with any sincerity.

"This isn't going to take long," Adrian replied.

He produced a copy of the Missing Persons flyer that Detective Collins had given him and handed it to Wolfe.

"That's who I'm looking for," he said.

Wolfe eyed the picture. "She's lovely . . ." The word *lovely* could have been a substitute for *ripe*. It sounded obscene coming from Wolfe's mouth. Adrian wanted to shudder. "A runaway, you say?"

"No. I didn't say that. I said she has been a runaway before. But now she's stolen."

Wolfe read through the details on the flyer, repeating them in a soft voice, *Five feet six inches, one hundred and seventeen pounds, sandy blond hair, no distinguishing marks, last seen . . .* Then he stopped reading.

"You know, with my . . ."—he hesitated—"*background*, if some cop was to find this flyer in my possession it'd be just as bad as . . ."

"We have a deal," Adrian said. "You don't want me to go to the cops and start talking about that other computer and what's on it."

Wolfe nodded, but his reply was far more chilling than the nature of their agreement.

"Yeah, I get it. So this is the kid you think is being used. I'm to explore the Web."

"The alternative is, you see . . ."

"Yeah. She's been fucked and killed. Or worse."

Wolfe twitched slightly. Adrian couldn't tell if this involuntary motion was caused by distaste or pleasure. Either seemed possible. Maybe the territories defined by both sensations existed simultaneously inside Mark Wolfe. Adrian suspected that was the case.

"You know, all that crap about snuff films, you know that was all urban legend mythology. Totally bogus. Bullshit. Untrue."

He repeated words for emphasis, creating the opposite impression. *Look behind the words, look behind the way he's standing, the tone he uses, the way he shifts about.* Adrian thought this was what Cassie would say to him, and it was as if the thoughts in his head had her musical tone of voice.

Adrian stared at the sex offender and then lifted his glance. The sky above them was a wide, cloudless expanse of blue, a promise of fine weather to come. High across the sky, Adrian could see a jet's vapor contrails drawing a straight line in billowing white against the pale background. People traveling at high speed, to varied destinations. He realized he would never ride on another plane, never have a chance to visit someplace exotic. He was nearly overcome with the direct path the airplane flew so effortlessly; he seemed to be caught up in a mire of disease and doubt. He wished he knew exactly what steps to take, in what direction, and how many miles he had left to travel.

"Audie, pay attention!"

He heard his brother's sharp words, bringing his vision back down from the skies.

"*Come on, Audie, focus!*"

"You okay, professor?"

"I'm fine."

"Well, the hassle is trying to determine what's real and what isn't. That's the trouble with the Internet. It's a place where lying and fantasy and all sorts of deceptive stuff exists right next to real good, solid information. Hard to separate the two. Even in the sex world, you know. What's real. What isn't."

"Snuff films . . ."

"Like I said, big phony. But . . ."

Wolfe hesitated. He rolled his words over, as if he tasted each before speaking, and added, "But all those myths, well, they only create *opportunity,* if you know what I mean, professor."

"Explain."

"Well, snuff films don't exist. But as soon as the FBI or Interpol says, 'Snuff films are an urban legend,' it only encourages people to try, professor. That's the thing about the Internet. It exists to make something out of something else. You say something's untrue, and someone else, maybe on the other side of the world, is out there trying to prove you wrong. Like, maybe killing porn for real doesn't exist, but . . . You pick up the paper in the morning what do you read? Some kids maybe in Eastern Europe filmed themselves beating someone to death. For kicks. Or maybe some guys in California filmed themselves killing a hitchhiker after making her perform all sorts of acts. Or . . . well, you get the idea. A terrorist takes a hostage and cuts his head off on film. It gets posted on the Internet. Well, the CIA and the military are all over it. But who else? It's out there for anyone."

"What are you telling me?"

"I'm saying that if little . . ."—he looked at the flyer and a lascivious grin broke out on his face before continuing—"Jennifer is being used, it makes sense. And it could be coming from next door or maybe on the other side of the world."

"How will you look?" Adrian asked.

"There are ways. You just keep punching those keys. It might cost some money."

"Money? How so?"

"You think that people exploit other people for nothing? Maybe just because they like it? Sure, maybe some do. But other people, they want to make a buck. And getting in to those sites, well . . ."

"I'll pay."

Wolfe smiled again. "It can be pricey . . ."

Again he heard his brother echoing commands in his ear. He reached into his back pocket and pulled out his wallet. He removed a credit card and handed it to Wolfe.

"What password shall I use?" the sex offender asked.

Adrian shrugged. He could see no need for deception. "*Psychprof,*" he replied. "And keep a written record of every place you use it. Any excess charges and I'll go straight to the cops."

Wolfe nodded but even this motion might have been a lie. Adrian didn't care. *I'm not going to live long enough to worry about these bills.*

"You have to move fast. I don't know how much time she might have."

Wolfe shrugged. "If she's someone's toy, and he wants to share her—"

"He and she," Adrian interrupted.

"That's right. Two people. That might make it easier. Anyway, if they want to share her, well, that's good, because that's what you want, because she will be there, somewhere."

He laughed again. Adrian thought Wolfe had the type of laugh that penetrated through walls, like a weapon fired at close range, before steering itself back into a cynical giggle, as if he always knew some extra secret that he was unwilling to share.

"You got one thing going for you, prof," he said, grinning.

"What's that?"

"This is what the world is now. Nothing takes place in secret really. Everyone wants to broadcast themselves. What was it? We're all famous for fifteen minutes? Well, it's true."

Warhol, Adrian thought. A sex offender quoting Warhol.

"One problem, though."

Or was it Marshall McLuhan? Suddenly Adrian couldn't remember. Maybe it was Woody Allen. He fought himself back to focusing on Wolfe.

"What's that?"

"Get close, try to break down that old electronic barrier, and whoever it is that's got her just might figure it out that someone is looking for her and then all of a sudden she's likely to be damaged goods."

Adrian took a sharp breath.

"And damaged goods . . ."

The sex offender continued to speak but Adrian noticed that his voice had changed, so that his lips moved with the words yet they sounded like his brother was speaking them. Adrian warned himself not to look confused but simply to listen.

"Well," Wolfe said slowly, "I don't know about you, but when something goes bad in my refrigerator I throw it out."

31

Jennifer was perched on the bed, her eyes shut tight behind the blindfold, trying to picture her room at home. She had started to envision things remembered, detailing with draftsman's precision every angle, every shape, and every color. Toys. Pictures. Books. Pillows. Posters. The desk was positioned just so, the colors of her bedspread were red, blue, green, and purple, all shaped in interlocking squares in a quilt. On a bureau there was a five-by-seven snapshot of her at a youth soccer game heading a ball. She took her time, piecing each element together; she did not want to forget even the smallest item. She luxuriated in each memory—the plot and characters of a book she read as a child; the Christmas morning when she had been given her first pair of earrings for her newly pierced ears. She slowly painted her past in her mind's eye. It helped to remind her that she had been Number 4 for only a few days but for many years she had been Jennifer.

It was a constant fight.

Sometimes, when she awakened from dozing, it took an immense effort to recall anything from her past. What she could feel, smell, hear—everything that she had memorized from her prison room and what she knew was being captured by the camera—all circumscribed the immediacy of her situation. She was afraid there was no Jennifer yesterday. No Jennifer tomorrow. There was only Jennifer right that second. It would have been easier to be a lost sailor cast adrift in a winter sea. At least then, she thought, it would be obvious that she had to fight the currents and the waves and that if she couldn't stay afloat she would drown.

Inwardly, she sobbed. Outwardly she kept herself calm.

She told herself, *I'm only sixteen. A high school student.* She knew she did not know much of the world. She hadn't traveled to exotic places or seen unusual sights. She wasn't a soldier or a spy or even a criminal—anyone who might have some experience that would help her understand her jail. This should have crippled her but, oddly, it didn't. *I know some things,* she told herself. *I know how to fight back.* Even if this was a lie, she didn't care.

Part of that approach required her to imagine everything about the life she had been a part of, all the way up to the moment the van had stopped and the man had leaned out toward her.

Next to the bureau there is a black metal floor lamp with a red shade. The rug is a multicolored throw that covers some dingy old tan and stained wall-to-wall shag. The worst stain is from where I spilled tomato soup, which I wasn't supposed to take out of the kitchen but I did. She yelled at me. She called me irresponsible. I was. But still I argued with her. How many arguments were there? One a day? No. More. When I get home, she will hug me and tell me how she cried when I went missing and that will make me feel better. I miss her. I didn't think I'd ever say that. I miss her. She has some gray now in her hair, just a few strands that she forgets to color, and I don't know whether I should tell her. She could be beautiful. She should be beautiful. Will I ever be pretty? Maybe she's crying now. Maybe Scott is there. I hate him. My father would have found me already, but he can't. Is Scott even looking? Is anyone even looking? My father is looking for me, but he's dead. I hate it. I was robbed. Cancer. I wish I could give cancer to the man and the woman. Mister Brown Fur knows. I would put him to bed beside me. He remembers what the room looked like. How are we going to get out of here?

Jennifer knew that the camera would catch a vision of anything she did. She knew that the man and the woman—she wasn't certain which one scared her more—might be watching. But quietly, as if by being silent somehow she wouldn't attract attention, she began to run her fingertips over the chain around her neck and the eyelet where it was attached to the wall.

One link. Two. She felt each. They were slick beneath her touch. She could picture them. They would be silver and shiny and they probably bought them in a pet store. The links weren't pit bull or Doberman heavy and strong. But they were probably strong enough to hold her.

She touched the eyelet screwed into the wall. Plaster board, she guessed. Drywall.

Once, when she had a fight with her mother—she had stayed out past her curfew—she had thrown a paperweight at the wall. It had hit with a solid thud, and then dropped to the floor, leaving a wide hole. Her mother had to call a handyman to come fix it. Drywall isn't strong. Maybe she could rip the eyelet out? She could feel her lips moving as she asked herself the question. The man would have thought of that. *I didn't throw that paperweight like a girl,* Jennifer reminded herself. *My father taught me to throw a ball when I was little. He loved baseball. He gave me my Red Sox hat. He taught me the right way. Pull back hard. Arm crooked at the elbow. Shoulder locked. Drive through the throw. Fastball. Painting 95 on the black.*

She smiled, just a little, stopping herself because she didn't want the smile caught by the camera.

Maybe I can be a little pit bull, she thought.

Jennifer ran her fingers over the leather collar around her neck.

She imagined the pet store conversation: "*And what sort of dog is it you want to chain up, ma'am?*"

She pictured the woman standing at a counter. *You don't know,* Jennifer thought. *You have no idea what kind of dog I can be. And what my bite is like.*

She took her fingernail and started to scrape away at the collar. It felt like cheap leather. She could feel a small lock, the sort that someone would use to secure luggage. This was supposed to keep the collar in place. She scraped a little harder, just enough so that she could find the same spot again. Maybe, she thought, she could rub it into pieces.

She told herself there had to be steps to freedom. She tried to formulate a series of moves. First, she had to get loose. Then she had to get through the door. *Was it locked?* She had to get up out of the basement room. *Where are the stairs? They have to be close by.* She had to find a door to the outside. Then she would run. It made no difference what direction. Just get away. That was the easy part, she thought. *If I can just get free enough to run no one will catch me. I'm fast. On every field, in every game, I was the fastest. The cross-country coach wanted me to run for the high school, but I told him I wouldn't. But I could beat all those other girls and most of the boys too. All I need is the chance.*

Jennifer lowered her hands from the chain and collar and started to stroke her bear. She whispered to Mister Brown Fur, "Just one step at a time. We'll make it. I promise."

Her voice resounded in the room and she was surprised she had spoken out loud. For an instant she thought she had screamed it out. Then she imagined it was a whisper. It echoed around her, filling her ears with sound until a different noise penetrated her consciousness. Someone was at the door. She twitched, bending her head toward the noise.

She bit down on her lip. She had not heard a key in a lock. She had not heard a deadbolt open. She tried to remember the other times the door had opened. Had she heard something different? No, she was sure, it was just the sound of the door handle being turned. *What did that tell her?*

Before she had even the millisecond necessary to answer her own question, she heard the man's voice.

"Stand up. Remove your underwear."

Michael and Linda understood that *Series #4* was not merely about sex, it was also about possession and control. The sexual component was critical and, they believed, the fulcrum on which the success of the show depended. Michael had spent hours studying every frame of the *Hostel* movies, which he thought had degenerated into bloodbaths that narrowed their audience down to teenagers who placed primary value on gore. But when the blood started spurting, the tension dissipated. Linda, for her part, considered those movies repulsive and instead had read, and then reread, virtually every book about Patty Hearst and the Symbionese Liberation Army she could lay hands on. What fascinated her was the way that the heiress had been altered psychologically into Tania, the erstwhile revolutionary. While they didn't have any need for Number 4 to numbly take up an unloaded weapon and join in some half-baked bank robbery and feed-the-people revolutionary scheme, what Linda found fascinating was the way that Hearst had been driven into giving up her own identity. Isolation. Constant threat. Physical abuse. Sexual pressure. Each part had chipped away at who Patty Hearst had been and turned her into the blankest of pages that her captors had then exploited. These were elements she knew could be manipulated into their show. She simply assumed that her fascination was easily the same for viewers around the world.

Of course, the more she felt compelled in this way, the crueler she became. She wanted to both possess Number 4 and hurt her. Sometimes, when Michael was asleep, she would crawl from the bed, wrap a blanket around her naked form, and go to the monitors and watch. The quickening in her heart was like those of the anonymous people watching. It was a different kind of intimacy. She would be aroused in a way that her lovemaking with Michael couldn't duplicate. Her breath would come in short bursts. She had a fierce desire to touch herself, made even more electric by her refusal to do this.

She denied herself so that when she gave in to Michael it was even more passionate. She knew this surprised him—the reckless abandon that she displayed—but he kept his mouth shut and performed.

The Virginity Clock had been her idea.

It was a simple addition. A timer joined to the outgoing feed. Viewers were asked to gamble on the exact time that Number 4 would be forced by her masked captors to give up her virginity. It was a little like an office betting pool, except that it wasn't a football match or a basketball game being bet on. It was rape.

There was no way of telling when it would happen. But it engaged the viewers in an interactive way. When the details of the clock and the way to post an online bet had first appeared on the site it had immediately boosted the e-mail traffic.

Lots of people like a lottery, Linda thought.

The key thing was to keep up a near-constant tease.

As always, throughout *Series #4,* suggestion was paramount, mixed liberally with explicit actions. Linda was sensitive to the idea that they were required to keep the viewers from both boredom and climax. Everything was about working all the people watching into the fabric of Number 4's story so that, in addition to lust, people became fascinated with twists and turns, as if the imprisonment of Number 4 were a soap opera that was real, and yet unreal, playing out in front of them.

The Virginity Clock was just a small set change. It appeared in a corner across from the regular *Series #4* duration clock, in red, steadily counting the hours that Jennifer had been in their control.

"Good," Michael said. His voice was rough-edged and deep. Number 4 was standing stiffly, self-consciously, at the end of the bed, like a soldier at attention except that her hands tried to cover her nakedness just as they had before, when she'd bathed.

He knew this was involuntary on her part. He also knew that this coyness would electrify most of the viewers. They were so accustomed to seeing the porn industry's eagerness to disrobe and be explicit that Number 4's reluctance to show what they wanted to see would be titillating.

"Hands to the side, Number Four," he said coldly.

He could see her shiver. He moved slightly to his left, just to be sure he wasn't blocking the camera view, and much closer. He wanted Number 4 to sense his presence. Maybe even feel his breath against her cheek. He trusted Linda to keep moving the other camera shots around. She wasn't as good as he was with the cinematography but she knew enough to keep changing angles.

Caress her with the camera, Michael thought. He was trying to send this message to Linda and he imagined he was successful. When it came to these things, they functioned on an intuitive wavelength.

"Look straight ahead."

Number 4 did as she was told. She was biting down on her lip. He hoped that Linda got a close-up of that.

"We have some more questions, Number Four," he began. She didn't nod in agreement but he saw her head turn slightly toward him.

"Tell us, Number Four, what did you imagine your first time would be like?"

As he had suspected, the question took her off guard.

Her mouth opened slightly, as if words were leaping forth but stopping at her lips.

He prompted her.

"Did you think you would fall in love? Did you think it would be romantic? Moonlight on the beach on some warm summer night? In front of a burning fireplace, in some cozy cabin, the winter weather closed away?"

He smiled. The imagery had been Linda's idea.

"Or maybe some sort of rough coupling in the back of a car? Or at a party surrounded by other teenagers, where you give in because of insistence or booze or maybe some drug?"

Number 4 didn't reply.

"Tell us, Number Four. We want to know what you imagined it would be like."

"I never, I didn't . . ." she started hesitantly.

"Of course you did, Number Four," Michael growled. He installed as much menace in his voice as he could. "Everyone does. Everyone imagines. Only the reality is never like the fantasy. But we want to know, Number Four. What did you dream about?"

He watched as she stiffened.

"I thought I would fall in love," she said slowly.

Michael smiled beneath the mask he wore.

"Tell us, Number Four. Tell us about what you think of love."

Jennifer told herself, *It's not me standing naked in front of the world. It's Number 4. I don't know who she is. She's someone else. Someone different. I'm still me. This is someone else talking.*

Then she thought: *Give him what he wants.*

She began to lie.

"There was a boy in my school, his name was—"

Michael stepped forward rapidly and grabbed her chin. His grip was taut and he squeezed savagely.

Jennifer inhaled sharply. She froze. She could feel the pressure on her jaw tightening. It was not so much pain as the suddenness of his motion that startled and frightened her. But as he squeezed the hurt began. She could see colors behind her blindfold, a kaleidoscope of reds and whites and finally a black, deep hurt.

"No. No names, Number Four. No places. No little details that you think someone might hear that might cause someone to come looking for you. I will not tell you again, Number Four. The next time I will really hurt you."

She could sense his strength. It was like having a dark thundercloud hovering over her.

She nodded agreement. She could feel the hand grasping her face slowly release, and the feeling was restored throughout her body. It was as if she slowly became aware again that she was naked, reminded by the dropping away of pain.

"Continue, Number Four. But cautiously."

She could sense that he had not moved more than a foot or so back. He was still hovering over her. She did not want to be hit again. So she invented.

"He was tall and skinny. And he had a goofy smile that I really liked. He liked action movies and was real good in English class. I think he wrote poetry and he would wear a funny hat in the winter with flaps that came down over his ears, so he looked a little like an elephant without a trunk."

The man laughed briefly.

"Good," he said. "And you imagined what, Number Four?"

"I thought if he asked me out, I would let him kiss me after the first date."

"Yes. And?"

"And if he asked me out again, I would kiss him again and maybe let him feel my breasts."

She heard the man slide closer. He was speaking in a soft, whispery voice, almost as if his anger had fled, replaced by something only the two of them could share.

"Yes, tell me more, Number Four. What would happen on the third date?"

Jennifer was staring straight ahead. She knew she was facing the camera. She suspected when she had used the word *breasts* that the camera had focused on hers. *Except,* she insisted to herself, *not mine. Number 4's.*

Behind the blindfold, Jennifer squinted, trying to picture some teenage boy who didn't exist.

No one had ever asked her out. And other than a spin-the-bottle party when she was twelve, no one had ever wanted to kiss her. At least, no one that she knew about. It had made her think sometimes that she wasn't pretty. It had never occurred to her that the opposite might be true, that she was too pretty and too different and too rebellious, and that all these things were intimidating and had driven her classmates toward easier challenges.

She invented. She drew upon every presleep fantasy. Movies. Books. Anything that had an easy-to-remember romance.

"And if he called again, and I could get things right . . . a place where we could be alone and it was quiet . . . I thought we might . . ."—she hesitated—"go all the way."

"Go on, Number Four."

"I wanted it to be in a room. A real bedroom. Not on a couch or in a car or in some basement. I wanted it to be slow. I thought it would be like a present I was giving. I wanted it to be special. And I didn't want him to run away afterward. I didn't want it to be scary."

The man moved closer to her. She could sense him maneuvering about. When his fingers touched her arm she nearly screamed. She was taut with terror.

"But it won't be like that, not now, will it, Number Four? This boy from your school, he's not here, is he? And do you think he will ever know what a treat he just missed out on?"

She didn't reply. She felt his fingertips just glassing over her skin. They circumscribed her body, as if drawing attention to each part. The shoulders. Down her back and across her buttocks. Around her waist and pausing on the flat of her stomach. Then lower. She shuddered. With someone she loved, Jennifer knew it would have been erotic. With the man, she could feel darkness shading her. She twitched and had to fight off the desire to shrink back.

"Do you want to get it over with, Number Four?"

"I don't know . . ."

The man repeated his question word for word: *"Do you want to get it over with, Number Four?"*

Jennifer hesitated. Would *yes* invite him to grab her right then? Throw her down and force himself on her? Would *no* be an insult? It might just bring about the exact same result. She breathed in sharply, holding her breath as if choking herself might help her to see what the right answer was, if there was one.

She twitched through her shoulders. *Afterward what would be left? Would she have any value?*

"Answer my question, Number Four."

She took a breath.

"No," she said.

He was still whispering. "You said you wanted it to be special."

She nodded. The man continued speaking in low tones filled with restrained hate, not love.

"It will be. Just not *special* in the way you thought."

He laughed. Then she sensed him stepping back.

"Soon," he said. "Think about that. Very soon. It could happen *any minute*. And it will be hard, Number Four. It will be nothing like you ever imagined."

And then she heard him cross the room.

Within a second another sound. The door opening and closing.

She remained standing, still naked. She waited for what seemed like several minutes, not moving. Then, when the silence built up around her into a scream, she breathed out slowly and groped around for her underwear. She pulled them on and returned to the bed. She could feel sweat dripping down under her arms. It wasn't the heat that caused this. It was the threat. She found her bear and whispered to him, "This isn't happening to us, Mister Brown Fur. It's happening to someone else. Jennifer is still your friend. Jennifer hasn't changed."

She wished she could actually believe this. She understood that something was in balance, teetering back and forth. A seesaw of identity.

She did not know if she could keep her equilibrium.

The room beyond the blindfold must have been spinning. She felt dizzy and flushed, as if every place the man's hands had swept over her had left red striations and scars.

She pulled Mister Brown Fur close.

Fight what you can fight, Jennifer. The rest doesn't mean anything.

She nodded her head, as if she agreed with herself.

Then she insisted deep into her core: *Whatever happens, it doesn't mean anything, it doesn't mean anything, it doesn't mean anything. Only one thing is important: stay alive.*

32

Adrian spent much of the weekend locked in his house, not by any deadbolt or keyed chain but by his illness. He barely slept, and when he did it was unsettled by vibrant dreams. Much of the time he paced erratically from room to room, pausing only to speak with Cassie, who did not answer him, or to plead with Tommy to emerge so that he could embrace his son once again. That thought kept racing through his head *one more time one more time one more time* but, despite his entreaties, his son remained silent and invisible.

When he spied himself in the mirror, he thought he was seeing a shadow. He was dressed in a torn pajama top and faded jeans, as if he'd been caught halfway between dressing or undressing. His hair was matted with sweat. His chin was stubbled with gray. He felt like he was trapped in the midst of an argument, that there was a loud and insistent part of him telling him to forget things, while a different half insisted he keep his head clear, control his thoughts, and manage his memories. One side was yelling and screaming while the other was speaking calmly, quietly. Every so often this reasonable side of his personality would remind him to eat something, to go to the toilet, brush his teeth, shower, shave—all the small routines of life that everyone thinks are normal traffic, and which Adrian knew were becoming increasingly hard and discouragingly complicated.

He wanted to shift responsibility to his wife. Cassie was always good at remembering every appointment for the two of them. She had a terrific recall for the names of people met at cocktail parties. She remembered dates, places, the weather, and conversations with a stenographer's accuracy. He had always marveled at her ability to summon up what he considered the most trivial aspects of life instantly. His own imagination was cluttered by so many measurements taken during lab experiments, and by words that he might try to string together into a poem. It was as if he had no space left inside his brain to remember the name of the adjunct faculty member's wife, whom he'd met at a year-end department barbecue, or when to change the oil in the Volvo.

Tommy had developed his mother's ability to summon up names and places effortlessly. It had helped him with his camera work. This shot was taken at this speed, with this shutter setting, with this lighting. He was encyclopedic about his craft.

Either one of them, he thought, would have been better searching for Jennifer. Each would have been adding details together, stringing observations into facts. They would be like Brian, able to compile small things into a larger picture.

He was envious. They were all better detectives than he was.

Adrian once again looked hard across the space to the favorite Queen Anne chair where Cassie should have been but wasn't.

He was only vaguely aware that his house was showing the same wear that he was. He knew the dishes were piling up in the sink. He knew soiled clothes were stacked in the laundry. He knew the vacuum cleaner and the mop were calling out to him, although he didn't exactly know what sort of language appliances might use. Some sort of disembodied metallic voice, like an announcement in a train or bus station.

Adrian told himself that he had to keep his mind functioning, and so, after abruptly standing up in the center of his living room and shouting,

Look, damn it, Cassie, you need to help me remember this crap! he located a broom and started sweeping. He couldn't find a dustpan so he pushed some of the debris under the carpet. This made him laugh, and he sensed his wife's disapproval. A ghostly nagging *Oh, Audie, how could you* seemed to echo around him, but she didn't appear, and he felt like a young child who had managed to get away with some small infraction of the household rules.

Then he set the broom aside, dropping it onto the floor, where it made a banging sound against the worn wood. He went into the kitchen. He managed to get one load started in the dishwasher, and then he began the washer and dryer. He was exceptionally pleased with himself that he was able to measure out detergent, put it in the proper receptacle, and then punch the right series of buttons to start the washing machines.

It was extraordinarily mundane, irrepressibly lonely work.

This was all unfair, he argued with himself. He needed them and they weren't here.

And then, as the washing machine began its *pocketa-pocketa* noises, filling with water and suds and cleaning his clothes, he realized they were.

He was never alone.

All the people he loved and cared about were beside him.

In that second, he understood that hearing them wasn't about *them*, it was about himself. He turned around sharply, pivoting as if he'd been surprised by a noise. Cassie was behind him. He broke into a wide smile; it was the young Cassie. She was wearing a loose-fitting summer dress, and he saw that she was pregnant—far along, maybe only days, or *minutes*, from Tommy's announcement that he was arriving in their world. She stood next to the wall, leaning up against the door of the kitchen. She smiled at him, and when he eagerly took a step forward, reaching out for her, she shook her head and wordlessly pointed to the side.

"Cassie," he said. "I need you. You've got to be here with me to help me remember . . ."

She smiled again. She continued to gesture to the side. Adrian didn't quite understand what she was pointing at, and he moved closer, reaching out with his hands widespread.

"I *know* it wasn't always perfect. I *know* there were arguments and sad times and frustrations and you used to complain about being stuck in a little college town where nothing ever happened and that you deserved to be a prominent city artist and that I held you back. I *know* all that. And I remember it was hard, especially when Tommy had his rebellious times and we fought about him and what to do. But now all I want to remember is what was great and wonderful and ideal . . ."

She pointed again to her side, and he could see exasperation in her eyes, as if his long self-serving speech wasn't important. She flashed with demand. Black eyes, he saw, that could resonate like thunder when she wanted.

"What is it?" he asked.

She smiled and tossed back her head again, shaking her long hair as if he were a child that couldn't quite grasp something pathetically simple in a classroom, like two plus two or the shape of the state of Massachusetts.

"What," he started, and then he saw what she was pointing at. The telephone attached to the kitchen wall.

Adrian listened carefully and, slowly, like the volume on a stereo being adjusted, he heard a distant ringing becoming louder and louder. He seized the receiver and held it to his ear.

"Hello?"

"So, professor, been waiting for me to call? You want to get together? I've made some progress."

It was the sex offender. Unmistakable tone of voice. Like thick oil bubbling up out of the earth, he thought.

"Mister Wolfe."

"Who'd you expect?"

"Did you find her?"

"Not exactly. But."

"Well, what is it?"

Adrian thought his voice had a no-compromise toughness to it. He wondered where that came from.

"I think, professor, you might want to help out now. I've found a few . . ." He stopped. Wolfe hesitated. "Well, I've found some things worth seeing," he said. "And I'm thinking you might be the person who needs to see 'em."

Adrian looked over at his wife. She was stroking her enlarged stomach, her hand making round circles across the swollen belly. She looked up at him and nodded eagerly.

She did not need to say *Go, Adrian.*

"All right," he said. "I will come over."

He hung up the telephone. He wanted to embrace his wife, but she made a gesture toward the door. "Hurry," she finally said in her singsong voice. He was overjoyed to hear her speak. The silence had scared him. "Always hurry, Audie."

He looked over at her stomach. What he remembered were the last days before their only son was born. She was hot, uncomfortable, but all the things that should have made her short-tempered and impatient seemed to be shunted away into some hidden box. She sweated in the summer heat and waited. He would bring her ice water and help her when she launched herself from her chair. He would lie beside her at night pretending to sleep, listening to her roll and shift trying to find a comfortable position. There was no way to express sympathy back then, because there really was nothing to be sympathetic about and it would just have made her angry. She was already working overtime to keep her emotions in check.

Adrian took a step forward.

"You can't just remember the good things," Cassie said. "There were lots of troubles too. Like when Brian died. That was bad. You were drinking heavily for weeks, and blaming yourself. And then, when Tommy . . ."

She stopped.

"Why did you . . ." He started to ask her the question that had lingered over the last weeks of her life but he could not. He saw that Cassie had dropped her eyes to her waist, as if she could see everything that was to come, and it made her both joyful and irrepressibly sad all at once. And then, Adrian thought, that must be what *he* felt, every second of every day, both in his sanity and in his madness.

He thought that he had been wrong to go on with life after Tommy and Cassie died. That had been his time. He should have followed them immediately, without any hesitation. Living had been the coward's way out.

When he looked back at Cassie, she was shaking her head.

"What I did was wrong," she said slowly. "But it was right too."

This made no sense at the same time that it made perfect sense. As a psychologist, he understood how grief could trigger a near-psychotic, suicidal state. There was significant literature in his field on this subject. But when he looked across the room at his wife and she seemed so young, so beautiful, and she reflected all the possibility that they had in their lives together, all the clinical studies in the world didn't help him to understand why she had done what she did.

Adrian squeezed his eyes tight. He wanted to ask her why she had left him alone, and then he thought he must have spoken the words, because her voice penetrated past his reverie. "When Tommy died, I became a shadow," she said. "I knew you were strong enough to see something left to living. But I was weak. I couldn't be in a house where there was so much pain and memory. Everything reminded me of him. Even you, Audie. Especially you. I looked at you and saw him and it was like something was torn from inside me. So I drove the car too fast one night. It seemed right."

"It was never right," Adrian said. He slowly opened his eyes, drinking in the vision of his young wife. "It could never be right. I would have helped. We would have found something together."

Cassie touched her stomach. She smiled.

"I forgive you," Adrian blurted loudly. He wanted to cry. "Oh, *Possum,* I forgive you."

"Of course you do," Cassie replied, matter-of-factly. "But you cannot waste these moments on me. You have a more important job. Don't you think there is another mother somewhere, Jennifer's mother, who feels like I did?"

"But," he started.

"Get cleaned up. You can't go out looking like this," Cassie said.

Adrian shrugged and went into the bathroom, lathered his face and grabbed his razor. He brushed his teeth and washed his face. Then he hurried into their bedroom. He rummaged through drawers until he came up with a clean pair of corduroys, fresh underwear, and a pullover that passed a quick nose test. He pulled on the clothes rapidly, knowing that Cassie was watching him.

"I'm hurrying," he said.

He could sense her laugh. "Adrian, moving quickly was never your forte," she said.

"All right, all right," he replied, a little exasperated. "The man makes me feel dirty, Cassie. It's hard to hurry to go see him."

"Yes, but he's the closest thing you have to an answer. Who knows better how to start a fire, Audie, the arsonist or the fireman? Who's the better killer, the detective or the assassin?"

"Your point," Adrian said, as he grunted, tying his shoelace, "is well taken."

"Puzzles. Mazes. Games. Brainteasers. Mental twisters. Adrian, see it all the way you saw *everything*. Pieces that add together and tell you something. Work hard, Audie. Make your imagination work for you."

Adrian thought his wife was clearly right. He sighed, wishing to stay longer, get more answers to all the questions that he already knew the answers to, instead of heading off into the night to try and find answers that were hidden. He trudged to his door, pulling on a tweed jacket, and exited into bright midmorning sunshine, momentarily surprised that the midnight darkness he'd expected seemed to have been strangely misplaced.

It was against departmental policy but it was the sort of rule that was frequently broken and rarely enforced. Terri Collins had brought the Jennifer Riggins case file home for the weekend, hoping that an examination of all the disparate details accumulated on various pages might lead her in some positive direction. She sat with it all collected on her lap while her children played outside with friends, making an acceptable racket, background banging and shouting, and, so far, she thought blissfully, no tears of conflict.

Her own frustration had redoubled. The technicians at the state police had managed to enhance the security video just enough so that some facial details were recognizable, but only in the most limited way. *If* she knew the man's name, it *might* prove helpful in a court of law. It *possibly* might have allowed her to ask some hard questions, if she had the man in a seat across from her. But so far as identifying who he was and what he was actually doing in the bus station and whether it had some real connection to Jennifer's disappearance was relatively impossible. Maybe if she had access to sophisticated antiterrorist software and banks of computers, it might have meant something. But she did not.

She recognized the classic cop's dilemma. If something else has provided a suspect, with a name and a link to a crime, backtracking into accumulating evidence was a tricky, though manageable, process.

But stare at a fuzzy, barely focused still frame ripped from a security video and try to guess if this anonymous individual had anything to do with a disappearance in another part of the state, and who it might be, and why he was there . . .

Terri stopped staring at the picture and shoved it aside.

Impossible, she thought.

She looked down at her file.

Dead ends and unlikely connections.

There was little enough to go on, and what little she had made little sense. She shook her head and wished that she had the professor's single-mindedness.

Terri thought, *He might be right but it's still impossible.*

Serial killers in Britain in the sixties. A couple in a panel truck on a suburban street. And then an impossible crime. A random nightmare. A milk carton disappearance.

She imagined that her career was about to be as dead as Jennifer Riggins. This was a terrible thing to predict—equating her paycheck with a sixteen-year-old's life—but it still rose into her imagination.

Maybe the professor's right about everything, she told herself. *But it still doesn't mean I can do anything about it.*

For a second she was angry. She wished she had never heard of Jennifer Riggins. She wished she hadn't responded to the teenager's first attempts to run away from home so that her name was linked to the official record of the teenager's misadventures. She wished she had refused to take the dispatcher's summons calling her to the scene of the latest flight. She wished she'd had nothing to do with the family that was about to undergo all the terrible uncertainties that the modern world can deliver.

Closure is a word that gets bandied about, she told herself, as if it somehow puts things right. We learn what happened to our child, we understand a disease, we comprehend the flag-draped coffin coming back from Iraq or Afghanistan. Someone says we have closure and that's like a get-out-of-jail-free card—except it isn't. Nothing is ever quite that compact and simple.

Terri clenched her hand into a fist. She discovered that she was staring at the Missing Jennifer flyer.

She abruptly dropped the file to the floor and almost kicked at it. Absolutely no leads to follow up, she thought. No telltale indicators of one thing or another. No obvious path to follow. No subtle trail to examine.

She sighed and stood up. She went to the window and stared out, idly watching the children at play. Everything, she believed, was utterly normal for a weekend morning.

She guessed that the same could not be said for the Riggins household. She breathed in deeply and understood that it was soon to be her job to take Mary Riggins aside and say that until some concrete piece of evidence surfaced they were at a standstill. This was not a conversation she looked forward to having. Police are well versed in the ability to deliver bad news. It is something of an art, expressing the details of the overdose or the accident or the murder, giving out information yet not overwhelming the victim's family with the capriciousness of life. The emotional content of these conversations was better left to priests and therapists. Still, it would fall to her to tell Mary Riggins that she was at a dead end, which probably meant that Jennifer, if she still lived, was also at a dead end.

302

It seemed unfair to her.

So many tragedies in life were preventable, Terri thought. But people are passive. They let things accumulate into disaster. She watched her own children. She wasn't like that, she told herself. She had taken steps to avoid everything that could go wrong.

This was reassuring to think, although she knew it was only partially true.

We like to tell ourselves lies, she admitted to herself.

She collected all the material and decided she would see Mary Riggins and Scott West that day. She would update them with nothing, and let them begin to see what Terri thought was the inevitable vision to come: Jennifer was gone.

She did not like to use the word *forever*. No policeman does. So she did not allow that word into the vocabulary of what she intended to say.

33

Jennifer was daydreaming about home before her father died, fantasizing about food and drink—what she wanted more than anything was a cold Diet Coke and a sandwich made with peanut butter, avocado, and sprouts—when she heard the sudden explosion of a distant door being slammed and voices rising in an argument. As when she'd heard the baby crying, and then the sounds of children playing, she craned her head toward the disembodied racket, trying to make out exactly what was being said, but spoken words were elusive in the torrents of noise, though the emotions were not. Someone was very angry.

Two someones, she told herself. The man and the woman. *It had to be.*

She stiffened, turning her head right and left, muscles tensed. She was only peripherally aware that she might be the cause of the argument. She listened and she heard high-pitched anger fading in and out of her ability to understand, and she felt herself clawing at every noise, trying to decipher what was happening.

She could make out obscenities: *Fuck you! Motherfucker! Cunt!* Each jagged-edged word sliced at her. She grasped at overheard phrases: *I told you so! Why would anyone listen to you! You think you know everything but you don't!* But it was like leaping into the midst of a story, the ending uncertain and the beginning long disappeared.

She stayed frozen on the bed, alert, Mister Brown Fur in her arms. The pitch of the argument seemed to increase, then decrease, ratchet up, then down, until she abruptly heard the sound of a glass shattering.

Her mind's eye pictured a tumbler being thrown across a room, smashing against a wall, pieces flying in all directions.

This was followed rapidly by a thudding sound, and then a near scream.

He hit her, she thought.

Then she doubted that. *Maybe she hit him.*

She grasped at any certainty that might penetrate the walls of her prison, but none arrived, except that whatever was happening outside her darkness was violent and intense. It was as if somewhere beyond her things were erupting, the earth shaking and the ceiling threatening to cave in. She barely realized it when she swung her legs over the bed and stood beside the nearest wall. She pushed her ear up against the board, but that seemed to make the noises fade farther away. She stepped in different directions, trying to gain some sort of purchase on the sounds, but like every other game of blind man's bluff she'd played since she arrived in the room they remained outside her grasp.

Jennifer made calculations in her head.

A baby cries.

School yard sounds of play.

A vicious argument.

All this had to add up into something. All of it had to be parts of a portrait that would maybe tell her where she was and what might happen to her. Everything was a piece of an answer. She staggered about the room, to the limit of the chain, trying to find something in the air in front of her she could touch that would steer her into some sort of understanding.

She desperately wanted to lift the edge of the mask and look around, as if by being able to see she would be able to comprehend. But she was too scared. Every other time she had snuck a view—seeing the camera that relentlessly eyed her, seeing her clothes folded on a table, seeing the parameters of her cell—it had been a quick, surreptitious glance. Every other time, she had tried to conceal what she was doing so that the man and the woman wouldn't know and wouldn't punish her. But this time her desire was framed by the intensity of the argument that echoed somewhere right outside her reach. There was something unsettling, something deeply frightening about the fight. Another sound of something breaking filled the room—a chair? A table? Did someone smash dishes?

She reeled. All the fights she had once had with her mother seemed to encapsulate her. She tried to measure what those battles had meant. She could think of only one lesson: *After a fight, people are mean. They want to hurt. They want to punish.*

She shuddered at the idea that whoever came through the door to her prison next would have nothing but pent-up rage, and she would be where it was delivered.

This thought made her retreat back to the bed, as if that was the only place she could be safe.

She cringed. Fear and uncertainty overcame her. She could feel tears forming and her breath came in sharp, small bursts, as if whatever the fight was about it involved her. She wanted to scream, *I've done nothing wrong! It's not my fault! I've done everything you wanted!* even if these protests weren't completely true.

She was enveloped by the darkness of her blindfold, but she couldn't hide. She shrunk back, dreading the next sound, whether it would be the door or another obscenity or something else breaking.

And then she heard the gunshot.

Two second-semester juniors at the University of Georgia were lounging inside their room at the Tau Epsilon Phi house when the unmistakable sound of the gun being fired crashed through the speaker set. One student lay on a metal frame bed beneath an army recruiting poster urging readers to "Be All That You Can Be." He was flipping through a copy of a magazine called Sweet and

Young, *while his roommate was seated in front of an Apple laptop computer at a scarred and battered brown oaken desk.* "Jesus!" *the first student said as he lurched up.* "Did somebody shoot somebody?"

"Sure sounded like it."

"Is Number Four okay?" *the other demanded quickly.*

"I'm watching," *replied his roommate.* "She seems okay."

The first student was lanky, long-legged. He wore pressed jeans and a T-shirt that celebrated "Spring Break in Cancun." *He crossed the room rapidly.*

"But scared?"

"Yeah. Scared. Like usual. But maybe more so."

Both boy-men leaned forward, as if by moving closer to the screen they could put themselves into the small room where Number 4 was chained to the wall.

"What about the man and the woman? Any sign of them?"

"Not yet. Do you suppose one of them shot the other? Remember they had that big fuckin' gun they were waving in Number Four's face earlier."

These were questions they didn't answer, because they knew enough to wait. The two students were prelaw and business management, which made them mildly sensitive to the legal issues associated with what they were watching, but not so outraged that they did anything other than pay the money—as they had to numerous pay-for-entry porn sites—and pay attention, which they did religiously. They, like so many of their classmates, had been raised on video games and were accustomed to spending hours engaged with a computer screen and some unfolding interactive drama, such as Grand Theft Auto or Doom.

"Watch her. See if she hears anything else."

The two roommates listened as carefully as Number 4. They were unaware that they mimicked her movements—craning their heads, bending toward sounds. From down a hallway in the fraternity house, someone started up thumping Christian rock music, which made the roommates curse in unison. Hearing what was happening in Number 4's small world was critical, they both thought, without saying this out loud.

"It's going to scare the piss out of her," *one said.* "She'll head to the toilet."

"Nah, it'll be the bear. She'll start talking to the bear again."

307

On the screen, the camera angle changed to a close-up of Number 4's face. They could see anxiety and tension in the set of her jaw, even with her eyes hidden. Each of the roommates imagined that Number 4's skin was prickling with fear. Each of them wanted to reach out and stroke the small hairs on her arms. Their frat house dorm room seemed just as hot, just as stifling as Number 4's cell. One of the students touched her on the screen.

"I think she's fucked," one said.

"Why?"

"If the man and the woman are really fighting, maybe it's because they've got some sort of disagreement over the entire show. Maybe it's the rape. Maybe the woman is jealous of the man getting it on with Number Four . . ."

They both glanced at the clock ticking in one corner of the screen.

"Did you put down our bet?" the roommate asked abruptly.

"Yeah. Twice. First time was far too quick. We lost. It was your fault. Just because you wouldn't waste any time if Number Four was here." He paused, and both frat boys grinned at the suggestion in his words. "Anyway, you had to know they would string it out. Makes good business sense. Now we're locked into an hour tomorrow or the next day, I think."

"Show me."

The first student clicked on a couple of keys and the image of Number 4 in her room instantly compressed into a smaller screen. A single message played across the remaining page. It was in a Bodoni Bold Italic script. It said: "Welcome TEPSARETOPS. Your current wager is HOUR 57. There are 25 Hours remaining before your wager is in play. Your wager position is shared with 1,099 other subscribers. Total pool is currently above euro 500,000. Additional wager positions remain available. Wager again?"

Below the message were two boxes. YES and NO.

The student moved the cursor over to the YES box and turned to his roommate, who shook his head. "Nah. I think my card is close to maxed out. And I don't want my folks asking questions. I told 'em that this was an offshore poker site and they gave me a really long and exceedingly boring lecture and told me to quit making bets."

"They'll probably follow up with something about a twelve-step program and wonder if you're going to church on Sunday."

He shrugged, moved the cursor to NO, and clicked. Once again, Number 4 immediately filled their screen.

"You know, this would be a lot cooler on a big LED flat screen."

"No shit. Call your folks."

"No way they'd spring for it. Not with my last semester's grades."

"So," the first student said, as he leaned back, "what happens next?" He glanced over at a wall clock. "I've got that damn Uses and Abuses of the First Amendment seminar in half an hour. I hate missing anything."

When he said "missing" he wasn't talking about the lecture.

"You can always go and watch anything you missed in the catch-up window."

The student clicked another couple of keys and again relegated the real time image of Number 4 to a corner. As before, a Bodoni Bold Italic message appeared. This said: MENU and contained a number of smaller images. They each had a title like "Toilet Use" or "Number 4 eats" or "Interview #1."

He clicked out of the menu, back to the full screen.

"Yeah, but I hate that. The fun is watching in real time."

He reached for a pile of textbooks. "Shit. I've got to go. If I miss another class, it will cost me a half-grade point."

"Then go."

The student shoved books into a backpack and grabbed a tattered sweatshirt from a pile of laundry. But before exiting he leaned forward and kissed the image of Number 4 on the screen. "See you in a couple of hours, darlin'," he said, adopting a fake southern accent. He actually hailed from a small town outside of Cleveland, Ohio. "Don't do anything. At least, don't do anything I wouldn't do. And don't let anyone do anything to you. Not for twenty-five hours."

"Yeah. Stay alive and stay a virgin while my asshole roommate goes to his class so he doesn't flunk out and end up flipping burgers for a living."

They both laughed, although it wasn't totally a joke.

"Let me know if you see something. Text me right away."

"You got it."

His roommate stroked the screen and settled into the chair in front of the computer. "Hey," he said, "your disgusting wet French kiss left a mark."

The roommate gave him the finger and exited. The remaining frat boy imagined that the echo of the gunshot still reverberated in the cell. He tried to picture what he would do if he heard someone firing a gun in another room. He believed that he would have many options, including flight. That this wasn't available to Number 4 only fascinated him more. He loved what he considered her resourcefulness, while at the same time he really didn't want to miss the rape when it took place. He found himself fantasizing, wondering whether it would be quick and violent or some protracted theater of seduction. He suspected the latter. He wondered whether she would give in and just let it happen or whether she would fight and claw and cry. He wasn't sure which he wanted. On one hand, he loved the domination of the man and the woman over Number 4. On the other, he sort of liked rooting for the underdog, which she clearly was. It was what he and his roommate loved about Series #4. Everything was predictable yet completely unexpected. Sometimes he wondered whether there were other students on campus paying to watch Number 4. Maybe we all love her, he thought. She reminded him a little bit of a girl he'd known in high school. Or maybe of all the girls he'd known in high school. He was uncertain which. The one thing he was sure of was that Number 4 was doomed.

The gunshot might have been the start of the end, he thought. But then maybe it wasn't. He couldn't tell.

But he knew she would die in the end.

He looked forward to seeing how it happened. He was an aficionado of jihadist tapes and YouTube–type postings of gory auto accidents. He loved television shows like Cops and First 48 and he secretly wanted to be on Survivor more than any other aspiration he might have had about his future. He absolutely 100 percent knew that if he went on the show he would win the million-dollar prize.

Number 4 was shaking again. He had come to anticipate her loss of bodily control. It told him that her fear wasn't faked.

He loved this.

So much of what he watched was fake. Porn stars faked orgasms. Video games faked deaths. Television shows faked drama.

Not Whatcomesnext. Not Number 4.

Sometimes, he believed, she was the most real unreal thing he'd ever watched.

His speculation stopped abruptly. There was some movement in the room. He saw Number 4 turn slightly. The camera panned with her. Something was happening.

He heard what she heard. The door was swinging open.

Jennifer twitched to the sound.

She could hear the crinkling noise that told her the woman in the jumpsuit was entering the room. But instead of moving slowly her pace seemed to be hurried. One second she was at the door, the next she was hovering over Jennifer, her face only inches away.

"Number Four, listen carefully. Do precisely what I say."

Jennifer nodded her head. She could hear anxiety in the woman's voice. The ordinary cold, modulated tones were accelerated. The pitch had gone up, even with the whisper that she used. She could sense the woman had lowered her lips very close to her forehead, so that hot breath swept over Jennifer's face.

"You are not to make a sound. You are not to even breathe heavily. You are to remain exactly where you are. Do not move. Do not shift about. No noise whatsoever, until I return. Do you understand what I am saying?"

Jennifer nodded. She wanted to ask about the gunshot but she didn't dare.

"Let me hear you, Number Four."

"I understand."

"What do you understand?"

"No noise. Nothing. Just stay right here."

"Good."

The woman paused. Jennifer listened to her breathing. She was unsure whether it was her own heartbeat or the woman's that pounded, reverberating in the small room.

Suddenly Jennifer felt her face being grabbed. She gasped. She froze as the woman's fingernails dug into her cheeks, squeezing her skin tightly. Jennifer shivered, fought off the urge to tear at the hands that seized her, tried to toughen herself to the abrupt delivery of hurt.

"If you make a sound, you will die," the woman said.

Jennifer shook, trying to reply, but she could not. The quivering that raced through her body must have been enough of a response. The woman's hand relaxed, and Jennifer stayed rigid in position, afraid to move.

The next sensation she felt was unfamiliar, yet fierce. It was a sharp point. It started at her throat and then traveled down her center, circumscribing her body—her neck, her chest, her stomach, her crotch—in a steady, sliding movement, accentuated by small jabs, like a needle being touched against her skin.

Knife! Jennifer realized.

"And I will make your dying terrible, Number Four. Is this clear?"

Jennifer nodded again, and the knifepoint scraped against her stomach a little deeper.

"Yes. Yes. I understand," she whispered.

She could sense the woman withdrawing. The crinkling noise she made when she walked faded. Jennifer listened for the door closing but she did not hear it. She remained frozen on the bed, bear in arms, trying to figure out what was happening.

She listened intently, and just as she formulated the thought that something wasn't right, she felt a hand grasp her throat and she was being choked. She could feel an immense force, stealing every bit of air from her chest. She felt like she was being crushed beneath a huge concrete slab. Fear and surprise threatened to make her pass out. Pain sheeted behind the blindfold, red as blood. She kicked out, at nothing but air. She reached up without thinking but her hands stopped when she heard the man's voice.

312

"I can do just as bad, Number Four. Maybe I can be worse."

Her body quivered. She thought she would black out in the darkness of her blindfold, and then she wondered whether she *had* blacked out, as she choked on slivers of breath.

"Don't forget that," the man whispered.

She shuddered at the sound as much as the message.

"Remember. You are never alone."

The man's hands suddenly relaxed. Jennifer coughed, trying desperately to fill her lungs. Her head reeled. She'd had no idea that the man—dressed in his skintight black balaclava and long underwear, ballet slippers on his feet—had silently trailed the woman into the room. Now everything was disjointed, disconnected. An argument, a gunshot—that had invented one scenario in her imagination. But both of them in the cell together, acting in unison, acting in tandem, acting in a coordinated fashion, simply pitched her into a vortex of confusion. She could feel herself spinning and she struggled to hold on to anything that might stop her from falling into the pit of darkness.

"Silence, Number Four. No matter what you hear. What you sense. What you think is happening outside. Silence. If you make a sound, it will be the last thing you do on this earth, other than experience unimaginable pain."

Jennifer squeezed her eyes tightly together. She must have nodded slightly. She did not think she had spoken out loud. But she heard the door close. The man, she realized, had crossed the room without her being able to hear a thing. This was as terrible as any of the explicit threats.

She remained in the darkness, as if encased in ice.

A part of her wanted to move. A part of her wanted to peek out. A part of her wanted to leave the bed. These were the dangerous parts, which warred against the safe parts that told her to do exactly as she'd been told.

She tried to listen for the man or the woman. No sound greeted her.

But this thick absence of any noise except for her own labored breathing didn't last.

What she heard was something familiar. Something that was both awful and frightening in its own way. It took her only seconds to realize what it was.

A siren. A police or fire siren.

It was distant but closing rapidly.

34

Adrian swerved hard to avoid the other car and was greeted with a horn blasting, tires squealing. The noise resounded through the Volvo's interior, and it wasn't hard to imagine the accompanying angry curses and shouted obscenities. He glanced up and saw that he had clearly run a red light, and he avoided an accident only by a couple of lucky yards. He muttered, "Sorry, sorry, my fault, I didn't see it change . . ." as if the other driver, who was speeding away, could actually hear him or see the apologetic look on his face.

"That's a bad sign, Audie," Brian said from the passenger seat. "Things are sliding. You need to stay sharp."

"I'm trying," Adrian replied, a touch of frustration creeping into his words. "I just get distracted. Happens to everyone at some point or another. It doesn't mean anything."

"You're wrong about that," his brother answered. "You know it. I know it. And probably the guy in the other car knows it now too."

Adrian drove on, more than a little angry, deflecting fears about his own capabilities into fury at his brother.

What Adrian wanted to say was that Brian, like Cassie and Tommy, had left him alone with nothing but questions. Every question was its own mystery. But he couldn't quite say that for fear he would be demanding too much of his dead brother.

Brian was quiet for a moment. Adrian steered the car down the roadway. A sheet of bright noonday sunshine filled the window in a flash, and then faded, as he maneuvered the car around a bend. They were only a few blocks away from Mark Wolfe's house, and Adrian thought he should be formulating what he was going to say to the sex offender. He reminded himself that a proper detective would be anticipating whatever it was that Wolfe had uncovered in his computer searches, because whatever it was it had caused him to summon Adrian to his house.

Adrian glanced to the side. His brother was dressed in his usual subtle blue pinstriped Wall Street lawyer's suit. He was natty. Well put together. But his voice was filled with a softness that Adrian hardly recognized. His brother was always dynamic, the one who made tough choices and fought loudly and fiercely on behalf of clients and causes, and to hear him sound so pummeled by defeat was alien, impossible.

Adrian gasped. Brian's face was streaked with blood. The front of his white shirt was stained deep crimson. His hair was tangled and matted. Adrian could not see the hole in the side of his head that the bullet had made, but he knew that it was there, just out of his sight.

"You know what surprised me, Audie? You were always this academic, intellectual type. Poetry and scientific studies. But I had no idea how tough you were," Brian continued, a flat, journalistic tone in his voice. "I couldn't have survived Tommy dying over in Iraq. I couldn't have gone on after Cassie drove into that tree. I was selfish. I lived alone. What I had were clients and causes. I wouldn't allow people into my life. It made it all so much easier for me because I didn't have to worry about who I loved."

Adrian shifted his eyes back to the road. He double-checked to make sure he was doing the speed limit exactly.

"Wolfe's house is just up there," Brian said. He was pointing ahead. His finger was bloody.

Adrian saw that his brother started to brush the front of his shirt, as if the bloodstains were like breadcrumbs. "Look, Audie, you can handle this guy. Just keep in mind what every detective knows: there's always one link. Something is out there that will tell you where to look for Jennifer. Maybe it's right here and coming up fast. You just have to be ready to spot it when it flashes by. Just like that car at the stoplight. You have to be ready to take action."

Adrian nodded. He pulled the car to the side.

"Just stay close," he said, hoping that his dead brother would think this was an order, when actually it was a plea.

Wolfe, Adrian saw, was standing in the doorway, watching for him. The sex offender waved in his direction, like any good neighbor on a weekend morning.

Adrian was taken aback by the cheeriness inside Wolfe's house. Things were clean and neatly arranged. Sunlight poured through open blinds. There was a springtime smell in the house, probably installed by a liberal spray of canned air freshener. Wolfe gestured toward the now familiar living room. As Adrian stepped forward Wolfe's mother emerged from the kitchen. She greeted Adrian warmly, with a kiss on the cheek, although she clearly had no recollection of his prior visits. Then she bustled herself off to a back room to "do some straightening up and fold some laundry," which Adrian thought was some sort of prearranged behavior. He imagined that Wolfe had coached his mother carefully about what to say and do when Adrian arrived.

Wolfe watched his mother disappear through a hallway and shut a back room door behind her.

"I don't have that much time," he said. "She gets restless when I leave her alone for too long."

"What about when you go to work?"

"I don't like to think about that. I have one of her friends stop by every other day. I keep a list of women she knew before all this started to happen who are willing, so I call them as much as I can. Sometimes they'll take her for walks. But because of my"—he hesitated—"*problems* with the law most of them don't want to be seen over here. And so I hire a neighbor's kid to come around after school and check on her for a couple of minutes. The kid's parents don't know we have this deal, because if they did they'd probably stop it. Anyway she can't remember his name nine times out of ten, but she likes it when he stops by. I think she believes the kid is me, only twenty years ago. Anyway, that sets me back ten dollars a day. I leave a sandwich out for her lunch. She's still capable of eating without supervision but I don't know how much longer that will last, because if she chokes . . ."

He stopped. The vise that he was in was obvious.

Adrian wasn't exactly sure what all this had to do with him, but he heard Brian's voice saying, "You know what's about to come, don't you?"

Seconds later, Wolfe turned to Adrian.

"I know we had an agreement, but . . ."

He could hear his brother's snorted laugh.

". . . I need more. Just promising you won't go to the cops isn't enough. I need to be paid for what I'm doing. It takes up a lot of time and energy. I could be working an overtime shift at work, making extra cash."

Wolfe moved into the living room. He took out his mother's laptop computer from the knitting bag and began to wire it into the flat-screen television.

"What makes you think—" Adrian began before he was interrupted.

"I know about you, professor. I know about all you rich academic types. All of you have money socked away. All those years getting government research grants, all those state benefits. Your colleagues over in the business school probably steered you into some pretty good investments. You know, that old Volvo. Those ratty clothes. You might look like you haven't got a dime but I know you've probably got millions socked away in some account."

Adrian thought that people who say *I know all about* something or someone generally didn't know anything. He kept this opinion to himself.

"What are you looking for?"

"My share. A proper fee for my time."

Brian was whispering instructions in Adrian's ear. Adrian could sense some glee in his brother's voice. A lawyer's delight: setting a trap.

"This sounds to me like extortion."

"No. Payment for services rendered."

Adrian nodded. Everything he did was at the direct behest of his brother, who was filling his ear with rapid-fire instructions. "*Get his phone!*"

Adrian did as he was told.

"Well, do you have a cell phone—I'm afraid I never carry one—so I can make a call."

Wolfe smiled. He reached into a pocket and produced the telephone. He tossed it to Adrian. "*Start to bluff.*"

"Call away," he said.

Adrian was momentarily confused by what his brother meant by a bluff, but he saw his own fingers punching numbers on the keypad. For a second, he thought it was Brian's hand that was steering his. He dialed 911.

"*You know who to ask for,*" Brian said briskly.

"Detective Collins, please."

Wolfe looked surprised.

"*Maybe* I've found her," he spoke rapidly, almost panicky. "But if that call goes through, *maybe* I haven't."

Adrian hesitated, heard a distant hello, and immediately clicked the phone shut.

"*That will make things tricky,*" Brian said softly. "*Pay attention. I've done this before. Step one: make him get specific.*"

"Well, Mister Wolfe, which is it? Have you found her or not?"

Wolfe shook his head. "It's not that simple."

"Yes it is."

"*Good,*" Brian said.

"Have you found her?" Adrian persisted.

"I know where to look."

"That's not the same thing."

319

"Yeah," Wolfe said. "But it's close."

"*Okay, Audie, keep going. You're controlling things.*"

"Do you have a proposal?" Adrian asked abruptly.

"I just want to be fair."

"That's a statement. Not a proposal."

"Professor, we both know what I'm talking about here."

"Well, Mister Wolfe, then why don't you describe to me what you think is fair?"

Wolfe hesitated. He was grinning. He had a look like the old Disney version of the Cheshire cat, who faded into nothingness, leaving only his wide, unsettling toothy smile behind on the movie screen. Adrian remembered watching *Alice in Wonderland* with Tommy, and then remembered spending more than a few hours trying to explain to his small son that the likelihood of him falling down a rabbit hole into a world where a Red Queen wanted to cut off people's heads prior to trials was small. When his son was very young, fantasy scared him, not reality. He could watch a show about shark attacks in California or hungry lions on the Serengeti and it would fascinate him. But hookah-smoking caterpillars left him tossing and turning and crying out in the dark instead of sleeping.

"*Audie, don't let your mind wander!*"

Brian was insistent. Alert.

"You know, professor, I'm not exactly sure just how much my time is worth . . ."

"Well, you put a price on it yourself. Double time at the store where you work."

"But this is specialized work. Highly specialized. That requires some" . . . he hesitated . . . "premium."

"Mister Wolfe, if you're going to try to extort money from me, please be precise."

"*Good,*" Brian said. "*That will upset him.*"

His dead brother, Adrian thought, knew much more about criminal psychology than he'd believed he did.

"Well," Wolfe said, "what's it worth to you?"

"Success is invaluable, Mister Wolfe. Priceless. But, on the other hand, I'm not willing to pay you for failure."

"Put a price on it," Wolfe said. "I want to know how hard to work."

"You will merely change whatever number I come up with at a later point. I say a thousand, ten thousand, or a million and you are just going to double it or triple it when you have something for me. Isn't that true?"

Wolfe turned away briefly. Adrian knew he'd scored.

He couldn't believe he was coldly negotiating over something as elusive as Jennifer's disappearance. It surprised him.

"Tell you what, Mister Wolfe. We shall have a reward. This is like those old-fashioned Wanted Dead or Alive posters from Western movies. Say twenty thousand dollars. That's a substantial sum. If you develop information leading to her discovery and return home—that's *if*—then I will pay you twenty thousand dollars. Help save Jennifer, make a pile of money. Play games, screw around, come up with nothing and you'll get nothing. There's your financial incentive. I doubt that if I were you I would take your pathetic efforts at extortion to her family or anyone else because the cops will be less sympathetic than I am, and you will land in prison. But I'm a little different, a little bit crazy . . ." Adrian smiled like the villain on a stage might. "So I will permit you to extort some money from me."

"How can I trust you?" Wolfe said.

Adrian burst out with a harsh laugh. "That, Mister Wolfe"—he imposed academic stentorian sounds into his words so that he came across as a pompous lecturer at a podium—"is of course *my* question."

Wolfe looked consternated.

"You aren't really good at this, are you Mister, Wolfe?"

"Good at what? When it comes to computers and surfing the Web I'm a goddamn *expert*."

"No. I meant being a criminal."

Wolfe shook his head. He turned back to his computer.

"I'm not a criminal. I never have been."

"We can debate that some other time."

"It's not a *crime*, professor. What I like. It's just . . ." He stopped, but whether it was because he knew how stupid he sounded or not Adrian couldn't tell.

"All right, professor. As long as we understand each other. Twenty grand."

Adrian expected some additional threat, some sort of *if you don't pay me, I'll* . . . but he wasn't exactly sure what either of them could do. Wolfe wanted the money. But Wolfe knew that Adrian could walk out the door. He thought they were ideally balanced. Both had needs.

So they would play a game.

He had no idea whether he even had twenty thousand dollars sitting in a bank account, and whether he would pay Wolfe *anything*. He doubted it. He could feel Brian's hand on his shoulder and he heard his brother's voice: "*He knows that, too, Audie. He's not stupid. So that means he will have another move. You've got to be ready for it when he makes it.*"

Wolfe missed Adrian's slow nod.

"I'm not a bad person," Wolfe said. "No matter what those cops say."

Adrian didn't reply.

"I'm not the bad guy here," Wolfe said, nearly repeating himself. He was talking quietly, as if he didn't really care what Adrian thought.

"I never said you were," Adrian responded. This was a lie and he felt foolish for saying it out loud.

The computer keys clicked like a soft drum roll leading into a symphony.

"Is that her?" Wolfe asked abruptly.

It was late in the afternoon and Terri Collins sat in her car outside the Riggins house mustering the confidence to walk up to the doorway and dispense bad news. On a nearby tree trunk someone—she assumed it was Scott—had stapled a homemade flyer with a picture of Jennifer and the word MISSING in large bold letters. It had a *Last Seen* section and an *If spotted, please call* followed by telephone numbers.

She was a little surprised that he hadn't called the television stations yet. The natural inclination for people like Scott was to turn a disappearance into a sideshow. Mary would stand in front of the lights and cameras, teary-eyed, wringing her hands, begging whomever to *just let little Jennifer go*. This, Terri knew, was both useless and pathetic.

Terri gathered up some police documents and copies of the "Be On the Lookout For" Missing Persons sheet. It was a collection that would create the impression that she had been busy working the case, when all it represented was frustration after frustration. She had left in her office anything about the security bus station tape and anything stemming from her conversations with Adrian Thomas.

She exhaled slowly and looked back at the Riggins house. She wondered what she would do if one of her children went missing. She would be caught, she understood, wanting to get away from every memory written throughout the house and unable to shed the hope that she *had* to be there, waiting, in case the unlikely actually happened and the missing child walked back through the door.

Impossible, she thought. *That much pain and uncertainty.*

She wished she were better at what she had to do.

As she stepped from her car and walked up the sidewalk to the Riggins house, she was struck by the isolation. There were people outside the other homes using the last hours of daylight to rake dead leaves left over from the winter or plant perennials in gardens that were finally stirring with spring. She could hear sounds of power tools and mowers as people finished up the inevitable suburban projects that had been postponed through the short dark days just passed.

The Riggins house, in contrast, displayed no signs of activity. No noise. No movement. It looked like a house that had been buffeted by high winds and torn at by the claws of winter.

She knocked and heard a shuffling before the door swung open.

Mary Riggins stood in the doorway. No greeting. No pleasantries. "Detective," she said. "Any news?"

She could see both hope and terror in Mary Riggins's eyes.

Terri looked behind her. Scott West was at a computer desk in front of a screen. He turned away from what he was doing to stare at the detective.

"No," Terri said. "I'm afraid not. I just wanted to update you on what we've done."

And then she asked, "You haven't heard anything? Any contact? Anything that might . . ."

She stopped when she saw the emptiness in Mary Riggins's face.

She was ushered into the living room, where Scott West showed her a Facebook page and a dedicated website that he'd established for information about Jennifer. So far, neither had produced much, but Terri dutifully collected a printout of all responses at either location. She knew that Facebook would cooperate with any police inquiry, and she also knew she could track any of the website connections if they appeared promising.

The problem was, most of the responses were along the lines of *We're praying for her soul. Jesus knows there are no missing children, only children he's called to him* or *I wish she was missing all over my face. Yum yum.* These vaguely obscene replies were utterly predictable, just as predictable as the religious ones. There were also some of the *I know exactly where she is* entries, but these all seemed to want money for a further explanation. Terri made a mental note to turn over anything that even smelled like extortion to the FBI.

She stared at all the material on the computer and realized that she could devote her life to chasing down every response. That was the problem—from a detective's point of view—with opening those doors. If there *was* someone out there who actually knew something, it was hard to distinguish him from the nuts and the perverts who were drawn so readily to grief. *The world,* Terri thought, *likes to redouble tragedy. It's not as if the first blow is enough. It has to add stings and insults to injury.*

She wondered whether this was the unique province of the Internet. When you exposed something personal it allowed strangers to leap in.

"Do you think any of this can help you?" Scott asked.

"I don't know."

He looked at the computer screen. "I do," he said glumly.

Scott hesitated as he looked across the room. Mary Riggins had gone to fetch coffee for the three of them.

"I did this for her. It made her feel like she was helping to do something to find Jennifer. It's a little like driving around the neighborhood, as if we could spot her like a lost pair of gloves lying on the road. But it won't work, will it, detective?"

"I don't know," Terri lied. "It might help. There are cases where it has. But then . . ."

Scott jumped in, finishing her statement, as he usually did, ". . . far more often it's just a futile exercise. Right, detective?"

Terri wondered for an instant what sort of person used words like *futile exercise* in conversation. She maintained a calm, inexpressive look as she nodded in agreement.

Scott seemed to have a foundation in reality that played out as a kind of coldhearted, disconnected cruelty. She imagined this came through in his therapy sessions.

"I'm trying to help her face facts," he said. "It's been days. Days and days and days. Hours go by, we sit in here like we're waiting for the phone to ring and it will be Jennifer saying, 'Hey, can you pick me up at the bus stop?' But that call sure as hell doesn't come. We've heard nothing. It's like the earth swallowed up Jennifer."

Scott leaned back and waved his hand in the air. "It's a mausoleum in here. Mary can't just sit in the dark for the rest of her life waiting."

Terri thought that was exactly what Mary should be doing. Everyone always wants people to be realistic until it's their own child involved. Then there is no reality. There is only doing what you can.

And that will never end, she realized.

She did not think that talking about *facing facts* made any sense. But she realized that she was on the wrong side of the equation being written in the Riggins household. She took a cup of coffee from Mary Riggins's hand and watched as she sat across from her. *She will age fast now,* Terri thought. *Every word I speak will just add years to her heart. She will be forty when I start and a hundred when I finish.*

"I wish I had good news," she said quietly.

35

The siren sound reached a terrifying crescendo and Jennifer imagined that it was directly outside her cell. Suddenly, she could hear the deep *thud!* of several car doors slamming shut, followed rapidly by a machine gun–like pounding on a distant door. She could not actually hear someone calling out "Police! Open up!" but her imagination filled this in, especially when she heard hurried footsteps beating a drum cadence across an upstairs floor.

She stayed still, frozen, not precisely because that was what she had been told to do, but more because she was overwhelmed by images forming somewhere in the darkness directly in front of her.

The word *rescue* vaguely latched on to her heart.

Jennifer gasped, a sudden burst from within that became a sob. Hope. Possibility. Relief. All these things, and many more, flooded unchecked through her, a river current of excitement.

She knew the camera was watching her, and if the camera was capturing every movement she made, she knew also that it was coming up on a screen somewhere. But, for the first time, there was now someone else who might see her. Someone different from the man and the woman. Not someone anonymous and disembodied. Someone who might be on her side. *No,* she thought, *someone who is absolutely on my side.*

Jennifer turned slightly in the direction of the cell door. She bent forward, listening.

She tried to hear voices but there was nothing but silence. She told herself that this was good.

In her mind's eye, Jennifer pictured what was happening.

They had to open the front door. You can't turn down the cops when they knock. There was an exchange: "Are you . . . ?" and "We have reason to believe that you're holding a young woman here. Jennifer Riggins. Do you know her?" The man and the woman will say no, but they won't be able to get the cops to leave because the cops won't believe them. The cops will be tough. No nonsense. They won't listen to lies. They will force their way in and now they're all standing in some upstairs room. The police are wary, asking questions. Polite but forceful. They know I'm here, or maybe they just know I'm close by, but they don't know where yet. It's only a matter of time, Mister Brown Fur. They will be here any second. The man is trying to make excuses. The woman is trying to convince the cops that there's nothing wrong, but the police know better. The man and the woman—now they're getting scared. They know it's all over for them. The cops will pull out their guns. The man and the woman will try to run but they're surrounded. No place for them to go. Any second now, the cops will bring out their handcuffs. I've seen it in a hundred movies and a hundred television shows. The cops will force the man and the woman to the floor and slap on the cuffs. Maybe the woman will start crying and the man will be cursing, "fuck you fuck you . . ." but the cops won't care. Not at all. They've heard it all before a million times. One of them will be saying "You have the right to remain silent" while the others start to spread out, looking for us, Mister Brown Fur. Keep listening, we will hear them any second now. The door is going to open and someone will say "Jesus Christ!" or something like that, and then they will help us. They will break the chain around my neck. "Are you okay? Are you hurt?" They'll tear off the blindfold. Someone will shout, "We need an ambulance!" and another will be saying, "Take it easy, now. Can you move? Tell us what they did to you." And I'll tell them, Mister Brown Fur. I'll tell them everything. You can help me. And then, before we know it, they'll help me into my clothes and the place will be crawling with paramedics and other cops. And I'll be right in the middle. Someone will hand me a cell phone and it will be Mom on the other end. She will be crying she's so happy and maybe this time I'll forgive her a little bit, because I really want to go home, Mister Brown Fur. I just want to go home. Maybe because of all this we can start everything all over. No Scott. Maybe a new school, with new kids that aren't such bastards and everything will be different from now on. It will be like it was when Dad was still alive, only he won't be there, but I'll be able to feel him again. I know he's the one that helped them find me, even though he's dead. It was like he told them where to look, and they came looking and here we are. And then, Mister Brown Fur, the cops will take us out. It will be night and there will be cameras flashing and reporters yelling questions, but I won't say anything, because I'm going home. You and I, together. They'll put us in the back of a squad car and the siren will start up and some trooper will say, "You're one lucky little lady, Jennifer. We got there just in time. So you ready to go home now?" And I'll say, "Yes. Please." And in a week or two, maybe, someone from 60 Minutes or CNN will call up and say we're going to pay you a million dollars just to hear your story, Jennifer, and then, Mister Brown Fur, we can tell them what it was like. We will be famous and rich and everything will be different from now on.

Any second now.

She listened carefully, waiting for a piece of the fantasy to make a noise and confirm for her what she knew was taking place just beyond her reach.

But there were no sounds.

The only thing she could hear was her own breathing, fast, raspy.

Jennifer knew that they had told her to be quiet. She knew they were capable of doing almost anything. There were rules she couldn't break. Obedience was everything.

But this was her chance. She just wasn't certain how to take it.

Each silent second was sharp, prickly. She could feel herself shuddering, as familiar muscle spasms wracked her body. Holding herself still was nearly impossible. It was as if every different nerve ending, every separate organ within her, every pulse of blood through her veins had a different demand and a separate agenda. She thought she was being spun around, and it felt like the first moment on a roller coaster, when the tracks drop down and the car suddenly plunges headlong into noise and speed.

Jennifer waited. It was agony.

She felt as if she was inches from safety.

She craned her head, trying to hear something that would tell her what was happening. But silence crippled her.

And then she thought: *It's taking too long, Mister Brown Fur, it's taking too long!*

Panicky, she thought of all the things she might do. She could start to shout, *I'm here!* Or maybe she could rattle her chains. She could toss the bed over or kick over the toilet. Something so that whoever it was upstairs would stop and listen and know she was close by.

Do something! Anything! So they don't leave!

She could stand it no longer and she swung her legs over the edge of the bed, but it was as if they were weak, without any strength. She willed herself up. Everything was about to happen—she knew she needed to cry for help, make a thunderous noise, a shriek, a scream, anything that might bring help to her side.

Jennifer's mouth opened and she gathered herself.

And then, as swiftly, she stopped.

They will hurt me.

No. The police will hear you. They will save you.

If the cops don't come they will kill me.

Her breath was choking in her chest. She felt as if she was being crushed.

They will kill me anyway.

No.

I'm valuable. I'm important. I mean something. I'm Number 4. They need Number 4.

She was pinned between possibilities. Everything scared her.

Jennifer knew that she had to save herself. But behind the blindfold it was as if she could see two roads, each perilously close to a cliff, and she couldn't tell which was safe, which was right, and she knew that whichever she chose there would be no turning back, the path would disappear behind her. She could feel hot tears running down her cheeks. She wanted desperately to hear something that would tell her which road to take, the silence torturing her every bit as much as anything the man and the woman had done to her.

Jennifer thought: *I'm going to die. One way or the other, I'm going to die.*

Nothing made sense. Nothing was clear. There was no way to tell with any certainty what was right or what was wrong. She squeezed Mister Brown Fur tightly.

And then, as if it were someone else's hand pushing hers insistently, she lifted the edge of her blindfold.

"Don't do it!" the filmmaker shouted.

"Yes! Yes! Do it!" his wife, the performance artist, yelled.

The two of them were riveted in front of the flat-screen television mounted on the exposed brick wall of their trendy SoHo loft. The filmmaker was a thin, wiry man in his late thirties, who made a nice living by specializing in documentary films about third world poverty funded by a variety of NGOs. His statuesque wife—they had recently been married by a gay friend of theirs who had left the priesthood in frustration and who probably had zero legal right to perform a wedding—was equally thin, with a cascading Medusa-like tangle of curled black hair. She was a frequent performer at nightclubs and on small stages that were not the sort to be listed in The New Yorker, *which gave her some edgy credibility, although she secretly would have preferred to slide into the mainstream, where there was more money and greater attention.*

"She's got to fight her way free!" the wife said excitedly.

Her husband shook his head. "She has to outthink them. It's like facing down a man with a gun—" he started but was rapidly interrupted.

"*She's just a kid. Outthink them? Forget it.*"

This was the couple's second subscription to Whatcomesnext.com. They considered the money they paid to join the network to be work-related and therefore tax-deductible. Cutting-edge film, nouveau acting. Often, after watching Number 4, they had deep, meaningful conversations about what they had seen, and its relevance to the modern world of art. They both saw Whatcomesnext as an extension of Warhol's world and his Factory, which had been mocked decades earlier but which had grown over the years in prominence among critics and thinkers they followed. Number 4 clearly fascinated both of them, but they thrust their interest into an intellectual realm—not wanting to acknowledge the criminal or voyeuristic nature of their participation. They kept their subscription private from their friends, although each, at many a dinner party where the discussion turned to cinema techniques and the rise of the Internet as a place where film and art collided, had been tempted to blurt out their attraction to Number 4 and what she meant to them. But they did not do this, although they both believed that many of the people at the dinners probably subscribed as well. It was, after all, how they first heard of the website.

But as they had watched Number 4 over the days and nights of her captivity each had settled into a different relationship with her. The filmmaker had been protective in his responses, worried about what was going to happen to her, cautious, not wanting her to do anything that might put her in jeopardy or rock any boat unnecessarily; his wife, in contrast, wanted Number 4 to push things to their limits. She wanted Number 4 to take every chance. She wanted Number 4 to stand up to the man and woman and to fight back. She urged rebellion, while he spoke of being careful and obedient.

Each believed that what they shouted at the screen day and night was the only possible way for Number 4 to survive.

They had argued frequently about this. Every argument drove them deeper into the narrative surrounding Number 4. Each wanted his or her approach to be justified. The wife had crowed with success when Number 4 had first peeked beneath her blindfold, orienting herself to the cell and the main camera. The filmmaker had leaped up, pumping his fist with excitement when Number 4 had remained motionless, despite the man's lurking threats.

*The filmmaker would say, "That's really the only way she can control any-
thing. She has to be a cipher."*

*The performance artist would reply, "She needs to create her own story. She
needs to take charge of every little thing she can. That's the only way for her to
remember who she is and make certain that the man and the woman see her
as a person and not as an item."*

*"That will never happen," the husband replied. This—like all the other
exchanges—sounded like the start of a fight. But invariably it ended with him
stroking his wife's leg and her snuggling closer to him. Fascination as foreplay.*

*And now, in their loft, a fine dinner with an expensive bottle of white
wine behind them, they watched, half undressed, caught by drama in the few
moments before heading to bed.*

*"This is her chance, goddammit!" the wife nearly shouted. "Seize the
moment, Number Four! Own it!"*

She used the loose vernacular of the therapists they knew socially.

*"Look, you're wrong, just damn wrong," the filmmaker responded, his own
voice rising as he watched the screen. "If she doesn't obey them, she could be
opening herself up for almost anything. They'll panic. They might . . ."*

*His wife was pointing at the corner of the screen. Number 4 had lifted
both hands to the collar around her neck. This motion had gained their attention. Abruptly, the angle on the screen changed to an overhead view, slightly
behind Number 4, and held that position. The filmmaker noted this shift,
knew instinctively what it meant, and leaned forward eagerly. But the performance artist was pointing at something else.*

Jennifer tucked Mister Brown Fur under her arm and brought her hands
up to the collar and chain. She understood that she had three choices:
Make some noise. Try to run. Do nothing and pray for the police to
arrive.

The first was what they told her precisely *not* to do. She had no idea
whether the policemen upstairs would be able to hear her. For all she
knew, her cell had been soundproofed, just in case what was happening

did happen. She thought that the man and the woman had planned out so many things; she had to do something unexpected.

This thought terrified her.

She understood that she was at a precipice. She balanced everything, but frantic energy overcame her.

Jennifer started to tear at the dog collar.

Her fingernails ripped and clawed. She gritted her teeth.

Paradoxically, she didn't remove the blindfold. It was as if doing two things that were wrong was too much for her to handle at once.

Jennifer could feel her nails cracking; she could feel the skin on her throat being rubbed raw. She was breathing like a diver trapped beneath the waves, searching for a taste of air.

Every bit of strength she had left went into the assault on the collar. Mister Brown Fur slipped from her grasp and dropped to the floor at her feet. Beneath the blindfold she was sobbing with pain.

She wanted to scream, and in the second that her mouth opened wide she felt the material start to tear. She gasped and wrenched the collar savagely.

And suddenly it fell away.

Jennifer sobbed, nearly falling back on the bed.

She heard the chain rattle as it dropped to the floor.

Silence surrounded her, but inwardly it seemed to Jennifer that there was some great discordant overture of sound, like a blackboard being scratched or a jet engine passing only feet over her head. She clasped her hands to her ears, trying to shut it out.

She tried to steady herself; the sudden freedom made her dizzy. It was as if the chain had been holding her up like a puppet's strings, and now, abruptly, her legs went rubbery and her muscles flapped like a torn flag in a gust of wind.

The blindfold remained in place. Hundreds of thoughts raced through her head but screeching fear obscured them all. Hands shaking, she reached up and tore it away.

Pulling off the black sheet of cloth was like abruptly staring into the sun. She held her hand up and blinked. Her eyes were watering and she thought she was blind, but just as quickly her vision started to recover, racking into focus like a movie camera.

Jennifer looked around.

The first thing she did was freeze in position. She stared directly at the main camera a few feet away. She wanted to smash it but she did not. Instead, she reached down quietly and picked up her stuffed bear.

Then she slowly turned to the table where she had seen her clothes when she had peeked out from beneath the blindfold days earlier.

They were gone.

She staggered slightly, as if she'd been slapped. A wave of fright-nausea threatened to overcome her and she swallowed hard. She'd been counting on her clothes, as if putting on jeans and a tattered sweatshirt was taking a step back toward the life she had known, while standing near naked in the cell simply continued the life she had been thrust into. She tried to make sense of this division but could not. Instead, her head pivoted right and left, looking, hoping they had merely been moved. But the room was empty—save for the bed, the camera, the discarded chain, and the camp toilet.

A part of her wanted to reassure herself, *It's okay, it's okay, you can run just as you are,* but if this thought crept into her imagination it was hidden. She stepped forward.

Jennifer repeated to herself *get out get out get out* without thinking what she would do next. All she had was the vague idea of bursting free somehow and shouting for the police upstairs. Inwardly, her fantasy kept changing with every small action. Now she had to find them, not the other way around.

She took a deep breath and crossed the cell floor, bare feet slapping against cement, stepping past the camera and reaching for the door handle.

Don't be locked don't be locked . . .

Her hand wrapped around the knob. It turned.

Mister Brown Fur we're free!

Gingerly, trying to be as silent as possible, she pushed the door open. She tensed, telling herself, *Get ready. We're going to run. Run hard. Run fast. Run harder and faster than you ever have before.*

She had time for a single breath, a single vision of where she was. She saw a dark, shadowy basement, littered with ancient must, a wooden framed window filled with a black night sky and covered with cobwebs and dusty debris, before a light, brighter than any light she'd ever known, exploded in her eyes, blinding her instantly. She gasped, holding up her bear, trying to block the explosion. It was like a fire bursting toward her.

Suddenly everything went utterly black as a hood—like the hood that had encased her in her first second of captivity—was jammed down over her head, cutting off the light. Before she choked she heard the woman's harsh voice: "Poor choices, Number Four." For a second she struggled wildly, but then she was thrown down and clamped in a grip that was part pain, part vise. Whatever terror she had known in the days past gathered in a single horrible second and seemed to spiral into a great dark hole.

She plummeted helplessly after.

The performance artist shook her head. "Damn," she said, instantly sad but still fascinated. "Damn." The filmmaker husband sighed. "I told you so," he whispered quietly as they watched Number 4 struggle helplessly. "This is so wrong," his wife said. But she did not turn off the feed. Instead, she clutched his hand and shuddered as they settled back on their couch and, utterly unable to turn away, continued to watch.

At the same time, at the University of Georgia, in the Tau Epsilon Phi house, the frat boy frantically sent a text message to his roommate still stuck in a late-night class. It read: "No shit! We 1! It's goin down now. Yer missin it."

In the corner of the screen in front of him the Virginity Clock stopped on a number, which flashed red for a moment before going back to zero.

36

"No," Adrian said.

"No. No. No. No," he repeated.

Image after image of young women leaped onto the screen. All were involved in various sex acts or else posturing for a live webcam that captured them covered in suds while taking a shower, naked while they assiduously put on makeup or salaciously entertained a man or another woman. Usually a man with tattoos or a woman with billowy blond hair. Some were budding porn stars. Others were rank amateurs. There were college students and call girls. All seemed to play to the camera. Adrian thought they were all childlike and beautiful yet mysterious. He berated himself inwardly: *Years of studying psychology and you cannot tell why someone would expose themselves so intimately for any stranger to watch.*

Of course, he knew one answer. Money. But this made little sense to him.

Then he had a second thought: *The camera isn't public. It's only the means of distributing themselves.*

Adrian turned to the sex offender, who was ordering up each entry. He expected Mark Wolfe to look exasperated, to throw up his hands in frustration, because that was what *he* felt, but the sex offender did nothing of the kind. He simply continued punching computer keys and bringing up pictures, penetrating website after website. It was a cascade of pornography, flowing downhill into the computer. Wolfe had a maestro's style, clicking away, rarely pausing to take a lingering look at the sights or videos that flooded the screen, ignoring the constant moaning and groaning that came through the speakers. Adrian, too, had settled into a rhythm of viewing, paying little attention to the actual details of each image, as if the numbing repetition had somehow immunized him to what his eyes absorbed, watching instead for a telltale sign that they had stumbled on Jennifer.

He shifted about in his seat.

"Mister Wolfe," he said slowly, "are we going about this the right way?"

Wolfe stopped. He punched the key that cut the sound off from the computer, leaving a girl who seemed barely eighteen writhing with what Adrian assumed was the most phony of passions in the background. He held up a list he'd made on a pad of legal-sized paper. It was filled with dot.com addresses and website names such as Screwingteenagers.com or Watchme24.com. Adrian thought just about *any* combination of sexually suggestive words had evolved into a spot on the Internet map.

"I've got a lot of places yet to go," he started, before shaking his head.

Adrian tried again: "The right way, Mister Wolfe?"

"No, professor," he replied. Wolfe pointed at the woman in front of them. "And," he said slowly, "as you can probably tell by now, not too many of these people are being forced to do anything they don't want to do."

Adrian looked at the screen. He felt as if he'd been in a fight.

"No, I'm not exactly right," Wolfe continued. "Maybe they've been forced because they're broke, or forced because they don't have a job, or forced because it's the only thing they can do. Or maybe something inside them forces them, because it turns them on. Possible. But that sure ain't the case for little Jennifer, is it?" Wolfe finished his statement with a question.

Adrian nodded.

"Yeah," Wolfe said. "And even the amateurs, or the high school kids posting on Facebook, they're too damn old for the girl you're looking for. And all these sites, well, in order to keep from getting busted, they're pretty damn careful about making sure that even the teenagers taking pix with cell phone cameras and sneaking around so that Mom and Dad don't find 'em are at least eighteen. No one wants the heat that . . ." He stopped. Adrian looked over at him.

He stared hard at the sex offender. He realized that the places Wolfe had steered their inquiry were far too legal and mainstream. Adrian wondered whether the sex offender had been testing him.

"Mister Wolfe, you're the expert here. Give me some expert advice."

Wolfe appeared to be thinking, before reaching down to the floor where he'd stashed a bottle of water. He took a long pull. Then he crumpled up the sheets of paper filled with Web locations that he had been using as a guide.

"I've got one idea." He rocked back in his seat, thinking, before continuing. "Well, you know what date little Jennifer disappeared, so if she's somewhere in here it has to be a new posting. Most of these other sites have been around for a long time. The faces change. The action doesn't."

Adrian nodded. "Coercion, Mister Wolfe. A child being forced."

Wolfe picked up the flyer and stared at Jennifer's picture. "A child, huh? She looks pretty . . ."

Adrian must have looked oddly fierce, because Wolfe held up his hand. "I understand. You see a child. I see, well . . ." He hesitated. Adrian suspected he was going to say something that included the word *ripe*. "All right, professor. Now we're stepping into the dangerous part. You sure you want to go along?"

"Yes."

"Real dark places. Look at most of this stuff, professor. It might be explicit. It might even be disgusting to some folks. Or shocking, hell, I don't know. But it wouldn't be here if there weren't someone somewhere willing to pay for the opportunity to watch. And enough *someones* so that all the places we've been to are making money. So fit little Jennifer into that scheme and we'll know where to go.'"

"Stop calling her *little Jennifer,* Mister Wolfe. It makes it sound . . ."

Wolfe laughed and filled in the word: ". . . *trivial?*"

"That's good enough."

"Well, I'll try. But you gotta understand something. The Web makes everything trivial."

Wolfe looked at the entwined bodies on the screen.

"What do you see, professor?"

"I see a couple having sex."

Wolfe shook his head.

"Yeah, that's what I thought you'd say. That's what just about everyone says. Look closer, professor."

Adrian thought it was Wolfe speaking, but then he recognized Brian's voice. And it wasn't alone. It was as if behind the one hallucination there was a second, and he bent forward trying to separate out the tones until he realized that Tommy was echoing Brian.

"Look deeper," he heard.

For a moment he was confused, not sure where the insistence came from. And then he understood it *had* to be Tommy. He wanted to burst out in a laugh of delight. He had almost given up hope he would hear his son again.

"Look deeper," he heard a second time. "It's what I told you before, Dad. Use poetry. Use psychology. Think like a criminal. Put yourself in the rat's shoes. Why do they run down one maze corridor and not the other? Why? What do they gain and how do they gain it? Come on, Dad, you can do it."

Adrian whispered his son's name. Just saying the word *Tommy* filled him with a mixture of emotions, love and loss, all barreling around within him. He wanted to ask his son, *What are you saying?* but the words got lost on his tongue as Tommy's insistence interrupted him.

"The Moors Murders, Dad. What tripped up the killers?"

"They exposed themselves."

"What does that mean, Dad?"

"It means they were overconfident and weren't thinking of the consequences when they gave up their anonymity."

"Isn't that what you should be looking for?"

His son's voice sounded confident, determined. Tommy had always had the knack of expressing complete control even when things were disintegrating. It was why he was such a great combat photographer.

Adrian looked back at the screen.

"Hey, professor . . ."

Wolfe sounded unsettled. Adrian started to talk like a student being questioned by a teacher.

"What I see is someone who, for whatever reason, wants to be on that screen," he said. "I see someone who is playing by some rules, willing to perform. I see someone who hasn't been forced to scar herself."

Wolfe smiled. "That was poetic, professor. I think the same."

"I see exploitation. I see commerce."

"Do you see evil, professor? A lot of people would say they see depravity and something frightening and awful at pretty much the same time. And then they would stop looking."

Adrian shook his head. "In my field, we don't make moral judgments. We just assess the behaviors."

"Sure. Like I believe *that*." Wolfe seemed amused but not in an irritating way. Adrian thought that the sex offender had spent some time considering who he was and what he was drawn to. As Wolfe turned back to the computer keyboard, Adrian heard Brian whisper in his ear, "Well, so he's a pervert and a deviate, but lo and behold he's *not* a sociopath. Isn't that the damnedest thing?"

Brian's laugh faded as Wolfe punched some keys and the screen filled with red and black. It was a close-up of a dungeon, replete with whips, chains, and a black wooden frame, where a man wearing a skin-tight leather mask was being systematically beaten by a large woman, also encased in black leather. The man was naked and his body shuddered with each blow. Pleasure or pain, Adrian couldn't tell. Maybe both, he thought.

"This sort of dark place," Wolfe said.

Adrian watched for an instant. He saw the man quiver. "Yes. I see. But this . . ."

"Just an example, professor."

Adrian was quiet for a moment. "We have to narrow the search criteria down."

Again, Wolfe nodded. "My thoughts exactly."

He wanted to blurt out "*Where do I look?*" hoping that Tommy or Brian would know, but they frustrated him with silence. "We have to look for captives," he said.

Wolfe seemed to be thinking as Adrian continued.

"Three people. The two kidnappers and Jennifer. How do they enlist people in what they've done? They need to make money. Otherwise, this is a useless search. So find me the money, Mister Wolfe. Find me the way someone would use a girl they stole from the street."

Adrian was insistent. His voice had an authority that defied his disease. He could hear his brother and his son in some recess of his head, echoing applause.

Wolfe turned back to the computer. "Settle in," he said quietly. "This is going to be difficult, especially for an old guy like you."

"Not difficult for you, Mister Wolfe?"

The sex offender shook his head. "Familiar territory, professor. I've seen it all before."

He continued punching the keyboard. "You see, when you're like me, it's not as if you automatically understand precisely what"—he hesitated—"attracts you. There's an exploration involved. As your mind fills with ideas and passions, well, you search them out. You do a lot of traveling in your head and then on your feet."

He shrugged. "That's usually where you get caught. When you're not sure what it is you are looking for. Once you know, and I mean you *really know,* well, professor, then you're home free, because you can plan things with a concrete purpose."

Adrian doubted that any of the teachers in his former department could have given such a succinct analysis of the entangled emotional issues gathered around a variety of sex offenses and deviant behavior.

Wolfe suddenly stopped with his finger poised above a final key.

"I need to know you're gonna back me up," he said brusquely. "I need to know I can count on you, professor. I need to be sure that all this stays with us."

Adrian suddenly heard both Tommy and Brian urging him. *Go ahead and lie.*

"Yes. On this you have my word."

"Can you watch someone get raped? Can you watch someone get killed?"

"I thought you said that snuff films didn't exist."

Wolfe shook his head. "I told you that in the reasonable world they don't. They're urban legend. In the *unreasonable* world, well, maybe they do."

Wolfe took a deep breath and continued.

"You see, if I was ever caught with this stuff on the computer, or if some cop that monitors these things ever traced it back to me, I'd be . . ."

Adrian didn't have to fill in the obvious word.

"No. I'm the one demanding you do this. If anything comes of it, like the police, I will take all the blame."

"All the blame."

"Yes. And you can always tell the truth, Mister Wolfe. That I was willing to pay you to guide me."

"Yeah, except they got to believe me." Wolfe muttered these words and Adrian thought the sex offender was balancing on an edge. On the one hand, he knew the trouble he might be in, even with Adrian's cover. On the other, Wolfe clearly wanted to keep going. The places they were heading were destinations that Wolfe desired. Adrian could see this, in the hunched way the sex offender bent to the keyboard.

343

"All right, professor, now we're entering into the shadows." He smiled.

Adrian understood that Mark Wolfe was a frequent explorer in these worlds.

The sex offender punched a last key and young children came up on the screen. They were playing in a park on a sunlit day. In the background, Adrian could make out antique buildings and cobblestone streets. Amsterdam, he guessed. Mark Wolfe seemed to twitch at that moment, an involuntary movement that Adrian caught only out of the corner of his eye. Then both men swallowed hard, as if their throats were suddenly parched, although for diametrically opposed reasons.

"It looks innocent enough, doesn't it, professor?"

Adrian nodded.

"It won't be in a minute."

The sunlit day and the park dissolved into a white-walled room with a bed.

"Now watching this or owning this or even thinking about this," Wolfe said, leaning forward, "is absolutely fucking against the law."

"Keep going," Adrian said, but he hoped that it was Brian who was forcing him to continue, although he hadn't heard an insistent word from the hallucination in several minutes. It was as if even the brusque dead lawyer beside him was cowed by what appeared on the screen.

For hours, the two men wandered through a computer world that seemed to exist in a parallel universe, one that had different rules, different morality, and which played directly to aspects of human nature that Adrian believed were coldly outlined in textbooks he'd assigned in classrooms decades earlier. It was a world that had existed for centuries—there was little that was new, except the delivery system and the people engaging in it. He would have been unsettled by what he saw, except he felt a clinical detachment. He was an explorer with a single purpose and everything that passed in front of him that didn't fit into his theory of *Where Jennifer is* was discarded instantly. More than once, as he shifted about uncomfortably at the appearance of some awful exploitation, he thought himself lucky to be a psychologist and lucky to be losing his mind and his memory simultaneously. He was doubly protected, he told himself, and was able to watch things that redefined *terrible* because they would disappear from within him instead of becoming a nightmare.

Through the long day and into the evening, Wolfe's mother appeared from time to time at the living room door, hesitantly demanding access to her shows, only to be quickly steered aside by the dutiful son. Eventually he made her a small meal and put her to bed, following the usual nightly ritual, apologizing for monopolizing the television and promising her an extra-long sitcom experience the next day. Wolfe had seemed reluctant to steal those moments from his mother. Adrian noted this sense of empathy at the same time he noticed that Wolfe seemed to tumble with delight into the pictures they found. Sometimes Adrian would say, "Let's move on" but Wolfe would be slow to respond, reluctant to tear himself from the images. Wolfe was both stimulated and cautious. Adrian guessed that the sex offender had never sat next to another person as he examined the Web worlds.

It was, Adrian thought, exhausting in a numbing way.

They saw children. They saw perversion. They saw death.

It all looked real, even if it was faked. It all looked fake, even when it was real.

Adrian understood that the line between fantasy and reality was beyond blurred. There was no way for him to tell any longer if what he was seeing had actually happened or had been concocted with a Hollywood special effects master's skill. A terrorist executing a hostage—that had to be real, he thought, but it happened in some nether existence.

Wolfe continued to punch keys but he was slowing down. Adrian imagined the sex offender was fatigued just by the act of being on the precipice of so many of his own desires.

It was late.

"Look," Wolfe said, "we need to take a break. Maybe eat something. Get a coffee. C'mon, professor, let's give it a rest. Come back tomorrow, keep trying."

"A few more."

"Do you have any idea how much money you've spent already?" Wolfe asked. "Just signing up for these websites. One after the next. I mean, we're into the thousands . . ."

"Keep going," Adrian said. He pointed at a list that had popped up on the screen. I'lldoanything.com was followed by YourYoungFriends.com and Whatcomesnext.com.

Wolfe clicked on the last.

He sat up sharply. "Look at that. They want some heavy bucks to join. That's an expensive site," he said. "They must be offering something *special.*" This last word was spoken with a sort of excited energy.

There was only red writing on a black background and a price list, except for a duration clock. No indication what the site was selling, which told Adrian that visitors already knew what to expect. This intrigued him. At the same moment, Wolfe pointed at the duration clock.

It read: *Series #4.*

"Doesn't that fit with your girl's disappearance?" he asked.

Adrian did some quick math. It did. He leaned forward, filled suddenly with a different sort of enthusiasm than what he sensed from the sex offender.

"Pay the money," he said.

Wolfe typed in Adrian's credit card number. The two men waited for the authorization to come through. The room filled with Beethoven's "Ode to Joy" as the charge was approved.

"That's cool," Wolfe said as he typed in *Psychprof* as a screen name, and when a prompt asked for a password he typed *Jennifer.*

"Okay, professor, let's see what we have here."

Another click and a webcam image dominated the screen. A young woman, face hidden by a hood, sat on a bed. She was alone in a stark basement room and quivering with fear. She was naked. Her hands were loosely handcuffed to a chain that was fixed to a wall.

"Whoa," Wolfe said. "That's out there."

Below the image, the words *Say hello to Number 4, Psychprof* appeared.

Adrian stared hard at the image. His eyes traveled over the girl's skin looking for some telltale sign that might help him. He saw nothing.

"I can't tell," he said, as if answering a question that didn't need to be spoken out loud. He stood and closed in on the television, hoping that by moving closer he might see something clearer. The room on the television screen filled with the sound of heavily labored breathing and muffled sobs.

"Look there, professor. On the arm."

Adrian saw a tattoo of a black flower on the girl's arm. As he stared, Wolfe moved next to him. He pointed at the screen, touching it with his hand as if he could caress the person it showed.

Adrian saw what he was pointing at. A thin scar from an appendectomy on the girl's side.

"But she looks like the right age, huh, professor?"

Adrian picked up the Missing Persons flyer. There was no mention of a tattoo or of a surgical scar.

He hesitated. He saw Wolfe's cell phone on the table and he picked it up.

"Who you calling?" Wolfe asked.

"Who do you think?" Adrian answered. He dialed a number but his eyes were fixed on the naked, shivering girl in front of him.

Terri Collins picked up on the third ring. She was still seated across from Mary Riggins and Scott West, working her way through the same explanation for the hundredth time. Mary Riggins seemed to have an inexhaustible supply of tears that had been shed liberally over the hours that Terri had sat next to her. This didn't surprise the detective. She knew she would have had the same.

The caller ID on her cell phone came back with Mark Wolfe's name. This astonished her. It was very late and this made little sense. Sex offenders *never* called the police. It was the other way around.

She was taken aback when she heard Adrian's voice.

"Detective, sorry to bother you at this late hour," he started. He sounded oddly rushed. Terri Collins thought Adrian had usually seemed unsteady in the times they'd been together. *Hurried* was not a word she would have used to describe him in any of their meetings.

"What is it, professor?"

She was curt. The tears from Mary Riggins seemed the priority at that moment.

"Did Jennifer have a scar from an appendectomy? Did she have a tattoo of a black flower on her arm?"

Terri started to answer, then stopped.

"Why do you ask, professor?"

"I just want to be sure about something," he answered.

Sure about what? she thought. This raised her suspicions but she didn't follow up. She did not want to be cruel to the deranged old man, but neither did she want to distract the mother and erstwhile stepfather with anything that might be misinterpreted as hope.

She turned to Scott and Mary. "Did Jennifer have any scars or tattoos that you might not have mentioned?" She asked the question holding her hand over the receiver.

Scott answered swiftly. "Absolutely not, detective. She was little more than a child! A tattoo? No way. We would *never* have allowed that, no matter how many times she asked. And she was underage, so she couldn't get one without our permission. And she'd never had a surgery, right, Mary?"

Mary Riggins nodded.

Terri Collins spoke into the phone. "No to both. Good night, professor."

She disconnected the line, though not without a number of questions reverberating within her. But their answers would have to wait. She needed to extricate herself from the grief in the room, and she wasn't sure yet how to do that gracefully. Most cops, she thought, are real good at exiting as soon as they've delivered the blow. She wasn't.

Adrian clicked the phone shut.

He continued to stare at the screen. "You can't tell much," he said.

Wolfe was moving to the keyboard. "Look," he said, "they've got a menu. Let's at least check that."

He clicked first on a chapter heading "Number 4 Eats," which gave them a new screen. In it, the young woman licked at a bowl of oatmeal. Both men bent forward, because in these images a blindfold had replaced the hood. It gave them a few more features to examine.

Wolfe held up the Missing Persons flyer, pushing it right next to the television. "I don't know, professor. I mean, no tattoo . . . but Christ the hair sort of looks right."

Adrian stared hard. Hairline. Jawline. Shape of the nose. The curve of the lips. The length of the neck. He could feel his eyes burning into the images. He stiffened when he saw the tray of food being removed by a masked, jumpsuited person. *A woman,* he thought, as he measured her size and form, even if concealed by the folds of clothing.

When Tommy spoke to him, it seemed to come from within. *"Dad, if you wanted to hide someone's identity who you had to show to the world, wouldn't you take some precautions?"*

Of course, Adrian thought.

"Mister Wolfe, do you know anything about fake tattoos? Or Hollywood makeup?"

Wolfe looked closely at the television. He touched the appendectomy scar. "I got one of those. Looks the same. So this one doesn't look fake to me. But that's the point, ain't it?"

He clicked on the chapter heading "Interview 1 with Number 4."

They saw the young woman move closer to the camera. The jumpsuit was questioning her. They both heard her say "I'm eighteen" to the lens.

Wolfe snorted. "The *hell* she is. She's just been forced to say that bullshit. Two years younger, easy."

Adrian thought that there were probably few people he had ever known quite as expert as Mark Wolfe at recognizing a teenager's precise age.

Wolfe clicked on a chapter headed "Number 4 Tries to Escape." They watched as the young woman clawed her way out of a collar and chain around her neck. Just as she ripped off her blindfold the camera angle changed so that it was from behind her, obscuring her facial features.

"Escape, sure," Wolfe said cynically. "See how the front camera shut down and now we can see her only from behind? Can't see her face, can we? Somebody knew what they were doing."

Adrian didn't reply. He was trying to focus on something else. There was a piece of memory floating in his imagination and he couldn't get it to hold still so that he could examine it.

Wolfe watched as the young woman approached a door. From the rear, the camera tracked her. There was a flash of light and a masked man jumped into the image. Then the chapter ended. "The next one is 'Number 4 Loses Her Virginity,' professor. My guess is that would be explicit sex. Maybe it's a rape. You want to see that?"

Adrian shook his head. "Go back to the main screen."

Wolfe did. The hooded girl remained frozen in position.

Adrian had a thousand questions, all about who and why and what was the attraction, but he didn't ask them. Instead, he simply turned and examined Wolfe's face. The sex offender was leaning forward. Fascinated. The light in the man's eyes pretty much told him all he needed to know. He could recognize compulsion when it reared up in front of him.

Adrian wanted to turn away but he was unable. He suddenly heard a chorus of voices—son, brother, wife—all of them were shouting conflicting things, but all loudly told him to *watch and see*. The racket in his mind was ratcheting up in volume, steadily increasing, symphonic, all-encompassing. It screamed in his head and he clasped his hands over his ears but it did no good. Their cries redoubled painfully. The only thing he could do was stare at the screen and the young woman seemingly trapped there.

And, as Adrian watched, he saw her reach out blindly, feeling around, until her skinny arm wrapped itself around a familiar shape, which she hugged to her heaving chest.

It was a shape he had seen once before.

Once he had noticed a worn and tattered stuffed bear, a child's toy strapped incongruously to a backpack. *Same bear. Same bear. Same bear.*

The thought echoed in his mind, as if it were shouted by each of his ghosts, except this was his own voice now. He stared at the television screen. *It's the same toy bear,* he told himself inwardly.

Only now it was clutched helplessly in shaky arms.

37

In slippers and underwear, Linda was ensconced in front of the bank of computers, diligently taking care of some pressing *Series #4* business. Her white Hazmat suit had been tossed haphazardly onto the floor near the bed. She had pinned up her dark hair so that she looked a little like an undressed office secretary waiting for the boss to return from a meeting so she could give him a surprise. She was busy crediting the accounts that had picked the right hour in the rape pool, her fingers racing over a calculator keypad. She thought this was important. Their clientele would expect a rapid return on their wagers, and there was a sense of obligation involved. She was aware that there were any number of ways Michael and she could have cheated the winning subscribers out of their money, but this seemed distasteful and unfair. Honesty, she believed, was an integral part of their success. Repeat customers were important, as was word-of-mouth recommendations. Any good businesswoman knew that.

Michael was in the shower and she could hear him singing haphazard snatches of tunes. He never seemed to have any rhyme or reason for the songs he chose; one morsel of country and western blended into an

operatic aria, followed by something from the Dead or the Airplane—
"Don't you want somebody to love . . . Don't you need somebody to love." He
seemed fond of antique rock and roll from the sixties. She was the music
expert in their relationship and she was in charge of their iTunes account.

She hummed along as she glanced at one of the monitors keeping an
eye on Number 4. Because the blindfold had been discarded and Number
4 was back beneath the hood, it was more difficult for Linda to assess her
state of mind. Number 4 remained curled in a fetal position and very well
might have finally fallen asleep. As best Linda could tell Number 4 was
no longer bleeding. She did need a bath. But, more important, the girl
needed her rest.

They all did. She wondered whether any of the subscribers to *Series #4*
fully appreciated the constant effort and exhausting work that Michael
and she put in to bring the Web theater to its final curtain. They had to
battle their own fatigue, along with attention to every conceivable detail.
They were constantly alert to both criminality and creativity. *Series #4*
required that much and more. The subscribers ranged so widely in their
backgrounds and interests it was a never-ending chore to make sure all
desires and all fascinations that flooded through the interactive board
were accommodated. While there *were* similarities—a request from Sweden might be the same as a demand from Singapore—they tried to adapt
their responses, and Number 4's behavior, to the distinctions in cultures.
There was a worldwide audience and she had to be sensitive to detail. This
was tough work. That it was astonishingly rewarding, Linda thought, was
pretty much beside the point. Ultimately, Whatcomesnext.com was about
their dedication.

Video game designers, porn site maintenance—these were big, mainstream businesses that employed dozens or more. None was anywhere
near as edgy as what she and Michael had invented all by themselves. This
made her proud.

She listened for Michael, smiling as he butchered one tune after another.
They couldn't do this, she thought, if they weren't really in love.

Linda shook her head.

She couldn't help herself. She laughed out loud just as he emerged from the shower.

Over the years they had been together, she had memorized every routine step that Michael took in the bathroom. He would grab a threadbare towel and dry himself off, rubbing away the residue of his task with Number 4. He would emerge, shiny-skinned, refreshed, glowing a little red from the steamy heat, and naked. She could picture his lanky body as he dried his hair. Then he would stand in front of the mirror and painfully drag a comb through his tangled locks. Maybe afterward he would shave. Slicked down, clean-cheeked, he would step out of the bath and look at her with his endearing, lopsided grin.

He will be beautiful, Linda thought. *And I will be beautiful for him forever.*

Linda checked the monitors again. Nothing from Number 4, except for the occasional rabbit twitch. She wanted to speak to the image on the screen, very much in the same manner that she suspected the subscribers did: *You got through the tough part, Number 4. Well done. You survived. And it couldn't have been all that bad. It didn't hurt that much. I got through it once. Every girl does. And anyway, it would have been far worse in the backseat of some car or some low-rent seedy motel room or on the living room couch some afternoon before your parents arrived home from work. But it wasn't the biggest challenge you are going to face. Not by a long shot.*

Listening for the sounds of Michael's feet padding against the wood floor, Linda took a quick glimpse at the chat boards. There were hundreds of responses filling the queue. She sighed, knowing that the two of them would have to get to all of them promptly, because those responses would guide their next moves.

Did they want to see more?
Did they want it to come to an end?
Were they tired of Number 4?
Were they still fascinated?

She predicted that the end was closing in on Number 4, but she wasn't completely certain. Number 4 had been by far their most intriguing subject—if their bank account and the number of people who were drawn into the story were accurate ways of measuring. Linda felt a twinge of sadness.

She hated to see things come to conclusions. Ever since she was a child she had hated birthdays, Christmas, summer holidays, not because of what she had done or received on those occasions but because she had known that whatever fun and excitement accompanied them, it had to end. On more than one occasion she had sat as a child in hard-backed pews listening to priests' phony talk about eternal life standing over a coffin. Her mother's. Her grandparents'. Finally, her father's, which left her cold and alone in the world until Michael arrived. That was what she hated, the finishings.

Returning to normal disappointed her. Even if *normal* was going to be a fancy resort beach with a cold drink in hand and money in the bank—it was still something she didn't look forward to. In a way, she was already impatient and wanted to start planning *Series #5*.

She leaned back at the desk, eyes still traveling over the monitors, but in actuality she was thinking about who their next subject might be. Number 5 needed to be different. Number 4 had set the bar high, she thought, and their next show would need to surpass what they had done in the past weeks. She was extraordinarily proud of this. It had been her insistence that they move away from the prostitutes they had collected for the first three series and expand into someone totally innocent and significantly younger. Someone inexperienced, she had insisted. Someone *fresh*.

And random, she reminded herself. Utterly random. Hours spent cruising quiet suburban areas in a variety of stolen vehicles, slinking past schools and shopping malls, lurking around pizza joints, trying to spot the right person to snatch at the right time. It had been risky but she had known it would be rewarding.

Michael, in truth, had been the one who had said that *Series #4* should be the worst of middle-class nightmares. He had believed that the very surprise of it all would fuel the drama.

He had been right. Her idea. His refinement of it.

They were the best of partners.

She felt desire swelling inside her chest and she raised a hand and caressed her breast slowly.

Behind her, she heard a familiar shuffling from the bathroom. She quickly turned away from the computers and unpinned her hair, shaking her head seductively. Rapidly she shed her few clothes and, as Michael entered the room, tossed herself, giggling, onto the bed. She turned to him and crooked her finger, gesturing for him to join her.

He smiled and eagerly stepped toward her.

Linda knew that what Michael had done with Number 4 was an integral part of the job. It was critical that she make certain he never thought of it as anything except a duty he did for her. No pleasure. No excitement. No passion. Those belonged to her. Even as she had handled the camera capturing the job with Number 4, she had felt detached, clinical. He should experience no joy.

This was important, she thought, as she reached out to embrace him. She wanted to wrap her arms and legs around him with every muscle she owned, possessing him as deeply as she could, covering him with herself like a huge and powerful wave at the beach. She needed to make certain that the only thing he could feel, the only thing he could smell, the only thing he could hear was her and her caresses and her heartbeat.

"Well," Michael said, as he was dragged down onto her. He broke into a grin. "Well, well, well . . ."

She paused, stroking his cheek with her hand. She did not have to ask for love. She saw it.

What he had done earlier was just good business.

Linda lifted her lips to his. Only for a second did the next difficult job cross her mind. But she knew Michael would take care of that as well. She knew she would have to help. She always did. But she trusted him to do the hardest part.

Love and death, she thought. *They are a little the same.*

Then she gave in to all the explosive emotions reverberating within her, closing her eyes tight with girlish delight.

"Hey, Lin," Michael said, clicking computer keys. "What do you think of playing this *real* loud?"

He had risen from their bed after they had completed their lovemaking, drawn magnetically to the computers and the camera monitors.

The speaker system filled the room with the sound of someone singing. It was very country, Loretta Lynn wrapped around "High on a Mountain Top," which had an intoxicating, friendly *aw-shucks* beat and attitude, driving a listener with each note farther up into the Ozark or Blue Ridge mountains.

Linda shrugged. "You don't want to play the babies or the school again?"

"No," Michael said. "I thought something different. Something really unexpected and kind of crazy. I doubt Number Four has ever listened to old-time country music."

He paused, clicked a few more keys. Suddenly Chris Isaak groaning "*Baby did a bad bad thing*" filled the room.

"Our man Kubrick," Linda said. "That's part of the soundtrack from his last movie."

"Think it works?"

Linda made a small face. "I think she's already totally disorientated and completely lost. I don't think she has any idea where she is or even who she is anymore. Music, even if it just pounds her, I don't know . . ."

"We don't have many audible options left," Michael said. "I've got a few we haven't used but . . ."

Linda rose, naked, from the bed and went to his side. She rubbed his shoulders.

He looked up at her. "I've been reading through the chats," he said.

"So have I."

"Maybe we're near the end," he said.

He pulled up some of the comments on the monitor in front of them.

Don't stop. Make her pay!

Do it again! And again. And again.

357

"A lot like those," Michael said. "But these . . ."

The two of them bent forward reading words on the screen.

I thought she'd fight more.

Number 4 is broken now.

Number 4 is finished. Kaput. Finito. Toast.

Number 4 is over. She can't go back. She can't go forward. There's only one way out for her now. That's what I want to see.

The back and forth between clients seemed to reflect a sense of loss, as if for the first time they saw imperfections in Number 4's ideal figure. At first, she had been exquisite fine china; now she was cracked and chipped. Her being chained in the room, knowing what *might* happen, anticipating it, had fueled their fantasies. Now that the inevitable had taken place, it was as if she had been soiled and they were ready to move on to what they had always known would come next.

Both Linda and Michael saw this.

They might not have been able to fully articulate it but they both understood. There was only one step left.

Linda stopped rubbing Michael's shoulder and squeezed it as hard as she could.

He was nodding his head. He loved many things about Linda, but chief among them was her ability to say so much without words. On stage, he thought, she would have been special.

"I'll start scripting the exit," he said. "We need to be careful."

Both of them knew that, even with all the planning they had put in, Number 4's popularity had created a situation where the last act had to be special.

"What we need to be," Linda said slowly, "is memorable. I mean, we can't just *Wham! Bam!* End it. We have to do something no one will *ever* forget. That way, when we get series number five rolling . . ."

She didn't need to finish her thought.

Michael laughed. Linda drove them creatively, which, he thought, was a kind of lovemaking all of their own. Once he had read a lengthy, appreciative article about the artist Christo and his wife, Jeanne-Claude, who partnered with him in inventing many of their huge projects—draping wide canyons with orange sheets of fabric or encapsulating bay islands with pink rings of plastic—and then, a few weeks later, removing every-thing so that whatever had once been art was restored to the way it had been. Jeanne-Claude got less credit in the art world, but more credit in the bedroom, he guessed. Regardless, Michael thought the two of them would understand what Linda and he had accomplished.

He cut off the music coming through the speakers.

"All right," he said. He had a mocking tone in his voice, as if making a joke that would amuse only the two of them. "No Loretta Lynn for Number Four."

Jennifer could no longer tell whether she was conscious or not. Eyes open was a nightmare. Eyes shut was a nightmare. She felt damaged, as if a leech were slowly but surely sucking all the lifeblood from her veins. She had never thought much about what it felt like to die, but she was sure that this was what was happening to her. If she ate, it did nothing to prevent her from starving. If she drank, it didn't stop her from dehydra-tion and dying of thirst. She clutched Mister Brown Fur, but now she whispered to her father, "I'm coming, Daddy. Wait for me. I'll be there soon."

They had allowed her only once into his hospital room. She'd been young and frightened and he'd been trapped on his bed by late-afternoon shadows, surrounded by machines that made strange noises, tubes run-ning from his thin, skeletal arms. The arms seemed like a stranger's. She knew he was strong, able to lift her up and swing her around the room. But the arms she saw couldn't have mustered the strength to stroke her hair. It was her father, but it wasn't, and she'd been scared and confused. She had wanted to touch him but she was afraid she would break him into pieces even with the smallest caress. She had wanted him to smile, to reassure her and to tell her that everything would be all right. But he couldn't do that. His eyes fluttered and he seemed to slide in and out of sleep. Her mother had said that was the drugs they were giving him for pain, but she thought then that it was death just trying him on, like a suit of clothes. They had hustled her out of the room before the machines announced the inevitable. She remembered thinking that the man on the bed wasn't the man she knew as her father. He had to be an imposter.

But now, she thought, the same thing had happened to her: all the parts that made up *Jennifer* had been erased.

There was no escape. There was no world outside the cell and nothing past the hood over her head. There was no mother, no Scott, no school, no street in her neighborhood, no home, no room with her things. None of that had ever existed. There was only the man and the woman and the cameras. It had always been that way. She was born in the cell and she was going to die there.

She imagined she was becoming like him in the hospital. Sliced away slowly, inexorably.

Jennifer pictured the moment early on when her father had come to her and told her that he was very sick. "*But don't worry, beautiful. I'm a fighter. I'm going to fight like hell. And you can help me. I'm going to beat this with your help. Together.*"

But he hadn't.

And she hadn't been able to help. Not a bit. She was sorry. She had told him she was sorry hundreds, thousands of times in her head where she stored all her memories.

For the first time throughout her confinement, she suddenly no longer felt a need to cry. No tears on her cheeks. No sob crushing its way through her throat. The muscles in her arms and legs, her rigid spine, had relaxed.

As hard as he had battled, there was nothing he could do. The disease was just too powerful. It was the same for her. There was nothing she could do.

She had a single additional thought: if she had the chance to fight and die, that would be better than simply letting them kill her. That way when she saw her father again, she could look him in the eye and say, "*I tried as hard as you did, Dad. They were just too strong for me.*"

And then he could tell her: "*I could see. I saw it all. I know you did, beautiful. I'm proud of you.*"

That would be enough for her, she insisted silently to her bear.

38

Adrian felt as if electric current had replaced the blood in his veins. He stared at the television screen and felt years dropping away from him, and he knew that he could no longer afford to be old, sick, and confused. He had to find the part of him that once was but had been lost within layers of age and disease.

"You want me to try another website?" Wolfe asked. It was hard for Adrian to tell whether the tone of the sex offender's voice reflected late-night exhaustion or a genuine desire to move ahead. When he looked at Wolfe, he saw him still leaning toward the image of the hooded girl on the screen. Adrian understood that Wolfe, even if this *wasn't* their quarry, was definitely returning to Whatcomesnext.com as soon as Adrian left him alone. Wolfe's voice had a dry sound to it, like a parched man but one who excitedly sees an oasis ahead. It was as if fascination, like a powerful smell, had been released in the room.

Adrian hesitated. He could hear Brian nearly screaming caution in his ear, words that demanded he watch his step. The dead lawyer brother was almost frantically insisting on a contradiction: *Move fast but move carefully!*

"Look," Adrian said slowly, as if by speaking in a matter-of-fact tone it would add weight to his lie. "I don't think this is the right place . . ."

"Okay," Wolfe replied, reaching for the keyboard.

"But it's close. I mean this is what we need to be looking for."

Wolfe did not look at Adrian but let his eyes absorb the image on the screen. Adrian saw that there were moments in the sex offender's life where it made no difference how tired he was, or how depleted, if he was hungry or thirsty or distracted by anything in life—if desire was triggered he would find himself driven by the infinite resources of compulsion every time.

Wolfe said, "It can't be *close,* professor. Either it's little Jennifer or it isn't."

Adrian ignored the sex offender's *little Jennifer*.

"I understand, Mister Wolfe. It's just I saw her only briefly and I'm not completely sure."

But he was sure. He just didn't want to say it out loud.

"Well, that tattoo, either it's real or fake. Same for the scar. When she tells the camera she's eighteen, well, that's either the truth or a lie and it sure as hell looks to me like a lie. But you tell me, professor, which is it? That's *your* area of expertise. Anyway, it's late and I think we need to wrap this up for today."

Truth or a lie. Adrian still needed the sex offender's help. He glanced at the hooded figure on the screen. Whoever she was, she lived right at that moment trapped on one riverbank. Adrian realized that it was up to him to find a bridge.

"But just so I understand what we're facing, if I wanted to know where this website was located, how would I . . ."

He tried to make his question sound innocent and ordinary and no matter what he said he thought it was totally transparent. He persisted anyway, counting on Wolfe's fatigue to help conceal his interest. "I mean, we've been surfing back and forth, but how will we actually know where to physically go to find Jennifer once we spot her online?"

The sex offender gave a small dismissive laugh of disbelief, his eyes never leaving the screen. "It's not that hard," he said. "Except it sort of depends on the people running the site."

"I don't follow," Adrian said.

Wolfe spoke the way a really tired third-grade teacher would to a student more interested in passing notes than in math. "How criminal are they?"

Adrian rocked back and forth. "Isn't that like asking if somebody's *a little* pregnant, Mister Wolfe? You're either . . ."

Wolfe pivoted in his seat, fixing Adrian with a crisply cold look.

"Haven't you been paying attention, professor?"

Adrian remained in his seat, thoroughly confused. His silence became a question that Wolfe seemed eager to answer.

"How much do they want the world to know they're doing something illegal?"

"Not very much," Adrian started.

"Wrong, professor, wrong, wrong, wrong. The shadow world. In there, you need credibility. If people think you're completely legit, well, where's the fun in that? Where's the excitement? Where's the edge?"

Adrian was taken aback by the sex offender's pointed accuracy about human nature.

"Mister Wolfe," he said cautiously, "you impress me."

"I should have been a professor, just like you," he said. Wolfe's face creased into a smile, which Adrian genuinely hoped was a different smirk than those he wore when he was engaged in what he truly wanted to be doing.

"Okay, professor, you understand that every site has an IP address? Some server has to put it out there. There's a pretty simple program that gives the GPS location for each server. We can look this one up pretty quickly, except . . ."

"Except what?" Adrian asked.

"Bad guys—crooks, terrorists, bankers, you name it—know this too. There are programs you can buy to keep yourself anonymous while viewing or broadcasting, except . . ."

"Except what?"

"As soon as you buy something that is supposed to hide who you are, well, it doesn't really. Anything can be broken down eventually. As soon as you use the Web . . . Okay, it really depends on the persistence of whoever is looking for you. You can encrypt things—if you're a corporation or the military or the CIA, you're pretty sophisticated about hiding things. But if you're a site like this . . ."

He pointed at the hooded girl.

"Well, you *don't* want to hide. You *want* people to find you. Just not the *wrong* people. Like the cops."

"How do you prevent that?" Adrian asked.

The sex offender rubbed his hands across his face slowly, before replacing them on top of the keyboard.

"Think like a bad guy, professor. You do what you're doing. Hell, we already paid out money. They've got your subscription fee. So they stay at whatever it is that attracted folks just long enough to fill the old bank account. And then *poof!* they exit, stage left, lickety-split, before they've attracted the wrong sort of attention."

Adrian looked at the screen. He saw the *Series #4* duration clock.

Adrian took a deep breath. Psychology professor that he once had been, he could see it. He remembered the Moors Murders. Half, maybe more, of that couple's excitement came from risk. It was what fueled the relationship and drove it deeper into perversion. He looked at the television. The huge screen was filled with the hooded girl. All the danger accentuated passion.

His head reeled. Adrian felt beaten and twisted by what he knew and what he saw. He tried to steel himself inwardly, to maintain control.

Wolfe started punching keys. The hooded girl disappeared, replaced by a search website. He continued to punch keys, then paused, as he stared at the information that came up in front of them. Wolfe wrote down a sequence of numbers on a pad of paper. Then he went to a second search engine and typed those in spaces conveniently provided. A third screen came up, demanding a fee for the inquiry. "You want me to run it?" Wolfe asked.

Adrian looked up, not unlike a tourist staring at the Rosetta stone, knowing that it was the key to languages but unable to comprehend how.

"I suppose so."

They waited through an authorization for his credit. Within a few seconds they were accessing a site that also wanted a screen name and password. Wolfe typed in the now familiar *Psychprof* followed by *Jennifer*.

"Now, that's damn interesting," Wolfe said.

"What is?"

"Someone really knows his way around computers. I wouldn't be surprised if there was some really top-of-the-line hacker connected to this site."

"Mister Wolfe, please explain."

Wolfe sighed. "Look at this," he said. "The IP address changes. But not too fast."

"What?"

"It's possible to put in links, shift the IP address from place to place, especially running it through server systems in the Far East or Eastern Europe that are very difficult to trace because they cater to less than legal activities. Of course, the problem with doing *that* is you raise an electronic red flag, professor. If you set up your site so that the IP address changes every two or three minutes, then it's pretty damn clear to any Interpol people—and even more clear to their computers—that someone's doing something *nasty,* which, as you can imagine, grabs their attention. Next thing you know, you have the FBI and CIA and MI6 and German or French state security all over your little porn site. Don't want that. No sir. Don't want that at all."

"So . . ."

"Whoever set this place up is pretty clever and he must have known that. So he's got just half a dozen servers set up. Look, he bounces back and forth between them."

"What does that mean?"

"It means that it's a trick to backtrack. And my guess is, if you do the GPS search on all of them, you will find a bunch of computers sitting in an empty apartment in Prague or Bangkok. His main broadcast is emanating from somewhere else. It would take the cops—or a bunch of Delta guys working for the CIA if we were talking terrorists here—time to figure out the real *where,* if you follow."

Adrian looked at the screen.

The real where. He thought the sex offender had been strangely literate.

He paused, and a question seemed to flow through his thinking. It had an obvious quality.

"Are there any IP addresses here in the States for that website?" he asked.

Wolfe smiled. "Ah," he said slowly. "Now, finally, the professor is learning."

He clicked on some keys.

"Yeah," he said. "Two. One in"—he hesitated—"Austin, Texas. I know that one. It's a big pornography server. Handles dozens of *watch me* webcam sites and dozens of *post yourself and your girlfriend fucking* sites. Let me see where the other IP address is listed." He punched keys and then said, "Well, I'll be damned."

Adrian stared at the GPS coordinates the computer had found.

"That's a New England cable system," Wolfe said.

Adrian thought for a moment, then spoke very quietly.

"Where is that, Mister Wolfe?"

A rapid-fire *click-click-click* filled the room.

The screen changed and more GPS information arrived on the screen.

"You want to know where Whatcomesnext.com is broadcasting to the Web, this program will tell you."

Wolfe punched another set of keys. Yet another GPS location appeared on the computer. Adrian stared, memorizing numbers. He told himself, *Get them straight. Don't forget. Don't show him anything.*

"Have I earned my twenty grand?" Wolfe asked. "Because, professor, it's late."

"I don't know, Mister Wolfe," Adrian lied. "It's a fascinating process. I'm impressed. But I agree with you. It's very late and, you know, I'm not as young as I used to be. I will meet you tomorrow and we can continue this."

"The money, professor."

"I need to be sure, Mister Wolfe."

Wolfe clicked the keys and the hooded girl jumped to the screen in front of them.

Both men stared at the girl. She shifted position, bringing her legs up underneath her, as if shivering with cold.

Wolfe moved slightly, like someone charged with watching two things at once and worried that either one might slip something past him. His wariness was in his eyes and in the tone of his voice. Adrian thought he should simply continue to lie, as much as he needed, but he knew that Wolfe wasn't buying very much of it, if any.

"I will bring a portion. Consider it an honorarium, Mister Wolfe. Although I doubt that we've found what I'm looking for."

Wolfe leaned back, stretching like a cat awakened from sleep. Adrian couldn't tell whether the sex offender even cared about believing him. He—or more precisely his credit card—had opened up a few new avenues for Wolfe to travel. Whether he gave a damn about *little Jennifer* or Adrian or anything other than his own interests was unlikely.

"Sure," Wolfe said, making no effort to hide his skepticism. "If that's not little Jennifer, then *whoever it really is* is someone who needs a hand, professor. Because I'm thinking that what comes next for this little gal is going to be damn unpleasant."

Wolfe laughed. "Get it?" he said. "A little late-night pun. No wonder the place is called Whatcomesnext."

Adrian rose. He took a last look at the figure of the hooded girl, though he somehow believed that by leaving her behind with the sex offender, encased in Wolfe's computer, he was consigning her to evil. As he watched, it seemed to him that she was reaching out, through the screen, directly to him. He didn't move—at least he didn't *think* he moved—because he didn't want Wolfe to know how energized he felt. As with one of his poems, he started to silently repeat the GPS coordinates over and over. At the same time, in the back of his head, he could hear Brian issuing commands: *Do this! Do that! Get going! Time is wasting!* But it was not until he heard his dead son whisper *You know what you see* that he forced himself to turn away from the picture and shuffled out of the sex offender's house.

39

Michael was seated at a scarred white Formica kitchen table that wobbled unsteadily, one leg just millimeters too short, a laptop in front of him, taking what he liked to think of as endgame notes. The bouncing table irritated him, so he took a 9mm pistol out from beneath his belt, ejected a single live round, and by wedging the bullet under the short leg managed to steady the surface.

"Mister Fix-it," Linda called out as she passed through an adjacent room.

Michael grinned and continued to work. Outside the window above a sink littered with filthy plates and glasses he could see a cloudless, afternoon blue sky. Thankfully, the ground would still be soft from early season rains and the slow process of melting snow in the northern regions, where summer took a long time to arrive. That was where he was heading. He wasn't exactly sure when—maybe the next day or the day after—but very soon.

Number 4, he thought, was growing old.

Not old in terms of years but old in terms of interest. While he knew that she definitely had good days left, and there was *always* the possibility that a novel twist to the story would occur to them, which might drag things on longer, he also knew the audience had to be left with a sense of completion. This was tricky. The clients had to be satisfied but teased. There had to be both an ending and a promise.

Linda was the business brains, and she had explained this to him. "Repeat customers are the lifeblood of any enterprise." He liked listening to her when she adopted her junior executive tone of voice. She usually did this when they were naked and the contradiction between their unbridled sex and her dedicated, mechanical, well-thought-out observations excited him.

He wanted to get up from his chair and embrace her. She usually melted when he showed spontaneous Valentine's Day greeting card affections.

Michael was halfway out of his seat when he stopped himself.

More planning. Less distractions. End Series #4 *strong.*

He almost laughed out loud. Sometimes *sexy* is simply getting the job done.

He turned away from the window and got busy applying his organizational qualities to designing the disposal of *Series #4.* He took time to map out a route leading more than two hundred miles away from the farmhouse that would take him deep into Maine's Acadia National Park. It was a spectacularly wild area that the two of them had scouted two summers earlier like a dedicated granola and wheat germ pair of young outdoorsy types—deer, moose, eagles winging through the air, fast, frothy rivers filled with wild salmon and trout, and totally isolated.

The state forest was crosshatched with old and abandoned logging roads that penetrated deep into the wilderness. He needed truck access, even if this meant traveling across rock-strewn, rutted, overgrown roads.

He would need privacy.

It was a fitting place for Number 4 to spend her coming years. Not much chance she would ever be found—and if some stray hiker came across bleached bones dug up by wildlife, well, by that time they would be on to *Series #5* or maybe even *Series #6.*

Michael worked hard to identify all the police substations along his anticipated route. He'd determined the patrol routes for all the state police barracks along his drive, as well as the local cop departments that covered the rural areas he would pass through. He'd even checked on the staff and operating hours for any park ranger stations. He made an Internet inquiry at the American Automobile Association about traffic stops along the path he expected to follow and identified the hours least likely to result in being pulled over. It was the sort of preparation he enjoyed—keeping lists, making rapid computer searches. He sometimes thought he should have been a mountain climber who led expeditions to the highest and riskiest peaks. He was meticulous and filled with the energy of numbers. It gave him a sense of precision about death.

He also made a list of the right equipment—shovel, saw, hammer, pickax, wire—for Number 4's last few scenes. He did not know if he would actually use everything he listed, but he believed in preparation for all contingencies. He checked the small, handheld Sony mini-HD video camera that he would take with him on Number 4's last ride. He had backup batteries and extra tapes and a small tripod that he could mount the recorder on. He made a note to spray the connecting clamp with some WD-40 to make sure it was operating smoothly.

When he'd finished with every detail, going over each element two or three times in his head, he pushed away from the table and went to find Linda.

She was at the monitors, yawning and stretching with exhaustion, half-heartedly watching Number 4. Michael paused. He could sense that some part of her that connected with Number 4 had come loose. He did not assign this to the rape she had dutifully, expertly filmed.

He had two lists, a *His* and a *Hers*. Linda read through both rapidly, nodding in agreement.

"You leaving now?" she asked.

Michael glanced at the monitor where Number 4 was huddled. "This seems like a good time," he said.

"Hurry back."

"There are still final-scene details to work out," Michael replied.

In her hand she had another sheet of paper, a partial script that Michael had written the day before. She'd added some elements of her own, like a producer going over a screenwriter's first rough draft. The margins on the page were cluttered with Linda's pinched, elegant handwriting.

"I know," she said. "I'm just not satisfied we've got it right yet."

She walked him to the door and the two of them hesitated. This was the first time they had been apart since the first hours of *Series #4*. Indeed, during the duration they had hardly even been outside, so that the light breeze and mild temperatures riding on the clear air were heady, intoxicating, and they breathed in clarity.

Michael looked around at the old farmhouse. It was a battered place, dusty and much the worse for wear.

"We're lucky we haven't spent the entire series sneezing and coughing in this old dump," he said. "I won't be sad to move the hell out of here."

Linda squeezed his hand. "Don't be long," she said.

"I won't be. You need anything from town?"

The conversation was typical of any young couple in love parting while one ran some boring weekend errands.

She shook her head. "No. I'm good." She glanced around. From where they stood, she could see trees lining a distant field, waves of green grass, and weeds cluttering a rolling countryside stretching back beyond the ramshackle faded red barn where they'd parked their Mercedes. Broken wooden fences and rusted barbed wire stood marking enclosures that had once held cows or sheep. The long dirt and gravel drive up to the farmhouse wound through haphazard bits of leftover forest, which hid the main road from their sight and created a partial tunnel. The nearest adjacent home was close to a mile distant and barely visible through underbrush and tree branches. Like so many places in New England that fall into disrepair, the setting looked both old-time idyllic and worn and tired. That was the beauty of it, Linda realized; concealed within all the age and splintering, they had created an ultra-modern world. The surroundings were a perfect camouflage for what they were doing. "Look, I don't want Number Four to hear the truck starting up. The thing makes a racket. You know, *rattle, rattle, ka-pow, clickety-click, vroom*. So count to ninety before you turn the ignition key. That will give me enough time to play something that distracts her."

Michael thought that Linda often anticipated small but significant problems. "All right," he said. "I can't believe you would criticize my truck, it's been totally reliable." He joked and they smiled like any pair of lovers amusing each other with back-and-forth banter. "Okay. Ninety seconds, starting . . ." They both began to count, only Michael started at ninety and was going backward while Linda began with one and started up. They giggled like a pair of first-graders.

"Again," he said. "But from ninety . . . *down.*"

She was shaking her head, tossing her hair back in the breeze. Then she started to count out loud as she made a rapid about-face and headed into the farmhouse. Michael scurried across the damp, muddy ground to the old truck, counting silently with each step.

They were having fun again. They could both see the end of *Series #4* and this made them both relieved and excited.

As he settled behind the wheel, he imagined Linda at the computer. *Music?* he wondered. *Maybe the playground again?*

Whatever she chose, it would erase any noise he made with the truck pulling out.

Actually, Linda combined the two. Still counting out loud, she had settled down at the main computer bank and punched up some keys. First she played the sound of someone banging loudly on a door, which made Number 4 twist about suddenly on the bed. This was instantly blended with the raucous opening chords of Led Zeppelin's "Communication Breakdown." She saw Number 4 cover her ears with her hands, which was difficult but just possible with the handcuffs and chains that now made up the limits of her freedom.

Michael hurried through the warehouse home and hardware store, pushing a large orange shopping cart and purchasing many of the same materials he'd used to burn the stolen van.

He tossed items into the bed of the truck like a number of other do-it-yourself types and contractor's assistants who were exiting the store along with him. He was aware that the chain had security cameras by the doors, in the aisles, and out in the parking lot. He kept his hat scrunched down on his head and his chin tucked in. He had turned his shirt collar up. He didn't want any of the items traced back to the store, and he didn't want any cop going over the tape and maybe identifying the truck.

Everything had to be erased. It was a constant fight for him to identify even the smallest of items that might serve for a link. Hair stuck in a comb? That might provide DNA. Fingerprints on the slick surface of a tabletop? He worried about some cop connecting prints to his old teenage arrest report. A sales receipt from a high-end New York City camera store? He always paid cash, no matter the cost. The hard drives from their computers? They needed special disposal attention. *Hard work,* he thought, *making sure that absolutely nothing is left behind when you disappear.*

Michael stopped at a self-serve gas station and fueled up both his truck and half a dozen red plastic canisters with gasoline. He topped off all the tanks.

Graves to dig, trails to burn, he thought. Tickets to purchase. He knew he had to work out times and distances, dovetail them with airline flights and auto miles.

Disassembling *Series #4* was as difficult as planning it. The timing was tricky. Everything he had built had to be taken apart and erased. Lots of work, he thought, and coordinated efforts. Never quite enough hours in the day to do it all.

He drove, sticking religiously to the speed limit.

The farmhouse was several miles out of the small town, down a side road and just visible from the highway. As he pulled in, Michael could not imagine what it looked like when it had been a functioning farm. Now it was awaiting the arrival of a wealthy type who would want to rebuild it with high-end European kitchen appliances and imported hardwood floors, wrought-iron chandeliers from Vermont Castings and probably with a home theater in the basement that had once been Number 4's cell. The house was perfect for some rich city couple looking for an isolated weekend retreat. They would want to replace one sort of theater with another. They would get out of the demands of their busy lives and want a place surrounded by nature—not wild nature but tamed ex-farmland nature—where they could have guests and watch Blu-ray movie discs and have no idea what real drama had been created in the very same spot. Everything about the rebuilt farmhouse would be fake and contrived. And in Michael's imagination this trite and trendy couple would not have the slightest clue as to what truth had actually been witnessed in the same location.

Michael wondered if after they left the place would be haunted. He burst out in a small laugh: ghosts would probably disappoint his imaginary couple.

He stopped the truck near the front, carefully turning it so that it was pointed down the drive. He left the keys in the ignition. He liked the truck and would be sad to abandon it. He did not think about what he had to do to Number 4. Like the truck, she was now a commodity that was nearing the end of her usefulness. For an instant, he found his mind wandering. He was having difficulty remembering Number 4's real name.

Janis, Janet, Janna—no, Jennifer.

He smiled. Jennifer. *Goodbye, Jennifer,* he thought.

Linda rocked in her fancy desk chair.

She was unsure playing the two injections of sound was a wise idea. The subscribers preferred the noise of Number 4's labored breathing, which she suspected they considered a type of music. On the other hand, everyone seemed to get energized when they used one of the other disorientating sound effects. These triggered their fantasies, just as they did Number 4's. Linda made a mental note that in the future they should increase the variety of added noises. Playgrounds and babies crying were good, police sirens were excellent, but they had to expand their repertoire. Number 5 needed to be surrounded by constantly shifting fake worlds.

Linda believed that they learned something new with each series as she picked up Michael's outline for the last hours of *Series #4*.

They were getting better and better at what they did but she simply wasn't satisfied with the way he'd outlined the denouement. It didn't have the right *passion*.

Bad memories, Linda thought. *Number 4 deserves a better send-off.*

Number 1 had died accidentally. The rope they'd used to confine her snagged and throttled her when she tumbled from a bed in the midst of a nightmare. Michael and she had not been paying enough attention and it brought their first series to a premature ending. Her death had really upped the devotion they paid to monitoring *all* activities.

Despite their plans, Number 2 had died offscreen. Their initial scenario had been to combine rape and murder in traditional snuff terms—but it had devolved into a fierce cat fight, and Linda had been forced to cut the outgoing feed and help Michael with the knife. It had been sloppy and grotesque and unworthy of their professionalism. A huge mess to clean up, Linda remembered. It had left a decidedly sour taste in their mouths and had been a very poor business decision. They had been more careful with Number 3. They had spent hours working on the smallest details of her death, only to be cheated when she got precipitously sick. Linda had suspected that the illness was somehow related to the beatings they'd administered. They had overemphasized the physical aspects of submission. These mistakes were why they had been far more cautious with Number 4. Hurt but not *hurt*. Torture but not *torture*. Abuse but not *abuse*.

Never before had the end actually played out on camera as designed, while everyone watched, glued to computers and television screens. She knew the clientele wanted this—no, *demanded* this. They wanted action. They didn't want accident, or severed feeds, or excuses and they sure as hell didn't want Number 4 to simply stop moving, choke up some blood, and die as her predecessor had.

But they also didn't want Michael to simply execute her on camera. Linda even found this distasteful. It would make them little more than terrorists. They had to be far more sophisticated.

376

Linda glanced around the room and spotted the table filled with their collection of weapons. The beginnings of an idea formed in her imagination. She rose up, went to the table, and grabbed a .357 Magnum revolver. With an expert flick of the wrist, she opened the chamber and checked to see if it was loaded. Smiling, she replaced the pistol on the table and grabbed a stray pad of paper. She scrawled some notes, suddenly excited. A challenge, she thought. A unique challenge for the viewers. But even more so for Number 4.

Linda lifted her head. She heard the truck arriving outside. She bent to the task of writing, thinking, *Michael is going to love this.*

It was like a present.

40

Adrian could feel Cassie moving about just behind his head. He leaned back in his seat and felt her fingers running through his hair. Then her arms wrapped around him, hugging him like a child. She was crooning to him, as once upon a time she had with Tommy, when he was young and feverish. It was probably a lullaby but he couldn't make out the tune. Still, it calmed him, so when he heard her whisper "It's time, Audie. It's time," he was ready.

Mark Wolfe was no longer important. The sex offender's house, his mother, his computer—all the unsettling spots they had visited electronically— seemed to be sliding into a distant recess. Detective Collins was no longer important. She was confined by procedures and too worried about the wrong things to help. Mary Riggins and Scott West were no longer important. They were handcuffed by arrogance, uncertainty, and runaway emotions. The only person remaining actively hunting for Jennifer was Adrian, and he knew he was teetering on the precipice of madness.

Perhaps madness would be an advantage, he thought. His dead wife and his dead child and his dead brother jumbled together with the image of the hooded girl reaching out through the computer screen directly to him. It was like listening to two instruments playing the same piece of music but in different keys and different octaves.

He pushed himself reluctantly out of his wife's embrace. He could feel her hands slipping from his skin, leaving it on fire with recollection of happier days.

"You have enough to go on, now," she said, prodding him.

"I think so."

On a piece of scrap paper he had written the GPS coordinates for the website Whatcomesnext. He went over to his computer and hesitated.

"You know what you have to do," she said cautiously, urging him to action. "Maybe not like Wolfe or the detective but you know enough. They would take what you've learned, Audie, and they wouldn't stop until it was all over."

He was thinking, *One would do something evil, the other would do something good. One was a criminal. One was a cop. But both would want Jennifer, even if for different reasons.*

"Adrian, love . . ." Cassie was cajoling him forward. "I think you need to hurry."

He looked down and saw his hands reach toward the keyboard. Cassie was steering his fingers. *Touch an E. Type an R. Spell a word. Click the mouse.* He thought he had become trapped between worlds. At first the disease had chipped away only simple things that most people would take for granted. Now it was stealing them wholesale. Inwardly, he stiffened. He told himself that it was only a matter of being tough and determined. He muttered, "You will not stop. You will not hesitate. You will do this just like you used to be able." The sound of his own voice echoed about his book-lined study, almost as if his words were shouted at the edge of a deep canyon.

Adrian put aside doubts and employed Google Earth.

An address came up on the screen. He used that to get to a real estate listing.

A dozen color pictures of an old, ramshackle two-story farmhouse appeared in front of him. There was also a name and a telephone number for a real estate agent. He clicked on the agent's smiling picture and saw that she managed many properties. Each of the places was described in glowing, desirable terms. The companion photographs made every listing seem quaint and solid, the type of investments that would inexorably rise in value. Adrian didn't believe much of what he saw. Realtors could make even the most depressed and neglected New England rural area sound like *the next big real estate opportunity.*

He could sense Cassie looking over his shoulder. She must not have believed what she read either.

"Isolated places," Cassie said. "Poor places that want richer people to show up, set down roots, start spending money, and save everyone already stuck there."

Adrian could see that, and he nodded.

"These are places where no one gives a damn what you're doing," Cassie continued, "as long as you're doing it quietly and you're all paid up. No nosy neighbors or curious cops, I'd guess. Just a lot of quiet, hidden spots off the beaten path."

Adrian hit the PRINT button and his printer started to whir.

"Especially the pictures. You are going to need the pictures," Cassie insisted. It was like being reminded not to forget something at the grocery store.

"I know," Adrian replied. "I've got them."

"You have to go now," Cassie urged. There was a *no-debate* tone to her voice that he remembered from times when Tommy had gotten into trouble. These hadn't happened often but, when they did, Cassie put aside the artist and became as stern as a black-robed Methodist minister.

He stood up and grabbed a coat from the back of a chair.

"You'll need something else," she said.

Adrian nodded because he understood precisely what she was talking about. He was pleased that his strides across the room seemed steady. No drunken wavering, no hesitant steps. No old man's unsteadiness. He took a long look around the house, standing in the front doorway. Memories seemed like a thunderous waterfall of noise around him; every angle, every shelf, every space and inch loudly reminded him of days that had passed. He wondered if he would ever return home. As he paused, he heard Cassie whisper beside him. "You need a verse," she said quietly. "Something stirring. Something brave. *'Half a league, half a league, half a league onward'* or *'fought with us upon Saint Crispin's day.'*"

Adrian heard the poems resonate within him and they made him smile. *Poems about warriors.* He stepped outside into early morning light and realized that for some unfathomable reason his wife remained at his side, suddenly cut loose from the home they'd shared. He didn't understand why she was no longer locked inside but the change made him happy and excited. He could feel her stepping in place with Brian and he guessed that Tommy wasn't far away.

Adrian and his dead past marched swiftly across the yard to his old Volvo waiting in the driveway.

Adrian's voice on the sex offender Mark Wolfe's cell phone had stuck in an unsettled part of Terri Collins's mind since she'd heard it. She had hoped that the old professor was finished with meddling in Jennifer's disappearance. And she thought that Mark Wolfe had been questioned and cleared and had no connection other than coincidence with the situation. She could not see any reason to put the two of them together asking questions about tattoos and scars.

She was en route to her office. It was morning commuting time, which crowded the main streets even in the precious little college town. In Terri's mental list of things to do, at the top was to find out what the professor was up to. It wasn't exactly like he could mess up her investigation. That was at a standstill. She looked around at people behind the wheels of cars and she slowed to a halt to allow a school bus to swing into the drop-off lanes at an elementary school. This reminded her to increase heat on Mark Wolfe. She didn't see any way she could make enough trouble that he would pack up and leave *that day*, taking all his perverse desires to a different community where some other local police force would have to deal with him—*passing the trash* was the phrase cops used for this type of jurisdictional release of responsibility. But the day when his mother was shipped off to a nursing home—*that* was the day she would damn well make sure Mark Wolfe began to think moving was a really good idea.

She drove past the school, glancing quickly to the side when she saw the yellow bus disgorge its load. A pair of harried teachers steered unruly children toward the front doors. The start to a typical day. Absolutely nothing out of place. She knew her own children were already inside. She imagined them sliding noisily into classroom seats. There would be art and math and recess and at no time would any of the children have the slightest inkling that just on the periphery all sorts of dangers lurked.

The police headquarters was only a couple of blocks from the school, and she pulled her car into the rear parking lot. She grabbed her satchel, badge, and gun. She figured the professor would require another stern *stay away from police business* half lecture, half threat. It was mild outside. *Burglaries,* she thought. The rise in evening temperatures invariably encouraged more overnight break-ins. Frustrating crimes. Insurance paperwork and angry home owners.

Fully expecting to spend her day taking reports and maybe going out to a few houses or businesses and inspecting a shattered window or splintered kitchen door frame, Terri Collins walked into the headquarters. Her eyes fell first on the shift sergeant, ensconced behind a security glass panel at a desk in the main vestibule. The sergeant had a paunch and gray hair but a practiced manner with citizens who stomped in through the front entrance with some loud complaint or another—generally these were dogs off their leashes, loud students urinating in public bushes, or cars parked illegally. But as soon as their eyes met, the sergeant pointed to the side, where a dozen stiff plastic chairs were gathered against a wall. This was what passed for a waiting area.

"This guy's been waiting for you," the sergeant said through his safety glass.

Terri hesitated as Mark Wolfe stood up.

382

He had an upset, not much sleep and out of sorts look on his face. She didn't start with any greeting and she cut him off before he could speak. "How come Professor Thomas used your cell phone to call me?"

Wolfe shrugged. "I've been helping him with research, and he asked me for it—"

"What sort of research?"

Wolfe shuffled about.

"Mister Wolfe, *what sort of research*?"

"I've been helping him look for that girl. Little Jennifer. The one that went missing."

"What do you mean *helping him*? And what do you mean *look*?"

"He thinks the kid will show up on some porn website. He has some pretty far-out theories about why she was taken and . . ." Wolfe stopped.

This made little sense to Terri Collins, especially the phrase *far-out theories*.

"So why are you here? You could have just called me."

Wolfe shrugged. "The old guy didn't show," Mark Wolfe said. "He told me he was gonna come to my house this morning so we could make some more progress. I even called in sick at work, damn it, and we were supposed to . . ."

Wolfe said nothing about the money he expected.

"Supposed to what?" Terri asked sharply.

"I've been showing him around the stuff on the Internet." Wolfe spoke slowly, cautiously. "He wanted to see, well, you know, some pretty weird stuff. I mean, he's a psychologist, for Christ's sake, and I was just helping him out. He didn't really have a clue where or how to surf around and—"

"But you did," Terri said stiffly.

Wolfe gave her a *What can you do?* look.

"Don't get me wrong. I kinda like the old bastard." Wolfe's voice had a curious sort of affection within it. "Look, you and I know he's crazy. But crazy determined, if you know what I mean." Wolfe hesitated, measuring Terri's blank cop poker face. He seemed to shift gears and spoke forcefully. "I need to talk to you," Wolfe said. "But in private."

"Private?"

"Yeah. I don't want to get in trouble. Look, detective, I'm trying to be the good guy here. The professor is pretty shaky. Hell, you must have seen that." Wolfe eyed Terri to see if she agreed. "And, look, I got worried about him, okay? Is that so goddamn terrible? Why don't you cut me some slack?"

Terri paused. She wasn't sure she believed the sex offender had suddenly become a proper, attentive, straitlaced citizen of their community. But something had driven him to police headquarters and whatever the *something* was, it had to be a powerful incentive because a man like Mark Wolfe *never* wanted to have anything to do with the police.

"All right," she said. "We can talk in private. But first you tell me why?"

Wolfe smiled in a way that made her even more suspicious.

"Well," he said, "my guess is that our friend the professor is about to go shoot someone."

Wolfe didn't know whether this was actually true or not. Adrian had spent enough time waving his semiautomatic pistol in the sex offender's face that it wasn't an unreasonable conclusion to draw. In fact, Wolfe believed if one considered the possibility that the professor could *accidentally* fire the weapon while it was pointed in the general direction of another person then the death odds increased significantly.

They drove over to the professor's house, even though Wolfe insisted they weren't going to find him there. As he'd told the detective, the car was gone and the front door open and unlocked. Without hesitating, Terri Collins pushed inside, Mark Wolfe a stride behind. One realized that she was breaking a pretty clear-cut departmental rule, the other was intensely curious.

"Jesus," Wolfe muttered, "this place is a mess."

They were greeted by disarray. Terri shrugged it off, although she realized that it had disintegrated further from when she had first visited the professor. Any semblance of straightening up or cleaning had vanished.

Clothes, dishes, debris, papers cluttered every surface. It seemed as if there had been a storm inside that just minutes earlier had passed through.

Terri bellowed out, "Professor Thomas?" although she knew he wasn't there. She walked through the living room, repeating, "Professor Thomas, are you here?" while Wolfe stepped into a side room.

She shouted at the sex offender, "Hey, stick with me!" but he ignored her.

"This is what you really need to see," Wolfe called out loudly.

She went to his side and saw that he had already seated himself at a computer in the professor's study. Wolfe was typing furiously.

"What are you going to show me?" she asked.

"I suppose you want to see the website that got him all excited. He told me it wasn't the right one, but then he called you about the damn scar and the—"

"Yeah, the tattoo, keep going."

She bent to the computer screen, leaning over the sex offender's shoulder.

The welcome page for Whatcomesnext.com came up in front of them. Wolfe typed in the password *Jennifer* and *Greetings Psychprof* appeared before the image of the young woman came up on the screen. It seemed grainy, shaky, as if out of focus to Terri Collins, although she could feel her pulse accelerate, so it was more likely that it was *her* that made it difficult to see, not the high-def feed.

She saw a naked young woman, chained to a wall, handcuffed and hunched in a fetal position, clutching a stuffed animal. The figure of the young woman was partially turned away from the camera, so making out the details of her body was difficult, and a dark hood obscured her face. Terri could see the black flower tattoo on a scrawny thin arm, but not the scar that Professor Thomas had asked about.

"Jesus," she said. "What the hell is this?"

"It's a live webcam feed," Wolfe said. He sounded a little like the professor. "The world wants everything to be live, immediate. No delays. Instant gratification."

Terri continued to stare, trying to collate the image of the young woman with her memory of Jennifer, unconsciously duplicating precisely what Adrian had done earlier.

"It's got to be an actress," Terri said, disbelieving.

"You think?" Wolfe snorted. "Detective, you don't know anything about this."

He clicked on the keys that brought up the menu. He chose a random chapter and the two of them were suddenly watching the blindfolded girl bathe herself, trying to hide her nakedness from prying eyes. The figure of a man swept in and out of the camera feed. This time, Terri saw the scar in addition to the tattoo.

"Those don't fit," she said out loud, although there was hesitancy in her voice.

"Yeah," Wolfe said. He spoke rapidly, excited. "That's what you told the professor last night, except it was pretty damn obvious to me that he didn't believe it. Or he thought these were Hollywood-type makeup."

"I need to see her face," Terri said. Her voice had dropped almost to a whisper.

"Can do," Wolfe said. "Sort of. They keep her masked." He brought up the chapter where Number 4 was interviewed. There was a little distortion in her voice as she answered questions, and Wolfe the expert explained, "They probably just tweaked the audio feed a little so that you couldn't just listen and recognize what she sounds like."

Terri stared at the blindfolded girl, paying careful attention to each word she spoke. She thought of the times she had sat across from Jennifer. She tried to hear something in the voice that would confirm that her Jennifer memory and what she was seeing now were the same person.

It has to be her, she thought, astonished, even when she heard "I'm eighteen" tumble from the girl's mouth.

"Where . . ." she started.

"That's the thing," Wolfe said. "It's not in LA or Miami or Texas. This damn website is about two hours from here."

Terri could see a map in her head. *Does it take two hours to drive someone into purgatory?* she wondered.

"I've got the GPS," Wolfe continued. "Same as the professor does. Probably that's where he's headed. In fact, I'd count on it. He's just a little bit ahead of us. But I bet the old guy won't be driving as fast."

No. He will, Terri thought. She did not say this out loud. She pulled out her cell phone to call him but Wolfe shook his head. "He's not that modern," the sex offender said, as if replying to the obvious question. He reached into his pocket and plucked out his own cell, the one Adrian had used.

"All right, then. Let's get going," Terri said.

Wolfe clicked the mouse and the website closed down with a cheery *Goodbye Psychprof.*

The detective and the sex offender hurried out of Adrian's house, running across the driveway to Terri's car, almost step for step in the same path Adrian had taken a short time earlier. Had they been a little slower to act and instead lingered in fascination in front of the computer screen for a few more seconds, they would have seen the hooded girl suddenly stiffen with alarm as the door to her cell opened.

41

Jennifer shrank back, although with her back against the wall, and chained to the bed, there was nowhere left for her to retreat. She listened to the now familiar sounds of the woman crossing the room. She felt beaten, abused, starved. The bleeding between her legs had stopped but she remained raw and sore. She understood that she was only a skeleton barely clinging to a pretend life, and when she moved she expected to hear her bones clacking together. She assumed the man was right next to the woman, although she couldn't hear him. He always traveled silently, which would have terrified her more except she had gone past whatever line existed between rationale and fear. It was no longer possible for her to be more scared, and so, curiously, she was hardly frightened at all. She was too young to articulate to herself that she was resigned, but blackened defeat swept over her.

She thought: *When you know you're dying, there's nothing really to be afraid of. My dad wasn't scared. I'm not scared. Not anymore. Whatever you're going to do to me, go ahead and do it. I don't care. Not anymore.*

She could sense the woman moving close, and then she was hovering over her.

"Thirsty, Number Four?" the woman asked.

Jennifer suddenly felt her throat was like sand.

She nodded.

"Then drink, Number Four."

The woman pushed a bottle of water into her hand. The hood still had the small slit cut into it over her mouth from when she had been drugged her first day as Number 4. She struggled to get the bottle to her lips, and even when she'd succeeded water dripped down through the hood to her chest and for a moment she wasn't refreshed so much as she thought she was drowning. She caught her breath and kept gulping at the water bottle until it was empty even though she figured it was probably filled with drugs, for she believed that would be a good thing, because anything that numbed her to pain and to whatever was about to happen to her was absolutely fine with her.

"Better, Number Four?"

Jennifer nodded, although it was untrue. Nothing was better. She was suddenly almost overcome by the desire to scream out *My name is Jennifer* but she could no longer even form these words with her tongue and push them past her parched lips. Even with the drink of water she was still mute.

There was a momentary pause, and Jennifer heard a scraping sound of wood against the hard concrete floor. She knew what it was. The silent man had moved the interview chair into the customary position. In seconds, the woman confirmed the image that had already jumped into Jennifer's mind's eye.

"I would like you to move to the end of the bed. The chair that you sat in before is there. Please find it and sit down. Relax. Face the front."

The woman's orders were straightforward, spoken almost softly. To her surprise, Jennifer could hear a modulation in the woman's voice. The punishing monotone that had sounded so harsh over so many days of captivity had softened. It was almost receptionist-office friendly, as if the woman were asking Jennifer to do nothing more complicated than taking a seat while waiting for a long-scheduled appointment to begin.

She did not trust this new sound in the slightest. She knew she was still hated.

"It is time for a few additional questions, Number Four. Not many. This won't take long."

Jennifer lurched and crawled from the bed, her restraints rattling, as she made her way to the chair. She dragged Mister Brown Fur with her, like a soldier trying to haul a wounded buddy out of the line of fire. She no longer cared about her nakedness or the camera probing her body with its insistent curiosity. She groped the air until she found the seat and slipped onto it, staring straight ahead to the spot where she knew the lens was focused on her.

There was a momentary pause before the woman asked, "Tell us, Number Four . . . do you dream of freedom?"

The question took her by surprise. Like every other time the woman probed her feelings, Jennifer couldn't see what the *right* answer was.

"No," she said slowly. "I dream of going back to the way it was, before I came here."

"But you told us that you despised that life, Number Four. You told us that you wanted to escape it. Was that a lie?"

"No," Jennifer answered quickly.

"I think it was, Number Four."

"No, no, no," Jennifer responded, pleading, although what she was begging for she didn't know.

The woman hesitated, before continuing. "Number Four, what do you think is going to happen to you now?"

Jennifer felt as if there were two of her in the room, occupying the same space. Half of her was dizzy, head spinning, confused by the small shift in the woman's tones, while the other half was cold, nearly stiff with frozen feelings, knowing that no matter what she said, or what she did, she was near the end, although she didn't want to imagine what the end would be like.

"I don't know," she replied.

The woman repeated herself: "Number Four, what do you think is going to happen to you now?"

Demanding an answer to that question was as cruel as anything that had happened to her, Jennifer thought. Responding was worse than being beaten, chained, humiliated, raped, and filmed. The question required her to look into the future, which had the emotional impact of being sliced with a razor blade. Jennifer realized that when she lived in the absolute moment it was terrible. But speculation was worse.

"I don't know, I don't know, I don't know," she said, words rushed, exploding from her chest, high-pitched so that they defied the muffling from the hood.

"Number Four . . . let me try one last time . . . what—"

Jennifer interrupted. "I think," she replied quickly, "that I will"—she slowed her words down—"never leave here. I think I'll be here for the rest of my life. I think this is my home now, and there is no tomorrow or the next day. There wasn't a yesterday or the day before that. There isn't even a new minute waiting for me. There's just this. Here. Now. That's all."

The woman remained quiet for a few seconds, and Jennifer imagined that either she liked what she heard or she hated it. Jennifer didn't care either way. She had managed to respond without saying *I'm going to die,* which was the only real answer.

Then the woman laughed.

The sound carved right through Jennifer. It was almost painful.

"Do you want to save yourself, Number Four?"

What a dumb question, Jennifer thought. *I can't save myself. There has never been a way to save myself.*

Although these words rattled in her imagination her head nodded up and down.

"Good," the woman said. There was another brief hesitation.

"I have a request, Number Four," the woman continued. *A request? She wants a favor? Impossible.* Jennifer bent slightly forward. Her nerve ends were on edge. Every word the woman said was somehow cheating her, but of what she wasn't sure.

"You will do what I ask?" the woman continued.

Jennifer nodded again. "Yes. Whatever you ask, I'll do."

She didn't think she had any alternative.

"Anything?"

"Yes."

The woman paused. Jennifer expected some new delivery of pain. *She's going to hit me. Maybe the man will rape me again.*

"Give me your bear, Number Four."

Jennifer didn't understand.

"What?" she said.

"I want the *bear*, Number 4. Right now. Hand it over."

Jennifer nearly panicked. She wanted to scream. She wanted to run and hide. It was like being asked to give up her heart or her breath. Mister Brown Fur was the only thing that reminded Jennifer that she *was* Jennifer. She could feel the toy's rough synthetic fur against her naked skin. In that instant, it seemed more intense, as if the stuffed animal had cleaved to her body, fused together with her. *Give up Mister Brown Fur?* Her throat closed. She choked and gasped and rocked back in her seat as if she'd been punched hard in the chest.

"I can't, I can't," Jennifer moaned.

"The *bear*, Number Four. So I have something to remember you by."

She could feel tears welling up in her eyes and nausea filled her stomach. She thought she was going to be sick. She could feel the tiny toy arms of the stuffed animal clutching her like a baby's. She wanted to fall into a hole.

"The *bear*, Number Four. This is my final request."

She did not know what else she could do. Slowly, she pushed Mister Brown Fur away from her breast and extended him outward. Her shoulders were wracked, shaking, and she could not withhold her sobs. She felt the woman's hand brush against hers as Mister Brown Fur was taken from her. She tried hard to stroke the toy's fur as it slipped from her grip. Her loneliness was complete. Nothing except *I'm sorry I'm sorry goodbye goodbye goodbye* formed in her mind. She barely heard the next words from the woman.

"Thank you, Number Four. Now, Number Four, we think the time has arrived for the end. Would that be acceptable to you?"

The question stifled her. She felt more naked than ever before.

"Acceptable, Number Four?"

Mister Brown Fur, I'm sorry. I failed you. It was all my fault. I'm so sorry. I wanted to save you.

"The time to end, Number Four?"

She could tell this was still a question that demanded a response, but as usual Jennifer didn't know what to reply. *Say yes and die. Say no and die.*

"Would you like to go home now, Number Four?"

What little breath she had left within her caught sharply in her throat. She thought it was hot and steamy and fiercely cold, blizzard-like, both at the same time.

"Would you like to be finished?" the woman persisted.

"Yes," Jennifer managed to squeak out, sobbing.

"The end then, Number Four?"

"Yes, please," Jennifer said.

"Very well," the woman said.

Jennifer couldn't understand or believe what was happening. Fantasies of freedom cluttered her imagination. She twitched, and suddenly she felt the woman's hands on hers. It was like touching a live wire and she shuddered through her entire body. The woman slowly undid the handcuffs, dropping them with a clanking noise to the floor. The chain rattled as it too dropped away. Jennifer felt dizzy, almost seasick, pitched back and forth, as if the chain and the cuffs had been holding her upright.

"The hood stays in place, Number Four. You will know when you are free to remove it."

Jennifer realized she had lifted her hands to the black sheet covering her head. She instantly complied, dropping her hands into her lap, but she was terribly confused. *How would she know?*

"I am placing the key for you to leave this place in front of your feet," the woman said slowly. "This key will open the only door still locked between you and freedom. Please remain seated for several minutes. You should count out loud. Then after you think enough time has gone by, you may find it and decide if you think it's time for you to go home. You may take as much time as you like for this decision."

Jennifer's head reeled. She understood the *remain seated* portion of the command and the *you should count*. But the rest of the orders didn't make any sense.

She remained locked into position. She heard the woman shuffle across the cell and the door open. This was followed by the sound of it closing and a bolt being thrown.

Her imagination seemed feverish, filling with images. The key was supposed to be right in front of her. She thought, *They're leaving. They're running away and they just want me to wait until they've gone. That's what criminals do. They need to make their getaway. That's okay. I can play that game. I can do what they ask. Just go. Leave me behind. I'll be okay. I can find my own way home.*

"One one thousand. Two one thousand. Three one thousand . . ." She was whispering.

She could not help herself. Hope raced through her, alongside guilt. *I'm sorry, Mister Brown Fur, you should be with me. I should be taking you home too. I'm sorry.*

She convulsed. Head to toe. She imagined that Mister Brown Fur would be placed in front of a camera and tortured in her place. She thought she would never forgive herself for giving up the bear. She didn't think she could go home without him. She knew she could not face her father again without him, even if her father was dead, although that impossibility didn't seem a hurdle. Every part of her tightened like a screw being driven into wood.

" . . .twenty one thousand, twenty-one one thousand . . ."

She told herself, *Let enough time go by. Let them run. Let them go. You will never see them again.*

It made sense to her. *They've finished with me. It's all over.* She started to sob uncontrollably. She did not allow herself to form the words *I'm going to live* in her mind, but that feeling soared through her, keeping pace with the numbers of her self-clock.

When she had slowly and painstakingly counted to two hundred and forty, she could stand it no longer. *The key,* she told herself. *Find the key. Go home.*

Still seated, she bent down, leaning over, stretching her hand out, like a penitent churchgoer lighting a devotional candle on an altar in front of her. She groped around and her fingers came up against something solid, metallic.

Jennifer hesitated. It did not feel like any key she'd ever touched. She reached out farther and her hand wrapped around something wooden.

Her fingertips swept over the form of the key. Something round. Something long. Something awful. She recoiled sharply, gasping, as if her fingers were burned by heat.

She thought, *The baby's cries. They were a lie.*

The children playing. They were a lie.

The sound of the argument. That was a lie.

The police upstairs. That was a lie.

A key to set yourself free . . .

The worst lie of all.

It was not a key to a locked door at her feet.

It was a gun.

42

Adrian took at least three wrong turns and got thoroughly lost once on a series of potholed roads that meandered through small towns that would have been Norman Rockwell pretty if not marred by an insistent undercurrent of hard times and poverty. Too many old rusted-out cars up on cinder blocks in side yards, too many abandoned pieces of farming machinery leaning up against rickety fences. He passed faded red barns that hadn't been painted in dozens of years, with rooflines that sagged from the burdens of too many harsh winter snows, next to double-wide trailers adorned with satellite dishes. Hand-painted signs for *authentic* maple syrup or *authentic* American Indian artifacts sprouted up frequently.

He was on roads that didn't lead to popular destinations. These were winding, narrow, two-lane trails that pushed away from the parts of New England that make up the tourist brochures for each state. Great stands of tangled forest trees swept in patches away from the highways, their leaves filling in with vibrant greens. Fields that had once seen dairy cows and sheep rolled between the tree lines. These were ignored parts of America that people hurriedly pass through while trying to get somewhere else, usually to an expensive lakeside summer home or a high-end ski condo. He was forced more than once to backtrack after pulling to the side to painstakingly inspect the old-fashioned tattered paper map he'd retrieved from his glove compartment.

He didn't really have a plan.

His erratic path, filled with old-man missteps, had delayed him significantly. He knew he was in a flat-out hurry. He steered the car and pushed on the gas pedal like someone in a panicky *get-to-the-hospital* rush, jerking the car forward one minute, then braking hard when he thought he would lose control on some sharp corner. He kept reminding himself not to take another mistaken turn. *A wrong turn might be fatal,* he said to himself, sometimes breaking out loud with a grunted "Get going, get going . . ."

Adrian tried to keep thinking of Jennifer, but even this was slippery and difficult. There were warring images: *Jennifer determined in pink Red Sox hat, when he'd first seen her; Jennifer in the smiling false picture that adorned the police Missing Persons alert resting on the seat next to him; Jennifer blindfolded and nearly naked, staring out at the camera while being questioned by a concealed interrogator.*

He knew which Jennifer he would find when he located the farmhouse.

What was left of the reasonable professor of psychology, onetime department chairman, the thoroughly respectable part of him, told him that he should be calling Detective Collins and letting her know where he was and what he was doing. This would have been the prudent thing to do. He realized he could even call the sex offender and fill him in on where he was. Either Wolfe or Terri Collins would certainly have a much better idea about how to proceed than Adrian did.

But Adrian had decided to give up on being reasonable at the very moment he set off in the car that morning. He did not know if his behavior could be assigned to his disease. *Maybe,* he considered. *Maybe this is just the craziest part of it all coming out and taking over. Maybe if I took a handful of those pills that don't work I would be doing something different.*

Maybe not.

Adrian dramatically slowed down the old Volvo so that he was creeping down a small, two-lane back road, looking right and left for something that would tell him he was close. He half expected some pickup truck to come whipping around a corner, horn blasting, angry that he was crawling dangerously along. He suspected he didn't have far to go. He wondered if he should have called the realtor, gotten good directions, maybe even asked her to meet him and show him the way. But there was an insistent voice within him that told him everything he was doing was better done alone. Brian, he suspected, was behind this advice. He was always the type that trusted himself the most and others much less. Maybe Cassie, as well. She had an artist's *I need to be by myself* approach. Certainly Tommy, who was always wonderfully self-reliant, would contribute.

He steered the Volvo into a school bus turnaround by the side of the roadway and ground to a halt, tires crunching on loose gravel. According to his torn map, and to the GPS coordinates that he'd obtained and all the real estate information he'd printed out, the driveway leading to the farm was a quarter mile up the road. Adrian stared in that direction. A single battered blue mailbox, angled like a drunken sailor after a night on the town, marked a solitary entrance.

His first inclination was simply to drive up, get out, and knock on the door. He started to put the car in gear but a hand touched his shoulder and he heard Tommy whisper, "I don't think that will work, Dad."

Adrian paused.

"What do you think, Brian?" he asked. He used the same tone he would have when running a long-winded faculty meeting, opening the floor for complaints and opinions, of which there would be many. "Tommy says not to just go up to the front door."

"Listen to the lad, Audie. Frontal assaults are usually easily beaten back, even when you have the element of surprise. And you know, you don't really have any idea what to expect."

"Then what . . ."

"Stealth, Dad," Tommy chimed in, although he was still speaking in a very low voice. "You want to sneak up on them."

Brian quickly added, "I think this is the time to move cautiously, Audie. No bluster. No demands. No sudden *Here I am where's Jennifer?* sort of attack. What we need is to go get the lay of the land."

"Cassie?" he asked out loud.

"Listen to the two of them, Audie. They have much more experience than you in this sort of operation."

He wasn't certain this was precisely true. Sure Brian had led a company of men through the jungle in a war, and Tommy had filmed numerous military operations before he went out on the assault that killed him. But Adrian had imagined that Jennifer was more like one of his lab rats. She was in a maze and he was watching the experiment unfold. This thought made some sense to him. He was accustomed to patiently observing matters, and finding a place where he could once again watch seemed natural.

Adrian took another long look at the pictures from the realtor's website. Then he folded them all up and stuck them in the inside pocket of his coat. He was halfway out of the car when he heard Cassie whisper, "*Don't forget it.*"

Adrian shook his head and muttered, "Stay focused!" He thought he was down to maybe fifty percent ability to reason and think straight. Maybe less. Without her warning, he would have been lost. "Sorry, Possum," he replied. "You're right. I'll need it." He reached back into the car and grasped his dead brother's 9mm Ruger from the passenger seat.

The gun's heft seemed familiar. He thought he'd had much more use for the weapon than Brian ever had. His brother had used it only the one time to kill himself. Adrian had used it to *almost* kill himself, and then to repeatedly threaten Mark Wolfe, who had helped lead him to this moment, and now he might have occasion to use it again. He tried to put it in his jacket pocket but it would not fit. He tried to jam it into his pants belt but what seemed so easy for television and movie stars made him feel unbalanced, and he thought it would slip out and he might lose it. So, gripping it tightly, he kept the gun in his hand.

Adrian lifted his head. He could hear a small breeze moving through tree branches. Shafts of sunlight and dark shadows swayed back and forth, shifting positions defined by the wind. A flock of coal black crows raucously rose from a bloody highway meal when he startled them. He trotted across the road and started to make his way toward the driveway. He was glad no one had come along, because he thought he looked either totally ridiculous or deadly insane.

Terri Collins drove hard, pushing her small car well past any limit that might be safe. Mark Wolfe gripped the handhold above the passenger seat, a wild grin on his face and eyes wide open with what seemed like roller-coaster excitement. Miles swept underneath the wheels. For much of the trip they traveled in silence, broken only by the seductive, metallic voice of the GPS directions that came over an application on her cell phone.

She did not know how much time they had made up on the professor. Some, but enough? She was sure this was an emergency, but she would have been hard pressed to explain exactly why it was so urgent. *Prevent a half-crazed psychology teacher from shooting someone innocent?* That was possible. *Find a runaway teenager being exploited on a porn website?* That was possible. *Do neither and make a fool out of herself?* Likely.

At one point Wolfe had laughed. She had been doing close to a hundred miles per hour, and the sex offender thought this incredibly amusing. "Some trooper would have busted me, for sure," he said. "And gotten a big surprise when he ran my plates and license. Guys with records like mine *never* talk their way out of a speeding ticket. But you're lucky."

Terri did not think she was fortunate. In fact, she would have welcomed a state police car surging up fast behind her. It would have given her the excuse to ask him for assistance.

She wasn't sure she needed help. She wasn't sure she *didn't* need help. It seemed to her that she was caught up in some sort of curious quest, accompanied by the most distasteful Sancho Panza ever, in pursuit of a Quixote that didn't even have the literary knight-errant's loose connection to reality.

The GPS voice steered them off the interstate and onto back roads. She drove her car as fast as the narrow roads would allow. Her tires complained. Wolfe swayed in the passenger seat, driven first right, then left by the force of momentum.

A shifting landscape of idyllic isolation swept past the windshield. The forests and fields should have been peaceful and beautiful, but instead they seemed to the detective as if they were hiding something. For a moment she thought she had stepped outside of reason, not knowing that the same thought had crossed Adrian's mind earlier. Everything in the town where she worked and where she had her family made sense to her. Maybe everything was not always ideal but she understood all the dark undercurrents and shadows that she dealt with on a daily basis so they didn't seem unusual or frightening to her.

This trip was something far different. These were dark notions that were far beyond any black horizon she had ever experienced in her years as a cop. She shook her head, as if she were replying to a question, but none had been asked.

Mark Wolfe stared down at directions. "Ten miles on this road," he said. "Actually, ten point eight, according to this. And then one more turn and another four point three and we should be there. Assuming this is correct and all. Sometimes MapQuest is, sometimes it isn't." He laughed. "I never thought I'd be a cop's navigator."

She ignored this comment although she followed his directions while waiting for the GPS voice to confirm what the sex offender had already told her.

* * *

Adrian found a path that seemed to parallel the driveway, leading through the trees that marked the side of the road to the farmhouse. He took that route, maneuvering over fallen trunks and tromping on spongy damp earth. Scrub brush tugged at his clothes, and within a few minutes the path narrowed and grew more tangled, and he found himself fighting against the spring growth.

He wove in and out, thorns grabbing at his pants and hands, pushing brush away, turning right, then left, trying to beat a trail that one instant seemed open and accessible and then, a few yards farther on, became impassable. Nature's obstacles conspired to make progress increasingly hard, and while Adrian would not concede that he was lost again he knew he was being forced in directions that took him away from where he wanted to go. He had hoped for a straight path but discovered instead that he was being twisted about. He struggled to keep his sense of direction intact as he bushwhacked his way forward. He expected Brian to tell him something about how the jungles in Vietnam were far worse, but he could hear only his brother's hard, quick, exhausted breathing beside him, except that when he stopped for a moment's rest he realized it was his own.

He felt trapped. He wanted to start shooting the 9mm as if bullets could clear a trail for him. Sweat dripped down from his forehead even with the mild temperatures. It was like being in a fight, and he punched out, pushing a limb from his face, kicking at thorn brush that clung to his pants.

Adrian took a second to look up. The blue sky seemed to light his way. He forced himself forward, although he understood that the concept of *forward* might have meant sideways or even backward. He was turned around completely, defeated by tangled forest. For a second he was filled with fear, thinking that he'd launched himself into a no-man's-land he could never get out of and that he had been abruptly destined to spend whatever time he had left on earth lost in a thick mess of trees and bushes, doomed by a single poor choice.

He wanted to panic, scream for help. He grabbed at branches and pulled himself in whatever direction was manageable. He slapped away dead wood and tripped more than once. The fight bloodied him; he could feel scratches on his hands and across his face.

He cursed his age, his disease, and his obsession.

And then, as swiftly as the forest had seemed to entangle him, he felt it thin, as if loosening its grip on him.

Suddenly, the spaces grew wider. The ground beneath his feet firmed up. The thorns seemed to release him. Adrian looked up and saw the way out. He pushed forward, like a drowning man gasping for air as his head breaks the surface of the water.

The tree line ended, giving way to a muddy green field.

Adrian fell to his knees like a supplicant, filled with gratitude. He breathed in and out rapidly, trying to calm himself and figure out where he was.

A small, rolling rise stretched in front of him and he climbed up the side, feeling sunlight on his back. There was a faint smell of damp earth. At the top, he stopped to get his bearings. To his astonishment, below him he could see the barn and a farmhouse. Reaching into his jacket, he pulled out the sheaves of real estate brochures and frantically contrasted what he saw with what was depicted.

I'm here, he thought suddenly.

His meandering battle through the forest had pushed him past the house, which lay in a small dip below him. He was facing the side of the house, almost around the back, with the barn closer to him. He was at least fifty yards away from the two buildings.

It was all open space, a muddy field that once had been home to livestock.

He didn't ask his brother for advice.

Instead, Adrian dropped down to his knees and then lowered himself to the soft ground and started to crawl toward the place where he absolutely knew he would find the missing Jennifer.

43

Jennifer picked up the revolver, surprised at how heavy it was. She had never before held a deadly weapon in her hand and she had the mistaken idea that something murderous should be light and feathery. She knew nothing about how to handle it, how to crack open the cylinder, how to load it or thumb back the hammer. She could not tell if the safety was on or off, or whether there was one cartridge in the chambers or all six. She had seen enough television to know that probably all she had to do was point the gun at her head and keep pulling the trigger until she no longer needed to.

A part of her screamed inwardly, *Get it over with! Do it! End this now!*

Her own harsh feelings made her gasp. Her hand shook slightly and she believed she should act fast because there was no telling what the man and woman might do to her if she hesitated. Somehow the equation *kill yourself so they won't hurt you* made a curious kind of logic.

Contradictorily, she was being extremely deliberate, as if the last minutes should be played out in slow motion and she had to examine each facet of each motion: *Reach out. Grab the gun. Lift it carefully. Stop.*

She felt utterly alone, although she knew she wasn't. She knew they were close by.

A sensation of dizziness made her head reel. She found herself replaying things that had happened to her since she was stolen from the street. It was like being struck again, raped again, mocked again. At the same time, she discovered that she was filling with disjointed images from her past.

Her imagination warred within her. The problem was, every one of these memories, seemed to be retreating steadily down a tunnel so they were getting harder and harder for her to see.

It was as if *Jennifer* was finally leaving the room and Number 4 was the only person left behind.

And Number 4 had only one option remaining.

The key to go home. That was what the woman called it.

Killing herself made by far the most sense.

She did not see or imagine there were any alternatives.

Still she hesitated. She did not understand where the combination of resiliency and reluctance came from but it remained within her, shouting, fearful, arguing, battling against the urge to end Number 4 right then. She could no longer tell which was the brave thing to do. To shoot herself or not? She hesitated because nothing was clear.

And then Jennifer did a surprising thing, which she could not have explained but which shrieked in her head as necessary and important and to do without delay.

She cautiously placed the gun on her lap and raised her hands up and began to undo the hood covering her head. She did not know it, but this had all the Hollywood romanticism of the brave spy facing the firing squad and refusing the blindfold so that he could stare death in the eye. The hood was fastened tightly, and she painstakingly struggled to untie the knots that held it in place. Some wayward thought about not going directly from one kind of darkness into another ricocheted within her. It was slow work because her hands trembled wildly.

* * *

405

It was Linda who first spotted what Number 4 was doing. The two of them, like virtually all their subscribers, were riveted to their monitors, watching the slow yet delicious pace of Number 4's end. It was inevitable. It was tantalizing. The chat rooms and instant messages about the last act were filled with subscribers typing furiously about what they were watching. There was a frantic electronic din of responses. Exclamation points and italics were abundant. The words flowed like water bursting through a dam.

"Jesus!" Linda said. "If she takes that off . . ."

In a world dedicated to fantasy, Number 4 had inadvertently injected a reality they had to deal with. Linda had not anticipated this, and she was suddenly tossed into a sea of fear and waves of concern.

"I shouldn't have uncuffed her hands," Linda said angrily. "I should have been more explicit."

Michael moved to the keyboard and grabbed a joystick. He was about to kill the main face front camera, but then he stopped.

"We can't cheat the clients," he said abruptly. "They are going to demand to see her face."

All he could see was the rage that would follow if Number 4 did as they expected her to but he and Linda concealed the last act with clever camera work and oblique shot angles. "Not good," Michael muttered. "They will want it to be absolutely clear."

"Do we . . ." Linda started, but she stopped. "They got a flash when she thought she was going to escape. There might have been a second or two before the feed got switched to the behind view . . ."

"Yeah. And the responses were pretty clear. They hated covering up her eyes. They *wanted to see*," Michael replied.

"But . . ." Linda paused a second time. She could see all the ramifications in what Michael said.

"This is a big goddamn risk," she whispered. "If the cops ever saw this—and Michael, you know they goddamn will, sooner or later—they can freeze the image. Do an enhancement on the picture. They'll know who they're looking at. And that might, I don't know how, but it might some way make them think of whom to look for."

Michael was absolutely aware of the dangers in letting clients see who Number 4 actually was as she died. But the alternative seemed worse. All the other numbers had died more or less anonymously, their true identities concealed right through the end of the show. But both Michael and Linda were thoroughly familiar with the passion and sense of intimacy evoked in clients by Number 4. They *cared* about her. So much was at stake as Number 4 continued to struggle with the binds that held the hood in place.

"She doesn't realize," Linda said slowly, "she could probably just rip the thing apart. It would be faster than what she's doing. That might be good. Visually, I mean."

"Wait. Keep watching. She might figure it out. Stay ready. We might have to cut that main camera feed fast. I don't want to, but we might."

Michael kept his fingers on the right keys. Linda was at his side. He considered taping the final scene at the farmhouse, then broadcasting it later, after they had disposed of Number 4 and covered all their tracks. But he knew this would infuriate the subscribers. Safe in their own homes in front of their computer screens, they desperately wanted *to know*. And that required them *to see*. Michael felt his muscles tighten with tension. *No delays,* he thought. *We'll just have to deal with things as they happen.* The uncertain turn energized as well as concerned him. He glanced at Linda and imagined that more or less the same thoughts were pummeling her. Then he turned back to watch Number 4 as he and Linda fastened on what they could see and what they were sending out into cyber world.

He took a deep breath.

For the first and only time in *Series #4* Michael and Linda were hesitant. It was as if the uncertainty that had trapped Number 4 throughout the show had finally caught up with the two of them. Their own confidence wavered and, also for the first time, they bent to the screen without any insight as to what was actually going to come next.

* * *

Mud caked on his clothes, covered his hands, and made the handle of his 9mm seem slippery. The rich smell of the earth filled Adrian's nostrils as he snaked forward, foot by foot, heading patiently toward the farmhouse. The sun beat down above him, and he thought that, if anyone looked out of any window, even his low profile might be spotted. But he crawled forward inexorably, covering the open space as efficiently as he could, his eyes focused on his destination.

He did not stand until he reached the corner of the barn, where he was able to duck behind the wall, concealing himself from the house. He was breathing heavily, not from exertion but from the feeling that he was plunging headlong into an irrevocable fight that pitted his illness against all his failures as a husband, a father, and a brother. He wanted to turn to his ghosts and say he was sorry, but with what little sensibility he had he knew he had to keep going. They would come with him regardless of what silly apologies he made or didn't make.

Everything within him told him that the lost Jennifer was only yards away. He wondered if any rational person would have reached that same conclusion as he crept to the edge of the barn and peered cautiously around.

He could see the back of the farmhouse. There was a single door that he guessed would lead into a kitchen. In front, at least according to his pictures, there was an old porch that once upon a time had probably seen a swing or a hammock but now was just another roof that leaked.

There was no sound. No movement.

Nothing that indicated anyone was inside.

If it weren't for the old truck parked in front, he would have thought the place abandoned.

The doors, he knew, would be bolted and locked. He wondered whether he could use the butt of the 9mm to break in. But noise was his enemy and frontal assault . . . his brother had already explained that was a mistake. The idea that he would get so close only to fail frightened him.

Adrian kept inspecting the house, and then he saw what might be possible access. Off the kitchen was a set of rickety wooden steps with a banister that appeared broken. But just to the side, right above the ground level, there was a small dirt-stained window.

His own house had the same narrow single pane of glass that allowed some light to circulate into the basement.

Adrian made a calculation: *If the man and the woman who stole Jennifer are like most people, they will remember to lock the front door and the rear door and they will throw the sash locks on the living room and dining room and kitchen windows. But they won't have remembered the basement window. I never did. Cassie never did. I can break in there.*

It would take a fast sprint across open yard. As fast as he could muster.

Alarm system? *Not in such an old house,* he lied hopefully to himself.

Run hard, he warned. Then he would throw himself down by the foundation of the house and try to work the basement window open.

It wasn't much of a plan. And if that didn't work he didn't know what he was going to do as an alternative. But he took some comfort in the idea that he'd spent his academic life not prejudging the results of experiments. He had lectured endlessly to generations of graduate students to *never anticipate the result, because then you won't see the real meaning in what takes place and you won't see the excitement in things unexpected.*

Once he'd been a psychologist. And when he was young he'd been a runner. He gritted his teeth, took a deep breath, and launched himself forward. Adrian ran, arms pumping wildly, toward the farmhouse and the small ground-level window.

44

They were still moving fast down a two-lane narrow back road when Mark Wolfe spotted Adrian's car abandoned in the school bus turnout. Terri Collins braked hard when the sex offender burst out "Hey! That's it!" but still she swept past the old Volvo and had to make a tire-squealing U-turn before pulling in next to the car.

Her legs quivered as she jumped out from behind the wheel. Too much anxiety, too much forced speed; she felt a little like someone who had swerved to avoid an accident.

Wolfe lurched from the passenger seat and stood beside her.

There was no sign of Adrian. Terri approached the Volvo carefully, inspecting the ground around it in much the same manner she would gingerly examine a crime scene. She peered down through the safety glass. The inside of the vehicle was cluttered with typical debris. An ancient Styrofoam coffee cup. A half-finished bottle of spring water. A newspaper that was months out of date and a *Psychology Today* that was over a year old. There were even a couple of long-neglected parking tickets. The car was unlocked and she pulled the door open and continued to check the inside, hoping an item left behind would tell her something she didn't already know.

"Looks like he's been and gone," Wolfe said slowly, elongating each word. He used a fake southern accent to cut through the tension. The sex offender laughed sharply.

Terri stepped back. She turned and stared down the road. The look in her eyes asked the question *Where?*

As if to answer, Wolfe trotted back to the detective's car and seized maps and the cell phone. He did a quick survey and punched some keys before pointing down the tree-lined roadway. It was like giving directions from shadow to shadow.

"Down there," he said. "That's the place he's heading. At least, according to all this it is. You can't always trust what they tell you. It sure as hell doesn't look like the place a really sophisticated webcast would originate."

"What do you think they're *supposed* to look like?" Terri asked.

"I don't know," Wolfe replied. "California strip malls? Big city photo studios?" Then he shook his head as if he were responding to an argument that hadn't been made. "Of course, maybe not for the type of broadcast these guys are making."

Wolfe followed Terri's eyes. "I guess the old guy went on foot," he said.

Terri Collins could see that as well. She peered forward and saw the battered mailbox that marked the entry to the farmhouse, just as Adrian had earlier.

"Maybe he decided to sneak up on 'em," Wolfe said. "Maybe he actually knows what he's doing and just hasn't let on to you or me that he does. One way or the other, he doesn't exactly know what sort of greeting he's going to get up there, but whatever it is it won't be real friendly."

Terri did not reply. Every time Wolfe made an observation that mirrored her own, or was accurate to any degree, she felt a mixture of disgust and anger. That they were on the edge of territory he just *might* know better than she did infuriated her. She rapidly turned away from the sex offender and started calculating in her own head. She faced more or less the same dilemma that Adrian had.

411

She hesitated. She took the cell phone from Wolfe's hands. There were well-established procedures for this sort of thing. Her department was forever putting out expansive memos underscoring correct legal approaches to crimes in progress. Investigation should have been processed and evidence collected. Reports needed to be filed. Her boss should have been informed. Warrants should have been acquired. Maybe even SWAT should have been contacted—if there even was a local SWAT team. She doubted it. Getting a well-trained team to this location would require numerous phone calls and lengthy explanations, and even then they would have to come from the nearest state police barracks, which had to be thirty minutes, maybe more, away. There was rarely any need for special weapons and tactics in rural New England. And when they arrived they would need to be briefed. *There's a retired and possibly nutty university professor with a loaded gun somewhere around here.* She doubted they would think this was much of a reason for body armor, high-powered automatic weapons, and military-type planning.

So, no SWAT, she thought. And she had no idea if the local police even had more than one patrolman on duty, and he might be miles away. She knew she was way out of her jurisdiction and she ought to have local assistance. In fact, she knew that legally she *had* to have local assistance.

Nothing she was doing fit into any procedure she had been trained for. *If* Jennifer was here, *if* Adrian was assaulting some criminals holed up in a farmhouse, then she should be following a well-defined, mapped-out approach. Just steaming up to the front door might be every bit as dangerous as whatever it was that Adrian was doing. She was caught in a tangle of indecision. Missteps were inevitable, she expected to be second-guessed, but she realized that she had committed herself to doing *something*. She just needed a moment to figure it out but every moment that she took might be the last moment available to her to act.

She cursed loudly. "Goddammit!"

Lost in all this decision making, assessment, and impossible choices, she barely heard the distant popping noise.

Wolfe did, however.

"Jesus!" he said abruptly. "What the hell was that?"

But he knew the answer to his question.

Adrian moved crablike, crouched over, pinning his back to each board on the exterior of the farmhouse. He could feel sweat gathering on his forehead and dripping down under his arms. It was like being caught in a spotlight; the heat and glare were overpowering. He clutched the 9mm in his right hand and crept along until he reached the basement window. He was acutely aware of sounds and he sniffed the air like a dog. He thought he was more alive in that moment than he had been in weeks or maybe even longer.

He dropped to his knees in the soft ground and set the gun down. Inwardly, he was pleading with whatever god there was that watched over old men and teenagers. *Please let it be open. Please let this be the right place.*

He worked his fingers up under the edge of the window frame and tugged. It moved a quarter inch.

Adrian slid sideways, facing the window, trying to get a little more purchase on the frame. He pulled again and he heard a half-creaking, half-splintering noise as the tired, decayed old wood gave way. Another half inch.

His fingernails were instantly torn and he could feel sharp pain in his hands. Wooden ridges had cut his fingertips and he looked down and saw that blood was already welling up from scratches and cuts. For an instant, he closed his eyes and told the pain to disappear, that he had more important things to do than to feel hurt at that moment. He decided that no matter what happened he would ignore all discomfort from that point on.

He grasped hold of the window a third time and leaned back, using every ounce of strength he had. He heard the wood crack, and then it came free, and he skidded back as he fell over. He scrambled to his feet and grabbed at the frame, lifting it up.

The window was narrow and small. It was no more than a foot high and twenty inches wide.

But it was open.

Adrian bent over again. It had not occurred to him that he might not fit through the small space and for a moment he tried to measure his shoulders against the opening. He told himself that whatever it was he would force himself through. *Round peg, square hole,* it made no difference. He looked down into the basement, his eyes adjusting to the variegated lights that poured in over his shoulders. His first impression was that the basement below him was dark, abandoned, and smelled of damp age. But as he swept his vision through the corners he saw lines of high-tech wiring snaking through the ceiling. None of the wires was coated with the dust that everything else was.

He looked harder and he saw that there were walls built out from a corner. The front wall had a single cheap wooden door with a bolt lock on it. It looked like a flimsy, rushed construction project that had been stopped well before the painting and decoration stage.

It was a cell. It reminded him of a larger version of the boxes he'd used with lab rats.

Adrian groped around and grabbed up his automatic. Cautiously, he pushed his legs through the small opening. There was no way to prop it open, so it bumped up and down on his back as he tried to lower himself through, knocking against his shoulders and then his head. Someone wiry, a gymnast or a circus performer, would have launched himself into the basement without difficulty. Adrian, however, was neither. He struggled to keep his balance, trying to lower himself like a mountain climber that had run out of rope.

His toes stretched into the void. He swung a few inches to the right, and then the left, trying to find something that he might be able to drop to, but his feet flailed the air uselessly. He could feel his grip sliding on the window frame. He did not know how far down the floor was, perhaps only a few feet, but it felt like he was balancing above a crevasse that fell a thousand. Gravity pulled at him, and he took a deep breath and dropped.

He hit the cement floor hard, his ankle buckling beneath him, and pain shot through his leg.

But the crash of his fall and his sudden gasp of pain was obscured by a sudden high-pitched scream of animal agony that came from behind the bolted cell door.

The final knot fell apart, and Jennifer realized that the hood was loose. It was only a matter of lifting it up and removing it.

She hesitated. She no longer cared if she was breaking any of the rules. She no longer feared what the man and the woman might do to her. There was only a single option remaining. But she was caught in a tangle of thoughts that somehow she didn't *want* to see her world in her last seconds. It would be like standing on the edge of her own grave and peering down into the dirt-rimmed hole that welcomed her. *This is where Number 4 dies. As expected.*

And then these feelings were replaced by an overwhelming anger welling up within her, unchecked and bursting like water through a broken pipe. It was not as if she wanted to fight back any longer—that opportunity had disappeared minutes, hours, days earlier. It was more that she couldn't stand not being who she really was as she took her final breaths.

And so . . .

She screamed.

Not words. Not a sentence. Not anything other than a huge cry of disappointment and rage. It was a noise that gathered all she would miss of life in the years to come and remade them into a long, drawn-out cry of despair.

It was muffled by the hood but still it filled the room and soared past the walls and up through the ceiling.

Jennifer was only barely aware that the sound belonged to her. She had no idea *why* she had let loose. But as the scream faded from her lips she reached up and tore off the hood.

As before, at the end of the small wonderful moment when she'd thought she was escaping, light blinded her. At first she thought it was the man or the woman flooding her with a spotlight. But almost instantly she realized it was just the regular bath of illumination that had constantly filled the cell while she had been confined in blindfolded darkness. She blinked rapidly. She shielded her eyes with her free hand and then rubbed her face. The entire room suddenly seemed a different quiet than before. She had to strain to hear her own rapid-fire breaths as they came in short bursts.

It took seconds to adjust sight, sound, and hearing, but when she did she saw the gun and it seemed far uglier than it had when she first blindly discovered it at her feet and could understand it only through touch. It was jet black and evil and glistened in the harsh overhead lights. She looked away and suddenly caught sight of Mister Brown Fur, tossed cavalierly to the side of the room, a discarded lump of twisted brown. She didn't know why she hadn't heard the woman drop the toy, but without thinking she jumped up and crossed the few feet, grabbing him up and cuddling him to her chest. She stood, rocking sideways with joy that she was no longer alone. Then she reluctantly returned to the interview chair, plopped down, and picked up the gun.

Jennifer and Mister Brown Fur stared at the camera.

She wanted to kick it over but she did not.

One more time, she looked around. Every wall was solid. The door, she knew, was locked. There was no exit. There never had been. She'd been a fool to imagine there had ever been any way out of the room other than the one she was about to follow. "I'm sorry," she whispered, apologizing to herself and to her companion. She hoped no one else heard her.

She lifted the gun and started to tremble. Her hands were quivering and she clutched the bear even tighter, as if Mister Brown Fur could help settle her twitching muscles and steady her shaking hands.

She put the gun to her head, hoping she was doing it right. She stared into the camera lens.

"Are you getting all this?" she asked. It sounded weak.

She wanted to be defiant but she could not find it inside her. A huge wave of sadness and defeat washed over her, drowning all her thoughts of anything that was once Jennifer.

It's all over now, she insisted to herself.

"My name is Number Four," she said to the camera.

She was too scared to shoot and too scared not to shoot, and in that momentary hesitation she heard something that confused her even more. It was a single word and it seemed to come impossibly at the exact same time from someplace very far away and someplace extremely close. It was a long-forgotten memory calling to her and it echoed in the room around her.

"Jennifer?"

Michael suddenly bent to the computer monitor.

"What the hell was that?" he said quickly.

Linda crowded beside him.

"Did you play any effects?" he demanded.

"No! I was watching, same as you. Christ! The same as *everybody*!"

"Then what—"

"Look at Number Four!" Linda said.

Jennifer was shaking wildly, like the edge of an untrimmed sail flapping in a powerful breeze. Her body quivered, head to toe. The gun, pointed at her forehead, seemed to droop down slightly, and her head turned toward the sound of her name.

"Jennifer?"

She wanted to cry out *I'm here!* but she didn't trust that what she imagined she heard she actually did hear.

Instead, she told herself, *It's them. They're lying again. It's just another fake.*

But slowly she shifted in her seat and stared at the door. She heard the lock turn and the door started to open.

Jennifer realized that this time *she* had a weapon. *They've come to kill me,* she imagined. She moved the gun away from her forehead and trained it on the door.

I'll get one of them, Mister Brown Fur. I'll at least take one of them with me.

She sighted down the barrel.

Kill them! Kill them!

The door swung open slowly.

Adrian peered around the corner.

The odd thing was he didn't know what to expect.

He kept telling himself that he'd seen her on the street, and then in pictures at her house. He'd seen her on the computer with Mark Wolfe at his side. He'd seen the room and the bed and the chains and her mask, so he should have been able to picture what he was opening the door to, but all of these things had dropped away and he felt as if he were opening a door onto a blank slate. The only thing he was able to remind himself to do was to keep his own weapon ready.

What he saw first was the gun aimed directly at him.

His first instinct was to jump back and his muscles gathered like those of a mongoose suddenly spotting a cobra about to strike, but then he heard his son's calm voice coming from a canyon within, saying, *It's her.*

"Tommy," he whispered out loud, followed rapidly by, "Jennifer?"

The question hung in the stale basement air.

She remained seated. Naked, one arm wrapped around the bear, the other shakily training the gun on Adrian as he tentatively stepped forward. Pain was shooting up from his torn and probably broken ankle, but true to his promise to himself he ignored it.

Jennifer knew she was supposed to ask something, say something, but she couldn't form the words in her head. She knew that something had changed, but she could not tell what it was. She understood that something was happening that seemed far different and out of synchronization with everything else that had happened to her and she struggled to wrap her head around whatever this might be. It was dreamlike, unreal, like the noises of children playing or babies crying, and she suddenly told herself not to trust what she saw. It had to be a hallucination. Everything was untrue.

She saw his gray hair. *That isn't right.* She saw an old, weathered face. *That's not the man. That's not the woman.*

That the person seeping into the room in front of her was someone new, someone different, only encouraged panic. She was fighting hundreds of sensations within her, all vaguely connected to terror.

"Jennifer," the person in front of her said slowly. But this time he said her name not as a question but as a statement of fact.

Her throat was dry. The gun in her hand seemed to weigh a hundred pounds. A part of her screamed, *He's one of them! Kill him! Kill him now before he kills you!*

The barrel of the pistol swayed back and forth as she warred within. The idea that someone had come to help her was impossible to comprehend and far too dangerous to allow. *Much safer to shoot.*

Adrian saw the gun, saw the teenager's eyes widen, and he knew that she was in a sort of victim shock. He thought of all the years that he had spent studying fear in cloistered academic situations. None was as electric as the moment right then in the little cell, across from a wild-eyed naked girl he'd expected to be blindfolded but who was pointing the evil end of a large revolver directly at him. All his clinical truths gathered over so many years meant absolutely nothing. The reality in front of him meant everything. He understood in that second that he must have seemed as frightening as anything that had happened to her.

He knew she was going to pull the trigger, like a trapped lab rat who had learned to ring a bell for safety.

Common sense told him to dive aside and hide. "*No, Dad, keep going. Just like I did.*" It was Tommy. "*It's the only way forward.*"

Imagining that he might be putting his own death on film, Adrian moved into the room. All his education, all his experience screamed to him to find the *right* thing to say so that they had a chance to save both their lives. He somehow felt as naked as she was.

"Hello, Jennifer," he said very slowly and quietly, his voice barely above a whisper. "Is that Mister Brown Fur?"

Jennifer's finger tightened on the trigger and she took a deep breath. And then she looked down at the bear.

Tears welled up in her eyes, burning across her cheeks.

"Yes," she said, her voice creaking. "Have you come to take him home?"

45

Inside the large modern apartment overlooking Gorky Park in Moscow, the svelte young woman and her barrel-chested companion were alone on the oversized bed. It was night outside and city lights blinked and sent piercing glows through darkened shadows. Cheerful music was playing on one street, but in the apartment the only brightness came from a flat-screen television mounted on the wall. The two of them were naked and staring up at the shifting and unexpected picture of the familiar homemade cell, the teenager they had signed on to watch through the duration of Series #4, and the sudden arrival of an old man. The television was flanked by two large modern paintings by well-known artists that commanded seven figures but the gray-tinged images on the screen dominated the art.

Silk sheets were tangled around the couple, but not from lovemaking; the young woman had clutched at the bedclothes more than once as she watched, riveted by the action in front of her. The man was equally possessed. They had not said much for the past hour, although they both felt that much had passed between them. The man—part criminal, part entrepreneur—had muttered the make and caliber of the weapons he'd seen, both the Colt .357 Magnum *that Number 4 gripped so tightly and the Ruger 9mm that he caught a glimpse of in the old man's hands. Neither he nor his beautiful young companion recognized this new character. The camera caught only his profile as he approached Number 4. To the couple, he seemed fascinating, angelic, and their own pulses raced with trying to comprehend what it meant to the show. The man wondered whether he should grab his computer keyboard and demand to know "Who is this?" but he could not tear his eyes away from what was happening. And any thought he might have had about an interactive demand was erased instantly when his lover seized his hand and pulled it tight to her breast, just as Number 4 had clutched her toy bear.*

They had both thought minutes earlier they were to witness Number 4's death. From the beginning, they had believed she was destined to die. But something was playing out that seemed beyond any script they might have imagined. The man felt a surge within him. He had thought that he, too, owned Number 4, just as he did the priceless paintings, his gold Rolex, his large Mercedes, and his own Gulfstream plane. But now he felt Number 4 slipping from his grasp, and to his immense surprise he wasn't angered or disappointed and he found himself urging her forward, but exactly toward what he could not tell. His lover felt many of the same things, but she was more vulnerable to the sea change, and she whispered to the screen, much as she would have to the man when they were locked together. But instead of endearing words of passion, she reverted to the rural Russian of her childhood and pleaded, "Run, Number 4! Run now! Please."

Everything now taking place was utterly incomprehensible to Michael. Everything had been scripted and this wasn't. Everything had been planned and this wasn't. He always knew more or less precisely what was going to happen at all times, with the injection of each new element, but now he didn't. He stared at the monitor screens in front of him as if he were watching something unfold that was taking place somewhere else, somewhere around the world, not mere yards away, in a room beneath his feet.

Linda was only slightly faster to react.

Her first instinct had been that her nightmare fantasy detective—part Sherlock Holmes, part Miss Marple and Jack Bauer—had finally shown up unexpectedly. But just as swiftly she dismissed this, because she could tell from the B camera angle that whoever this was in the cell with Number 4 he was no cop, even if he did have a gun in his hand.

No fleet of squad cars had arrived outside, sirens blasting. No loudspeaker demanding they surrender could be heard. No helicopters were circling overhead.

Linda jumped to a window and quickly surveyed the world beyond the farmhouse walls.

No one.

She pivoted back to the screens.

"Michael," she said. "Whoever the hell it is, he's alone!"

As she spoke she leaped across the room to the table with the weapons.

Michael thrust himself out of the fancy desk chair and jumped to her side. He did a fast inventory of the array, then pushed the AK-47 into her hands. He knew the thirty-shot banana clip was full and he stuffed a second into his pants pocket. He quickly cracked open a revolver, checking to make sure it too was fully loaded, and jammed it into the belt of her jeans so that Linda had a second weapon. He seized the twelve-gauge shotgun and rapidly began thrusting shells into the breech. But after it was filled, and he'd cocked it with a single, violent up-and-down motion, instead of grabbing one of the semiautomatic pistols from the table he picked up a small Sony HD camera.

"We've got to get this all down on video," he said. He seized one of the laptops and a cord that he rapidly plugged from the camera into one of the computer jacks. He knew he would have his hands full, between the shotgun and the camera and computer, but sending out images was critical.

In Michael's mind *killing* and *filming* had coalesced into something of equal importance.

Linda understood instantly. There would never be a *Series #5* if they didn't produce the ending to Number 4. Their clients needed finality.

They needed to *see,* even if it came in some less than perfect cinematic form. They expected an ending, even if it wasn't precisely the one Michael and Linda had devised.

Without speaking out loud, both were flush with concern, surprise, but also a creative kind of excitement. In Linda's mind, as she clicked off the safety on her automatic weapon, they were drawing true art.

She imagined a performance that no one watching would ever forget.

Armed with deadly weapons and artistic drive, Michael and Linda ran to the stairs that led to the basement. Their feet thundered against the worn wooden floorboards.

The chorus of ghosts filled his hearing with soft-spoken commands, all urgent, all whispered. *Be gentle. Be careful. Reach out.*

"Yes," he said slowly. "I think Mister Brown Fur needs to go home now. I think Jennifer should come along too. I'll take you both now."

The pistol in the teenager's hand suddenly drooped down to her side. She looked quizzically at him.

"Who are you?" Jennifer asked. "I don't know you."

Adrian smiled. "My name is Professor Thomas," he said. This sounded terribly formal for an introduction given their circumstances. "But you can call me Adrian. You may not know me, Jennifer, but I know you. I live close to your house. Just a few blocks away. I'll take you there now."

"I'd like that," she said. She held out the gun. "Do you need this?"

"Just put it down," Adrian replied.

Jennifer complied. She dropped the gun onto the bed.

She could feel sudden warmth, a tumbling backward in time to when she was a child playing outdoors on a hot summer day. She was still naked but she had her bear and a stranger who wasn't the man or the woman and so whatever was going to happen to her now she was willing to accept. She thought that she might be dead already. Perhaps, she mused, she had actually pulled the trigger of the gun and this old man was really a sort of companion-helper who was going to take her to her father, who was waiting eagerly for her to join him in some better world. A guide during the transition between life and death.

"I think it is time for us to leave," Adrian said.

He gingerly grasped her hand. Adrian had no idea what he should be doing from the police perspective. He thought he should be acting like some television cop, speaking loudly, taking charge, brandishing his own weapon, and saving the day with Hollywood bravado. But the old psychologist in him told him that no matter what the hurry was he had to move gently. Jennifer was extremely fragile. Taking her from the cell and from the farmhouse was like shipping unstable but extraordinarily valuable cargo.

Adrian steered her through the door into the shadowy damp basement. He had no plan. He had been so intent on finding Jennifer that what he should do afterward hadn't occurred to him. He hoped that his ghosts would tell him what steps to take. Maybe they were doing that already, he thought, as he helped the teenager forward.

She leaned against him, as if she was wounded. He limped from his ankle injury. He could sense bones grinding at the bottom of his leg and he knew it was fractured. He gritted his teeth.

As they exited the cell they heard the terrifying *rat-a-tat* of footsteps, moving fast, coming from directly above them.

Jennifer instantly froze, bending over as if someone had punched her in the stomach. A sound came from deep in her chest—not a scream but a gurgling noise of despair, guttural, primal, filled with terror.

Adrian turned in the direction of the sound.

In the corner of the basement was a single stairway of rickety wooden steps. He had some vague idea that he would lead Jennifer up and out of the basement, through the kitchen, and out of the house as if they were suddenly invisible and there were no one there who might not want the two of them to leave. They were only a few feet away from the bottom of the stairs.

As he watched, he saw a sudden shaft of light race down the shadow against the wall. He heard a creaking sound and he knew that it was the upper door opening.

As he stared up, locked in on the light, he was abruptly pulled back hard.

It was Jennifer, clutching his arm, tugging him away. She figured that whoever the old man was, he had to be better than the man and the woman, and she knew it was the two of them just past all the darkness in the light waiting at the top of the stairs. Survival instincts took over as she pulled Adrian deeper into the basement.

Adrian let himself be carried backward. He didn't know what else to do. And as he hesitated, insisting inwardly that he needed to make some sort of plan, the world around them exploded.

A cascade of bullets roared down the stairway. The basement was enveloped by noise and smoke. High-powered 7.62mm shells ricocheted off cement walls and screamed haphazardly through the dusty air. Debris flew up in the air around them as the small, tight space of the basement was savagely ripped apart.

Adrian and Jennifer slammed sideways, ducking against the wall farthest away from the shots. Both screamed as if they'd been hit, but they had not. That they hadn't seemed both impossible and lucky, but Adrian could see that the firing angle down the stairs limited the effectiveness of the barrage even as military-issue rounds exploded against walls and floor and tore into the shadows and darkness.

He knew the obvious: *They could not go that way.*

The only remaining route out was the path he'd used to enter. The small basement window glowed with outside light. To get to it was a risk—if the people firing came even one or two steps down, they would be able to cover the entire basement. The only place to hide would be back in Jennifer's cell, but Adrian knew that the teenager would not retreat there, nor could he ask her to. He had pulled her out. He could not ask her to return. No matter if the cell was the only safe place—and that was questionable—Jennifer could never see it that way. She was huddled by his side, clutching bear and hand. She was whimpering.

A second volley crashed down the stairs, whining shots scouring the thickening air. Smoke curled around them, bitter smells and dust, and both coughed. It was hard to breathe.

One exit. One exit only. He gently pried Jennifer's fingers from where they were digging into his arm. She seemed panicky and didn't want to let go, but when he pointed with his gun toward the window it seemed as if she understood.

"We have to get up there," he whispered, his voice hoarse against the noise from the automatic weapon.

At first, Jennifer's eyes were clouded with fear. But as she glanced toward the window, perhaps nine or ten feet up on the wall, her vision cleared, and Adrian could see understanding. She also seemed to toughen, almost as if she had abruptly aged in that precise second, passing from innocent childhood to nearly adult, all because of the cascade of gunfire.

"I can do that," she said softly, nodding. She should have been yelling above the weapons fire but Adrian understood her response with the clarity that danger brings.

He uncurled from where they had huddled against a wall and began grabbing at old and abandoned furniture, misshapen items that once had been part of living in the farmhouse—a broken-down washbasin, a pair of wooden chairs—and pulled them desperately across the basement, throwing them against the wall beneath the window. He had to find enough that they could ladder their way up and reach the window. His fractured ankle screamed at him, and for a moment he wondered whether he'd been shot. Then he realized it made no difference.

At the top of the stairs, Michael was shooting with the camera over Linda's shoulder as she loosed each burst from the AK-47. He made certain that the camera didn't catch her face so she could be recognized. The explosions deafened them, and when she stopped they both leaned forward. He doubted that they'd managed to kill Number 4 and the old man. Wound them, possibly. Scare them, certainly. He was acutely aware of the gun in the old man's hand. He thought Number 4 might be armed as well. After all, she'd had the Magnum she'd been given for her on-camera suicide.

He was trying to be logical and to think things through, even as adrenaline pounded away within him and he kept his right eye glued to the viewfinder.

"The gun you gave Number Four . . ." he said to Linda. He kept his voice low, hoping that the camera mic wouldn't pick it up, although he knew some of his words would undoubtedly be recorded and were heading out over the Internet. "How many shells were . . ."

"Just the one she needed," Linda said.

She placed the AK-47 at her hip and tightened her finger on the trigger. Just as Adrian had observed, she knew that if she stepped down a few feet she would be able to cover the basement effectively. But the angle would be very difficult for Michael to film behind her.

Like a cinematographer preparing each shot for a complicated action sequence—one with racing cars, explosions, and actors scurrying pell-mell in every direction—she did quick calculations in her head. "If we rush them—" she began, but he cut her off.

"Listen," he said. "What's that sound?"

The two of them tried to force comprehension past the ringing in their ears caused by the explosions from an automatic weapon fired at close proximity.

It took a few seconds for the two of them to realize that what they were listening to was the scraping sound of junk being hauled across the cement floor and thrown against a wall. At first Michael imagined a barricade and thought the old man and Number 4 were going to try to hide themselves and fight it out below.

In his mind's eye, he reconstructed the basement, trying to see the most advantageous spot for a makeshift foxhole and a pair of cornered rats. And as he did this he saw the small cobwebbed window in his mind's eye. The window was the only remaining route out or, if Linda and he got there first, the means to shoot down—both with his camera and with all their weapons.

He touched his lover on the shoulder and lifted his finger to his lips in the universal signal for stealth and quiet. He gestured for Linda to follow, but first to let go another burst. She did this, sweeping the AK-47 back and forth down the narrow corridor of the stairwell, raining bullets into the basement until the clip was empty.

She grabbed the second clip from Michael's pocket and expertly slammed it into place, pulling back the bolt so that she was ready to fire. Then she hustled after him.

It took a few seconds for Terri Collins to understand what was happening. From where she and Mark Wolfe were standing next to Adrian's car the shooting noises seemed disconnected, like hearing things on a television set in another room. What she could hear had to translate into a picture in her head, which would prompt a clear-cut response. Even muffled by the house, the noise of automatic weapons fire was unmistakable. Years earlier, she had spent too many hours waiting with small complaining children in her old car for her ex-husband to finish up on a military firing range where cutting loose with hundred-shot barrel clips at fixed fake terrorist dummy targets was the norm.

She pivoted toward Mark Wolfe. Recognition like electricity flowed through her.

"Call for help!" she shouted.

He fumbled with the cell phone as Terri sprinted to the back of her car. She jacked open the trunk and removed a black bulletproof vest that she kept there. It had been a gift from her neighbor Laurie many years back when she was still a patrolwoman, and she had not worn it once since unwrapping it at a Christmas morning gathering.

"Give them the right address," she shouted back over her shoulder. "Tell them we need everybody. Tell them there are automatic weapons involved. And an ambulance! If you have to, tell them an officer has been shot. That will make them move fast."

She fastened the Velcro closings, snugging the vest to her chest. It felt terribly small and flimsy. Then she chambered a round in her pistol.

She heard a second distant volley of gunfire. Without thinking about what she was doing beyond knowing that she had to get to where the firing was taking place, she started running.

The last command, which she threw back over her shoulder, was "Wait there. Tell 'em where I've gone!"

Moving as fast as she could, gun clutched in hand, Terri raced toward the driveway and the road up to the old farmhouse.

Wolfe was busy calling for help and watching as she disappeared around the corner. When the local police dispatcher came on the line he was clipped and precise.

"Send help," he said. "Lots of help. A police detective is in a shoot-out."

He gave the dispatcher the address and he heard the shocked and instantly breathless woman say, "It will take time for the state police to respond to that location. At least fifteen minutes."

"There isn't fifteen minutes," he curtly replied, then disconnected the line. *She's never had to handle a call like that one,* he thought.

Wolfe looked up, his eyes staring at the path that Terri Collins had just raced. She had vanished around the corner, just past the battered mailbox. The forest by the entranceway was too thick for him to make out her progress; it appeared to him as if she had been immediately swallowed up. He was torn. He had been told to wait and the half coward in him was perfectly willing to stand back in a shady safe spot and allow whatever was happening to happen without any more direct involvement on his part. But this natural sense of self-preservation warred with another part of his personality, the part that wanted *to see* and was willing to take all sorts of risks to indulge that particularly demanding curiosity and unrelenting desire.

Everything important in his life was about being *within reach*.

Taking a deep breath, he started to run after the detective, although he kept repeating to himself, in time with each stride, to stay back, stay hidden, and let it all play out in front of him. *Get close,* he insisted, as his legs stretched into a sprint of his own, *but not too close.*

Adrian balanced on misshapen debris and helped Jennifer up next to him. Everything was unsteady beneath their weight, and he could feel the entire panic-built structure swaying and threatening to collapse. He stuffed his gun in his pocket and hoped it would not fall out, and then he cupped his hands together and made a step for the naked teenager. She lifted her foot and placed one hand on his shoulder to steady herself, but she kept the other hand clutching her bear. With a single grunting force of strength, he launched her rocketing upward toward the window. She grabbed at the frame. Adrian saw her thrust the bear hand forward, throwing the toy outside as she grasped the splintered wood. Jennifer teetered for an instant, and then, kicking and scrambling like a fish floundering on the deck of a boat, she forced her way up and out.

Adrian gasped with a sense of relief. He was a little astonished at what he'd done.

He did not know how he would manage to get himself up the same distance. From where he was perched—like a bird on an unsteady branch—he looked around for something he might add to the pile and gain the necessary feet.

He saw nothing.

Resignation began to gnaw at his stomach.

She can run. I'm stuck here. I'd like to get out, but I can't.

As these defeated thoughts crept into him he heard a sound from above. "Professor, quick!"

Jennifer, who had disappeared through the window, was now leaning back in, half in, half out, reaching her skinny arm down toward him.

He didn't think she would have anywhere near the strength to help him.

"Try, goddammit, Audie! Try!"

Brian was shouting in his ear.

Adrian looked up. Only this time it wasn't the teenager leaning through the window, reaching for him, it was Cassie. *"Come on, Audie,"* she begged.

He didn't hesitate. He grasped at her arm, clawed at the wall, pushed as hard as he could with both his broken and unbroken legs. He felt the pile of debris crashing behind him and for a moment he seemed to float in the air. But as rapidly as that sensation came, he felt himself slam against the cement, and he thought he was falling until he realized he wasn't, that he had hold of the window frame, digging his bleeding nails into the wood. He kicked his feet wildly. He did not think he had the strength to do the chin-up that was required, but he felt himself being lifted up, partly by the teenager grasping hold of his jacket collar, partly by what little power he had left, but also by all his memories.

Wings, he imagined.

And suddenly he saw sunlight above.

He crawled through the window, Jennifer hauling him the last couple of feet.

The old man and the naked teenager slumped exhausted against the farmhouse wall. She was drinking in fresh air like it was the finest champagne, sunlight splashing across her face. She told herself, *Just one more breath, and then I can die, because this tastes wonderful.*

Adrian scrambled to organize his thoughts. He could see the barn across the same open area he'd run earlier. From the far side of the barn the safety of the tree line was closest. If they could get there they could hide. As he grabbed at Jennifer's shoulder and started to frantically point *that's the direction we want to go* a thunder of bullets from the AK-47 smashed into the wall above their heads and tore into the ground near their feet. Clumps of dirt flew up into their faces, shards of wood and insulation rained down on their heads. It was like being caught in a tympani-drum being beaten madly. They jerked back, huddled together, and Jennifer started to scream again although her voice wasn't powerful enough to rise above the insistent racket of the machine gun. It seemed as if the deadly hammering of the gun were coming out of her open mouth.

Linda and Michael had split up. She had gone to the back and was aiming the rifle around the corner of the house, which gave her a firing angle on the two of them. It was hard to shoot accurately without exposing herself, so she relied on the volume of fire to do the job.

Michael had run to the front, past his old truck, which gave him just enough cover to keep filming. He had lowered the shotgun and lifted the HD camera, sticking the laptop on the roof of the truck cabin.

All he could think of was *what a show*.

Jennifer was shouting and holding her hands over her ears as bullets showered their position. She pressed against Adrian.

He was holding his forearm across his face, as if that might ward off the rain of automatic weapons fire. His eyes were closed and he expected to die any second.

"Audie, listen to me! It's not over!"

He turned to the side and saw Brian. It was the Vietnam Brian, a young officer of men at war only a little older than Jennifer. His fatigues were covered with grime and his tin pot helmet was pulled down over his head. He was sweat-streaked, filthy, and he lay prone on the ground as he jammed a magazine into his M-16. His face was set with determination. Brian didn't seem frightened in the least.

"Come on, Audie! Return fire, goddammit! Return fire!"

Brian let loose with a furious volley, his own weapon on full automatic. Adrian suddenly saw the edge of the house where Linda was drawing down on them exploding in fragments. A window shattered, glass flying up into the sunlight. He looked down and saw that he had tugged his brother's 9mm pistol from his pocket and somehow managed to get into a kneeling position. The bullets striking the house were his own.

Linda reeled back, gasping. One shot had creased the frame just above her head and she felt a splinter slice her cheek. She hugged the wall to get out of his line of fire and touched her scratch, seeing blood on her fingertips. It enraged her.

"*Outstanding!*" Brian screamed. "*Don't let them flank you, Audie. Keep up a masking fire!*"

Adrian pulled the trigger again and again. Spent shells fluttered around him. He heard Tommy yelling in his ear, "*Now, Dad! Now's her chance!*" As he fired he shouted to Jennifer, "Now! Now! Run for it! Go!"

Jennifer did not understand what he was saying but the implication was clear. Get to the barn. Use it for cover. Race to the woods. Get away. Hide.

Outrun death.

She scrambled to her feet and without hesitation sprinted. She ran as hard as she could, as hard as she ever imagined she could, as hard and fast as she had once hoped to run when she'd been trapped in her cell. She could feel wind caressing her, like a hurricane breath blowing at her back and pushing her forward as she dug hard for the safety of the barn.

Adrian struggled to his feet behind her. He ran, too, but his was a staggered, ancient limp, as his fractured ankle tripped him up with every stride. He fired as he ran, trying to blast the corner, hoping that some lucky unaimed shot might strike home.

He'd made it only halfway when a sudden, immense blow like a lightning strike seized him, lifting him up and then throwing him effortlessly to the ground. His face thudded against the moist earth. He could taste dirt, and his ears rung, and pain shot through his legs, right up into his midsection and finally to his heart, which he believed was going to come to a grinding halt. He could not form the words *I'm shot* in his head, though that was what had happened.

His eyesight was unfocused and shaded, as if night had abruptly fallen across his face. He wondered whether Jennifer had made it to the barn, the first step to safety. He hoped that Cassie and Brian and Tommy would take her the rest of the way, because he knew he no longer could.

He closed his eyes and heard an evil sound. A *clickety-click*. He did not know it was the noise made by a shotgun when a spent round is ejected and a fresh round chambered, but he understood that it was the sound of dying.

When Adrian had launched himself into his race across the open space, Michael had set the camera down on the hood of the truck. He'd hit the auto switch so that it would continue to film. It was like a director's Dutch Cut, the image on a sharp angle. But it still captured the action from behind him as he stepped forward. He knew he remained anonymous. All that any of the clientele would see was his back.

He had fired a single blast from the twelve-gauge.

The steel pellets had caught Adrian around the thighs and hips, lifting him up and dropping him to the ground with a linebacker's force or a professional soccer player's violent red-card sliding tackle.

Michael carefully ejected the shell and lifted the weapon to his shoulder, this time taking careful aim at the figure crumpled to the dirt in front of him.

Finish this show, he thought.

He did not hear the person behind him until the high-pitched order sliced the air.

"Police! Freeze! Drop your weapon!"

He was astonished. He hesitated.

"I said drop your weapon!"

This simply wasn't a part of what he'd imagined.

Thoughts pummeled him. *Where's Linda? Who is this? Number 4 is finished now. What's going on?* But the flood of questions that ricocheted off into recesses within him were empty and irrelevant. And instead of doing as he was ordered, Michael pivoted abruptly, swinging the shotgun barrel toward the strange sound of someone trying to give him commands. He had no intention of doing anything other than shooting to kill and getting back to the far more urgent and important business of completing *Series #4.*

He did not get the chance.

Terri Collins was crouched in a firing position near the back of the truck. She had both hands on her pistol and had taken careful aim. Michael seemed to her to be moving in slow motion, exchanging the broad back that she'd taken a bead on with his chest.

She could not understand why he didn't drop the shotgun. He had no chance.

She fired five times, just as she had been taught. *Make no mistakes. Put the subject down.*

The police detective's pistol roared. She had not once in all her years as a member of the small college town force ever had the occasion to remove it from its holster at any moment other than practice time on a firing range. Now, at this first opportunity that it was drawn in seriousness, she was trying to remember everything she was supposed to do and to do it right. She knew from instruction that there were no second chances. But the weapon seemed to have a helpful mind of its own. It seemed to take aim and fire without her; she was only barely aware that she had pulled the trigger.

Steel-jacketed rounds slammed into Michael. The force of the close-range shots lifted him up and threw him backward. He was dead before his eyes caught a last glimpse of the sky.

Terri Collins breathed out hard, exhausted.

She took a step forward, dizzy. Her head spun but every nerve within her was on some razor's edge.

Her eyes were locked on the figure in front of her. A huge puddle of blood had replaced his chest.

The sight of the man she'd killed was mesmerizing. She would have remained locked in position like a hypnotist's subject if not for the sudden scream.

Linda took in her lover's death from her spot at the other end of the farmhouse. A single, awful sight.

She saw the policewoman standing above Michael. She saw the blood.

It was as if the most important part of her had been savagely ripped from her heart.

She ran forward, her eyes instantly filling with tears and panic, screaming "Michael! Michael! No!" as she fired off every remaining round in the AK-47.

High-powered bullets crashed into Terri Collins. They slammed into her vest, spinning her around like a child's top. She could feel her own weapon flying from her hand as one of the bullets crushed into her wrist. Another caught her as she tumbled, right above the top of the vest, slashing her throat like a knife.

She landed on her back, eyes fixed up on the sky. She could feel hot blood gurgling up in her chest, choking her, and every breath grew harder to steal from the air. She knew she should be thinking of her children, her home, and all that she was going to miss, but then pain sheeted down, black and irreversible across her eyes. She did not have the time to say to herself *I don't want to die* before her last breath rattled out.

Linda was still running. She threw the machine gun aside and pulled out the pistol that Michael had placed in her jeans belt. She wanted to keep shooting, as if by rekilling the policewoman, over and over, she could somehow reverse time and bring Michael back.

She went straight to his side.

Linda threw herself down on her lover, embracing him and then lifting him up, like Michelangelo's Mary cradling the crucified Jesus. She ran her fingers across his face, trying to scoop blood away from his lips, as if that might restore him. She howled with pain.

And then her pain was replaced by blind rage. Her eyes narrowed with unrestrained hate. She scrambled to her feet and grasped her pistol. She could see where the old man was sprawled on the ground. She did not know who he was or how he'd managed to arrive there, but she knew he was totally to blame for everything. She did not know if he was alive or not, but she did know he did not deserve to be. She knew that Number 4 had to be close by as well. *Kill them. Kill them both. And then you can kill yourself, so you can be with Michael forever.*

Linda raised her gun and took careful aim at the old man's body.

Adrian could just see what she was doing. If he could have moved, crawled somehow to safety, or gathered his own weapon and taken aim he would have, but he could do none of these things. All he could do was wait. He thought it was okay to get shot and die right there, as long as

437

Jennifer got away. It was what he'd meant to do to himself all along. But his suicide had been interrupted when he'd seen her get stolen from his very own street, and that hadn't been fair, it had been terribly wrong, and so he'd done everything that his dead wife, brother, and son had wanted. It had all been a part of his dying and he was okay with it. He'd done his very best and maybe Jennifer could get away now and get to live and grow up. It was all worth it.

Adrian closed his eyes.

He heard the roar of the pistol.

Somehow death did not arrive milliseconds later.

He could still feel the damp earth against his cheek. He could feel his heart pumping and the pain from his wounds coursing through his body. He could even feel his illness, as if insidiously it was taking advantage of all that had happened and was now demanding prominence. He did not understand why, but he could feel memories slipping away and reason departing. He wanted to hear his wife just one more time, his son, his brother. He wanted a poem that would ease him into madness, forgetfulness, and death. But all he could hear inside himself was a waterfall of dementia thundering down, erasing the few parts of Adrian that grasped life.

He blinked his eyes open.

What he saw seemed more a hallucination than any of his dead family.

Linda was facedown on the ground. What was left of her head flowered blood.

And behind her: Mark Wolfe.

In his hand was Detective Collins's pistol.

Adrian wanted to laugh because he thought dying with a smile made some sense.

He closed his eyes and waited.

The sex offender surveyed the carnage outside the farmhouse and muttered, "Jesus Christ, Jesus Christ, Jesus Christ," over and over, though the words had nothing to do with faith or religion and everything to do with shock. He lifted the detective's pistol a second time, not really aiming at anything, before lowering it, because it was obvious that he wouldn't need it again. He saw the laptop computer on the roof of the truck and the camera that was faithfully recording everything in its view.

The silence seemed complete. Gunshots echoed off and faded away.

"Jesus Christ," he repeated again.

He looked down at Detective Collins and shook his head.

Then he walked slowly over to Adrian's body. He was surprised when the old man's eyes fluttered open. Wolfe could tell he was badly wounded and he doubted that he could survive. Still, he spoke encouragingly as he bent down beside him.

"You're a tough old bird, professor. Hang in there."

Wolfe heard the sound of sirens approaching fast.

"That's help coming," he said. "Don't give up. It'll be here any second." He was about to add *you owe me a lot more than twenty grand* but he did not.

Instead, what crowded into his thinking at that moment was a burst of pride and a truly wondrous realization: *I'm a goddamn hero. A goddamn hero. I killed someone who killed a cop. They're never going to hassle me again, for no reason at all, no matter what the hell I do. I'm free.*

The sirens whined closer. Wolfe looked away from the wounded professor and what he saw made his mouth widen in astonishment.

A stark-naked teenage girl emerged from behind the ramshackle barn. She made no attempt to cover herself, other than to hold her stuffed teddy bear close to her heart.

Wolfe stood up and stepped aside as Jennifer crossed the open space. She knelt down at Adrian's side, just as the first state trooper's squad car rounded into the farmhouse drive.

Wolfe hesitated, but then he stripped off his lightweight jacket. He wrapped it around her shoulders, partially to cover her nakedness but more because he wanted to touch the young woman's porcelain skin. His finger brushed against her shoulder and he sighed as he felt a familiar deep, unbridled electricity.

Behind them police cruisers ground to ragged tire-squealing stops and officers waving weapons leaped out, shouting commands, taking positions behind open car doors. Wolfe had the good common sense to throw the detective's pistol down and lift his hands in a surrender that wasn't in the least bit necessary.

Jennifer, however, didn't seem to see or hear anything other than the raspy breath coming from the old man. She took his hand and squeezed it hard, as if she could pass some of her own youth through her skin and give him a little more strength.

Adrian looked at her like a man awakening from a long nap, unsure whether he was still dreaming. He smiled.

"Hello," he whispered. "Who are you?"

EPILOGUE

The Last Poem Day

Professor Roger Parsons read through the entire term paper, then read it a second time, and finally with a red pen in hand he opened to the last page and wrote *Outstanding, Miss Riggins* at the bottom. He took a second to consider what he was going to write next, looking up at the framed, signed *Silence of the Lambs* movie poster displayed on his office wall. He had been teaching his Introduction to Abnormal Psychology course for first-year potential psychology majors for nearly twenty-two years and he could not recall a finer freshman-year paper. The topic was "Self-Destructive Behavior in Adolescent Youth" and Ms. Riggins had deconstructed several types of antisocial activities common among teenagers and fit them into psychological matrixes that were far more sophisticated than he had any reason to expect from a first-year student. Clearly, Professor Parsons recognized, the young woman who always sat in the front of the classroom and was first with quick, pointed questions during the Q and A period at the end of each session had read all the extra-credit articles and many more books besides those he had listed on the course syllabus.

And so he wrote: "Please see me at your earliest opportunity to discuss the psychology honors major program. Additionally, perhaps you would be interested in a summer clinical internship. Usually this goes to upperclassmen but we might make an exception this time."

Then he gave her the grade: A.

He had a reputation at the university as an exceptionally tough grader, and he could recall giving out only a few such high grades in his years teaching, and never before in a freshman survey course. Young Ms. Riggins's effort was a match for the papers he anticipated from the juniors and seniors taking his advanced Abnormal Psych seminars.

Professor Parsons added the paper to the top of the stack he expected to return to the other students after the next lecture, which would be the last before the summer break was upon them. He was reluctant to pick up another teenager's effort and start the assessment process again. When he did, he grimaced widely and groaned loudly, for the next paper had an obvious typo in the very second sentence of the opening paragraph.

"Haven't they heard of spell-check?" he muttered. "Don't they bother to read through their work before handing it in?"

With a flourish he circled the error in dramatic red.

Jennifer hurried out of her Social Trends in Modern Poetry class and rapidly made her way across campus. She had a set routine that she followed every Thursday, and even though she knew there would be some necessary changes this last time she wanted to make certain she stuck to it as much as possible.

Her first stop was a small florist in the center of town, where she purchased an inexpensive bouquet of mixed flowers. She always chose the brightest, most vibrant colors, even in the dead of winter. Whether it was bitterly cold or sunny and mild, as it was this particular start-of-summer day, she wanted the arrangement to jump out.

She took the flowers from the nice saleslady who recognized her from her many visits but who had never asked her why she needed the flowers with such impressive regularity. Jennifer simply assumed that the lady had accidentally noticed where she placed them, and that was why she'd never intruded by asking what they were for. The saleslady thought the girl was interesting, because everyone else buying flowers in the shop was ordinarily quick to loudly state their purpose. A wedding anniversary luckily remembered. A birthday. Mother's Day.

Jennifer's flowers were for something different.

She took them wordlessly, hurried back outside into the midafternoon sunshine, and dropped them on the seat of her car. She drove directly across town to police headquarters. Usually there were parking spaces close by, and the few times the street had been crowded, patrol officers had waved her into their private lot behind the station.

This last day she was fortunate, easily finding a spot right in front of the modern-design brick and glass entranceway. She didn't bother to feed the parking meter; she simply jumped out, flowers in hand.

She crossed the broad sidewalk to the front doors. Just outside there was a large bronze plaque mounted prominently on the wall. It had a glistening gold star at the top that trapped rays of sunlight and highlighted the raised inscription.

> *In Memory of Detective Terri Collins.*
> *Killed in the Line of Duty.*
> *Honor. Dedication. Devotion.*

Jennifer placed the flowers beneath the plaque and took a quiet moment. Sometimes she recalled the detective seated across from her during one of her aborted runaways, trying to explain why escape was such a poor idea when clearly she didn't really believe that herself. She would say to Jennifer that there were other routes out. All she had to do was search hard for them. This, Jennifer had learned in the three years since the detective died rescuing her, was true. So often she would whisper to the plaque, "I'm doing exactly what you said, detective. I should have listened to you. You were right all along."

More than one police officer had overheard her say this, or something similar, but none had ever interrupted her. Unlike the florist who expected her on Thursdays, they all knew why Jennifer was there.

"It's Thursday, it must be poem day," the nurse said in a friendly, welcoming lilt. She looked up over some paperwork and a computer screen at the main desk inside the wide doors of a squat, unattractive cinder-block building off one of the main roadways leading into the small college town. The doors had been designed to accommodate wheelchairs and gurneys and were equipped with electric open assists that *whooshed* when anyone pressed the right button.

"Absolutely," Jennifer replied, smiling in return.

The nurse nodded, but then she shook her head, as if there was something both happy and sad in Jennifer's arrival.

"You know, dear, he might not understand anything much anymore, but he really looks forward to your visits. I can tell. He just seems a little more with it on Thursdays, waiting for you to come by."

Jennifer paused. She turned for a second and looked outside. She could see sunlight diving between the branches of trees that swayed in a light breeze, their full green leaves wrestling with breaths of wind. From where she stood, she saw the sign outside the building: Valley Long-Term Care and Rehabilitation Center.

She looked back at the nurse. She knew that everything the nurse said was untrue. He wasn't *more with it*. He was deteriorating a little more each week. *No,* Jennifer thought, *every hour more drops away.*

"I can tell, too," she said, joining in on the lie.

"So who did you bring along for today's visit?" she asked.

"W. H. Auden and James Merrill," Jennifer replied. "And Billy Collins because he's so funny. And a couple of others, if I have the time."

The nurse probably didn't recognize any of the poets, but she acted like each choice made absolute good sense. "He's out back on the patio, dear," she said.

Jennifer knew the way. She nodded to a few of the other staff she passed. They all knew her as the Thursday poetry girl and her regularity was more than enough reason for them to leave her absolutely alone.

She found Adrian seated in a wheelchair in a corner shadow.

He was bent over slightly at the waist, seemingly inspecting something directly in front of him, although the angle of his head told Jennifer he couldn't even see the fine afternoon sunlight. His hands quivered and his lip twitched with Parkinson's-like symptoms. His hair was completely white now, and the fitness that he'd once relied upon had faded. His arms were like sticks, his thin legs jumped nervously. He was cadaverously underweight, and he hadn't been shaved, so gray stubble marked his sunken cheeks and chin. His eyes were cloudy.

If he recognized Jennifer there was no way for her to tell it.

She found a chair and pulled it up next to the old professor. The first thing she said was, "I'm going to get straight A's in my major—no, *our* major, professor. And next year will be the same. I will keep at it however long it takes, and whatever you started I will finish, I promise."

She had worked on this speech in her head for some days. She had not told him this before. Mostly, she had been preoccupied with simpler things to tell him about, such as how she had finished high school and getting into college and then what courses she was taking and what she thought of the teachers who had once been his colleagues. She sometimes talked about a new boyfriend or something as mundane as her mother's new job and how she seemed to have recovered from exiting her relationship with Scott West.

But mostly she read him poetry. She had become quite good at inflections, rhythms, and language, finding the subtleties in the verses and capturing them for the old man—even if she knew he could no longer hear or understand anything she said. It was, Jennifer knew, the *saying of it* that was important.

Jennifer reached out and took his hand. It seemed paper-thin.

She had done her research and confirmed it with conversations with the rehabilitation center staff. Professor Thomas was simply and inexorably sliding into death. There was nothing anyone could do about the torture except hope that as his brain functioning had evaporated he wasn't in terrible pain.

Except she knew he was.

She smiled at the man who had saved her. "I thought maybe a little Lewis Carroll today, professor. Would you like that?"

A small stream of spittle appeared at the corner of his mouth. Jennifer took a tissue and carefully wiped it away. She thought he had been through much near-death, the disease and the wounds from the shootout that should have killed him, but didn't, although they had left him crippled. It did not seem fair.

She reached down to her backpack and removed a book of poems. She took a quick glance around. A few other patients were being wheeled through the nearby garden, admiring the flowers laid out in rows, but on the patio the two of them were alone. Jennifer thought she would not have a better moment to read to the professor.

She opened the book but the first lines came from memory: " 'Twas brillig, and the slithy toves did gyre and gimble in the wabe . . ."

The poetry book was thick—a compilation of generations of English and American poets—and she had slid a small syringe between the pages. The syringe had been lifted during a visit to campus health services six months earlier, a bit of sleight of hand while coughing with a faked case of bronchitis.

The syringe was filled with a mixture of Fentanyl and cocaine. The cocaine had been easily obtained from one of the many students "working" their way through college. The Fentanyl was harder to acquire. It was a powerful cancer drug, a narcotic used to mask the harshness of chemotherapy. It had taken her a few months to befriend a girl who lived down the hallway from her and whose mother was suffering from breast cancer. On a weekend visit to the girl's house in Boston, Jennifer had managed to steal half a dozen tablets from a medicine cabinet. This was more than a lethal dose. It would stop his heart within a few seconds. She had felt bad about the theft and betraying the confidence of her new friend, but it couldn't be helped.

She kept reciting as she rolled back the professor's shirtsleeve.

"Beware the Jabberwock, my son! The jaws that bite, the claws that catch!"

Jennifer took a final glance around to make sure no one was watching what she was doing.

"One, two! One, two! And through and through the vorpal blade went snicker-snack!"

She had no experience giving injections but she doubted this would make a difference. The professor didn't flinch as the needle penetrated his flesh and found a vein. She plunged the concoction home.

Nothing remained of Adrian's imagination save a dull gray. He could see diffuse light, hear some sounds, understood that words resonated inside a part of him hidden by disease. But all the sheaves that, bound together, had made him into who he was were now scattered and broken. And yet suddenly all the opaque waters within him seemed to come together like a wave, and he managed to lift his head just a little bit and see figures in the distance, beckoning to him. Illness and age dropped aside and Adrian ran forward. He was laughing.

'And has thou slain the Jabberwock? Come to my arms, my beamish boy! O frabjous day! Callooh! Callay!'

Jennifer watched carefully, her hand on the old man's pulse as it faded away. Then, when she was absolutely certain that she had set him as free as he had set her, she closed the book of poetry. She bent down, kissed him on the forehead, and quietly repeated, "O frabjous day! Callooh! Callay!"

She replaced the syringe and the poetry book in her backpack and then wheeled the professor into a bright spot on the patio and left him there. She believed he looked peaceful.

On the way out, she told the nurse on duty, "Professor Thomas fell asleep in the sun. I didn't want to disturb him."

It was, she thought, the least she could do.